Sweet Rafter Jesus!

BUTTERFLY IN AMBER

SPOTLESS SERIES, BOOK 4

CAMILLA MONK

TABLE OF CONTENTS

Ce livre est dédié à Benoît, qui a supporté mes sautes d'humeurs, les dîners McDo pour cause de manuscrit, les affrontements épiques avec l'éditeur, les crises de nerfs quand la deadline approche et que le disque dur crame, qui a supplié pour lire chaque livre de la série, m'a trollé sans pitié, s'est vu interdire de les lire, les a lu quand même, et sans qui rien de tout ça n'aurait été possible.

On t'aime.

BUTTERFLY IN HELL

He'll go against mountains and cross rivers,
he'll tread a pathway through heaped-up snows,
he'll set sail, neither fearing Eurus's raging east winds,
nor waiting for stars propitious for his voyage.
Who but a soldier or lover could endure the chill of night,
and torrents of mingled snow and rain?

—*Ovid*, Amores, Elegy IX: Of Love and War

Leaning against the wall, his arms crossed, his captor had yet to speak. Instead he observed through tranquil icy blue eyes that gave no signs of impatience or even anger. The man people called Auben knew better. The plastic sheeting covering every surface of the empty and windowless room spoke louder than any threat to come.

A soft patter somewhere above him caught Auben's attention. A butterfly had managed to get trapped in hell with him, drawn by the single lamp hanging from the ceiling. It kept hitting the scalding glass desperately, eager for the light to consume it. He willed his body to relax in the ropes holding his four limbs tightly strapped to a steel chair. Bolted to the floor. Auben recognized the eye for detail of a consummate professional. He drew a steady breath. Death he did not fear. It was part of the job, both the sentence and the reward, a leap into blessed darkness. Everything in between now and death . . . was another matter.

As he had been taught, he closed his eyes and mentally let go of his body. There was only so much pain the flesh could take, and he knew—or rather trusted—that beyond that threshold would come a sense of numbness. It would help. He repeated in his head, like a mantra, that he had led a good life, all forty years of it, that whatever his executioner sliced, broke, or tore would be useless meat scraped from a body that was already dead.

After a prolonged silence, spit-shined brogues shifted on the plastic. The man came out of the shadows and walked across the room, his stride slow, predatory. He went to open a black suitcase resting on an instruments tray, a few feet from the chair.

"I heard you were dead," Auben remarked, his tone cordial even as a drop of sweat burned its way down his temple.

His host never stopped searching the case, moving aside a compartment where two semiautomatics and their suppressors lay encased in foam. "You shouldn't believe everything you hear, *broer.*"

Auben managed a chuckle, even as nausea lapped at the back of his throat. "You know I can't tell you anything."

"You *won't.* But you can, and I'll make you."

The case snapped shut. Auben caught the menacing glint of a pair of pruners in the man's latex-gloved hand.

Now came the moment to breathe, to let go, despite every single muscle contracting in his limbs, the stifling weight of fear crushing his chest. The sleeve of a navy jacket brushed his arm, carrying in its wake a clean, almost medical scent, like those hand sanitizers they sold everywhere these days. Seconds after, hands gripped his left thumb and forced it into the cool embrace of the pruners' blades. Through the blood roaring in his ears, Auben had to remind himself over and over that this body was dead already. It didn't matter that he lost the use of his hand. It was a transitional state. It meant nothing.

"My apologies," the man said evenly. "I'd usually start with something more . . . benign, but I'm in a bit of a hurry. I've heard you recently came back from a mission in Finland. Can you perhaps share some of the details with me?"

No.

Auben gritted his teeth and breathed hard, fast through his nose. He looked up at the blinding orb of the lightbulb above him to find the butterfly gone. In a single snap, agony shot through his hand, thundered all the way up to his shoulder. He bit back a howl, tasting blood in his mouth. Years of training had him able to ride the waves of pain flowing from the wound, but no amount of past fractures could have prepared him for the horrific awareness of the missing finger, the odd weight of his hand, the sudden absence.

Auben watched, in a state of shock that overrode the pain itself, as his captor dropped the bloodied thumb in a plastic bag filled with crushed ice and sealed the package in a cooler waiting under the steel tray.

With absolute detachment, the man glanced down at the box at his feet. "You have four hours to tell me where she is. We'll be moving on to the right hand, so please be ready."

ONE
THE GLASS DOLL

I didn't mean to, but I just dropped my glass again. It still happens—less than it used to. From time to time, my hands will shake uncontrollably, and whatever I'm holding will go crash, splatter, scatter on the floor, for Stiles to pick and clean up, as always.

"I'm sorry," I say, without looking at him.

As he carefully mops the purple mess of broken glass and grape juice on the tiling, he smiles that sweet, empty smile he always gives me. Faded, like his baby blue eyes. "It's all right; we're good. That marble has seen worse."

I mumble another apology, gazing past him and through the bay window, at the ghostly silhouettes of the snow-covered pines surrounding the castle. You can't see the Baltic Sea, but it's there, beyond the trees, encircling the island. My father sent me here to rest because he says it's quiet; it'll help me find myself again. "An island for Island," he said, and it made him chuckle. When I'm depressed though, which is more often than I like to admit, I think my world has shrunk to a mile-long rock.

"Island, are you still with me?"

I look up at Stiles and nod automatically, but in truth, for a second I didn't recognize him. I mean, I did, but it's his voice or, rather, his accent. He told me once that he was born in a place called Denton, in Georgia, where time trickled slowly and people squeezed their pennies so hard the eagle screamed. He said he spent sixteen years there, hunting quail, skipping church, and waiting for something to happen—according to him, the rest of the town is still waiting. All he kept from his hometown is a soft drawl that will occasionally weigh on his vowels. There's nothing wrong with that, but every time he opens his mouth, it's like my brain is expecting something more, someone else, until the feeling is gone, and I remember that it's only Stiles.

I don't know; it's just one of the many things that are wrong with me. I guess I'm still pretty messed up since my accident. I feel slow, confused most of the time. Everybody tells me it's normal, that eight months is not much to recover from the kind of trauma I went through, that maybe it'll take years. I hope not. I turned twenty-six in September, and I'd rather not stay a convalescent child for the rest of my life.

Once he's done wiping the last pinkish smear, Stiles wastes no time crossing the kitchen and opening the fridge to grab the bottle of juice again. He reminds me of a big robot: The man is cut like a Terminator, and he never gives up, never gets distracted. I drop the glass where he put my meds? He'll fetch another one. I never tried, but I'm pretty sure that if I dropped it ten times, he'd fix it all over again ten times too. Always the same gray dress pants, white shirt, and black tie every day, always the same blond crew cut I suspect never grows. I could complain he also looks forty every day, but that'd be unfair: it's not like I've known him for so long.

My heart skips a beat at the distressing thought. I have. I've known him almost all my life, since the day my father hired him to take care of me. Bodyguard, nanny, nurse . . . friend, maybe?

How could I know? I don't remember any of that.

•••

Stiles is always here, through good and bad. When I wake up at night, screaming because I think we're still in April and I'm drowning in the dark waters of the Pacific, he's at my side. He was there too in the very beginning, when a helicopter brought me to Ingolvinlinna, my head still bandaged after the cranial surgery that saved my life, my left wrist shattered so bad they had to put a plate in it.

In many ways, it was the first day of my life, or rather the first I remember. I don't like to think about it; there's no word that could possibly describe how it felt, blinking awake in a bed one morning in that white hospital room, with my long-term memory entirely flushed down the drain. "Lost" isn't even close.

I know my name, I can brush my teeth, I know what matricial calculus and JavaScript are, like I know the difference between a strawberry and a mushroom, and I can understand many languages, among which are bits of Finnish, but also French, Afrikaans, or even Japanese—found out about that one a few weeks ago when reading the label of a box of matcha in the kitchen.

But how I acquired those motor skills and procedural knowledge, my job or my years of college in New York, the childhood I spent traveling the world and learning those languages with my mom before she died and I went to live with my dad, past lovers, forgotten friends . . . all of that is lost. I am a territory whose map is blank. I know only what I've been told by my father or Stiles. And so, day after day, I collect each memory, each passing mention of past events, like pearls on a string, to reclaim my life.

That being said, Stiles is also in for the good times, and I'd say today is good enough: It'll be Christmas in a couple of weeks, my mind is clear, and my legs are steady. I think I'm getting better.

Sitting cross-legged on an antique red brocade sofa in the salon, I go through the cardboard box he went to fetch from the attic. *You gotta be kidding me . . .* I hold the ratty silver garland in front of me with a frown. There's also a grand total of seven worn golden balls and one angel figurine whose wig and wings fell off at some point over the past forty years and who now looks like a cancer patient with its white shirt.

I cringe. "That's it?"

He responds with an apologetic wince. "I think one of the men in the security team has a mini plastic tree in his room too."

"Aw, come on . . ."

I blame it all on Stiles. He's the one who said, "Hey, let's decorate a Christmas tree," and I said, "Okay." But as it turned out, my father and I never celebrated Christmas here at Ingolvinlinna. You'd think it was the perfect place for that, but apparently no one ever told him Santa *himself* lives in Finland: Nineteen rooms and no trace of any ornaments. No mysterious box long forgotten in a dusty attic, zip, nada. I'm disappointed, but I can't say I'm surprised. My father isn't what you might call the fun type . . .

So here we are standing in the salon, going through our options over Stiles's meager loot. I like this room, the dark wood paneling, the way everything is steeped in a rich, smoky scent coming from an enormous fireplace. Most of the castle dates back to the seventeenth century, and everything inside has been carefully preserved, from the tapestries covering the walls to the soft brocade wing chairs. As the flames consume a log in the hearth with soft cracks and pops, Stiles's usual smile has been replaced by pursed lips. Annoyance? A rather extreme emotion coming from him.

He sighs. "Island, your idea with the toilet paper and the aluminum foil . . . I'm not sure about that."

"But you're the one who came up with the Christmas tree idea," I counter.

He crosses his arms over today's black tie. "Well here's a better one: I'll send someone to town to find ornaments."

I know what he's going to say next, but I jump at the occasion anyway. "Then why don't you just take me there so I can choose myself? I need some fresh air."

Before I'm even done talking, his lips part to form the word *No.*

This time, I decide, I won't step down. "I'd like to discuss this with my father. I get that you have instructions, but I'd like to remind you that I'm an adult."

Stiles gives me the softest smile . . . and shakes his head. "Island, you know what Dr. Bentsen said about taking it slow." He pauses with a long sigh. "I honestly don't want to see you come apart in the middle of a Christmas market."

"But you say that for everything," I snap back. "It's always too early for . . . for *everything*, and I'm wilting in here." The frustration and resentment I try to keep at bay all the time swells, and I struggle to plead my case calmly. "I need to see people. I'm spinning around in circles, I don't have any friends, no one called me after my accident, no one gave a damn!"

He draws a sorrowful sigh. "Do you miss Joy?"

I don't think he does it on purpose, but he can be cruel sometimes. It's like he unconsciously knows which button to push to make me come apart. I try to take the hit and keep my composure, but I can feel my face bunching already, and tears blur my vision.

"I don't even remember her . . ." I sob.

And it'd make no difference, since she's dead.

Joy, my roommate and best friend back in New York. Perhaps my only friend, since everyone else seems to have abandoned me. We met in college, lived together, did everything together. Like going on a vacation to the Poseidon Dome, a dream-like tropical resort in French Polynesia. Under a magnificent glass dome . . . which collapsed, bombed by some crazy terrorist guy whose name I've forgotten again. I'll have to ask Stiles.

I don't remember any of it, just bits, flashes, senseless dreams reminding me that it's real, even if all that's left to hold on to are blurry shapes undulating in the fog of my mind. I know Joy is blond, and that the dome collapsed in April. To me, these do not come across as factual truths but rather sensory experiences, things engraved in my heart, in my bones. Notes of Mozart's Magic Flute I perhaps listened to back then, the screams and my terror when the glass cracked. I can still hear them, feel it.

I have no memory of what happened before that. Joy's face is an abstract construct in my mind, based on photos my father showed me. He told me about the week she and I spent together at the dome. He had pictures of me too, but I didn't recognize myself. I still don't: I avoid mirrors because the girl looking back at me unsettles me. Barely reaching Stiles's shoulder, she looks younger than twenty-six, which had me wondering about my own age in my worst moments of confusion. Pale, gaunt, with a gap tooth and round hazel eyes I find too big—probably because of the dark circles under them. The only thing reconciling us is the auburn waves falling on her shoulders. I feel their weight on mine too; I can actually look down at my own chest and see loose curls clinging to my wool dress.

That way I know who I am, which I should be grateful for, since according to the MRI Dr. Bentsen showed me, my medial temporal lobe is now made of sponge cake and confetti.

I look down at my hands. I thought I was doing well, but now I'm desperately trying to remember Joy's face, and they're shaking again, wet from the tears I just wiped.

Stiles's palm glides down my back, leaving a trail of shivers in its wake. On a conscious level, I recognize that his touch is gentle, inoffensive, but my distress knows no other outlet than anger: I shove him away weakly. He barely moves, his solid frame wedged into the marble floor.

"It's okay, Island . . ." He reaches for me again, more cautiously this time. His voice envelops me like a warm blanket, numbs me. This time, I allow his arm to wrap around my shoulders, maybe because I know there's no point in fighting him. "Come here. I'll give you something so you can rest a little before lunch."

TWO
THE KNIFE

"How do you feel today, Island?"

Like crap. *"Great."*

I know Dr. Bentsen doesn't buy it, not even with the smile I muster. That's why she'll remain silent for a minute or so to give me the opportunity to elaborate on this statement. Spoiler alert: I won't.

She leans back in the delicate armchair facing the sofa I'm sitting on. We always meet in the music room when she visits me: she once said that it's because it's brighter, cozier than the rest of the castle, and so she thinks it'll affect my mood accordingly. Possible—I'm not sure. I do agree that the atmosphere here is different from the rest of the building. The windows are much larger, and the pastel blues of the floral toile covering the furniture speak of a time when a certain *art-de-vivre* took over the necessity of fending off enemies and keeping halberds in every corner in case you needed to skewer someone . . .

Bentsen combs back a long, sleek lock of silver hair behind her ear. She must flatiron. There's no way her hair is naturally that smooth. Her smile reminds me of Stiles's: soft, patient—inescapable. "Mr. Stiles told me you were upset a few days ago. Is it something you want to talk about?"

Upset. Her favorite euphemism. Upset like when I woke up in her clinic in Helsinki, terrified, disoriented, and surrounded by complete strangers. My father, Stiles, her . . . they'd try to talk to me, show me faces and ask if I recognized them, over and over. To me, it was nothing more than words piling up meaninglessly, questions I couldn't answer, recounting of events that might just as well have been someone else's life.

She doesn't need to remind me how it was, how the fear and the emptiness quickly degenerated into rage and paranoia. Most of the time, I do a good job putting a lid on those memories, and lie to myself that I'm taking meds because I had brain injury and that's going to help, somehow. But of course, things look a little different from Bentsen's perspective, who received a glass full of water and pills in her face—more than once—and who had to call in a bunch of male nurses to strap me to my bed a few times because I was so sure she wanted to kill me that I decided to strike first—with a fork and a plate of green beans. It's the only thing I don't want to remember, those hours spent screaming at no one in particular, the despair and the exhaustion afterward . . .

I shift in my armchair, unable to meet her eyes. "It wasn't like that. I wasn't angry or anything. I just . . . I was frustrated that Stiles wouldn't let me out, and it all kind of . . . bubbled up."

"When Mr. Stiles mentioned Joy."

I look through the window. I want out, away.

"Island?" she probes gently.

"Yes. Yes, I lost it, okay?" I snap. "I know it sounds bad, but I *do* feel better. It's like you're holding it against me."

Her voice is warm, gooey honey as she tries to get through to me.

"No one is holding anything against you, Island. We only want to make sure you're safe. We're all worried about you."

"Then why don't you let me go back to New York? I don't need people to worry about me; I need fresh air."

It would probably take a lot more than a saucy attitude to make the slightest dent in Dr. Bentsen's super-psychologist armor. She all but ignores my irritation and keeps going, as if this were a conversation between friends. "You told me the same thing during our last session. What do you miss in New York, Island?"

She's trapping me. She knows I can't answer that, at least not really. What do I miss? Joy? Joy is gone, along with my memories of her. All there's left of her is an indistinct ache, a void inside me. My other friends, my colleagues? They're just names, smudges in my mind that could be faces. My job? Apparently I worked in IT, but I got fired not long before I took that vacation to the Poseidon Dome. In truth, everything that held my life together snapped when that dome collapsed, like dozens of frail strings. And yet . . .

"My apartment . . . I'd like to return there. I think it'd jog my memory," I say, truthfully.

That seems to catch Bentsen's interest. "Is there anything you remember specifically from your apartment, Island? Objects, maybe?"

"We have . . . *I had* a pink vegetable knife. I'm sure of that."

I close my eyes. What I see, *who I see*, the faceless, broad-shouldered silhouette standing in what I believe to be my living room, holding the knife . . . I can't tell Dr. Bentsen, not when I'm not even sure if it's a memory at all. Bentsen warned me a few times that my brain might be sorely tempted to make up its own stories to fill the blanks. *Horror vacui* and all that.

You're where my tape starts.

"Island? Island?"

My head snaps up. The moment I realize I zoned out, I have this irrational burst of fear and guilt in my chest, like I got caught . . . doing what, exactly? It's not like I'm under some sort of obligation to let everyone know every single thought that's going on in my mind at all times. I need time to make sense of whatever shreds of memory I grasp at. I straighten in my armchair and force myself to meet Dr. Bentsen's soft, querying gaze. "I'm sorry. I was just trying to visualize my kitchen, see if I remembered it."

"Do you?"

"No. Only the knife. Maybe it's because of the flashy color."

She seems satisfied with my answer. I breathe out. We're almost done.

"Your father will be here by the end of the week." Something flickers in her gray-blue irises as she says this, hesitation maybe. "I'll call him then. I'm thinking we could try a different approach . . . give you some space to heal on your own terms."

I sit perfectly still, even as an uncontrollable feeling of freedom sends my pulse to a frenzy. On my lap, my fists curl, bunching the material of my sweater in a supreme effort not to jump from my armchair. From a purely rational point of view, it's a tiny step. All it means for now is that I'll likely win the Christmas-ornaments battle. But it's a start: with some luck, maybe Bentsen will eventually deem me stable enough to go face the chaos of modern civilization and get my life back, dammit!

I hold back the grin I feel tug at my cheeks, schooling it into a meek smile. "Yes, I'd like that. Thank you."

She nods. Outside, the snow has started falling again; fat snowflakes drift past the windows, shrouding the castle's park in a pearly fog. Dr. Bentsen checks her watch. This time, we're done.

When she opens the music room's heavy doors, Stiles is here, waiting in the hallway, as usual. For once, though, I greet him with a beaming face. He cocks an eyebrow in question. I'll tell him later.

•••

"Slice the banana, and arrange the strawberries on top."

A monotone male voice rises from Stiles's tablet's speaker and resonates in the vast kitchen, to dictate precise cooking instructions. His tongue darts between his lips in a frown of intense concentration as he fixes us an elaborate fruit carpaccio for afternoon snack.

We *do* have a chef, French and all—Gwennaël. My mother was French too, so I like to chat with him when he's here. She died more than ten years ago in a car accident, and I can't remember anything about her, not even the fiery-red curls cascading down her shoulders in my father's pictures. I find comfort in the simple knowledge that I haven't forgotten the language though, its odd combination of soft sonorities. It makes me feel like there's a part of her inside me, something that transcends memory.

So yes, there's a chef. But Stiles likes to cook, or, to be precise, Stiles loves to cook with step-by-step videos—and that's not even his weirdest hobby . . . I watch him rummage through a massive fridge. The voice orders him to squeeze lime juice over his creation.

"Do you really feel ready for that?" he eventually asks. "Going out on your own?"

"Yes." My head bobs up and down like a rear-shelf dog's. "It's just not working, being here, resting all the time. So my entire adult life got flushed down the drain, and I'll have to live with brain injury. Tough hand, but okay, fine. I'll just have to build a new life. But I can't do that if I stay here. I need, um"—I ball my fists—"to, like, get back on the ring. And my meds are making me slow; I can't focus. I need to ease up on those too."

In Stiles's hand, a long Japanese knife stops halfway in the middle of the lime. "Maybe it's a bit early for that."

"Dad"—my voice catches on the word. Somehow, it still won't come out easily even after eight months—"Dad would tell you that's Dr. Bentsen's call," I say warily.

He sighs and finishes cutting the fruit. When he's done with his carpaccio, and he's about to put the knife away in the sink, he does that thing, spinning it in his hand. I have no idea how he does that; I can't even follow the movement of his fingers. Amazing.

The knife clanks in the sink. "If you say so."

We eat in silence. I know Stiles disapproves of Dr. Bentsen's project to open the doors to my cage, but it's Stiles; he's not gonna throw a tantrum about it. He's not going to say anything, actually. I get that he worries though and that he's responsible for me on a professional level too. If I lose my mind and somehow fall off a cliff, he'll have to answer to my father for it, and getting fired will be the least of his problems.

Honestly, my father is no worse than, say, Anna Wintour. I suspect he intentionally cultivates this cliché of the unfunny billionaire who'll pink-slip your ass in a heartbeat and sue your underwear off on top of it—the other day, I overheard a security guard hiss to another that "Mr. Keasler doesn't tolerate failure," like the guy would get thrown into a shark pool James Bond-style or something . . . The bottom line is that my father goes to great lengths to protect his private life—me included—because the world is full of people willing to kidnap a wealthy man's offspring and send him a big toe in guise of an invoice. And, yes, fed up as I am to convalesce here, I do understand that I and my fickle brain make an easy target.

"You know, I'm not gonna run off naked in the woods or something," I joke, playing with a slice of banana on my plate.

Stiles chuckles. "Please put on pants if you're gonna do that."

"We can find a middle ground," I add, in a more serious tone. "I need to stretch my wings. But I can definitely do with some help. Up to a point."

He raises a blond eyebrow. "Up to a point?"

As if to answer his question, a tremor shakes my hand when I raise my fork to eat. He sees it, and I can tell he'll be on his feet in an instant if needed. I shake my head negatively. "When my hands do that, for example, I don't want you to help me, because if you do, I'll never learn to live with it."

I gobble the piece of fruit, my gaze firmly planted on his. He gives a nod of understanding and stands to pick up our now-empty plates. Moments later, I see him open the fridge and reach for a bottle of apple juice. Knots form in my stomach.

I stare down at the ashen veins running across the marble tiles, unnerved by the sloshing sounds of juice being poured in a heavy crystal glass. Stiles reaches in his pocket for the pillbox that never leaves him, where each dose is ready. When he hands me the pair of white pills, I bite my lower lip, aware of the blood pounding in my neck.

"No, I'm good. I think we can skip them for today."

I register the faintest click of his tongue. "Island. I'm not sure we can find any . . . *middle ground* if you don't take your treatment."

"I want to see how I fare without the pills, just for a few days. I'll take them if I don't feel well."

Stiles takes a step forward, concern and some degree of annoyance wrinkling his brow. "Island, you're putting me in a tough spot."

I shake my head obstinately. He won't force me; I can't believe he would. Yet he takes another step, and I find him uncomfortably close. Stiles has touched me, carried me before, in the first months of my recovery, when my legs would sometimes betray me, but I've never experienced any real sense of threat at his proximity—except for the early days, when confusion and paranoia got the best of me. At the moment, however, he's towering over me, dwarfing me with his brawny build, and I'm acutely aware of the difference in physical strength between us.

There's no detectable anger in his gaze as he studies me but rather an odd tenderness. He's so close I can smell the notes of aftershave and some woody cologne, see each line of his face. I can't help but flinch when his left hand moves. Slowly, carefully, the back of his knuckles graze my cheek. I gasp, his hand drops, and it's over within seconds, before I can even process what happened.

"You were always trouble," he says, his baritone down to a thrumming whisper.

Was I? I don't know what to make of that. I don't think there's anything romantic about his gesture. I mean, if Stiles was interested, considering all the time we've spent alone together since I arrived at Ingolvinlinna, he'd have . . . Yeah. No. *This is about control.* The realization seems to pop out from a part of my brain I didn't even know still worked. I'm proven right when he reaches for the glass, now fully expecting me to submit.

•••

There's a rumor among the personnel that my father pays Stiles like Ronaldo to watch me 24/7. I have no idea whether this is true—I certainly hope so for him, since we're talking two grand an hour.

16

There are nonetheless levels of debasement no amounts of soccer money can buy. For example, Stiles never follows me to the bathroom. Well, *almost* never, if we take into account that time when I caught some kind of stomach bug three months ago. It was sad, ugly, and mildly traumatizing. The toilet bowl still remembers as Stiles held my hair while I threw up. He has made a point never to get directly involved with my bodily functions since. Can't blame him.

Barely ten minutes after lunch is over, I stand alone in front of the bathroom mirror, surrounded by the many shades of blue in the kaleidoscopic Moroccan tiling. I'm thinking that what Stiles doesn't know can't hurt him. This time, I need no help kneeling in front of the bowl. I stick my fingers down my throat, careful to stifle any undignified noises, even as my stomach starts heaving. And up goes the apple juice, along with Dr. Bentsen's med cocktail.

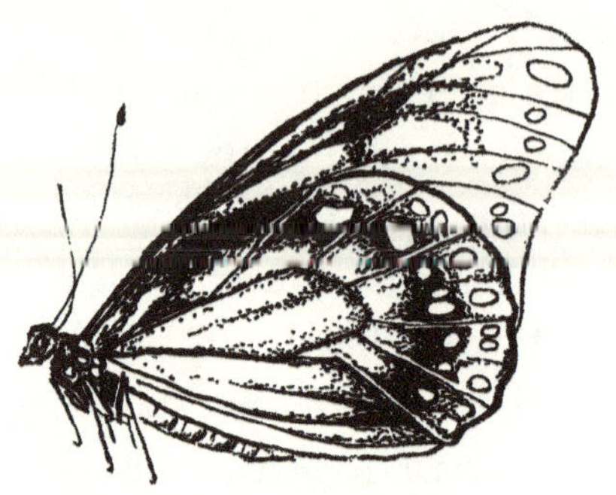

THREE
THE GREEN FAIRY

We're waiting for him.

My father should be here for dinner, so I went to curl up in one of the salon's armchairs with a book to pass time until he arrives. Night has fallen, and the room is plunged in a silence only disturbed by the occasional crack of a log in the fireplace. In comparison, the rest of Ingolvinlinna is in ebullition. As usual whenever my father visits, security appears to have doubled, and you can't go ten feet without seeing black uniforms. On the second floor, maids hustle to make sure that my father's room is ready to welcome him, while in the kitchen, Gwennaël is putting the last touch to a haute-cuisine feast he said would be a welcome change from "Internet recipes"—Stiles took the jab well, like he takes everything else, really . . .

Speaking of the devil, he's checking his phone while I flip through a painfully detailed account of the disastrous Arctic expedition led by a certain Sir John Franklin. After some prolonged typing, Stiles puts his phone away to dedicate himself to one of his favorite activities . . . staring. If I didn't know any better, I'd say he's bored and wants to make small talk, but I recognize his attentive gaze for what it is: he's monitoring, analyzing, gauging my mental state—no doubt to later provide a detailed report to our lord and master.

My father is away most of the time, conducting business all over the globe—it's actually been almost a month since his last visit. He rarely calls me, which I'm willing to blame on work and time difference rather than the product of an aloof and secretive personality. That's just the way he is: he never calls to chat, he calls when it's 2:00 a.m. in Shanghai and he needs to hear my voice—in which case I'm the one who does what little chatting I can. Even so, I don't mistake his introversion for indifference: I'm well aware that he keeps a close watch on me through his favorite snitch . . .

The culprit tilts his head at me with a soft smile. "Watcha reading?"

I hold up the book so Stiles can see the cover. "It's about the lost Franklin expedition."

"I heard about it. They found the ships a while back, right?"

"Yeah, it was an arctic exploration mission led by the British in 1845. They sent two ships that never came back, and it took almost one hundred and fifty years to figure out what happened to the crew."

"And what happened?"

"Bad karma. They ended up stuck in ice for two years, died from the cold, disease . . . some tried to walk south, and they all died on the way. The bones the scientists found showed traces of cannibalism too."

The way Stiles's eyebrows pinch tells he won't borrow that lovely tome.

"Actually, the most interesting part is that the men developed scurvy and pneumonia, but they had no idea they were also dying from lead poisoning from their canned food. Possibly from their tinned cans or the ships' water systems. Gruesome stuff."

As he listens to this, Stiles leans back in the couch and crosses his arms. "Interesting."

"There's also pics of the bodies," I say, flipping the book to show him the chilling rictus of death painted on the face of an otherwise perfectly preserved, frozen body.

Stiles shakes his head. "I'll pass, thank you . . . Besides"—he turns to the latticed bay window behind the couch. Outside, the faint droning of a rotor is growing louder by the second—"they're here."

He's right; moments later, the beam of a helicopter light swipes across the park and clouds of fresh snow swirl around the aircraft as it slowly descends. When the doors open, a few men jump to the ground. I recognize my father's bodyguards. Right afterward, a tall silhouette in a dark coat unfolds from the back seat and steps out from the chopper. His graying head turns to the castle; I wave at him. He doesn't wave back, but I know he saw me—there's very little that escapes my father's notice.

When a second figure steps out right behind him, I can't contain a wince. Even from here, I recognize the usual leather jacket, the shorter, slender build. I know that prejudice is the child of ignorance and all that, but . . . I don't like the pirate. He has a real name, by the way—Alexander Morgan. He's some kind of assistant to my father, and to be honest, I've never actually heard him say "aargh" or sing "Drunken Sailor." It's not his fault; I mean, I'm sorry that he's missing his right eye, and honestly, apart from that, he's like any guy my age. Not even bad looking, with his brown curls and soft—well, one soft—cinnamon eye. He's always nice to me, which makes me feel even worse for being creeped out like that.

Speaking of which . . . he too gazes in our direction. His face lights up. *Dammit.* Busted.

Next to me, Stiles acts like he didn't notice the pirate's grin and tips his head toward the window. "Let's go greet them?"

"Okay."

By the time we've covered the miles of hallway separating us from the entrance hall, I hear the heavy oak doors creak and slam closed. Cold seeps through my slippers as I come down the stone stairs alongside Stiles.

My father removes his coat and drops it in the awaiting arms of a maid he barely acknowledges. He's wearing his usual black mandarin suit underneath—he avoids white shirts, probably because otherwise people would ask to confess their sins to him. When he sees me, his features relax, an odd metamorphosis that smooths the sharp angles of his face and lessens the stern lines creasing the corners of his mouth. I wouldn't quite call it a smile, but it's an expression reserved for me solely; I know that much.

"You look radiant, Island," he says, his peculiar accent betraying his South African roots.

I respond with an awkward thumbs-up as he pulls me to him. I allow the embrace even if I don't fully return it. This is another bridge that collapsed, and that'll take time to rebuild. To be honest, I wonder if we were ever that close before my accident. I lost my mother when I was only fifteen, but when he showed me his old pictures of her, with her flaming-red locks and those features in which I could find a little bit of myself, I had this instinctual certainty—literally a gut feeling—that she was important, that our bond was important.

On the other hand, ever since I blinked awake for the first time at the clinic and found myself staring into those hazel eyes that mirrored mine, I've been grappling with whatever daughterly instinct was left in me in the absence of any memory of this man. I've learned again his calm, inscrutable mask, his brief hugs, or the peculiar smoky, peppery scent of his Vetiver cologne—I read the plant makes a great bug repellent, but I don't think it influenced my father's choice.

"I guess I'm doing better," I say when he releases me.

A dry cough shakes his frame as he replies, "I can see that."

"How have you been, Island?"

A prickle down my spine alerts me to the pirate's close proximity before I've even turned. I really need to get over that. He's a human being. With an eye patch. It's not the end of the world. I force a grin on my face. "Great, thanks!"

He steps forward, carrying with him a whiff of leather and outdoors. I didn't notice the box in his hands until now. He hands it to me with an easy grin. Tightly wrapped in a golden ribbon is a box of Italian gianduiotti.

"Early Christmas present," he explains.

"Um . . . wow. Thanks."

I'm torn. I don't want any gift from him—I'm not even sure I should accept it—but my mouth is watering already, and I know that I'm gonna hit that candy like Floyd Mayweather Jr. as soon as I'm alone. Morgan takes another step forward, right into what I deem my personal space, and my uneasiness returns full force. He always looms too close; I think that's why I have a problem with this guy.

"I'm really glad to see you like this, Island," he croons, plunging his gaze into mine.

I recoil with an unsteady smile that I fear is closer to a grimace. Part of me suspects that Morgan is hitting on me, while another counters that all he's really doing is sucking up to my father with his suave game and his candy. Either way, I could do without the attention.

"Island is delighted. Thank you." At last, my father's icy tone slices through the awkward silence. I let out a silent breath of relief as Morgan puts some distance between us.

On my father's face, the usual impassive mask has fallen back into place as he instructs Morgan. "Contact Jorge. I want a full report on the incident in Rio."

Morgan ducks his head. "Understood."

He strides past us with one last glance my way before disappearing behind the doors leading to the east wing. I'm not eating those gianduiotti. I'm strong enough for that.

Behind me, Stiles steps forward to greet my father. "Welcome back. Satisfying trip?"

My father's lips quirk briefly. "Very much so."

"Dr. Bentsen was hoping to speak to you. Would you like me to schedule a call?" Stiles asks.

A jolt of anxiety travels down all the way to my toes at the sound of her name. I had almost forgotten about that minor formality. She's going to report to my father on my progress, and how that meeting plays out will determine whether I can hope for a one-way ticket to

New York in the weeks to come . . .

My father's eyes are on me, kind and keen, as he replies, "I'll call her now." He pauses, bestowing his full attention on Stiles. "Once I'm done, you'll join Island and me for dinner, *broer*."

I blink. It's not the first time I hear my father call Stiles "brother," but an invitation to the dinner table is certainly something new. I shake my head with a secret smile. Stiles . . . ever the employee of the month.

•••

My father joined us after he was done with his phone call, and if I had a left nut to give, I'd trade it for a detailed recap of their conversation. *Right now.* But last time I checked, I was still a girl, and he won't talk until he's decided to. So instead I joined him with Stiles in the reception hall for what is shaping to be the longest dinner of my life.

My father sits alone at one end of the mile-long oak table, as usual, while I inwardly fret in a giant renaissance chair at the other, dwarfed by the massive chandeliers hanging from the coffered ceiling. I watch a stiff butler place three plates of beef tataki and julienned vegetables in front of us and dig in under the disapproving scrutiny of the giant portraits lining the walls—not ancestors, just paintings my father collected over the years. He doesn't like to discuss his hobby: I asked once, and he basically brushed me off and said they were forgotten warriors, no one history remembers.

I'd been hoping that Stiles's addition in the chair next to mine would bring a little life to this party, but the only sound in the hall is the soft clink of cutlery as we finish our plates. I still haven't fully adjusted to this strange ritual: my father always eats in complete silence. No use in trying to strike up conversation until dessert is finished: the best I can hope for is a nod, perhaps even a monosyllabic reply if he's in a particularly jolly mood.

Gwennaël earns a nod, by the way. My father loves crêpes Suzette, and they certainly taste even better when you have an actual Frenchman to flambé them right before you. I watch in amazement as the splash of Grand Marnier he pours over the crêpes ignites, and he serves us the flaming plates.

As expected, when the last bite of dessert has been gobbled and the plates are gone, my father rises from his chair and, at last, speaks. "We'll have a drink in the salon."

I bite back a sigh. "We" actually means "I": Bentsen doesn't want me to drink while I'm—supposedly—under treatment, and Stiles never drinks on the job. As we make our way across the lobby and to the east wing, I muse that sometimes my father reminds me of Louis XIV, "the Sun King." It's the way he orchestrates, ritualizes things around himself: the perfectly tailored mandarin suits or how he bestows his rare smiles like favors. Ice cold when business doesn't move fast enough, solar to those he deems deserving of his light.

I plop back in my favorite armchair while my father sits in his own, facing me. Behind the bar, Stiles begins yet another carefully choreographed ritual, setting a crystal glass and a flat, perforated silver spoon on the counter. Next is the bottle, which he frees from a lacquered box. He pours an ounce of the greenish liquid in the glass before he balances the spoon on top of it. Then the sugar cube, placed at the center of the spoon. Last is the fountain, an antique glass vessel resting on top of a finely engraved silver stand, with a silver tap designed to drip ice-cold water onto the spoon. Stiles checks that the glass is perfectly positioned and opens the tap. Drop after drop, the water hits the sugar and trickles in the absinthe glass with soft splattering sounds. My father watches as pale swirls form in the liquid and it turns milky. Another coughing fit shakes him, thunderous in this silent room.

Every time I witness this, I wonder if I should say something. He hasn't been well lately, and I doubt absinthe's legendary healing properties will do him much good. I glance at the spotted brownish label. Actually, I'm not even sure anyone should drink something that was bottled in 1907 . . . Once again, I respect the ritual though and sit still while Stiles serves him the glass. He raises it, toasting no one in particular—something common with him. "To *Odysseus*'s journey," he says before taking the first sip, his eyes closed.

That too, I won't try to overanalyze. My father is nothing but cryptic, probably by nature rather than choice. Often, he'll throw half a dozen words my way and be done, certain that his meaning and intent have been stated with absolute clarity. And I'll just blink, wondering what he was even talking about in the first place . . .

Once he's done and the bottle is back in its box, my father lets out a contented sigh. "Dr. Bentsen is pleased with your recovery."

My breath catches in my windpipe; I sit a little straighter.

"But she told me you've become restless and expressed boredom." He arches an elegant gray eyebrow. "Are you bored here in Ingolvinlinna, Island?"

If there's something I've learned over the past months, it's that litotes and diplomacy will get me nowhere. So, I look at him straight in the eye and say, "Yes."

"Have you visited the entirety of the island?"

"No . . ."

"Well then—"

"*Dad.*" My voice catches as I utter the simple and oddly foreign word, but I trudge on. "I want—I *need* my life back. I need to see people, to move, to work. I honestly think I've done all the recovering I can here." I try to smother the flicker of guilt at the back of my mind as I claim this. How pathetic is it that even I am not entirely convinced I'm stable?

At first, he remains silent, appraising me with unreadable eyes. When his lips part, I wrench my hands on my lap, hanging on to each word. "I suppose I can't keep you here forever, can I?" It doesn't sound like an actual question—because it isn't—I bite my tongue and allow him to go on uninterrupted. "Perhaps Mr. Stiles could start by taking you to Hamina for some Christmas shopping tomorrow."

A fist pump would certainly be inappropriate in this refined atmosphere. I go for an expression of sober wonderment. "Oh, I'd love that."

"Then that's settled."

Stiles watches our exchange from behind the bar. His mouth

twitches, and his right eyelid flutters in the briefest wink. I fight the urge to wink back at him.

My father's fingers rap on his armrest, and I almost think he's bored already and will leave for the night, but his gaze lights up in renewed interest. "I have a gift for you, Island."

I shake my head. "You need to stop spoiling me."

Not that he will . . . I'm not really worried about the money—obviously—rather, I'm kind of uneasy at the notion that he's offering me all that extravagant jewelry I won't wear anyway as a means to connect with me, to make up for everything I've lost. I don't need any of that, and it actually makes me feel a little guilty for not being able to return his affection on a deeper, more instinctive level.

Meanwhile, my father flicks his wrist to Stiles, who leaves the room and returns a few seconds later with a black leather box wrapped in a white satin bow.

He rises from his armchair to take it from him and places it in my lap. "I think you'll like it."

I tug at the delicate ribbon hesitantly. That stuff screams expensive again . . . but no. The box doesn't reveal the flare of an emerald necklace, like last time, but a simple pendant, held by a thin blue silk cord. At first glance, it looks like some kind of orange glass design, but when I take it out to examine it against the fireplace light, the translucent disc reveals veins and microscopic bubbles surrounding a delicate butterfly—trapped in amber, I realize.

I caress the cool surface with a mixture of awe and curiosity, inspecting the spotted wings, forever preserved. "Is it old?"

"Paleocene, a little over fifty million years old."

My mouth falls open in amazement. The longer I stare at it though, the more I struggle with a growing sense of discomfort, like a weight inside me, whose location I can't pinpoint. Maybe because it's basically wearing a dead insect around my neck.

Of course, my lack of enthusiasm doesn't go unnoticed. My father tilts his head. "You don't like it?"

"No, I do . . . Of course, I do. I guess it's just a little sad that it's dead," I muse, even as my mind pictures the butterfly being slowly trapped in the golden resin, struggling, and eventually giving up the fight.

He takes the pendant from my hand and holds it out against the light in his turn. "I prefer to think it's saved. Safe from predators that would have crushed its wings, freed from pain"—he bends toward me and, with careful gestures, secures it around my neck—"its beauty forever preserved."

And yet, I can't stop thinking that the butterfly is dead. I shiver. "Yes. You're right . . . Where did it come from, by the way?"

"Ecuador."

My ears perk up. "Where your factory is? Is that where you went this time?"

He lets his fingers trail in my hair, stroking it. "Yes. I'll tell you about it later, if you want. For now, you and I need some rest. Good night, Island. I'll see you tomorrow."

I don't take offense at this abrupt dismissal: this isn't the first time he's shut down on me when I want to hear about his business, and I know my father has been tired lately. That damn absinthe probably doesn't help either. "Okay, sleep well."

Stiles walks me back to my room, as usual. When I'm about to close the door, I hesitate before turning around to face him. My father's words echo in my ears. *Brother . . .* I wonder if this is all just a job to Stiles. How can he not see what's going on? I clench my fists. "You shouldn't give it to him. Even if he asks."

He tilts his head, as if waiting for the rest. We both know better; there's no misunderstanding between us at the moment.

"The absinthe," I insist. "It's shit, and you know it."

His lips curve in an apologetic pout. "Island, it's not my place to say anything."

"Then *who* will? You know he'll brush me off."

"Unlike me?" he asks—the undercurrent of irony is not lost on me.

My shoulders slump. "It's different for you . . ." I hate to admit it, but Stiles has a lot more reach than me, whom everyone around these walls regards as some kind of handicapped kid.

He inches closer, at the edge of my personal space, and places his hand on my shoulder. I can feel the heat of his palm through the light wool of my sweater, not quite intimate—no longer casual either. I'm wondering if I should say something, but then his head dips toward mine. My pulse picks up as his face draws closer, until his mouth hovers millimeters from my ear and his cheek grazes my hair. "I'll see what I can do," he murmurs.

After he's left and closed the door to my bedroom at last, I just stand there for several seconds in a state of mild shock, contemplating this new "incident." Maybe I need to tell him I'm not interested . . .

FOUR
PERILINEN

"Biscuit . . . wake up."

I jackknife up and shove the comforter away, its weight suddenly unbearable. Under me, the mattress feels like quicksand. It takes me a few seconds to figure that my good ol' canopy bed won't swallow me and that I haven't gone blind; it's just dark in here. My hair is matted to my neck by an uncomfortable sheen of sweat; my cheeks are hot. I will my heart to calm down with deep, slow breaths.

The sun hasn't risen yet. I squint at the window to my left and the dull, smooth immensity beyond—it's been snowing again. I glance at the glowing digits of the clock on my nightstand. 6:27. Stiles won't start the pancakes until 7. I hope we're getting normal ones today.

The chocolate and chorizo ones he tried last week probably fit the legal definition of cruel and unusual punishment. I rub my eyes and fall back on my pillows. Okay, I'm living a lie. I don't give a damn about the pancakes.

I stretch, sigh. I don't want to move just yet; my skin is still tingling—the dream lingers in my body in a warm, buzzing sensation. I've had dreams before—nightmares too—but never so vivid and not for three nights in a row like that. A little voice at the back of my mind quips that my new and questionable habit of throwing up my meds as soon as Stiles looks away might have something to do with it . . .

The biggest frustration is that I can never see his face. That fantasy guy of mine isn't really anyone I could identify. Similarly, there's no logic, no scenario to these dreams: it's not me being swept up by a brooding model and ravished on silk sheets. It's more like a patchwork of sensations, things I glimpse under a strobe light—hot skin, lips that search mine in the dark, and under my fingertips, a rug of chest hair so warm, so silky, so curly that I wish I could shrink to a microscopic size and live in there for the rest of my life. Kinda like a louse, technically.

God, it's in moments like this that I miss having someone to *really* talk to . . . Officially, my sessions with Dr. Bentsen are a "safe space," where I'm "free to bring up any subject, no matter how intimate." But I can't bring myself to tell Bentsen about that kind of stuff. It sounds so crude, so pathetic, even to myself. I've lost my best friend, my memories, my life. I need to focus on healing, rebuilding . . . and here I am, squirming under the sheets with a faceless incubus.

I did wonder if he might be the ghost of an ex, but I was apparently single when I had my accident, and no one has mentioned any significant relationship. According to my mailbox, I went on a slew of terrible dates through Yaycupid a year ago or so—no trace of any sex god with quiet dark blue eyes and epic chest hair though. It appears I also curated a large collection of research material on the subject of heterosexual romantic involvement, such as the *Forbidden MC Desires* series or *His to Save and Submit.* I'm kind of relieved that

I don't remember those books, because the very covers made me blush . . .

Anyway, pretty much like every time I try to dig up a little piece of my past self, I'm left with only one option: asking either Stiles or my father. *Or not.* This goes at the top of my personal list of conversations that won't happen. I shake my head to dispel the memory of his body against mine and hop out of bed. Under the heavy wooden doors of my bedroom, a thin ray of light filters that gilds the Persian rug. Shadows come and go as the castle awakens. On the other side of the doors, boots stomp by: Stiles never leaves the hallway unguarded—another detail that annoys me to no end, even if I know he means well.

I quickly shower, and by the time I'm done slipping into a pair of jeans and the blue cashmere sweater my father offered me a few weeks ago, there's a gentle knock at the door.

It's pancake time.

●●●

Raisins, dammit!

"Not hungry this morning?" Stiles asks as he watches me repeatedly poke with my fork the offending pile sitting on my plate.

"Not really." Because no one likes *raisins.* It's like vegan bacon and wet socks in your shoes: whoever pretends to tolerate those is just lying.

Culinary mishaps aside, I'm actually in a fairly good mood, sizzling with excitement at the prospect of buying Christmas balls. Outside, at last, back to civilization! Okay, with its twenty thousand souls, Hamina, the nearest big town—a few miles east—isn't exactly a megalopolis. Still, there are at least four supermarkets and a handful of kebabs whose ranking is a subject of hot debate among the castle's personnel. That'll be more human activity than I've seen in months; the thrill is real.

I dissect a pancake under Stiles's patient stare, extracting the raisins one by one. After I've gulped down the last bite, he takes my plate with a wink. "Please don't slam me on Yelp."

I give him a level stare. "It'd need to load for that."

He turns around with an air of contrition I know all too well. "Oh? They blocked it too?"

I glare at him. "We *really* need to do something about that firewall."

All I get for my efforts is a chuckle. "I e-mailed support again about that."

"I'm telling you that company is a joke. I don't even know how you put up with this."

"I use my data," Stiles replies with a shrug.

Because *he* has a phone, and I don't. Over the past few weeks, the Internet had become one of my primary sources of frustration, along with the general need to expand my horizons. I didn't think about it much until the end of October, mostly because before that, I'd been lying either in my bed or on a couch, oscillating between stages of mild apathy and crippling depression. I have to give credit where it's due: the meds helped in that regard.

As I got better though, boredom reared its head, and I quickly came to the conclusion that there wasn't much to do in the castle. I wanted Internet. Except we only have satellite-Internet access at Ingolvinlinna, one of the planet's many buttholes. Our signal is sketchy at best, and it doesn't help that we have a nazi firewall on top of it. Twitter and Facebook are a lost cause, but I do manage to load some pages on Wikipedia or CNN, and I even watched a few videos on YouTube. Most of the time though, the connection is so slow that I give up before the firewall can even kick me out—and our TV signal is hardly any better . . .

I've started filing regular complaints to the staff about this pressing issue. Translation: I bitch to Stiles that Facebook won't load. Every time, he assures me that yet another support ticket has been sent to our ISP, who will handle it ASAP. My best guess is that those tickets are remorselessly deleted upon reception by an employee who deserves to spend the rest of his life cursed with a nine-hundred-millisecond ping and no hope to ever load Facebook again.

I shake my head, ready to leave the table, when Stiles moves toward the fridge. The simple sound of the door opening makes me fidgety, but my recent transgressions have awakened the thug in me: I look at him in the eye as I take the glass of juice, knowing fully that today's meds will be on their merry way to the sewer system before we leave the castle.

After I'm done and he's put the glass in the sink, I spin on my heels. "I'll go get my coat." *And I'll make a stop to the bathroom . . .*

"Already?"

"It's not like we got anything else to do today. Plus it's Saturday: we better get there early, before the shops get super crowded."

"All right, but"—he points to the ceiling, or rather to the second floor, where my father has been locked in his study since the break of dawn—"he told me wants to see you before we leave."

•••

Absinthe isn't the only thing capable of lifting my father's mood: morning walks in the park can work wonders too. The sun peeks through the clouds to warm our cheeks as we tread down the French garden's central alley. Around us, the rows of perfectly round and evenly spaced evergreen shrubs look like ice-cream scoops with their smooth snow topping. I blow a little fog through my mouth with childish delight.

The faintest smile plays on my father's lips: now is a good time to chat—possibly the best. "So, how are your shipments going?" I ask, stroking my chin like I actually know what I'm talking about.

I don't—well, not really. My father owns stakes in a variety of industrial ventures, but he doesn't share the details of his business with me. That leaves me with the option of either eavesdropping or asking Stiles, who loves to pretend he's too dumb to understand all that complex financial stuff I shouldn't worry about anyway.

"We're almost done. We'll be ready to launch in less than two weeks."

But launch *what*? So far, none of my efforts to find out have been successful. I know he's been working on something big in South

America over the past year. I've also come to understand that the Big-Ass South American Project—BASAP—relies on complex logistics and requires many large shipments. My father's mood is linearly correlated to the speed and safe delivery of those shipments, and heads are expected to roll when they get late—which is apparently not the case this time.

"Still won't tell me what's the big reveal?" I give it a try, knowing full well it's useless.

"Not yet."

Yup, useless . . .

He offers me his arm as we reach the central parterre, a series of tightly clipped hedges forming arabesques around a wide, circular fountain. The four stone lions sitting in the center have stopped spitting water for the winter; they'll watch over this frozen Eden until spring returns. My father looks up at one of them. "It's perhaps a bit selfish, but I want to enjoy the surprise in your eyes when you see it for the first time."

When the meaning of his words registers, I nearly quiver with excitement. "You'll take me with you? To Ecuador?"

"Yes," he confirms.

I perform a mental fist pump. "When do we leave?"

His smile grows mysterious. "Chaque chose en son temps." *Everything in its own time.*

My father doesn't speak French, and his accent is pretty thick as he recites the old saying. Much like the gardens or Gwennaël's presence, it's a reminder that Ingolvinlinna was meant for my mother. She died before she could ever see it, in a car crash in Tokyo that I can't even remember, eleven years ago. My heart weighs a little heavier, as it always does when I think of her. It's an instinct that doesn't need words or even memories, a love that's part of me. I wish my father and I were that close . . .

"I can't wait," I tell him, looking up at the pearly sky. "I need a change of air, and that way Stiles can take some time off too." I didn't mean to make it sound like I want him gone, but I'm afraid that's exactly how it came out.

"He'll be joining us," my father replies, with a side-eye I'm not sure how to interpret.

"Ah."

"I was pleasantly surprised to see you so well. Joshua has been taking excellent care of you."

Joshua? Now that's new. I've never heard my father pronounce Stiles's first name before. To me, and everyone in the castle, it's Mr. Stiles, and while his affable manners are a hit with maids and contribute to earn him the security teams' complete devotion, no one gets too personal with him. He's built those invisible walls around himself, walls you hit soon enough—except he's let me in a little lately, I remind myself . . .

Gravel cracks under my boots as we stroll around the fountain. "Yeah, I suppose he's been very patient."

"Kindness and patience. All too rare qualities in our world."

I try, in vain, to decipher my father's shuttered expression. I'm not sure if he means in business, or if this is a general statement that all men are baboons except his favorite employee. Either way, I'm not entirely comfortable with the direction this conversation is headed.

"True," I say lamely, waiting to see where he'll go with this.

He nods. "He's proven trustworthy . . . and he told me he enjoyed spending time with you here in Ingolvinlinna."

My mouth falls open. I don't know what surprises me the most: Stiles's obvious lie or what I fear might be an awkward attempt from my father to play cupid.

Without warning, he pauses in his stride. A birdcall in the distance rips through the sudden silence. He gazes down at me with those unfathomable hazel eyes—almost golden, when the light is right. There's no spark to be found in them today though; he looks bone weary as he draws a long sigh that carries a whiff of herbs and alcohol. The peculiar scent of absinthe. "We don't live for ourselves, Island. We build for the generations to come."

I ponder the implications of this statement in the light of the recent changes in "Joshua's" behavior. If this means what I think it means, it's a no from me. He can date Stiles himself, since he likes him so much. I'm not sure my father would take that kind of snark well though, so when he resumes walking, I follow him back to the castle without a word. My thoughts drift to Pirate Morgan, with his gianduiotti box and his obsequious loyalty—I wonder if he understands he's not the chosen one . . .

FIVE

SPRINKLES ON TOP

The boat was a shock. It's nothing huge or anything: just a small navy blue yacht, fast and comfy, designed to cover the distance to the coast but not much more. No, what stunned me was the realization that there *was* a boat. Several, in fact, but also a road leading to the snowy pier, lined by barracks and a couple of stone houses in which I assume the castle personnel lives. There was an entire world at hand's reach, even within the confines of the island. A world I never suspected was there because, curled up in the fog of my meds, smoldered by Stiles's constant monitoring, I never made it beyond the fricking park. *Sweet Jesus*, I've been vegetating in a two-hundred-yard-wide perimeter since April . . .

As we trail across the gulf of Finland toward Hamina's harbor, I can't take my eyes from the windows, even for a second. Every detail of the barren immensity surrounding us feels new and awesome: the dark waters, the pristine floe blanketing the sea in the distance. Ingolvinlinna is part of a cluster of islands off the southern coast, most of them mere skerries. I never cared much for the local topography until now, but seeing them feels like a revelation, and I marvel at each snow-covered rock emerging from the water.

For a while, I'm barely aware of Stiles, sitting by my side on a long couch. It takes me a few minutes to notice that he's not looking at the scenery but, rather, at me.

"What?" I ask, fiddling with the white beanie and matching gloves I shoved in my parka pocket before leaving.

"Nothing. You look enthralled."

"And you look blasé. Don't you like it here?"

A brief wince twists his mouth before he readjusts his black leather gloves under the sleeves of a brown coat. "I'd have picked someplace warmer."

I think it's the first time I've ever heard Stiles express any disagreement with my father. Because we both know that's what he means by that. The island is my father's retreat—a cold, silent place most would find desolate but where he sees beauty and finds peace, to quote him. Which is why I'm here: for an old-fashioned patriarch, it goes without saying that what's good for him is good for his offspring.

"Where?" I prod, turning away from the window.

"Where what?"

"You said you'd pick someplace warmer. Where?"

His gaze grows unfocused, lost in the foggy horizon. "Savannah. Nice weather, even in December."

"Sounds good. Is that where you live?"

Stiles blinks—I've taken him off guard. On his face, the surprise quickly morphs into an impenetrable smile. "I live where my job takes me. Which is here, at the moment."

Gotcha. "Stop dodging the question. I'm talking about the place where you keep your cats."

His eyebrows shoot up. Here's another low blow he didn't expect. The Roomba cats . . . I have no idea if anyone knows about them besides me. They're his secret hobby, and it basically goes like this: Stiles has four cats, who live in the mysterious sunny place where he finds solace when he's not doing my father's bidding 24/7—they may or may not be the only thing he loves in this world. He trained them to ride on the many Roombas ambling around his house, and he buys silly costumes for them—mostly on Etsy, where the boldest names of feline fashion gather. Anyway, he dresses them up, lets them roll, and films the whole thing.

I love his stuff. You don't know the true meaning of *art* until you've seen a sphynx in a glittery unicorn costume sitting on a Roomba that repeatedly bumps against a fridge. The dreaded firewall did allow me to check some of his videos on YouTube, and his account is insanely popular. I have no idea how much he makes from online advertising, but he hit twelve million views for that vid of his tabby dressed up as a monkey and licking a banana, so I bet he could retire today if he wanted to.

"So," I insist. "Where does the magic happen?"

"I could tell you," he eventually says. "But where's the fun without a little bit of mystery?"

I'm tempted to give it another try, but I can tell he traced a line he doesn't want me to cross. Stiles works for my father, and what he does in his free time, or *where* he does it, is technically none of my business.

"I guess you're right," I concede as the first houses come into view, and the yacht slows down toward a small marina.

Stiles glances through the window and clasps his hands. "Get ready. It's adventure time."

Adventure it is, when our pilot helps me down a frosty pier. On a wooden shelter furnished with not one but two benches, a sign proudly reads Hamina Yacht Club. There's a parking lot lined with naked birch trees and a few traditional Finnish log houses, with their characteristic *falu* red paint and white trims and windows. I spot a café and, nearby, what appears to be a minigolf course, half-buried under the snow. Yes. *This.* This is something I'll need to investigate. Thoroughly.

With a nod to the pilot, Stiles leads me to the parking lot, where a black Jaguar sedan awaits. It's a short drive to downtown Hamina, past more wooden buildings, but also neoclassical ones, like the town hall and Vehkalahti Church—a stunning ensemble of arches and columns supporting a portico, all painted in bright orange with white trims: a Roman architect's dream . . . in the land of the Finns. Stiles takes his time driving us around and playing tour guide—I love that. I feel like my mind, my body are awakening at last, and I want to absorb everything, the lights, the sounds, the colors . . .

As we near the marketplace, the picturesque wooden houses are replaced by concrete buildings, restaurants, and shops. I rub my hands in anticipation when I notice a supermarket sign. Most of the place is occupied by a Christmas market—this too shall be visited extensively, I decide, eyeing the food trucks lined up around the place.

As soon as we're parked in front of a supermarket with an impossibly long name I instantly dub the S-Mart, I spring out of the car like a jack-in-the-box. "Let's grab the Christmas stuff first; after that, we can check the market and, um, I need to buy a phone too."

"A phone?"

"Yes. I thought about it yesterday. I haven't had one since I came to Ingolvinlinna, and I figure I lost mine back in April. But I need one." I swallow to catch my breath—my brain is working faster than my mouth, which is a welcome novelty. "I can't believe I spent so long without a phone, right?"

He gives a skeptical nod. "I don't know if that's something we can find—"

"We can probably find one there," I counter, pointing at a store across the street, whose sign features a yellow phone next to a big Ericsson logo.

A perplexed frown creases Stile's brow, before he nods. "All right, but let's go through your shopping list first."

I give him a thumbs-up and follow him inside. There, I make a beeline to the Christmas aisle and start filling our basket with a steady hand, piling golden balls, light garlands, little reindeer plushy ornaments . . .

Stiles watches me compare two stars with his arms crossed. After several minutes of silence, he cocks his head at me. "You've livened up lately."

He's right. I want this new energy I feel flowing through me. I love feeling so sharp, so pumped. My mind is stirring awake at long last, and I want out of the cocoon my father has crafted around me . . . I think of the colorful pills I threw up before leaving the castle and shush my conscience as I tell Stiles, "I told you I was feeling better . . . I kept blaming everything on my meds, but I just needed to give myself a kick. Rising up, back on the street, you know the drill."

Stiles chuckles, taking the glittery white star I picked. "I see . . . Got everything you need, tiger?"

"Yup." I take determined strides toward the register. "Now, all I need is a phone, and next time that crap firewall acts up, I'll just switch to my data."

His eyes seem distant as he places our loot on the conveyor belt. "Christmas market first, maybe?"

I grin. "You're tempting me . . ."

"Then let's go," he retorts with a wink.

After a brief stop to the car to load our purchases in the trunk, we're ready to take on the Christmas market, with its small wooden houses selling stuff no one needs yet everyone will buy. The heady scent of freshly baked pastries and fried food tickles my nostrils as I stop in front of a stall selling a multitude of flashy Peruvian beanies.

I'm so used to Stiles always hovering behind me that it takes me a whole minute to notice he's stopped a few feet away, in front of a different stall. His eyes dart my way—the professional never sleeps. I trot back to him to see what could have possibly distracted the steadfast Joshua Stiles . . . and stifle a laugh. Those tiny Christmas costumes were meant for dogs, as evidenced by the many pictures hanging on the shop's walls, but it won't stop him: I can already see the cogs spinning fast in Stiles's head as he examines a reindeer costume and its pair of felt antlers.

"Feeling inspired?" I ask.

He strokes his chin. "Could be."

While Stiles rummages through the owner's stock, a series of shrill sounds reaches us, coming from the direction of the ice-cream truck. We look over our shoulders to check the source of the commotion. Flash tantrum: a little girl just collapsed in the snow and is now emitting otherworldly screeches. Stiles returns to his shopping, but I keep watching, fascinated. Apparently they're out of strawberry cones, and the child is now attempting to tear off her clothes in a textbook case of possession.

The crowd too witnesses in consternation as the mom attempts to reason with the vile little turd writhing in the slush at her feet. Suddenly, a scoop of ice cream flies from the truck, fired at the kid with deadly precision. The shrieking stops. The air becomes still as the girl stares up at the old and burly clown leaning over the counter. Her round face is smeared with pinkish goo; she looks winded. Before she can open her mouth again, the clown finishes her with a handful of sprinkles that land in her hair and barks, "Seuraava." *Next.*

In the US, that would probably go all the way to trial, but instead the mom simply picks up her child with a solemn nod in the clown's direction. Tough shores. I look back to see that Stiles is paying for the reindeer costume. A cold flake lands on my nose. I look up; snow is starting to fall again, like a thousand stars tumbling down from above to melt at our feet. In the food truck, the clown is gone, leaving a young guy to serve the customers instead. I feel suddenly a little cold, despite the wool scarf around my neck. A shiver raises goose bumps on my arms. Something is wrong, but I can't put my finger on it. From the corner of my eye, I see Stiles taking a paper bag from the dog-costume seller. Around me, people walk, run, laugh under the snow.

That's when I notice that someone in the crowd isn't moving, standing still. I stare back at the man in a long black coat I am now certain is staring at me. My chest tightens. It's not real—I *know* it's not . . . Maybe I shouldn't have thrown up my meds because now I'm hallucinating hard. My pulse picks up, and I can't look away from the tall silhouette, the short chestnut hair. I'm certain his eyes are a dark blue, the color of the ocean, which is logically impossible to ascertain from this distance.

"Island?"

I whirl around to find myself nose to chest with Stiles. I stagger back, blink up at him, and immediately turn again to check the surroundings of the ice-cream truck. There's no one there. *God*, I have serious issues . . .

"Island, are you still with me?" Stiles's inquiry sounds muted, like I'm pressing my hands over my ears not to hear him. But my arms are actually dangling alongside my body, so it can't be that.

When I finally face him, he's studying me with narrowed, worried eyes.

I shake my head, struggling to calm my racing heart. "No, I mean . . . yeah."

He places a hand on my shoulder. "We'd better head back."

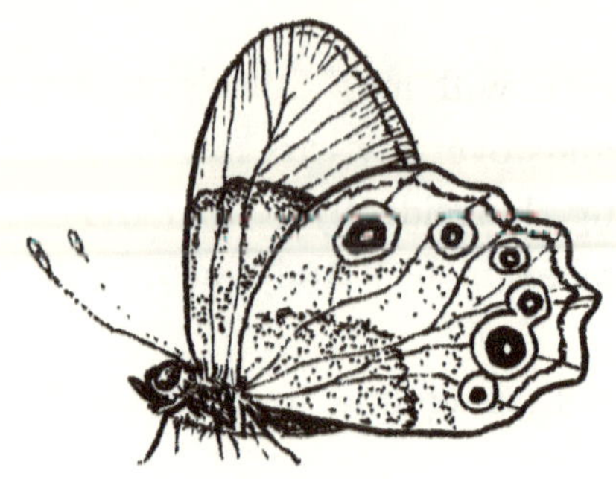

SIX

BEYOND THE GREAT WALL

Stiles didn't comment on the way I zoned out at the Christmas market, but I've been feeling his gaze on me all the way back to Ingolvinlinna. There was a point when the weight in my chest became too heavy, and I wanted to tell him about the blue-eyed ghost, ask him . . . if maybe he knows something about him. But it felt shameful, intimate, like pulling the scab off of a wound and baring it to him, so I sat by him in the boat in silence.

He went to see my father in his study right after lunch, and now it's 3:00 p.m., night is falling already, and they're still giving no sign of coming out. I paced in the salon for a while under the scrutiny of a pair of bodyguards standing in the doorway—I gather that's what Stiles means when he sometimes says he has eyes in his back. Pacing didn't help, so I tried to pick up my book about the Franklin expedition, paced some more, and eventually returned to my bedroom . . . to resume torturing myself with scenarios where Stiles tells my father I'm completely crazy, calls Bentsen to have her confirm his diagnosis, and concludes that I'd better stay locked up in the castle for the foreseeable future.

Yeah . . . maybe he didn't spend that long up there just to rat on me. I figure they're discussing business and going over the castle's expenses. But *I don't know*, and that's why I'm sitting on my bed in the penumbra of dusk, wrenching my hands. The room has progressively grown entirely dark, save for the eerie glow of the moon reflected on the snow outside. I let myself fall on my bed, palming the cool disc of amber resting between my clavicles as I summon a vision of my mystery man.

Unfortunately, the ceiling doesn't hold any answers as I wander through the empty aisles of my memory. Maybe he never existed in the first place. He could be someone I saw in an advertisement, or some guy I eye-banged in the subway once. But my instinct tells me this could be some sort of sign, a tiny fragment of the life I left behind. The need to know creeps under my skin, frightening and overwhelming . . .

I check the blue digits glowing in the dark on my nightstand. Only 4:02. I wish the sun would shine longer in Finland. I sit up and squint at the outline of the TV mounted on the wall opposite to my bed. Technically, it's not a TV, more like a screen connected to a hard drive and whose primary use is to watch series. But I can also use it to browse the Internet—or at least a fraction of it.

I'm thinking again of those e-mails about my Yaycupid dates I saw in my mailbox. There wasn't much, honestly. Just a handful of notifications confirming I accepted dates from "ElijahCool" or "LonelyAngara87," and subsequent mentions of those guys in my chats with Joy. Some convos were missing—likely deleted out of shame—so the exhaustive timeline of my romantic exploits was hard to follow, but from what I gathered, those encounters were disappointing at best and creepy at worst. Until now, I took it for granted that none of my suitors could be the mystery guy . . . but at the time I checked, I was depressed, shrouded in the haze of my meds, and honestly, that sheer mass of old e-mails and unknown faces scared me to the point that I hesitated to fully explore it.

No more.

I open the nightstand drawer to retrieve my keyboard and set it on the bed in front of me. Let's try this again. This time, I'll start by combing through my Yaycupid account. There must be some sort of log of the profiles I checked in there—Dear Lord Jesus, please let him not be ElijahCool, because even if he had blue eyes, he's apparently also the guy who cancelled our second date because his pet snake died.

The screen lights up with a tap of my finger on the keyboard's smooth glass surface. As soon as the browser launches, I crack my joints and type the URL . . . before stifling a groan. I just got swiftly kicked back to our firewall's warning page. I huff at the blank homepage and try again. One time. Two times . . . ten times. Again and again, in the bottom left corner of the page, I see my request to load Yaycupid being redirected to a local IP before my sorry ass lands on the firewall page again. I'm not sure why or after how many tries I get the idea to open the Developer Tools to check the network logs. Before I know it, my fingers are flying fast on the keys, testing the page, generating error after error, until I move to the big guns and launch the command line. I type a first string of code to retrieve info on the router and his goddamn firewall. The more I type, the more I feel . . . alive.

My entire body tingles from the excitement of yet another transgression, from the pride to discover that I can still do this; my fingers are going through the motions, and each new line of code calls for another. The router resists me. Not for long. Because I'm going to win this—I'm not just a lost girl with a damaged brain. I'm an engineer—I'm . . . more. A wonderful thrill licks down my spine when I make it into the router's admin. Here they are, the credentials I need to browse freely.

I launch a new window with a squeak of victory. Before my fingers freeze on the keyboard. The homepage has changed. A stack of colorful boxes now crowds the page, which I guess the firewall used to purge. Weather forecast, ads . . . news. Yaycupid can wait; first I want to click on all this! I load the news, scrolling through articles about the Finnish municipal elections, the latest antics of bizarre billionaire media magnate and part-time President Reginald Steed, who, when he's not battling accusations of conflict of interest, works on building a giant wall to "secure the Canadian border" and takes on whoever disagrees on Twitter—also that's a pretty fierce yellow toupee on his head . . .

I keep scrolling when my attention is drawn to a flash of turquoise blue. I draw an unsteady breath as I open an article about the dismantling of the ruins of the Poseidon. In the related links, I see dozens of old videos dating back from April. My fingers tremble on the touchpad. I think of Stiles's constant helicoptering, my father and Bentsen's reluctance to let me return to the noise of civilization . . . and for the first time, it occurs to me that maybe the firewall didn't kick me out because it was developed by monkeys; it did because they don't want me to face this.

My stomach twists into knots, but I know I need to know. I need to see it all to put the past at rest and move forward. I press play.

—Hi, I'm Karen Mills, and you're watching ABN Live News. All eyes are turned to Rangiroa in French Polynesia tonight as forty-six people are confirmed dead following the collapse of the Poseidon Dome, and thirteen are still reported missing. Local authorities announced that Dries Kovius, the man responsible for the bombing of flight DL504 four days ago, died in his successful attempt to destroy the resort. Over three thousand guests were safely evacuated before the dome's collapse. Hundreds have been injured, but according to Prefet Clément Martier, "No lives are in danger anymore." Three US citizens are among the victims. Fifty-four were wounded and are currently being treated at the CHPF in Papeete. If you or one of your relatives were—

I pause the video. Dries Kovius.

The name rings a bell. Probably because he's responsible for what happened to me. For my shattered wrist that took months to heal, for the memories I'll never recover. Dries Kovius. My stomach heaves as if I'm about to throw up. I need to see his face. I type his name in the search bar, and immediately, thousands of links appear. News articles, blog posts about conspiracy theories, all illustrated with what seems to be the only pic they have of the guy. A ten-year-old black-and-white portrait. I draw a shaky breath and zoom to better examine him. There's something familiar about his sharp features—the thick eyebrows over a piercing gaze, the straight nose . . . I can't look away from that man, who murdered almost seven hundred people in less than a week and would have killed three thousand more if the cops hadn't been able to evacuate the dome.

I scroll down the results of the image search, feeling sick and empty. It's an endless mosaic: faces, pics of the plane he bombed, of the remnants of the Poseidon Dome emerging from the water. And his face, over and over. My face too.

My face?

It's like a bomb detonates in my chest. I can barely breathe as I recognize myself among the many pictures Google dug up. My forefinger jerks and clicks before I've even consciously formed the intent. It feels so strange to see the logo of this company where I worked, that I don't remember at all. EM Group . . . It's a post on their PR blog, where CEO Hadrian Ellingham himself bemoans the loss of three of his employees, two in the plane crash, and one in the collapse of the dome.

My first reaction is a sort of remote disbelief. Maybe I'm still in Hamina, in the middle of the Christmas market. The snow is falling, I'm hallucinating things, and now I'm reading that I'm dead. No—that *Island Chaptal* is dead. A girl who looks like me, bears my name, worked where I worked, and grins happily on her corporate portrait. Her hair is shorter; there's more color on her cheeks. *It's a better version of me*, a remote part of myself notes, before the panic sets in. Pain flares in my veins as I type my own name in the search bar, like I have a few times before, in hope to pick up the scattered pieces of my past.

But this time, instead of a few meager links to my résumé or the Facebook account I haven't been able to access in ages, hundreds of pages of results pour in.

All saying I'm dead. *I'm dead. I'm dead* . . . I'm shaking too much to keep going. My vision is blurring, and wave after wave of nausea hits me, making me dizzy. *I'm dead. They're saying I'm dead.*

Lights blind me; someone just entered my room. A blurry silhouette approaches, and I'm too petrified to move, to speak. I recognize that fear—it's the same I experienced months ago, when I woke up and I thought nothing was real, when I screamed, fought back, writhed helplessly on my bed. The terror has returned; it's crushing my lungs and turning my blood to ice. But this time, I know it's not my brain making up imaginary threats.

It's all real.

A white shirt and black tie come into focus. The pounding in my head becomes unbearable as I crawl away from Stiles.

"Island," he asks softly. "What were you looking at?"

SEVEN
FALLEN AWAKE

"Stay away! Don't touch me!" My voice sounds unnaturally shrill, hysterical, even to my own ears.

In contrast, Stiles's is pure honey as he walks around the bed, looming closer. "Easy, Island . . . calm down."

I try to leap from the bed, but I'm no match for his speed and strength. I barely register his movements before I'm pinned facedown on the mattress, his body straddling mine. I thrash, fight his grip around my wrists, and scream until I feel my vocal chords might snap. Dark shapes move at the edge of my vision—several guards have entered my bedroom. Stiles barks for someone to go get Dr. Bentsen in Helsinki ASAP.

One of them leaves, but the others, they just watch. They won't help me. No one will . . . because I'm dead to them?

"Calm down," Stiles repeats with an exasperated sigh.

I'm hurting myself more than he is, writhing and straining under him in a futile attempt to free my legs and arms. Above me, a guard looms closer, and I hear Stiles snap, "Give me that."

A sudden sting of pain in my arm makes me bite down on the sheets with a long wail. There's a dampness on my cheeks—tears, mingled with sweat. He stabbed me with something, he's hurting me . . . yet the hold around me is easing already, and his touch grows softer. In a second of vertiginous despair, I understand that it's because I've stopped struggling. As my body is becoming numb, his voice drops down to a murmur.

"That's it. Easy, sweetheart . . ."

He's stroking my hair like I'm a dog, and I can't shove him away. I can barely blink, and no matter how much I will the room to come in focus, it's getting blurrier, like clouds of dark smoke are swallowing everything. Is this another dream?

No . . . this time I'm waking up.

•••

I don't recognize this room. It's not my bedroom; there's less furniture, and I never noticed cameras before in the castle. I watch black butterflies flutter and spin in circles on the ceiling. I think they can't get out because there're no windows, only four bare walls and an instruments tray nearby.

The butterflies won't stop spinning, and my body feels like cotton all over. I can't move, but I'm not asleep. It's because they strapped me to that stretcher. Large bands secure my torso, biting into my wrists and my ankles. There's a drip in my arm too, each drop falling in the tube like the water clouding my father's absinthe. Some distant part of me coldly concludes that I'm being drugged, and I wonder if I'm dying. If I am, it doesn't really hurt. All I can do is admire the dance of the butterflies and listen to the voices in my head. They're a little muted, as if my father and Dr. Bentsen were on the other side of the bubble I'm trapped in.

My father sounds angry. "What happened today will not happen again."

"She was perfectly stable when I saw her on Monday. The implant is still in place, but when I tested her tonight, her dopamine and serotonin levels were abnormally high." Bentsen's tone grows accusing. "Are you certain you gave her her treatment?"

"Yes." That'd be Stiles. He sounds so relaxed, as if this entire nightmare was normal.

"Have we considered the possibility of a dosage error?" Bentsen insists.

"There was none," Stiles replies.

"I find that hard to believe . . . In any case, what is done is done. The IV will stabilize her. After that we—"

The deep bass of my father's voice cuts her off. "Dr. Bentsen, can you operate on her here, in the castle?"

Operate? I shake my head weakly. I don't want her near me . . . I want to know what happened to me, what they're hiding.

My father's suggestion makes Bentsen angry. She's almost shouting now. "Certainly not! We've discussed this already. That sort of surgery is not . . . that's not the way."

Silence falls in the room. All I can hear is the frantic rustle of the butterflies' wings. They're desperate to escape.

When my father speaks again, I feel each word rasp across my skin, low, threatening. "You promised me results. And today she relapsed, hacked into our systems, and tried to escape. All this in less than fifteen minutes. No more experiments. Do what needs to be done."

I see a pale smudge stagger back. Dr. Bentsen. "No," She repeats. "Find someone else."

"Are you certain of your decision, Dr. Bentsen?"

"I won't do it. I specialize in neuroplasticity. I don't lobotomize patients," she hisses.

My fists bunch, and my body strains helplessly against the straps. *Lobotomize* . . . Is that what my father is asking? I want to scream, escape, but all I can manage is a broken moan, and my limbs won't move.

Footsteps echo toward the stretcher, and a shadow leans over me. Stiles's soft drawl fans against my cheek. "Shhh . . . it'll be over soon. Now, be a good girl."

Across the room, Bentsen is still arguing with my father; angry whispers drift my way that I struggle to piece together. "There would be significant risks . . . if anything happens, she might never be able to hold a spoon again . . . I know you want more than just a listless body to call your daughter!"

A listless body? Isn't that what I am already? Stiles's hand is resting on the stretcher like I'm not even here. I'm furniture. Horror blooms inside me, spills in my veins. The butterflies are still there, calling to me. I need to rise, to fly away too, but my body is too heavy and I can barely curl my fingers. I lie helpless, cool tears rolling down my temples.

"Joshua." I try to focus on my father's voice as he approaches the bed and talks to Stiles. "Dr. Bentsen will leave us tonight. See her out and take care of the rest. I want this solved in the next twenty-four hours."

"Understood."

With this single word, Stiles moves away from me and walks to Dr. Bentsen. I can make out his arm at her back as he leads her out. An ominous presentiment seeps into my bones . . . Stiles . . . she shouldn't go with him. I want to call her, tell her, but the whimper that makes it past my lips isn't enough.

They're gone now, and I'm alone with my father. He reaches next to my stretcher to turn off a lamp. His silhouette barely outlined by the light coming from the doorway, he too becomes a shadow. Like the butterflies.

I gulp and concentrate all my efforts on speaking. "Why . . . are you doing this?"

He kneels by the stretcher in a rustle of fabric and places his hand over my sternum—over the pendant. His palm is warm, and I desperately want to believe he's going to save me, free me.

"I gave you everything I couldn't give your mother, Island, and I'll give you even more. An entire new world. But I can't make you happy if you fight me." I feel his thumb caressing the smooth amber. "It can't work like that."

My mother? Thoughts collide in my head. She died when her car crashed into a gas station. He told me I was there, that I was wounded too. Did he . . . was there a doctor for her too? Did he lie to her too?

"I don't understand . . ." I whimper.

He rises to his feet and bends to place a kiss on my forehead. "There's no need to."

I strain against the straps keeping me prisoner. "Wait . . . Please!"

But he doesn't look back, and after the door slams closed, I'm alone in the dark.

•••

I must have slept. I feel dizzy as my eyes flutter open. The butterflies have vanished, and I've given up, having no sense of time in this silent and pitch-black room where I've been buried alive. I test my restraints, allowing some of the fog to clear in my brain. Like an electric shock, the panic returns tenfold, contracting my muscles. My father and Stiles . . . *they did this!* I was reading about the destruction of the Poseidon Dome, and then I saw myself on all these web pages saying I'm dead, and they won't tell me what's going on! They drugged me, locked me up!

And Bentsen said—*oh God*—she said she wouldn't lobotomize me. Was she being serious? Does that mean someone else will? Nausea swells at the back of my throat at the idea of someone gouging out parts of my brain to turn me into "a listless body." Soft clanks echo in the dark as my body starts trembling uncontrollably on the stretcher. I don't want this . . . It can't be real. It's like those dreams when I'm in an elevator and it falls, and I wake up the second my chest heaves from the sudden weightlessness. I'm going to wake up in my bed. Fighting the tears stinging my eyes, I squeeze them shut and will the nightmare to end. I'm going to wake up. I know I am . . .

The creak of the door opening sends my pulse into a frenzy. Light spills into the room, so bright it blinds me. Ghosts glide toward me. I recognize Stiles's voice, murmuring to a man in black fatigues to take me. I struggle against the straps holding me in place and croak, "No, wait! Please . . . J-Joshua!"

He heard me. The moment the plea bursts from my lips, a shadow drifts toward me. His face comes into focus, but instead of blond bristles, it's brown curls haloed by the light. I can make out the meek smile I know so well, and for the first time, it dawns on me that it's not real; it never was. Morgan shakes his head. "Oh, baby, I knew you couldn't behave that long."

A sob shatters my voice. "Please . . . don't let them take me!"

He moves away, and I register rustling coming from the general direction of the instruments tray. I crane my neck frantically to see what's going on. When he reappears in my field of vision, there's something in his hands, and they're descending toward me, ever closer, blurry.

My hands curl into fists, and my legs jerk in vain. I let out a series of incoherent wails. "No, no . . . please! Pl—" The word ends in a long howl, swallowed by the tape he smooths over my mouth.

"Much better," he jokes before trailing the back of his knuckles across my cheek. I feel everything, every single hair, every square millimeter of contact between our skin. I writhe in a desperate effort to escape his touch.

"No, no, no . . . You're not going anywhere, baby," he coos as he leans closer, enough for me to make out the jagged edges of a scar on his eyebrow . . . the eye patch. He's not wearing it. The area where his eye should be is shadowed, but I glimpse a mangled eyelid sunk into his empty eye socket. My stomach heaves with the need to throw up. His fingers glide to my temple and tap it delicately. "They're gonna clean up everything in there . . . I guess you won't remember me when you come back, but maybe we can start over. It wasn't so bad, you and me, right?"

All I can produce is a muffled moan of terror. What is he talking about? I just don't want him to touch me—please, *anyone,* make him *stop!*

But his hand won't go away, skittering across my jaw, my neck. My heart rams against my rib cage in panic when his fingers curl loosely around my neck, his voice down to a trembling whisper. "I'm going to wait for you, and when they bring you back, I'll tell you about my sister. Do you want to hear about Poppy?"

I pant and whimper under the tape, my chest constricting with each agonizing breath. I don't want to hear anything; I don't want his hands, his voice.

"Morgan."

My body jerks in surprise. I don't recognize that stone-cold tone, but the drawl is familiar. Stiles is calling him from the other end of the room. The light above is blinding me, blurring my vision: I can't see where he is. I screw my eyes shut and wait for Pirate Morgan to heed the call and get away from me. He does, his fingers trailing one last time along my clavicles before he retreats in darkness. Yet his absence brings me no relief. The stretcher clanks and moves; I'm being carted out of the room.

FEAR OF HEIGHTS

There's at least one person who cares: while his colleagues went outside to get the helicopter ready, one of the guards put thick socks and boots on my feet. I'm still wearing yesterday's jeans and sweater, but a fleece cover has been thrown over me, which this unexpectedly caring captor is adjusting around my body. I wish I could see his face, but like half of the men, he's wearing a ski mask that covers his nose and mouth. All I can see is a strip of ebony skin and watchful black eyes.

I swallow the lump in my throat and look away; like Stiles's kindness, the sliver of humanity I'm trying to grasp at is likely a figment of my imagination. Each breath I take through my nose because of the tape on my mouth, the painful hold of the straps securing my limbs to the stretcher: those are real. They're a constant reminder of what my father ordered them to do.

I hear the lobby's doors groan before a rush of icy air sweeps over me. Beyond the warm glow of the chandeliers, I see white stretching under a pink dawn. Someone unlocks the stretcher wheels and starts pushing. I pant fast and hard through my nose. They're taking me.

In the courtyard, the snow has been shoveled; there's nothing to hinder our progress toward the helicopter. When I see the blades hover above me like black wings, I can't hold back my sobs. I whimper, hiccup in vain against the tape. The tears streaming down my cheeks seem to turn to ice almost as soon as they touch my skin.

Within minutes, I've been loaded in the back of the aircraft, and four men have taken their places on a row of seats facing the stretcher. At least two of them carry assault rifles, something I've never seen around the castle. Were those purposefully hidden from me? Before the doors slam shut, I catch the blur of Stiles's brown coat as he climbs in the front, next to the pilot. I try to grip the sides of the stretcher and breathe my terror out as the cabin starts to vibrate and the roar of the rotor grows deafening. We're taking off.

All I can see of our journey is the morning sky through the window, turning a fiery shade of pink as the sun rises. I don't know where we're going or how long it is before I turn my head to look at the men my father paid to do this to me. The black guy who took care of me back in the lobby is looking at me, and so is the guard sitting next to him, I think. I'm not sure. My eyes are swollen with tears, and I need to blink those back, over and over, for their faces to come into focus.

I stare vacantly at the second guy, my brain like molasses as I try to pinpoint what it is about him that makes my skin prickle like that. It's his eyes—*dark blue* eyes, I realize, seconds before I notice the smoke. One of the men yells something in Afrikaans as an acrid white cloud quickly fills the cabin. *Oh my God . . .* what's going on? What's wrong with the helicopter? The fear of imminent death pumps in my veins, and I shake frantically on the stretcher. We're going to crash!

The next second is a blur during which the blue-eyed guy grabs one of his colleagues and slams his head against the wall. The guard quickly recovers and lunges back at him, raising the assault rifle he was carrying. Steadfast, his adversary grabs the barrel with both hands, and they start fighting over the rifle. The tape mutes my screams when gunshots crack in the cabin, the bullets clanking in the cart beneath me. I'm on the verge of a heart attack.

Twenty seconds ago, I thought I was on my way to be lobotomized on the orders of my own father. Ten seconds ago, I thought my luck was complete shit, and I'd die in a helicopter crash after all. Now the smoke is choking me while the black guy wrestles their remaining colleague, and I'm certain I'm gonna get shot dead. On a stretcher. In a fricking helicopter! In the midst of the confusion, I see a flash of brown. Stiles is trying to move to the back to stop the two men. A black-gloved hand rises through the smoke, holding a knife. It slices through black fatigues right before blood splashes all over my clothes. I arch against my restraints in complete panic until I'm sure my spine will break and . . . I'm free.

The straps have snapped. No. Something sliced through them—the bloody knife I glimpse in the hand of the blue-eyed guy, inches away from me. The smoke swallows him back almost immediately, and I recognize Stiles's arm, choking him. Amid a concert of groans and hoarse shouts, I count at least another gunshot, followed by a deafening crack—an explosion? Before I can make sense of the chaos surrounding me, icy wind rushes inside the aircraft. The double doors at the back of the cabin have been blown open, and I'm staring wide-eyed at the ground, miles under our feet. I curl up on the stretcher and shield my head, paralyzed by fear. I'm so sure the cart I'm still lying on is going to roll out from the helicopter, and I'll be ejected and fall to my death like a stunt dummy.

When an endless couple of seconds pass and the cart keeps shaking under me yet stays in place, I'm able to process that it's, in fact, secured to the wall. The smoke clears, and it appears that the two guards who were attacked are either dead or unconscious. Stiles is wrestling the black guy while the blue-eyed one is . . . right next to me. I try to sit up and crawl away from him, but his arms clamp around me, lifting me from the stretcher.

For a split second, I look straight into the blue eyes searching mine, and I feel like I'm drowning. I can't think, can't move a muscle as he hauls me away. Reality rushes back like a punch in the face the moment I feel my body tipping back and being sucked out. I'm falling. *We're* falling. Sweet goddamn baby Jesus, that psycho *jumped*!

My heart stops, and cold seeps through my bones as we tumble toward the ground. The wind bites my cheeks, numbs my fingers. My clothes are whipping around like they're about to be torn off of my body. I blink and see trees, white everywhere, before I squeeze my eyes shut and grip his shoulders so hard my fingers might snap. Time stretches infinitely, the world is upside down, and I'm gonna die. Around my waist, his hand reaches for something and gives a sharp tug.

All of a sudden, I'm pulled straight up, and the free fall stops—that bastard had a concealed parachute! Vertigo makes my head spin as we glide, swivel above the trees, and at last, the reality of what's happening hits me fully. I'm several thousand feet above the ground, his grip around me the only thing that keeps me alive. Adrenaline blazes through my system, and I'm going to be sick. A dark arc in my peripheral vision tells me that at least another man jumped.

"Lift your legs!"

My captor's shout draws my attention to how close the pines and the ground now look. Below us, a road stretches into the horizon.

"Your legs! Island, lift them! Wrap them around my waist!"

His bark jolts me into compliance. My legs jerk up, and I anchor my ankles to his thighs. Seconds afterward, trees flash past us, and we hit the ground. It's his body that takes the impact of landing, my legs safely wrapped around him as he instructed me to.

We collapse together on a bed of fresh snow, in a field, maybe. I can't stop the trembling of my limbs as he frees us from the parachute. It's like my brain has yet to land, and I can't fully process what just happened. A few yards away, the other guy has landed too with a soft rustle. With my body now free, the fight returns to me, pulses in my veins. I try to squirm away from the blue-eyed guy, but he pins me under him. My arms fly to shield my face when he makes an attempt to touch it.

"It's going to be all right, biscuit. Let me take this off," he says breathlessly.

Biscuit . . . The moment of surprise as the pet name registers and I try to place his accent is all it takes for him to rip off the tape. I yelp before any further protest dies on my lips when he pulls off his ski mask. Under me, the black parachute tarp suddenly feels liquid, alive, as if it might suck me in. For a second or two, all I can do is stare. I'm aware of the blood pounding in my temples as I take in every detail of the face I already know. The deep-set eyes whose color I can think of a thousand names for, the aquiline nose, the square jaw. The short chestnut hair. My eyelids flutter. It's not him. None of this is real. If I look up, I'll see snow falling, and I'll be back at the Christmas market. This time the nightmare will end. It has to. How long can one dream last anyway?

All of a sudden, the storm in my mind is silenced. By his mouth. On mine.

His lips are so warm . . . is what I think for half a second before renewed panic sets in, and I claw at his face to free myself. "*No! Don't* . . ." The word *rape* is on the tip of my tongue, but I can't say it. I don't even want to go there.

He lets me go with an expression of surprise. "Island, it's me."

Me *who*? How does he know me? I have no idea what's going on, and I'm suffocating, struggling for oxygen in rapid pants. My hands slip on the tarp spread all around us and tangle in nylon cords as I scramble away from him. "Stay back! Don't touch me!"

The hurt and incomprehension transforming his features seem genuine, like he doesn't get why society frowns upon predators who randomly kiss unsuspecting prey. "Island . . ."

Strong hands clasp around my shoulder to block my escape. "Time is running out, lovebirds. Our ride is here."

I look up; the black guy has removed his ski mask as well, revealing a mischievous gaze. He's maybe a little older than the blue-eyed guy—forty or so—and I have this odd epiphany that I expected that face too, the elegant features and the perfectly trimmed beard. My head is spinning like I'm standing in the middle of a funhouse mirror. I try to fight his grip, but he's hauled me back on my feet before I can land a single punch.

The one who tried to kiss me is at my side in an instant, his arm around my waist. "Island, we need to go."

"No! I-I . . ."

At last, I notice the car. A white SUV with tinted windows has stopped on the road, less than a hundred feet away. As if on a cue, the rear doors slide up and fold out in a silent invitation.

Someone inside shouts, "Porho, Fokken maak gou!" *Porho, hurry the fuck up!*

Afrikaans? So they are my father's men after all? Are they turning against him? *Whatever . . . They're going to take you. You literally skydived from the frying pan and straight into the fire.* The voice in my head is surprisingly calm and lucid about this—I'm not. I kick the blue-eyed demon in the shin and thrash in his arms in a desperate bid to escape him.

"March . . . clock's ticking," that Porho guy warns.

That's when my feet leave the ground. The one I now identify as March lifts me bridal style, ignoring my hands' poorly coordinated attempts to shove him away. He covers the few yards separating us from the car at record speed, and we land in the back seat together. Seconds later, the black guy has climbed in the passenger seat, and I'm propelled against March's chest as the SUV nearly takes off of the road.

"Don't worry." Porho laughs, winking at me in the mirror. "Dominik was born behind a wheel."

Dominik . . . I roll frightened eyes at our driver. He's wearing a white parka and looks pretty young, early twenties maybe. He too has a kind of buzz cut, but his skin is a lighter brown than his colleague's, almost golden. Almond-shaped green eyes meet mine in the mirror for a brief second. Focused, angry. Without thinking, I grip March's arm as we fly past a continuous ribbon of snow-covered trees. I'm alerted by red arrows blinking on the map displayed on the dashboard's touch screen.

Dominik glances at them. "Didn't take them long."

"Where is he?" Porho asks, casually loading a machine gun.

"Twenty miles north. Right on time," Dominik replies.

March's hold tightens around me, even as he pulls out a gun with his free hand. His chin brushing my hair, he whispers soft words of reassurance. "Don't worry; it's almost over."

He's lying.

On-screen, the red arrows are inching closer to the blue one I assume is us. And that new green arrow . . . it's driving straight toward us.

NINE
HARD SERVE

At first, I just stare at the dots on the map, growing ever closer. They're abstract, they mean nothing, and yet my heart is drumming so fast I'm gonna pop an artery at this rate. Then I hear it—the roar of an engine behind us. On the dashboard, the speedometer goes through the roof at the same time that my organs splatter against my rib cage. I hold on to March as hard as I can. Not because I trust him, but because I don't know if I'll still be alive in thirty seconds, and all that's left in me are primal reflexes.

We're driving way too fast, but still not fast enough: I glimpse a black hood to our left, before another acceleration crushes my lungs and our pursuant disappears from sight, as if swallowed back by the road. I experience five seconds of relief until I look up in the mirror. Two Hummers are following us. The closest is the one that tried to pass us.

March anchors me as Dominik swerves left and right to block them. I have this terrifying epiphany that if we can't escape them, Stiles will take me again, put me back on the stretcher, and . . . I squeeze my eyes shut and bury my face in the crook of March's arm. I just want this to be over.

I feel him squeeze me harder. "It's going to be all right. Trust me."

I don't. The car shakes, and we're being jostled like pinballs. I scream when we take a turn so sharp my body crashes against March's, and I'm sure the SUV has toppled over. Yet we're still driving. Loud clattering outside the car makes me peek up. Sweet Jesus, we're no longer on the road. Snow and dirt fly all around us as we race down a narrow trail leading to God knows where.

"Dominik," Porho shouts. "They got us."

"I know," the driver says through gritted teeth. "We just need to hold on a little longer."

As he says this, the car drifts to a stop. My eyes automatically dart to the dashboard's screen to figure out what that means. In my veins, the blood all but freezes when I see a third red dot that should be . . . right in front of us.

"Oh my God! There's another car . . ." I pop my head up to take a look through the window, only for March to immediately shove it down. A minivan has stopped less than twenty yards ahead of us on the trail. Behind us, the two Hummers have stopped as well. Panic swells inside me, squeezes my lungs. This time we're trapped.

"Island, stay down!" March barks.

In the passenger seat, Porho asks Dominik, "How long will it hold?"

"One minute tops," the guy replies, pulling out a gun from his parka.

I have no idea where the realization comes from, but I know with absolute certainty that they mean the car, or more exactly the windows. They're probably bulletproof, but if those guys outside shoot at us repeatedly . . . On the dashboard, the green dot is still inching closer.

The first shot crashes into Porho's window, and Sweet Jesus, the guy doesn't move, doesn't even blink while inches from his temple, a flower of shattered glass has bloomed. There's a beat of complete silence before all hell breaks loose. March folds his body over mine and keeps my head down, literally pressing my cheek into the leather seat as a deafening din tears our eardrums. We're being showered with a barrage of bullets that rattles against the side panels and turns the windows into an abstract pattern of circular impacts.

After several seconds of this treatment, the shooting stops—either because they need to reload or to assess the damage they've done so far, I have no idea. Under March, I wait, petrified, counting the seconds. I can feel his breath on my cheek, hot and unsteady. He smells of mints, like he ate an entire tube, really. In his hand, the gun is still here, and his black-gloved index rests on the trigger. Ready.

The last thing I expect to hear at this point is . . . "Jingle Bells." My eyes slowly widen as, indeed, the melody grows louder. And yes, the bells do jingle. Is this real life, or is someone going to slather their watch with butter and yell it's teatime? Outside, our attackers must be equally puzzled, because they still haven't resumed shooting. I squirm under March and see Porho and Dominik slump in their seats with . . . grins on their faces?

I'm not sure what comes first, the sound or the impact. There's a sort of . . . *whoosh*, and almost immediately, a massive explosion shakes the SUV, booming through my chest. I peek up at the windshield just in time to witness the surreal sight of one of the Hummers upside down, literally flying over us in a blaze of flames before crashing into the minivan that was barring our way.

Porho lets out a low whistle, and I shift under March to get a better look, but he hisses for me to stay down. Rightly so, since renewed gunshots crackle behind us. The bells keep jingling hard, and a second detonation shakes our car.

Through the windows, I glimpse flaming debris raining all around us.

I register Porho's laugh. "Didn't I tell you the truck was a great idea?"

The comment was apparently directed at Dominik, who straightens in his seat. "Not bad."

Above me, I sense March relax.

"Is it . . . over?" I squeak.

"Yes. But stay in the car, please."

Like I'd venture so much as a toe outside . . . March moves away from me to step out of the SUV. Porho and Dominik do the same. I can make out burning fragments littering the once-pristine snow, and swirls of acrid black smoke stretch around the car. I inhale some and cough my lungs out. The music sounds much louder now, covering what I recognize as groans of pain.

Painful chills cascade down my spine. What have they done? Those were my father's guards, men I saw every day. Stiles might even be among them . . . A mixture of emotional and physical distress squeezes my lungs as I try to make sense of the past few hours. These men I thought I knew and trusted would have hurt me. My father *ordered* them to. Stiles drugged me and let them strap me to that stretcher, and that turd Morgan taped my mouth shut so he wouldn't have to hear my screams. Enter my kidnappers—because they kidnapped me, right?—who act like they already know me, who technically *saved* me. But from what, exactly? And *why?*

The word *ransom* resounds in my head, loud and clear, like the obvious answer. I need to know what's going on. Against my best judgment, I crawl toward March's open door and risk a peek outside. My stomach heaves at the sight of the devastation surrounding me. As I feared, the two Hummers were somehow bombed one after another. There's the one that flew over our car, now a fuming upside-down carcass that destroyed the other van upon impact. Bloodied limbs dangle from the broken windows. Several men lie wounded in the bloodstained snow, some clutching their arms, their chests. The fog clouding the air around their noses and mouths tells me some of them are still alive. Tears bubble in my eyes, blind me. I can't handle this. I just wanted to be free; I never wanted *this* . . .

I let myself roll to the ground to get a better look at the source of the music. I fall face-first in the snow, shake my head, and scramble to my feet. It must be the meds. They put something in that drip. In no sane, rational universe should I be standing thirty feet away from the very same ice-cream truck I saw in Hamina. I stare at the colorful vehicle in a state of complete shock. One that doesn't get any better when I notice the retractable rocket launcher mounted on the roof.

So that's what happened. And that's the truck that was serving ice cream to kids yesterday. No, wait. They were firing ice cream scoops at the kids. My knees wobble. At least it all makes sense now, right? In a daze, I wonder if that kind of equipment is approved by the Finnish food-safety authorities when the truck's driver door slams open. Why am I not surprised to see the clown step out?

There's actually nothing funny about this man underneath the rainbow-striped jumpsuit and the red nose. I make note of his graying beard and hard hazel eyes—almost golden—before my eyes train on the gun in his hand. He takes a few steps away from the truck, contemplating his work with a chilling gaze. No trace of fear or remorse to be found there.

I shudder when he calls to the wounded men in a booming voice, "Who wants to live to carry a message for me?"

Without waiting for an answer, he aims at the man lying closest to him and presses the trigger. The single gunshot explodes in my ears. I see the jerk of the man's head, the crimson stain growing on the snow. None of it feels real. My mouth falls open, but no scream comes out; only icy tears stream down my cheeks as the clown growls, "Never mind. You are the message. All of you."

TEN
THE SPIDER

The clown just shot a wounded man before my eyes . . . I'm shaking, and there's an unexpected pressure in my bladder. I think I'm going to wet myself. *Oh God . . .* he's noticed me. His eyes widen, and his harsh features melt into a sinister parody of a smile, revealing a gap tooth—the only thing we could possibly have in common. When he takes a step toward me, the muscles in my legs coil with what I now recognize as the urge to run.

Slowly, he takes off the red nose. A tremor shakes his hand. "Little Island . . ."

As I discover his face in its entirety for the first time, I'm aware of every beat of my heart reverberating through my body, of the snow squishing under my boots. He must be pushing fifty, and he's about the same height as my father but a little beefier. I scan his sharp features, the straight nose and thick eyebrows. Save for the short beard, they could be brothers, really. I doubt they are though, because I'm almost certain I'm standing in front of Dries Kovius.

I look at the three men surrounding me frantically. They stay still, watching. My gaze searches March's. He of all people is going to say something; he's going to tell me what's going on. But he remains silent, a tired smile stirring his lips as the clown opens his arms as if to welcome me. All I can see is the gun in his hand. My breath coming in short pants, I scan the road, the bodies lying at our feet . . . the pines around us.

I can do this. Once I'm hidden in that thick tangle of branches, they won't be able to find me. It's only a few yards. I *can* do this. My rational mind shuts down, and my legs spring into action, the need to escape stronger than the fear pounding in my temples. I bolt between March and the clown and run as fast as I can without looking back. The surprise effect doesn't last; already I can hear them bark my name. Heavy footsteps crush the snow behind me. I run faster, my lungs burning with the effort of inhaling gulps of icy air. I desperately want to believe I'm going to make it. I'm almost in the woods; the first branches are lashing at my clothes. In my legs, the muscles protest against the sudden effort, and I can tell I won't be able to keep this up for long. I look ahead and spot an area where the ground seems to slope between two tall pines; with one last effort, I reach it and skid down, ankle deep in fresh snow.

It wasn't such a great idea, because the soft white mantle actually conceals . . . rocks. A searing pain tears through my right ankle, and I pray it's not broken. I can no longer run: I roll to the ground and let myself slide down the rest of the way, until I reach a stream. They're right behind me: over the sound of my own panicked breathing, I register branches creaking and hoarse shouts. Yeah, right . . . like I'm going to stop and come back! I limp toward the stream, intent on crossing it. I don't care that the water might freeze my feet: it's my last chance. Once I'm on the other side they'll give up, and I'll be free. Just free.

I lunge forward, but one of them catches me before I even touch the water, hauling me backward.

"No! Don't touch me!" I shriek and thrash against the powerful hold, vaguely aware of Porho saying to someone, "He's got her."

A whiff of mint identifies my assailant before I've even turned to see his face. March is holding me tight, blocking any possible escape. The silvery stream is mere feet away, but I'll never reach it. Air whizzes in my throat as I slowly give up the fight. I'm exhausted, and March and Porho top me by at least a foot, Dominik and the clown only slightly less: I'll never get past them, much less overpower them.

My legs give way under me, but I don't fall: March gets down on one knee and lowers us both to the ground. My breath coming in ragged gasps, I don't immediately realize he's pulled me back against his chest in the semblance of a hug. I feel him nuzzling my hair. "Island, please calm down. You're safe now; it's over."

I have no strength left to push him away, so I bury my face in my hands to block his presence. I just don't want him to kiss me again. "Who are you? Why are you doing this? Is this, like ... for a ransom?" I croak.

I register a sharp intake of air and March's hold tenses, like he just seized for a millisecond. Heavy steps crush the twigs on the ground somewhere to my left, and I look up to see the dreaded rainbow jumpsuit. Looming above me with the sun at his back, Kovius looks even more terrifying. He kneels in front of us and studies me with chilling eyes. "What's wrong with her? Is she high?"

March draws a heavy sigh, and his voice sounds almost strangled as he says, "I don't know. I don't think so ..."

•••

I'm not high. And yet I'm riding through the deserted Finnish backcountry in an ice-cream truck that's been modified to fire rockets ... Dominik took the wheel and Porho too went to sit in the front while I sit in the back, sandwiched between March and Kovius the clown. Ice-cream trays and equipment clank on the shelves as we progress on what I suspect is a trail.

They gave me a black men's parka in which I've huddled into a tight ball. Kovius won't stop staring at me, so I spent most of the trip with my head buried into my knees to block his scrutiny and March's repeated inquiries about my well-being. Yes, my ankle is fricking fine. No, I *don't* want him to "take a look." He doesn't even seem to realize that he and his little terrorist club kidnapped me—not that my future looked any brighter before their intervention. My eyes squeezed shut, I replay in my mind everything that happened since I hacked through that damn firewall. I'm missing something huge; I can't make sense of any of this, save for the chilling intuition that all I ever was to my father was a pet—one Kovius has now stolen, probably to extort something from him . . .

My head snaps up when I feel the truck stop. March's hand brushes my shoulder. "Island, we've arrived."

"Don't touch me," I hiss, for at least the tenth time.

He moves away with a sigh and gives me some space to scramble to my feet. When the truck's door slams open, the icy air bites my cheeks. I draw a shivering breath that fogs the air around me; it's much colder here than in Hamina. As soon as I step out, I'm greeted by the sight of a frozen lake, a white immensity stretching under a cloudy sky. On the shores, I see nothing but snow-covered trees for miles around. How I regret ever complaining that Ingolvinlinna was in the middle of nowhere. Not even close. This place—wherever we are—this is officially the frozen butthole of the world.

Nestled in a grove of birch trees, I spot a roof. There's a log cabin facing the lake—somewhere no one will ever find me. I ball my fists in my coat's oversize sleeves and when I remain frozen in place, March's hand hovers at my back in a silent invitation. I will my legs to move, their joints like rusty, reluctant gears. I'm not the only one struggling, by the way: I didn't notice before, but Kovius has a slight limp. His right leg looks a bit stiff, and as we climb the few steps leading up to the porch, he huffs and swears under his breath.

Once we're inside, it becomes obvious no one lives here. The sparse furniture looks clean—spotless, really—but impersonal and barely comfortable. A table and a few chairs, a kitchenette. Two doors—I'm guessing a bathroom and a bedroom. Someone turned on the heat, a small blessing in what otherwise looks like the setting to a horror movie. Plot twist: the bad guys win, the girl gets killed, and they bury her body in the woods. A century later, people sell books investigating the mysterious circumstances of her untimely demise, complete with gruesome details about the autopsy of her frozen body, perfectly preserved in the icy ground. I swallow back a wave of nausea—I should never have read that book about the Franklin expedition.

When Porho closes the door behind us, I notice that Dominik stayed outside. Through the windows, I see him climb inside the ice-cream truck.

"He'll get rid of it," Kovius comments.

He's looking at me again—scanning me, really. I'm wondering if he's starting to regret that he took me. He jerks his chin toward one of the doors, which Porho dutifully opens. March leads me into what is indeed a small bedroom, with bunk beds and a lonely chair sitting in a corner. My eyes dart over to the window, trying to assess the feasibility of breaking it with the chair. As if they'd leave me alone long enough for that . . .

Once the three of us are standing in the bedroom and Porho has closed the door, Kovius gestures to me. "We need to take a look at that neck. Take off your coat and sit on the bed."

Goose bumps rise all over my body in a prickling wave. I step back, only to bump into March's chest. "What are you going to do to me?" I'm trying to control my fear before it tears me apart, but already I can hear the tremors in my voice.

His hands creep up my arms. "Island, we only want to check something. We would never"—his voice catches . . . almost like he's afraid too—"no one is going to hurt you again."

"Then don't touch my neck!" I yell between panicked pants.

Kovius runs a hand across his face. "Little Island, believe me, I'd rather do this the easy way."

"Calm down," Porho says. "We're not going to try anything here. We'll need a surgeon for that. All we want for now is to take a look."

Okay. Now I know with absolute certainty that they *are* going to hurt me. My eyes dart at the cabin's door. Kovius and Porho stand in the way; I'll never make it.

My mind racing for a way out, I play my only card. I whirl around to face March. "Please don't let them do this!"

His eyebrows draw together in a pained expression. I have no idea what's the deal between us—or if there is one, for that matter—but there's a tenuous connection, I can tell that much. I just hope I'm not making a terrible mistake by staking my chances on a potential case of Lima syndrome . . . He takes a cautious step toward me. "Island, we only want to see whether there's any scar on your nape. Nothing more. I *promise* no one will hurt you."

A sense of impending doom grows inside me, like rocks piling in my stomach. "How . . . how do you know about that?"

March's features freeze, a tic in his jaw the only sign he's still alive. Porho, on the other hand, doesn't seem surprised by my answer—there's actually something smug about the way he arches one dark eyebrow. And Kovius . . . I'm pretty sure I just saw his hand shake.

"*How* do you know?" I insist.

"How did you get the scar?" Kovius counters.

"It was at the Poseidon Dome. I had a brain injury and . . . I got surgery," I admit. I hope he can read the hate in my eyes as I add, "You did this to me . . . when you blew it up."

His nostrils flare, and I'm scared he's going to hit me. "Is that what they told you?"

"It's all over the fricking Internet!"

"I see . . . Isiporho, show her."

I study the interested party warily. *Isiporho?* Not "Porho" after all . . . Meanwhile, he's pulled out a phone from his pocket. His fingers dance on the screen, and he hands it to me. "I snapped these back at the castle. They had a medical file on you. It's not a tracking device; that much we know."

I take the proffered phone hesitantly. On-screen is the hasty and poorly lit shot of an X-ray. I'm no medical expert, and one half is a little blurry, but I can still recognize a human head . . . and I know something doesn't belong in there. At first I think I'm seeing some sort of giant daddy longlegs, and I nearly drop the phone, but it's not that. *It's* . . . my skin crawls as I examine the white outline of some kind of narrow, rectangular device lodged right above the first vertebra. The legs are in fact long filaments reaching . . . inside the skull—possibly all the way to the ears; I'm not sure.

This time, the phone does slip from my hands, and March catches it before it reaches the floor. I reach reflexively to touch my neck and stagger back. "You're lying . . . it's not . . . it's not in my head!"

Kovius and March both move at the same time to catch me. I scramble away until the back of my knees hit the bed. My legs give way under me, and I let myself fall onto the mattress. "What the hell do you want from me? Why are you showing me this?"

March crouches to be at eye level with me. I retreat farther into the bed and huddle to avoid his gaze, the blue eyes I thought I recognized, which belong to a murderer, a kidnapper. Yet his voice is soft, coaxing, each deep vibration like a petrifying caress. "Biscuit . . . please look at me."

Biscuit. Far from reassuring me, the pet name he keeps using raises a trail of goose bumps down my spine.

"Biscuit—"

"That's not my name!" I scream, hugging my knees harder.

"Island," he tries again. At the same time, I feel something touch my leg. His hand. I kick blindly to get rid of it. "Island, it's me. I'm not going to hurt you. Please listen to me."

I hug my knees tighter and rock myself, in a desperate bid to shut him out. "Leave me alone. Let me go. Let. Me. Go!"

"What was in the drip?" I hear Kovius ask.

"A cocktail of anxiolytics and a light sedative. But I don't think that's what affected her memory like that. She didn't react when she saw me in Hamina either," March tells him.

His words send me spiraling farther down an abyss I don't think I'll ever reemerge from. It's him. It *was* him at the Christmas market. Watching me. Somehow March and I know each other . . . and every memory I might have of him is lost in the depths of the South Pacific, sleeping in the ruins of the Poseidon Dome. What *happened* there?

"I sent the files to Viktor; maybe he can tell us more about the implant," Isiporho adds.

"Island . . ." March croons, his voice barely above a whisper. "Are you certain you've never seen me before?"

Unable to look up at him, I let out a brittle, "No," even as the chills coursing through my body remind me that it could be a lie.

From the corner of my eye, I see Kovius step closer. "What about me?" he asks, his tone unexpectedly soft.

"You're Dries Kovius. You're the guy who bombed the Poseidon!"

His fingers slowly curl into fists. "I see . . . and do you know who kept you prisoner?"

Prisoner? I feel the room tilting around me as I hear my father ordering Bentsen to go ahead and lobotomize me. I see Morgan's terrifying smile while he taped my mouth. My skull is throbbing as if it's about to explode, and a wave of nausea makes my stomach heave. *Was I really . . . their prisoner?* "This is insane," I whimper. "This isn't real. It's not . . . real!"

March keeps stroking my hair, my shoulder. I wish he'd stop, but I don't have the strength to fight back.

Unlike him, Kovius doesn't lose sight of his goals. "Tell me who took you."

"You did!" I'm crying hysterically now, loud sobs shaking my frame.

"No, little Island. I *saved* you. *Anies* took you."

"I have no idea who that is!"

Kovius's voice deepens with anger. "No idea? What about Aidan Keasler?"

March protests. "That's enough. She's not in any condition to—"

"That's . . . my father," I manage, struggling through a hiccup.

My answer is met by several seconds of stunned silence. On my shoulder, March's hand stills.

Kovius eventually speaks, his voice clipped, each word like a countdown to an imminent explosion. "Say that again."

"I-it's my father's name. Aidan Keasler."

I vaguely register Isiporho swearing in Afrikaans while March remains silent, his breath slow and unsteady.

When I peek between my arms, I see Kovius's blurry form leave the room. Moments after the door has slammed behind him, something crashes to the floor, followed by a roar of pure bone-chilling rage. With a final glide of his fingers in my hair, March lets go of me. I'm not even sure I'm relieved: he scared me marginally less than his acolytes.

"I'll go talk to him. Isiporho, can you please watch over Island?"

I glance up at the two of them. The smug expression I thought might be permanently etched on Isiporho's face is nowhere to be found. He places his hand on March's shoulder and gives a brief squeeze before tipping his head to the door behind which Kovius is working on destroying the living room. "Go."

When March opens the door, I get a glimpse of Kovius standing among toppled chairs, dragging a hand across his face. Was it the mere mention of my father's name that set him off like that? Or maybe they have . . . the wrong person? Once the door closes behind March's departing form, I roll around to face the wall. I'm not in Kansas anymore; this is hell.

ELEVEN
THE TAN

Things have cooled down a little, but Kovius basically went berserk.
I heard furniture move and crash; glass shattered on the floor. He
shouted some stuff in Afrikaans, but I was terrified, and pressed my
hands over my ears to block his barking. I didn't care. Didn't want to
hear.

He seems to be done destroying the living room for now—
presumably because he went out: the ruckus ended right after the
front door slammed. Isiporho left his chair once to check on the
damage. I glimpsed Dominik helping March clean up everything. He
must have returned at some point after he got rid of the ice-cream
truck. There was something weirdly poignant about seeing March on
all fours, in his black fatigues, with a double holster over his
turtleneck . . . meticulously picking up each piece of a broken mug,
like it mattered if the floor was clean.

Now it's over, and the low hum of March's voice echoes through the wooden walls as he discusses something in Afrikaans with Dominik. I strain my ears to listen, grasp at anything that could give me a hint as to my immediate future . . . "Opstyg voor sononder" . . . "steek die grens oor." *Take off before nightfall . . . cross the border.* So there's a plane waiting for us somewhere—as for the border . . . I have no clear sense of time save for the certainty that the sun hasn't set yet. We didn't drive that long to reach the lake, and the helicopter must have still been in the general area of Hamina when we jumped. The closest point to cross the Swedish border must be four hundred miles away—Norway is even farther. That'd make it the Russian border then.

I know the puzzle's pieces are here somehow, scattered before me. But I can't make sense of any of it. Lying curled up on the bed, I study the knots and veins in the wooden wall. I'm no longer so scared those guys are going to kill me, but now that I feel more focused, I can't stop thinking about the scar on my neck, the spider on the X-ray. Maybe they're trying to mess with me. But if it's real, why would Bentsen have put that inside my head? They called it an implant. Maybe it's actually a plate, like the one in my wrist? No . . . wires snaking inside one's brain, I've never heard of anything like that. I touch my nape tentatively. I can't feel anything, only the inch-long vertical scar.

"You won't feel anything; it's deep."

I'd almost forgotten about Isiporho sitting in the chair across the room. I stare at the wall obstinately, ignoring him.

He sighs. "Not in the mood to chat, huh?"

Hardly . . . My thoughts drift to clown Kovius. I'm starting to suspect that this has nothing to do with ransom kidnapping. The way Kovius lost it when I mentioned my father; this is personal. Revenge, maybe? He said something about a guy . . . *Anies.* Maybe it's someone my father knows. In my mind, the dots, at last, slowly start to connect. My father did everything he could to isolate—well, *insulate*—me so I wouldn't hear about the Poseidon and remember Kovius, who knows him, and knows me too . . . Kovius, who was at the Poseidon at the same time I was and caused my wounds. But my father also let the world believe I'd been killed in the attack—yet another detail he tried to hide from me.

Then there's March: he doesn't act like we just met. I can still feel his lips on mine, the moment he ripped the tape. The warmth and the urgency . . . My eyes flutter closed. I don't know if I want to remember last night's dream or, on the contrary, wipe it from my memory for good. My rational mind fights the very idea, but every instinct I possess tells me it could really be my night visitor. That would certainly explain why I deleted all mentions of him in my mailbox . . . or did someone else take care of that for me? The Google results Ingolvinlinna's network were serving me were evidently fake until I hacked the router; how much of what I browsed over the past months was real then?

Goose bumps trail across my skin, carrying in their wake a fear I can't place, an intuition that once I know the truth, I won't like it. Ever since I woke up in the hospital and listened to my father's account of the fall of the Poseidon, I took for granted that I was but one of the many innocent victims of the disaster, but Kovius said he *saved* me; March and the others act like they know me already . . . Maybe my father wanted to save me too, in his own twisted way. From myself?

I gave you everything I couldn't give your mother . . .

I jerk to a sitting position. "Where's Kovius?"

Isiporho blinks as if I just rose from the dead before a warm grin pierces through his beard. "Probably smoking in the shed like he's sixteen again," he says with a wink in the direction of the window. Half-buried under a white blanket is a wooden roof I didn't notice before. "Don't worry; he's going to pull himself together." His lips go tight for a second. "This is a little too fucked-up even for a man like Dries."

"What? You mean that thing in my neck? Why did he lose it like that? Why did you take me?"

His smug expression returns. "Looks like Dr. Bentsen's magic cocktail has cleared out of your system . . . That's more like the girl

I know."

I decide not to probe where *he* knows me from: I've got enough thugs in my contact list for now. I stand up from the bed and look at the door. My hands are shaking again. I ball my fists. "I don't understand any of this," I eventually say. "I want to talk to Kovius. I—"

The door handle moving nearly sends me hiding under the bed, until I remember that I need to man up—or so to speak. I'll never get answers otherwise. So when March enters the room, I don't chicken out; I square my shoulders and give him a level stare.

"I need to understand," I say simply.

"Isiporho, can you please leave us?" March asks.

A silent question flickers in my warden's eyes, but he complies nonetheless, casting me one final glance before the door closes behind him.

As if prompted by the doorknob's final click, March moves closer. I stand still as a mouse, trying to appraise his mood. Unlike Kovius, whatever manic rage might simmer inside him he conceals under a perfectly calm façade. Yet in his silence, in the faint lines around his eyes, his mouth, I sense a weary sadness. It's that side of him that scares me. Dries and Isiporho I can deal with. The secrets they're hiding make my stomach churn, but I think the walls inside me are strong enough for me to face them. I won't let them get under my skin.

But March . . . everything about him feels personal, intimate— possibly is, for all I know. As he stands before me, studying me with equal interest, I struggle to keep my expression blank. My brain is working in a frenzy though, filing each detail to compare with whatever shreds of memory might still be lying around. His hair—I suspect he keeps it that short because it curls when it grows—the mesmerizing pattern in his blue irises, that faint bump on his nose: broken in the past?

I try to cross my arms so I won't fidget, but I end up wrapping them around myself. I hope that looking away from his face will help, but I find myself just as taken with the rest of him. He's rolled up the sleeves of his black turtleneck in perfectly flat and even folds. I perform a meticulous scan of the corded muscles, the veins running under his skin. I'm practically counting each hair on his forearms when I pause in my examination to glance at my own wrist and the chalk-white skin there. His is a dark shade of gold, almost coppery in places, on his hands, the bridge of his nose. There's a band of paler skin peeking from under the black bracelet of his watch.

"Looks like you're back from a vacation . . ." I mumble. I'm well aware that it's a disastrous start the moment the words leave my mouth, but I'm desperate to ease the tension building between us.

Dumb as it may be, the question seems to shake him a lot more than it should. One of his hands jerks, rises to touch me, but he hesitates, and it drops back to his side instead. I hold back a sigh of relief. When he finally answers, his voice is low, tight. "Island, I've been looking for you. *Everywhere.* I spent months following cold trails, until I managed to track down one of Anies's men in Rio. He was part of the team who transferred you to Ingolvinlinna. I questioned him." I notice the way his jaw works silently before he adds, "He spoke."

I'm not sure where the certainty comes from, but I know, without a doubt, that this man *tortured* someone to get here. To find me. To take me. I exhale slowly, inching away from him. "Who's that Anies guy? Does he have something to do with my father and Kovius?"

He tips his head to the bed. "Let's sit down."

"No. Answer me." Also, I'm not getting on a bed with him, but that's another matter . . .

"Anies is the man you call Aidan Keasler."

Kovius's angry accusation rings in my head. *Anies took you. I saved you.* I hate to prove March right, but my knees are wobbling, and I feel physically overwhelmed; I stagger back and sit on the bed. "Okay. So, you know him under that . . . code name."

"Yes," he answers, dragging the chair toward the bed to sit in front of me. He plunges his gaze into mine, and I can't look away, can't shut him out. I feel naked. "Island . . ."

Somewhere in the black hole that is my brain, a spark lights up in the darkness. My chest constricts like I'm standing on top of a cliff. I know what's coming next, as if I'd dreamt that very moment before. I'm not ready.

"He's not your father," March says quietly.

Part of me doesn't want it to be true. If it is, then I've truly lost everything; I'm just an empty shell with no past, no self. My friends, my real family—do I even have one?—I'm dead to them. I want to believe March is lying, but I can't fight this; already my mind is reorganizing itself around this new evidence.

Like something I'd remember after having forgotten it.

I breathe fast through my nose to hold back the tears I can feel building in my eyes. March extends a hand to wipe them. I push it away and do it myself, with my sweater sleeve.

"He said my mother was dead. Is that true?"

It's weird that once again, like a premonition, I already know—or rather sense—the truth. March nods once, and I feel my heart physically break over a loss I can't even remember, something abstract.

"Go on," I say, my voice cracking.

"Let's do this another way," he offers. "What do you need to know first?"

My mouth twitches bitterly. "You know, you can just say 'I have no idea where to start.' That works too."

He sighs. "Perhaps you're right."

"Why?" It's the only word I can force out. All encompassing. Why would my fath—*Anies*—do this? Why me? To what end?

March's gaze drops to his lap. He's searching his words. "First, you should also know that Anies is not a businessman. Well, certainly not in the conventional sense."

I nod, waiting for the rest with clenched fists.

"Does the word *Lions* ring any bell?" When I shake my head, he goes on. "They're a brotherhood of assassins and mercenaries. They've been around since antiquity, but today they're primarily—"

"South African," I complete, stating the obvious. I leaf through my recent memories. "They're . . . forgotten warriors. People history must not remember. He's one of them, Anies?"

"Yes, their commander, in fact. So he told you about them?"

"Not really . . . Sometimes he'd say things I wondered about. He keeps a lot of antiquities too. Old paintings, swords, that sort of stuff. That's what made me think of it."

March's eyebrows knit in an expression of disdain. "He probably helped himself to the temples . . ."

"The temples?"

"I can tell you about those later if you'd like."

"Okay . . ." I make a mental note to add antiquities looting to the dreadful résumé of a man I called father until last night, feeling sick to my stomach. "So, the investments, the industrial projects . . . it's all bullshit?"

"Not entirely," March explains. "Things have changed lately. The Lions have been branching into many sectors over the past decade, some legal, most not."

"They're growing," I conclude, thinking of the shipments. "My— *he* told me about his factory . . . in Ecuador. He's building something there." As I say this, I feel the butterfly still resting above my breasts under my sweater, strangely heavy. My fingers are itching to tear it off.

"I'm not surprised. Dries used to operate a few industrial ventures too. Biltong and rusks, mostly."

As soon as I hear Kovius's first name, I know what my next question is. "What happened at the Poseidon? Was I there . . . with Kovius?" *And you?*

In March's eyes, the nascent light instantly dies, and the lines around the corners of his mouth seem suddenly a little deeper. "You and I were there with Dries. We were trying to stop a man a named Lucca Gerone. He's the one who destroyed the dome."

I frown. "Not Kovius?"

"No. Anies framed Dries for flight DL504 and the Poseidon, to get rid of him."

I'm not sure why I didn't pick up on this before, but hearing both names in the same sentence, I see my father's face, Kovius's, the hazel eyes . . . almost golden when the light is right. The same eyes. It's like a drop of water hit the surface of a very quiet, very deep lake, and in the void of my mind, the ripples are spreading, growing into waves. He's not just a weird and violent ice-cream man with anger-management issues and a heavy rap sheet. I can't work the idea into words yet—I can barely breathe as it is—but I know I'm gonna have to turn that particular stone, and I'm scared of what I'll find underneath.

"Why would Anies do that? Why did he want to get rid of . . . Dries?"

"For power," March says. "Dries used to be the Lions' vice commander. They had different visions, and there was an old feud between them."

Anies on top. Dries second in command. Anies. Dries. The golden eyes and the sharp features. There it is, the stone I wish I could ignore. "They look like each other."

"Anies is Dries's elder brother," he replies, each word laced with sorrow.

"I understand." *Do I?* I can't fully process the implications of this news. I don't want to . . . I look away and focus on the window. The sky is turning pink. It must be 3:00 p.m., and I gather we'll be moving soon. I return my attention March. "So . . . you're a Lion too? And Isiporho and Dominik?"

"I used to be. Dries trained me—he trained the three of us. I left the brotherhood eleven years ago. Isiporho and Dominik were forced to . . . retire eight months ago when Anies turned on Dries and purged all his disciples."

"But you're an assassin. You can't stop." It hurts to say it. I'm not sure why, but I can feel the words rasping my throat.

"No." He sighs. "I suppose I can't stop."

"Why did you leave the Lions then?"

"Because I met you."

I welcome his admission with stunned silence. *You're where my tape starts.* The words I remembered during my last session with

Bentsen suddenly take a new meaning. The room seems to be spinning around me, and I feel . . . I don't know exactly. It's like looking through a frosted glass door. Deep down, I already know what I'll find on the other side, but for now, it's nothing but blurry, distorted shapes.

When I remain voiceless, March gets up from the chair and takes a tentative step forward, his hand reaching for my arm, as if he can't help himself. I freeze. "Island," he asks. "Do you remember—"

"Who am I to you?" My voice breaks before I can even finish my sentence.

I look at his lips, see him swallow. "You were—you *are* my girlfriend."

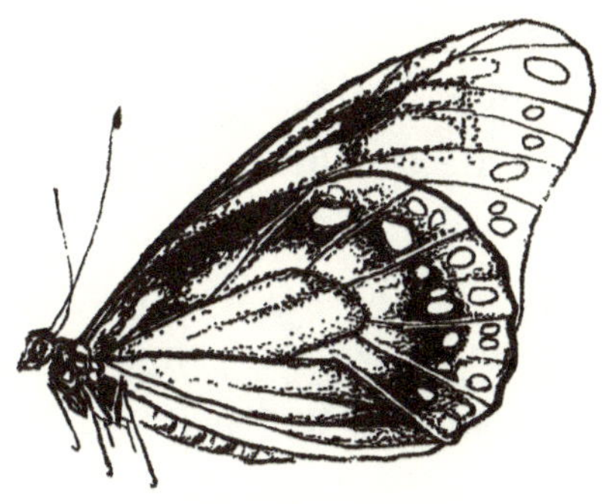

TWELVE
STOLEN

"I need to go to the bathroom."

I splash my face with cold water—no time for a shower, although I'd sell a kidney for one. I can't believe I said that to him. March looked at me, right after he'd dropped the bomb, and he waited, because I was supposed to say something. But after the accumulation of revelations of the past hour, after the base jump, the rockets, and the spider in my head . . . it was just too much. I couldn't handle that on top of everything else. I knew I'd cry again if I stayed in that room with him any longer. So when he told me he'd left a brotherhood of deadly assassins for me, and that I was his girlfriend, I balled my fists and said, "I need to go to the bathroom."

A round of self-applause is in order.

I didn't even look up at him as he opened the door for me—couldn't bring myself to, really. He made it clear he considers we're still together, but what can he possibly expect from me? I don't even remember him—*Yes, you do*, a douchey little voice reminds me. As if now were the moment to think of him, of us . . . doing *that*. An unwelcome flashback of his lips pressed to my neck has me squeezing my eyes shut in distress.

I splash water on my face again, pat at my cheeks with a clean towel, and stare at my reflection in the mirror. My hair is a tangle of dirty auburn curls springing in all directions. I sigh. I actually have leaves in there. And a twig too . . . I do a quick job of cleaning and untangling the unruly mass with my fingers and braid it hastily, securing the end with a bit of floss I found in a cupboard when looking for a toothbrush.

Once I'm done and I check the result of my efforts in the mirror, I'm filled with a sense of unease, something that weighs in my stomach like impending nausea. Maybe it's because of the braid . . . I don't recognize that girl. I thought I'd gotten over this, that I was getting used to seeing my own face, but it seems that feeling of being external to my own body is back. I trace the bridge of my nose, touch my lips, my chin, wondering what March sees—the same Island he used to know or a stranger wearing her face?

A low growl in my belly rings in the end of this distressing metaphysical debate. Time to exit the bathroom and face whatever awaits me on the other side of that door. Namely, Dominik, who was apparently tasked with guarding said door. I'm not certain how to interpret his shuttered expression when he sees me coming out: on a scale of one to Guantanamo, how captive am I? To be honest, March hasn't treated me like a captive so far. I'm on the fence about Isiporho, and Dries . . . having seen him shoot that wounded guy like he'd have stepped on a roach, I don't want to think about it.

"You hungry?"

My head snaps up; Dominik is talking to me. An embarrassing rumble rises between us, which is probably what tipped him off in the first place.

I nod. "Um, yeah."

"Come with me."

I follow him back to the living room, where I'm greeted by a splash of white. March and Isiporho have ditched their black fatigues for the same sort of white gear Dominik is wearing. The magazines perfectly lined on the kitchen table and the snow-camo pants tell me we're about to move.

"How do you feel, biscuit?" March asks, his voice tinged with concern.

There's a pang in my chest, an ache I can't quite place every time he uses that South African pet name. Maybe the other girl inside me regrets that past I can't remember. Did she . . . love him? I stare at the floor intently. It's all behind me; I prefer not to know. It'd only make me more vulnerable around him.

"I think I'm okay," I mumble while Dominik searches a backpack for peanut butter energy bars. He retrieves two, which he tosses my way. I catch them and examine the label. "Soldier Fuel." Huh? Yep, I need that right now.

"We're going to need you to change too," March tells me, gesturing to a remaining pair of camo over pants folded on a chair—whoever did that must have spent some time on it: they almost look like they were ironed.

I gobble down the last bite of my energy bar and take the pants, as well as the oddly stiff and heavy white parka he gives me—is that stuff bulletproof or something? "I'll go change in the bedroom."

March's mouth opens like he's about to object, and I'm reminded that I *am* under surveillance after all. Behind me though, the bedroom's door opens to reveal Dries . . . I'm actually glad March tried to stop me from walking into the Lion's mouth, or so to speak.

There's no trace left on Dries's features of the berserker rage he unleashed less than an hour ago. He's perfectly composed as he gauges me, his gaze settling on the camo pants in my hands, the same as he's now wearing. "Feeling better?" he asks.

I shrug in confirmation that yes, I'm alive, and I'm able to stand on my feet, at least.

"Good. Then come in. You and I are going to talk."

I take a step back instinctively. March's eyes meet mine, but he doesn't interpose himself. I'm on my own. I swallow and walk toward Dries, like a lamb headed to the slaughter. He moves aside to let me enter the room and closes the door behind me. I toss the parka and camo pants on the bed, and it's just the two of us, in that tiny space I now realize is permeated in a rich, smoky scent—he had a cigarillo in here too.

After a prolonged silence during which we size each other up warily, Dries shoots first. "You were always tougher than you looked."

Always . . . "March says we've met before, at the Poseidon."

His eyes narrow in interest. "Do you remember it?"

"No. All I have is his word for it."

"And you believe him?"

Do I? March said I was trying to stop the Lions from destroying the Poseidon, that the two of us were helping Dries at the time. Supposing this is true, that might have been enough for Anies to cage me and nuke my brain as retribution . . . But I can tell there's more to this. "I don't know," I say at last. "There's something that doesn't add up in March's story."

Dries crosses his arms. I don't like the way he's staring down at me; it's too . . . intense. "Go on, little Island."

I avert my eyes and wrap my arms around myself protectively. "All of what March said, the spider . . . if it's true, what Anies did to me was personal. It wasn't just about coming up with some sick punishment. He could have tortured me or even killed me, but he made me his daughter instead. He made everyone act like I was his child. He wanted something else from me." My stomach twists at the memory of his comments about building the future . . . about Stiles.

Dries's arms fall at his sides, his hands curling into fists. Fear surges inside me at the thought that he could hit me, but I stay still, pinned in place by the inexplicable certainty that he won't.

"He wasn't trying to punish you," he says, his voice suddenly low, harsh. "He took you to punish *me*."

What was it that March said? That Anies had framed Dries for the destruction of the Poseidon because of an old feud between them . . . There's a voice inside me screaming not to go there, that if I open that Pandora's box, it'll swallow me whole, engulf me in darkness. But I can't stop the movement of my lips as I ask, "What happened between the two of you?"

His expression softens. "We both wanted Léa."

I go rigid upon hearing my mother's name. He says it exactly the same way Anies does, the single syllable rolling off his tongue with an accent of tenderness.

"But she chose *me*. Island, you are *my* daughter."

I don't understand. I mean, he was perfectly clear, and it'd be rude to make him repeat what he just said. Right? But the words won't compute; they whirl around my head, paralyzing my lungs, my limbs. I see the hazel eyes, the gap tooth we share, notice for the first time that Dries has many little moles on his hands, his neck.

Like I do.

My body is shaking. I hear him again, howling, destroying everything in the cabin's living room after he realized my brain had been wiped clean. The words I wanted to block back then finally register in my brain, branding me.

Dogter . . . gesteel . . . *Daughter . . . stolen . . .*

Stolen.

Is that what Anies did? I feel numb, my brain working in vain to process the monstrous possibility. He needed a willing doll to play the part of the child he never had, and he took his own brother's child for that. *Me.* My legs are barely holding me up as the bedroom spins back into focus. In Dries's eyes, the anger has become raw pain.

"How do I know you're not lying?" I chew out each word slowly. They're burning my throat. When Dries's brow gives the faintest quiver, I add, "How do I know that any of this real?" I sniff back tears. "I thought everything was real at Ingolvinlinna! He told me about my mother too. He said he gave me everything he couldn't give her!"

Dries steps forward brusquely, his arms rising to pull me to him. I stagger back toward the door in distress. "I don't want you to touch me!"

Regret swells in my chest the moment the words burst out, and I wish I could breathe them back. Dries's arms fall back to his sides, and I don't miss the way his hands shake a little. I've hurt him, and I can feel . . . I feel his distress. I *care.* My brain won't hear Dries's truth, but my body knows—remembers? I realize I've never experienced anything close to that kind of primal response around Anies, and that's when I can't contain my tears anymore. They overflow and roll down my cheeks, my neck.

The bedroom door slams open behind me, and I whirl around to find March. He probably heard me yell at Dries, and now he's seen my tear-streaked cheeks. His hands reach for me; he murmurs my name. I don't want any of this; I raise my palms to keep him at a safe distance. "Please leave me alone . . ."—I spot the parka and camo over pants I tossed on the bed—"I need to change. I want to be *alone.*"

I sense reluctance in the air, but they both comply and exit silently, March's anxious gaze lingering on me for a second before the door closes for good. I grab the over pants and slip into them clumsily. My hands are shaking so badly I need to try several times before I manage to zip them.

I almost wish I could go back, never know the truth. Part of me is still fighting March and Dries's version of events, secretly hoping that there's another answer somewhere, a door I could open to magically get my life back. But what life? What is there to return to if all Anies ever told me were lies, if the only family I have are killers?

I bury my face in my hands and rub my eyes forcefully with the heel of my palm, but the headache won't go, threatening to grow into a full migraine. Soft rapping at the door makes me jump, soon followed by Dries's voice. "We're moving in five minutes."

I take several deep breaths and finish prepping. As expected, the clothes they gave me are too big, but once I've rolled up the pant legs and adjusted the belt and suspenders, I'm good to go. The gloves and thug balaclava are a welcome addition too, especially after I peek through the window and see that snow has started falling again, silently blanketing the lake under an indigo sky.

Buried under all those layers of clothing, I draw a trembling sigh.

Maybe it's for the best that I'm being given no time to process any of this; otherwise I'd curl into a ball for at least a week . . .

THIRTEEN
WINTER SPORTS

"Hurry up, little Island."

Dries gives a gentle nudge between my shoulder blades, but my body remains frozen, standing ankle deep in fresh snow. I didn't give much thought to how we would leave this place without the ice-cream truck until they led me to the shed, and Isiporho pulled off the tarpaulins covering three snowmobiles.

"Have I . . . ever ridden one of those?" I ask warily.

"No idea." Dries shrugs. "But it's either this or walking all the way to the Russian border, and I'd rather we move quickly. Our brothers are probably getting fidgety after all that ice cream."

I make a note that my guess about the Russian border was right and stare at Dries's profile while he secures a white helmet on his head. I don't get how he can be so composed after the emotional quake we both experienced less than ten minutes ago. I'm still in shambles, and back in that room, I could tell he felt something too. But now it's like he's gotten over it all already. He said he was my *father*—one all evidence suggests is hardly more trustworthy than the man who took on that role for eight months. And yet . . . Dries looked for me, came for me with his rockets and his clown costume.

In his own bizarre, dangerous way, he *cares.*

While I ponder what sort of relationship he and I could possibly have had before Anies took me, Dries climbs on a snowmobile and Isiporho settles behind Dominik on another. I consider the remaining sled's wide track and aggressive lines hesitantly.

"You'll ride behind me; it's safe," March says before he helps me adjust an unexpectedly light helmet on my head as well.

Once he's seated behind the handlebars, I climb onto the back seat and wrap my arms around his waist, gripping it tight. It feels a little strange to be suddenly so close to him, my body molded to his, but I'll grudgingly admit I feel a little safer holding on to him. I have no idea how fast this thing can go, and I can already picture myself toppling backward and being ejected from the sled and then somehow shredded by the track. Definitely no.

When the engine ignites and I feel the track's vibration under my butt, I squeeze him harder. The first minutes are pretty bumpy as we ride down a slope toward a trail running along the lakeshore. The sky is almost dark, which makes me realize how well the combination of white vehicles and camo works. In the powdery mist surrounding us, I can barely make out Dries's sled behind Dominik's, but I keep my eyes trained on his silhouette.

We're gliding fast down the trail under the moonlight, and I'm starting to think this isn't so bad. I might even enjoy the ride under different circumstances. The helmet does a great job protecting my face from both the icy wind and the motor's noise, and there's something soothing about the endless ribbon of trees stretching along the frozen lake's silvery surface. I feel a little numb—most likely from exhaustion—in a sensory bubble of sorts, even as we race in one of the harshest environments on Earth.

Against March's back, my body starts to relax when suddenly the terrain changes. An unpleasant rattle travels up my spine as the skis hit a hard surface. I look down and tense. We're crossing the lake—as in, we're riding on ice. *Please, please let it be thick enough!*

I hold on tighter to March's waist and gaze at the moon's pale reflection chasing us on this milky mirror. A thought bubbles up from a quiet, secluded part of my mind: I wish my mother were here so I could tell her everything that happened today, that I'm scared but the lake is eerily beautiful, and I met this strange ice-cream man who says he once loved her. Through the visor, I watch him gliding on the ice a few yards ahead of us. I wonder if my mother ever saw him like I did back at the cabin, wounded and overwhelmed under that thick shell of arrogance and violence.

After a while, I make a mental note that snowmobiles are actually much louder than I thought, and heavy too: under our skis, the ice seems to be quaking. I don't think March hears me as I yell, "Are you sure the ice is gonna hold?" especially since the engine's powerful roar is growing stronger with each second that passes. He doesn't answer but makes a hand gesture to his colleagues, and our sled speeds up. It takes me a couple of seconds to figure that we're parting from Dries and the others. They're still trailing fast at the center of the lake, whereas we're moving closer to the shore.

And the noise . . . I'm not so sure it's coming from us—it's not the same kind of engine; this sounds *bigger.* I instantly regret my decision to shift behind March to get a better look into the mirror. Glimmering in a storm of powdery snow, several pairs of headlights appear. Following us—and gaining speed fast. My heart plops to the pit of my stomach. Anies's men found us? How the hell? Did they track the ice-cream truck?

The answer to my questions comes in the form of a droning above our heads and a blinding beam of light swiping across the darkened woods ahead of us. I know if I look up, I'm gonna regret it, but I do, and my spine turns into a popsicle. Didn't Dries hint that "all that ice cream" would piss off Anies? Another peek in the mirror tells me just how angry we made the Lion in chief, and I hold on to March desperately as my brain does the math. One helicopter, three quads, and a . . . Sweet Jesus, that thing looks like a cross between the Batcar and a minitank, with a low, aerodynamic body mounted on huge tracks that make the ice shake under their weight.

I know what's coming next even before the first gunshots crack behind us. *Oh God, oh God, oh God . . .* I can practically feel my head retracting into my shoulders, like a turtle, as March keeps hitting the gas, and the wind lashes at us. Sparks somewhere to my right tell me that the guys on the quads are shooting at Dries, Isiporho, and Dominik while in the sky, the helicopter has locked its beam on us. Everything becomes blindingly white for a second, snowflakes glittering in my vision, when the light engulfs us. They *know.* They've figured I'm on this sled. Perhaps because I'm smaller, or because I'm not . . . sitting backward on my seat and firing at our pursuers with an automatic assault rifle like Isiporho. How does he do that? I can barely breathe let alone muster the courage to pop my head out long enough to check our surroundings.

I can see the trees more clearly: we're almost on the lake's shore when an ominous rumble behind us has me craning to try to locate the Bat-tank. Answer: right behind us. With insane acceleration I didn't even think was possible for that kind of vehicle, the tank explodes forward and passes us. It keeps going, and I almost believe they've got something more urgent to do than kill us, until the tracks take a mad turn and send the whole thing drifting on the ice until it stops. Straight in our way.

Okay, change of plans: I hold on to March in panic when he sends our own sled into a full 180, ripping the ice as we make a swift turn back . . . toward the helicopter. A dark shape hanging out from the aircraft is the only warning I get before shots clank against the snowmobile's hood and tracks. *They didn't kill us,* but our tracks are shaking weirdly and the sled is slowing down. It comes to a full stop a couple of yards away from the lakeshore and the safe shelter of the dark woods. I'm not given any time to think; in an instant, March jumps down from the sled, grabs a rifle and some sort of pouch from the back, and hauls me with him.

I register his voice at last. "Run, and don't look back!"

Against all odds, my legs find a will of their own and move, carrying me toward the trees even as I can make out a group of men coming out of the Bat-tank. At the other end of the lake, Dries and his men are still playing a game of cat and mouse with the quads. What if they kill him before I ever have a chance to know him again, talk to him? The helicopter's ominous droning above them has me feeling utterly powerless; I force myself not to look or else I know fear will overcome me and paralyze me. I nearly slip on the ice, catch myself, and run, run as fast as I can, holding on to March's hand, each breath made agonizing under the confines of my helmet.

The feel of snow under my feet is a small relief. We're gonna make it. I mentally rehash the same words over and over. *We're gonna make it.* I know the men who climbed out of the Bat-tank can't be far behind, but already the woods are enveloping us, sheltering us in darkness. I register rustling sounds among the pines, right before March pulls me to the ground with him. I fall on the bed of snow with a yelp and roll against him, clutching his arm like a lifeline.

I look up to see that we now lie hidden under the shadow of a huge rock. An old pine leans against it, completing this natural rampart. I can still make out the lake, but I don't think Anies's men can see us from there. I take a calming breath. This could work. Next to me, March searches the pouch he took with him for a small object— a black ball? No, wait—*a grenade!* He arms the rifle and whispers, "Stay here, and"—his gloved hand grazes my helmet—"don't take it off."

"But—"

"Island. I need to take them out before they surround us, and I can't do it with you in the way. Trust me."

I'm sure March didn't mean it like that, but all I hear is that we're in deep enough shit that he's willing to take the risk of leaving me here. I watch him move a few feet away around the rock, concealed by a tangle of bushes as he positions the rifle. When he raises his visor to better adjust his eye in front of the scope, I go perfectly still. The wait is the worst part: lying here flattened to the ground, feeling the cold slowly insinuate itself through each layer of my clothing, the distant noise of the helicopter, like a sword of Damocles hanging above our heads somewhere in the night sky. Is it searching for Dries and his men? Or coming back for us?

There's a noise. I clench my fists in a desperate effort not to move. The helmet is muting everything: the sounds, what precious little moonlight bathes the woods. Maybe I dreamed it. My eyes are glued to March's finger around the trigger, until he presses once. This time there's no mistaking the soft echo as the bullet rips through the long silencer. A brief groan reaches us before a body hits the ground with a muted thud. I can't precisely place the source of the noise, but somehow, around us the woods have come alive. There's the whisper borne from careful crawling in the snow, the occasional twig cracking under unseen boots. I feel the Lions' presence more than I hear it, in the shivers running across my skin, the tension rising from deep inside me.

When March shoots again, they replicate with a rattle of bullets that hit the rock shielding us and the trees surrounding it. Frosty bark explodes and rains on me. I curl and bite my lower lip hard not to scream. When I roll to my side to check on March, he's no longer here. *Oh God*, not that. I don't want to be alone in here. Under the helmet, I'm sweating, hyperventilating, and my visor is starting to fog, even though I'm pretty sure it shouldn't under normal conditions.

With excruciating care, I turn my head to look around and locate him, to no avail. He vanished among the trees, could be any shadow in those moonlit woods. I wince when a little snow makes it inside my collar, freezing my spine even faster than the sudden silence surrounding me. I crawl toward the pouch March left behind. What if he doesn't come back? If they . . . kill him?

A scream tears through the still air somewhere to my right, all the spark needed for terror to ignite in my veins. I scramble toward the pouch and rummage inside it amid renewed gunshots. After a few seconds, the shooting stops again, and March's personal trousseau lies scattered in the snow. Several magazines, two hand grenades, but also a tube of mints, a couple energy bars, a pencil, and a neatly folded piece of paper that I recognize as crosswords.

There's only one thing I need in there, but my hands are shaking so much I don't think I'll dare . . . What if it blows up in my face?

A faint creak makes every single muscle in my body freeze solid.

"Island . . . let me see your face."

FOURTEEN
HIGH FIVE

The voice is deep, its soft drawl a familiar caress. Fear crackles down my spine, rushes in my blood, paralyzing me. I don't want to look up, but it's like I'm no longer in control of my movements. I raise my head slowly and see black boots a few yards away. The same black fatigues all the guards wore at Ingolvinlinna. Faded-blue eyes and a smile so gentle you could almost forget the semiautomatic in his hand and its elaborate optical mount.

Stiles.

Blood pounds fast in my temples. *March* . . . Where is he? Did they kill him?

Through the panic fogging my brain, I register Stiles's black-gloved hand extending toward me. "Let me see your face, Island. Don't be scared. You can get up."

Because I don't want him to get any closer, I comply. I take off my helmet with trembling hands and scramble up. Once I'm on back on my legs, I keep my right hand clutched firmly against my stomach.

His smile widens—he doesn't get it. "It's gonna be okay . . ."

"Don't get near me. I'm not going back with you." My voice is surprisingly harsh and steady, considering that my knees are wobbling so badly I'm not sure I could bolt even if I wanted to. But he was ready to let some doctor lobotomize me, I remind myself—he was taking me there, in fact. Dries may not be the father of the year—but he, at least, didn't strap me to a stretcher and drug me out of my mind . . .

Stiles's brow wrinkles in something akin to the sad face of an adult scolding a child. Nothing like the kind of genuine hurt weighing on March's features. I won't fall for that shit anymore. "Island," he coos. "I couldn't tell you everything, and I'm sorry that—"

"Shut the fuck up, and you'd better not take another goddamn step forward, or I swear we both die here!"

I can barely recognize the roar coming from me. When did I get so radical? Doesn't matter: his smile vanishes as if it were never there in the first place. He's seen the grenade in my hand. That hard expression, the glint of surprise in his eyes: I'm meeting the real Mr. Stiles for the first time, it seems.

"Oh, Island, do you even know how to use that?"

Adrenaline gives terrible advice: it's the only explanation I have for that second of rage and bravado where I unpin the grenade and raise it, crushing the lever in my clenched fist. "Like that."

"All right . . ." A dry chuckle escapes him as he raises his palms, but there's no humor in his gaze. It's deadly cold. "Now we got another problem to solve. Don't move; I'm gonna walk to you slowly."

I take a step back. "Don't."

"Island, believe me, I'm your safest bet right now. But I can't help you if you fight me . . ."

Stiles is talking, but it's not him I'm hearing; it's Anies. *I can't make you happy if you fight me* . . . "And you'll help me how, exactly?

Strap me up to a stretcher again?" My voice breaks as I remember the dark room. "Have doctors turn me into a zombie?"

"No, Island. We're gonna talk about this—"

A row of bullets crashes into a nearby trunk, shredding its bark at the exact same time that Stiles lunges to the ground. I see a black silhouette collapse a few yards away—a man. I think he tried to cover Stiles from . . . the flash of white now dashing at him. March! I watch, frozen in place, as they grab each other and roll around in the snow, fighting for the gun in Stiles's hand. It's a mess of limbs and scary growls as legs kick and punches fly, and I have no idea who's winning until March inflicts a brutal head-butt upon his adversary—that's made only worse by the helmet he's still wearing.

Red splashes on Stiles's forehead, and this time it takes him too long to recover: the gun spins from his hand to March's in a blur, almost like a magic trick. Stiles blinks through the blood running in his eyes from a large gash above his nose, barely conscious as March presses the gun to his forehead. Stiles mumbles something to him in a barely audible voice—some sort of plea?

I feel the grenade still in my hand, my muscles aching from the effort to squeeze the lever shut. When I pulled the pin, I was so angry, so desperate that I thought I had it in me to kill myself and Stiles too. But now I see his bloodied face, the way his fingers clench and unclench in the snow, and I know I could never have gone through with it.

"No!"

March's finger pauses on the trigger, and his eyes dart over to me, turning wide when he sees the grenade. "Island—"

"Please don't do it," I whimper, air wheezing in my throat with each word. "No more killing."

His hand jerks, and I'm so sure he's going to kill Stiles after all, but I hear a loud thump as he knocks him out ruthlessly. March is on his feet right afterward and rushes to me.

"Unpinned?"

I nod with a gulp.

"All right . . ." I know he's trying to sound reassuring, but it doesn't work because I'm holding a fricking live grenade. "Just let me . . ."

March's hand wraps around mine carefully. I feel a tug as the grenade changes hands, and in the time it takes for me to release a breath I didn't realize I'd been holding, he's hurled it toward the lake. There's a distant clatter as it lands on the ice, and I count less than three seconds before a powerful explosion shatters the frozen surface in an eerie blend of light, smoke, and water.

I'm . . . stunned. A chilly wind cools the sweat on my temples, carrying snowflakes in my hair. I stare, oblivious of March's presence, until he removes his helmet, revealing taut, sweat-soaked features. "Can you run?"

"Yeah . . ." Or maybe not. I honestly have no idea.

"Good. We need to get away from here."

Against all odds, my body doesn't betray me; my legs don't collapse under me like I thought they would. Somewhere, in a part of me I had no idea even existed, there's still enough strength, enough will to run and survive. I can feel the burn in my calf muscles, the pain that comes with each exhausted gasp, but once again I grip March's hand and run toward the lake.

The thrum of blades whipping the air above us sends a burst of renewed energy through my system. At least now my mind is clear enough that I know why I'm running. My eyes screw shut, blinded by the helicopter's beam. Did it come back for us because they're done with Dries and the others? And yet . . . two quads sit abandoned at the other end of the lake, lifeless bodies lying sprawled on the ice next to them. Dries was here—I can tell that much.

"We'll take one of those," March shouts over the increasingly powerful droning following us.

I'll take anything at this point, even a skateboard, as long as they don't start shooting again. I don't want to look up; I prefer not to know whether there's an asshole ready to engage us up there.

Halfway to our goal, March's feet skid on the ice, and he stops. His hand squeezes mine so tight it hurts, but I'm too frightened and exhausted to say anything. He looks around and . . . listens. After a few seconds, I too pick up on a distant rumble. What comes next is something out of *E.T.*, except it's not a bike that bursts from the trees under a moonlit sky and crashes onto the lake with a deafening sound, but the Bat-tank.

Panic explodes in my chest as I watch it drift our way in a cloud of ice dust, the tracks spinning madly to outrace the cracks forming on the once-smooth surface. Whoever is driving this thing deserves to die with us! I feel my feet leave the solid ground when March hauls me out of the way. We can't run fast, this time, not against this monster. The three pairs of headlights are rushing toward us so fast all I can make out is a blinding blur.

March holds me as we roll out of the way . . . right before the tracks come to a brutal stop mere feet from us. We find ourselves bathed in the glare of the headlights, dizzy and, I suspect, both terrified. One of the doors folds up, prompting March to shield his eyes with the back of his hand to get a better look at the tank's occupants. Seconds stretch as the helicopter too closes on us, the rotor's powerful wind swiping icy dust in our faces.

"What are you waiting for? I don't have all night."

I recognize Dries's voice, but I can't move. I just stay curled against March like a dead, frozen thing as he pulls me up. I went through one too many brushes with cardiac arrest, and my legs won't support me, not even when the first round of bullets clanks against the tank's hood, shattering the ice less than three feet away from us. I feel like a sock tumbling in a washer as March lifts me in his arms and carries me inside the Bat-tank. There's a loud buzzing in my ears, and above me, March's and Isiporho's faces seem like glittering smudges.

A remote, rational part of me concludes that I'm in shock, but there's nothing I can do about it. I don't know how much time passes until the fog starts clearing in my mind. The helicopter . . . it's shooting at us, and we're making a daring escape. The maniac who made the tank jump at us is, unsurprisingly, Dominik, who seems delighted by the whole situation. The wheel spinning madly in his hands, he keeps yelling that it's "fokken Christmas" while we tear through snow, rocks, and branches toward a trail. In the passenger seat, Dries casually comments that this is, indeed, a nice ride.

I shake my head, blink, and look down at my hand, gripping March's so hard my nails dig into his skin. *Sweet baby Jesus*, we're racing outside authorized hiking trails. In the back seat of. A. Goddamn. Tank. Also, the helicopter is still thrumming above our heads, its blinding beams swiping across the trail in an attempt to lock in on us.

Dries looks up through the windshield, on which I'm only starting to notice the bullet impacts. "We need to take care of that. Dominik, how many Javelins do we have?"

"Four."

Next to me, Isiporho whistles while March raises an eyebrow at his boss.

I'm about to ask what's a Javelin, but that red button blinking on the dashboard with a missile icon on it is all the explanation I need. This is madness.

A bump sends us flying and crashing through barbed wires. That . . . was the Russian border. Dominik seems to barely notice that we're being shaken like martinis. He frowns at the dashboard. "Fok! Launcher's fingerprint locked too." He holds out his hand to Dries, who casually reaches under his seat and retrieves . . . a severed hand.

I swallow hard to contain a wave of nausea as Dominik arranges the bloody fingers flat on a fingerprint scan on the dashboard. A row of buttons starts blinking green, and he gives the hand back to Dries.

I register March's whisper in my hair. "I'm terribly sorry for that."

Not nearly as much as I am . . . Whirring sounds coming from the roof catch my attention. In the driver's seat, Dominik is busy steering with one hand and tapping repeatedly on a touch screen with the other—to adjust the missiles' trajectory, I gather, when I glimpse a 3-D rendering of the terrain around the tank.

I don't really panic until I see Dries holding on to both straps of his seat. Dries, who chopped a guy's hand to steal his tank, who was driving a rocket-launching ice-cream truck when we first met. *This guy* is bracing himself? He is, because Dominik suddenly slams on the brakes, sending us flying forward. March and Isiporho simultaneously hold on to the door handles and my body, preventing me from crashing through the windshield. Something weird happens with the tracks, like they're unable to grip the snow and are spinning uselessly, before the tank bolts into reverse, the sudden acceleration crushing us against the back seat.

Within seconds, the helicopter is no longer behind us but well ahead, and I watch in fascinated horror as on the dashboard's screen, crosshairs lock on to the aircraft and start blinking red. The moment Dominik presses the firing button, there's almost no recoil, only a brief vibration propagating through the roof, the seat, and ultimately my body. We did fire though: two fiery lights illuminate the night sky, tracing graceful arcs all the way to the helicopter. I shield my face reflexively when it explodes, the booming shock wave hitting the tank hard, along with a rain of burning debris crashing on our roof and windshield.

As the adrenaline rush recedes and my heart rate slows down, I notice the way March wrapped his arms around me. Almost like a hug. Now that we're no longer seconds away from certain death, this quasi-intimacy feels weird. Scary even, as if I were naked in his embrace. I squirm away tentatively, willing myself to ignore his sigh as he lets go of me.

Stoic, Dominik raises his right hand, palm turned to Dries, who considers it with a haughty twist of his lips. "You know I hate that. We're between gentlemen here."

The Bat-tank jolts and moves forward, ostentatiously crushing the flaming tail of the helicopter, which now lies wrecked across the trail. Dominik's hand stays in place though.

Isiporho's shoulders shake with quiet laughter. "I say the pup's earned it."

Dries's tongue clicks in annoyance, but he relents and high-fives his disciple.

At last, Dominik places his hand back on the wheel with a self-satisfied smirk. "Since none of you are going to say it, I will: that was fucking awesome."

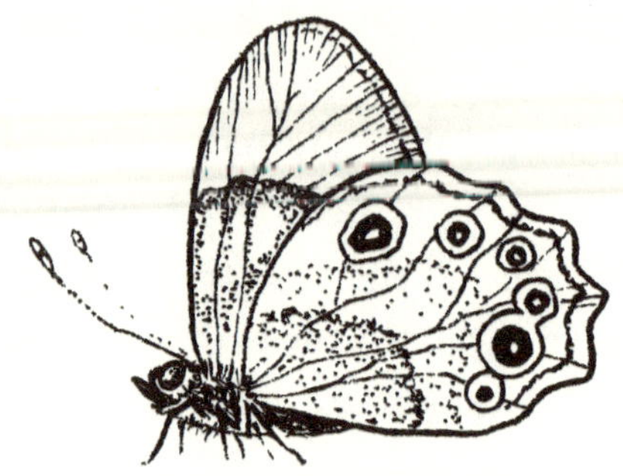

FIFTEEN
SURVIVAL OF THE FITTEST

We did pass a Russian border patrol a few miles east, probably sent to check on the gaping hole we left in their barbed wire fence. But there were three of them with only Kalashnikovs and a dog to defend their country, and, well, we had a Bat-tank. So they basically watched and pulled out their radios as we bulleted past them. I'm guessing that what happened there was something along the lines of, "Dude, I'm not paid enough for this shit."

Dries seems confident that we'll be "on schedule"—to quote him. He even retrieved a cigarillo from his breast pocket and is now busy slowly poisoning us under March's disapproving eye. I don't mind that much: there's something familiar, almost comforting about the sweet tobacco smell tickling my nostrils, like a childhood memory maybe—except I don't have any of those left, I remind myself bitterly.

It's been less than half an hour since we crossed the border, and under the tracks, the ground has gotten smoother. It's too dark outside to assess our surroundings clearly, but I'm not certain we're on the trail anymore. The woods have thinned, and at the end of the snowy road illuminated by our headlights, I can make out some sort of field, a white plain that seems to stretch until it blends with the inky sky. There's so many stars . . . I wonder if I'm seeing them for the first time. Was it that I never thought to look up, so numb that I was in my cage? Here, with the moon half-hidden behind distant trees, no clouds, and no light to distract my gaze, I'm spellbound, little more than a speck of dust under the infinity of the Milky Way.

I get too absorbed in my philosophical contemplation of the universe to notice the tank has stopped. March's gentle tap on my shoulder pulls me out of my daze. "Island, we're here."

Here?

I nod, but to be honest, "here" is . . . nowhere. He helps me climb out of the Bat-tank, and once we're standing at a safe distance, Isiporho arranges several loads of C-4 inside the vehicle. I watch him proceed with mild concern.

"We won't be needing it any longer," he explains, before pointing to the sky. "Look."

I squint at the horizon. Surely, a dark shape is flying our way.

Isiporho grins. "Right on time."

It's not until I see the plane clearly that I understand that the white expanse surrounding us is in fact an abandoned airstrip, as evidenced by the presence of a crumbling control tower in the distance, leaning on a hangar I didn't notice either because it's slowly being devoured by the forest and buried under a layer of fresh snow.

We watch the plane touch ground effortlessly despite the powdery clouds engulfing it. I don't think I've ever seen anything like it, with the engine placed atop the wings like that.

Next to me, Dries runs a hand across his face. "Where did he steal a Beriev?"

Isiporho shrugs. "Dikkenek works in mysterious ways . . ."

I look up at March. "Who's that?"

His expression softens. "One of your Facebook friends."

Okay. I used to cultivate ties to the criminal underworld on Facebook. I let that sink in. Deeply. A question forms on my lips, that I should have asked long ago. "March . . ." I gulp. "I'm not really a software developer, am I? Was I, like, an undercover spy?" CIA, Mossad, DGSI? I shudder at the endless list of equally frightening possibilities. Do I secretly know karate? Maybe not. I got caught by Stiles too easily for that.

Before March can answer, uncontrollable laughter erupts from . . . Dominik.

"Dominik, my boy, you vex me," Dries grumbles.

"Sorry, *baas*. It's just . . ." Aannd he's chuckling again, prompting Isiporho to do the same.

"No," March eventually answers. "You're a brilliant engineer . . . with a taste for adventure."

"*Trouble*," Isiporho corrects before his gaze darts over to our tank. Something seems to catch his attention—lights on the road. *Oh shit*, there's a bunch of cars driving our way. His eyebrows knit in annoyance. "Dries."

The culprit claps his hands. "Well, lady and gentlemen, now's the time to run."

I'm tempted to say, "Again?" but March takes my hand and drags me before I can voice any complaint. Our little group races toward the now-stationary Beriev while, behind us, voices bark in Russian— orders for us to stay where we are, I gather. A jolt of panic makes my legs work twice as fast when I hear gunshots . . . followed by an explosion—the tank. My legs falter and stumble before I catch myself; I nearly forgot about the C-4.

In the complete chaos that ensues, I glimpse a rudimentary ladder being deployed from the plane's side, and before I know it, March's hands are on my butt—helping me inside, actually. I fall face-first on a blue carpet in a dubious state of cleanliness. Dries hauls me to my feet . . . and that's when we're attacked by the dog.

Charging down the aisle with a terrifying bark is the fattest, ugliest bulldog I've ever laid my eyes on. And I'm pretty sure it'll also be the last thing I'll ever see, until an even louder bark explodes from the general direction of the cockpit: "Andrea! *Zwijg!*" Andrea! *Be quiet!*

The cerberus freezes at Dries's feet, its tongue dangling and drooling in a disgusting manner. Now that it's no longer trying to kill us, I notice the creature is wearing a knit Christmas sweater. On its back, snowmen and reindeers frolic among pines, and the red wool appears on the verge of ripping from the effort of containing "Andrea's" jelly.

I feel March's hands on my shoulders. "Don't be afraid; he's not dangerous, just a little . . ."

"Stupid." Dominik sighs, slamming the plane's door while, in the distance, a group of Russian soldiers runs toward the plane. Apparently they won't give up, even if the tank's explosion set one of their cars on fire.

Dries unceremoniously drops my ass in a row of blue-lined seats. "Buckle up, little Island."

I obey, fighting the urge to curl up when Andrea sprawls his big butt at my feet, panting heavily. I breathe a sigh of modest relief when March sits next to me. At least I have a bodyguard in case that monster tries to lick my hand. The cabin starts to vibrate, and the plane speeds up fast on the snowy tarmac, the engine's noise covering new gunshots coming from outside. I screw my eyes shut and block it all. I don't want to know; I'm at the end of my rope, too drained, too scared. My stomach drops as the Beriev takes off. The plane draws a wide curve above the airfield, allowing me one last glimpse of the flaming vehicles on the ground and the soldiers hurrying around them.

It dawns on me that my wish came true after all: I left Ingolvinlinna.

"Where are we going?" I ask March, after we've reached our cruising altitude and the engine's noise is down to a continuous hum.

"Constanta, in Romania." He checks the black chronograph around his wrist. "We'll land in four hours. Dries has a friend there who might be able to help with . . . what we saw on your X-rays."

"Is *he* a real doctor, this time?" When March doesn't answer and his brow lifts in puzzlement, I explain. "If Bentsen really put that device in my head and worked for Anies, I can't believe any kind of medical college allowed that . . ."

"Well, she started out as a promising neurosurgeon, but her license was revoked by the Norwegian Directorate of Health fifteen years ago."

Oh God . . . Bingo. *"Why?"*

Lines of concern form on March's brow. "I can't pretend to fully understand her research but . . . she was researching neuroinhibitors, allowing her to selectively manipulate long-term memory."

As his words sink in, I feel a tingling sensation in my neck. I know my brain is probably messing with me, converting the fear simmering in my stomach into vivid hallucinations. But I can feel the spider moving inside me, and none of the deep breaths I take through my nose help. On the armrest, March's hand tries to take mine; I snatch it away. I don't want anyone to touch me.

"So she was researching memory erasure, and what happened?" I snap, staring intently at my lap.

"She was supposed to target traumatic memories in a test group of mentally ill patients, but she experimented extensively on them."

"Like she did on me," I rasp out.

"Yes."

"Did any of them . . . recover?"

From across the aisle, I can feel Dries's scrutiny on me as March says softly, "I don't know."

I feel nothing. I don't know if I should be scared, angry, desperate, but the moment his words register, all I experience is a form of numbness, like I'm disappearing. Running from Anies and Stiles at least had the merit of giving me some sort of immediate purpose. Back in the woods, being alive made sense because the alternative was imminent death. Now that I'm no longer in immediate danger—save for the way Andrea keeps sniffing my feet—I'm trying to think of what it means to start all over being so empty, what kind of life I'll lead if I can never remember who I used to be, and really, I got nothing.

I look at March, and inside me something stirs. Anger. That sadness in his eyes, the way he seems to be constantly studying me, probing, waiting for some lighting strike that won't happen: it makes me feels uncomfortable, angry, and that's something already. A little anger is a good start, I decide, before I get up from my seat and squeeze past his legs into the aisle without meeting his gaze.

Dries watches me with a raised eyebrow. "Where are you going?"

I shrug in the cockpit's general direction. "March said he was my Facebook friend."

"Dikkenek?"

"Yeah, him."

Already, March is rising from his seat. "Do you want me to take you to the cockpit?"

I ball my fists. "That's approximately fifteen feet. I think I'll manage, thank you."

From the corner of my eye, I see his fingers twitch, but he doesn't insist and lets me walk past Isiporho and Dominik toward the cockpit door. The former is apparently busy reviewing something on a laptop while the latter is getting his ass handed to him by a giant cupcake at *Call of Duty: Candy War*. Serves him right for surrendering to a life of crime, I cheer internally.

I catch Dries muttering behind my back to March in Afrikaans. "Gee haar ruimte . . ." *Give her space . . .*

Exactly. Too bad the evening's only valuable piece of advice came from a dad with a rap sheet the size of Wikipedia.

I push the cockpit's door carefully, and I'm immediately greeted by the smell of potato chips. I spot the empty bag, discarded on top of a dashboard that blinks and gleams in the dark with every color of the rainbow. Sprawled in the pilot's chair is a blond giant I estimate to be in his late forties, early fifties at most. It's probably been a while since he last sat in a barber's chair, judging by the straw-like locks falling on his shoulders and the six-month beard.

Before I'm even through examining the colorful soccer patches on his leather jacket, Andrea drags himself to the cockpit too. The Viking welcomes him with a pat on the head and flings his hand at the free seat. "Make yourself at home."

His accent is much stronger than that of his teammates—must be South African too. It takes me a couple of seconds to realize that he's talking to me, not the dog, who's settled behind his master's seat and is now struggling to lick his own butthole.

I plop myself in the copilot seat, taking in the endless sea of clouds beneath us. "So you're a pilot?" I ask the Facebook friend I don't recognize and who doesn't give any sign that he remembers me either.

"Not really." He grunts.

I fasten my seat belt nervously. "You just took the plane?"

"Yeah."

"Dries says you stole it."

His lips tighten under that thick beard. "It's Russia. You can't steal anything here. They're communists; they share everything."

In that moment, I curse the devastation in my brain: I have this intuition that his story doesn't add up, but I can't provide any precise fact to back my point. I'm absolutely certain that Russia isn't communist, I know that Vladimir Putin is the president, and this guy named Dmitry Medvedev acts as his right nut, but there's a stupid hole in my memory, and I'd be incapable of explaining how I know that or precisely when communism ended in Russia. Here's something else I'll need to read about ASAP. Shaking my head in frustration, I resort to what I deem a shitty comeback. "I'm pretty sure they didn't want to share the plane with you."

A hoarse chuckle shakes Dikkenek's frame. "I made them change their mind."

His right hand moves to the throttle lever as he says this, and I register a whirring sound. Looking down, I discover that his hand is . . . fake, a sleek prosthetic whose fingers move with ease to flip a couple of switches on the dashboard.

When he notices the direction of my gaze, he shrugs. "Carbon fiber. All the way up to my shoulder."

"What happened?"

He looks away from the controls to study me. I make a note that he has clear eyes—gray, or maybe blue—and that he'd better watch where we're going. He eventually asks, "You ever been in a bare-hand fight with a capybara?"

My face bunches in confusion. "Um . . . obviously I wouldn't remember, but I don't think so."

He leans back in his seat and shakes his head. "Some things you'd best forget anyway."

I cringe. "That's what happened? A capybara ripped your arm off? I thought they were, like, big rabbits. Super cute and debonair."

"Nah. The arm, that's a different story—nothing I care to remember. But capybaras, they're vicious, you know. The males, they're territorial. You turn your back on them, and raaaaww!" He growls, mimicking some sort of alien attack with his hands. "It's over."

My mouth falls open. "*Over?* Like they eat you? But they're herbivores, right?"

"Herbivores, huh? Try hiking around with a ham sandwich in your backpack, and you'll see their true colors."

"Okay. You got attacked by an angry male capybara over a ham sandwich. Color me intrigued."

Again he lets go of the yoke and crosses his arms over his chest, his expression somber. "It was in Peru . . ."

"Shouldn't you be holding that?" I ask, pointing at the empty yoke now bobbling slowly in front of him.

He waves a dismissive hand. "It's a Beriev; it flies itself. So he sees me. He's twenty yards away, and his nose quivers. He's picked up on the sandwich's smell." He points at his eyes, forming a V with his index and middle finger. "Wrinkles his nose, clicks his teeth to challenge me. That's how I know it's on. When they attack you, you need to get them into a headlock before they can bite."

"So it charged at you or something?"

Dikkenek grazes the yoke with his palm, possibly preventing a future crash. "No. I was faster."

My hand flies to clasp over my mouth in consternation.

"Preemptive strike," he concludes soberly.

He goes on with the details of his fight, and I lose track of time, listening to his crazy tales. I decide I like Dikkenek—or rather *Jan*—who's actually from Brussels, launches preemptive strikes on capybaras and alligators alike, enters his dog in polenta-eating contests in Venice—where he lives—and claims to possess an autograph of a guy named Augusto Pinochet, who was apparently a huge deal in Chile in the eighties.

When he's finished telling me about his adventures in a Saudi prison, Jan goes silent for a while, his gaze lost in the night sky. Behind his seat, Andrea has fallen asleep.

"It's pretty bad, right?" he says.

I'm afraid I know what he means. I slump in my seat. "March says we were Facebook friends . . . before."

He grunts in confirmation and fishes a smartphone from his inner pocket. He swipes across the screen with his thumb and hands it to me. "I like those videos you sent me. I'm following the page now."

I look down at the screen and nearly drop the phone. In a nondescript living room, an orange tabby wearing a duck costume is riding a Roomba. Stiles's tabby. I swallow with difficulty. "I-I gave you that link?"

He nods. "In Venice . . . before all that shit went down at the Poseidon."

I return the phone to Jan and bury my face in my hands, gasping for breath. I knew Stiles, before Anies took me. Was it just a coincidence, because so many people shared his videos? No. I know it's more than that; I feel it in my bones. Jan has apparently no idea who Stiles is, but did the others tell me the entire truth? I have this intuition that Dries will dodge if I bring it up—I can't say I trust this newly found father of mine much . . . That leaves me with the option to ask March. It's not like he and I aren't gonna need to talk at some point, but the very idea makes me feel like I'm holding on to a lone branch dangling above a miles-deep pit.

Jan flashes me a worried look. "You okay?"

"Yeah . . . I just . . . maybe we can talk again later," I mumble before scrambling out of the cockpit.

In the cabin, four strangers await. Not really, but they all changed into civilian clothes, and it feels odd to see Isiporho and Dries in those impeccably cut three-piece suits. The latter is busy lecturing Dominik about his sneakers, cargo pants, and leather jacket—the sneakers appear especially problematic, since Dries keeps waving his forefinger at them and bitching in a low hiss. "Ons is nie gangsters nie . . ." *We're not gangsters . . .*

There's a lot that could be said about that particular statement, but Dominik appears suitably penitent while, at the back of the plane, March got away with wearing a black turtleneck and dark jeans—that being said, he does wear an old-fashioned plaid blazer, and his clothes look like he spent hours ironing them. Jesus, I don't think I've ever seen shoes shine so bright. I'm trying to figure what he's doing, hunched over his tray table and scrubbing something with intense concentration. Cleaning a gun.

I'm reminded of the way he cleaned the floor back at the cabin, and again he strikes me as this incredibly meticulous guy, what with his tiny brushes and spray bottles, or how he wipes the same spot of the barrel over and over, oblivious to the world around him. Over and over . . . and over. I frown, wondering if that's how he got his shoes so shiny.

Suddenly, he looks up from his handiwork with a start, and his gaze immediately settles on me, anxious, watchful. He quickly reassembles the gun and tucks it back in his holster. The cleaning tools and products are put away in a black suitcase just as fast and he walks up to me. "Is everything all right?" he asks.

"Yeah . . . there's something I need to show you but maybe later."

His brow wrinkles in suspicion. "It will be another fifteen minutes until we land; perhaps you can show me now."

My eyes dart over to Dries, who gave up on Dominik and is now observing our interaction with undisguised interest. I'd rather have this conversation privately however, especially because I have no idea where it'll lead us . . . I shake my head. "No. It can wait. It's not like we can do anything about it in a plane."

March nods, his gaze lingering on my wrinkled sweatshirt and camo pants. "We'll find you clean clothes as soon as we arrive."

"You don't have to . . ." I say, almost like a reflex. It's not that I don't need to change—although wearing dirty clothes for another day won't kill me. The thing is, with March, there's strings attached. I'm pretty sure that money isn't an issue, and I could ask for whatever I need, but anything he gives me will only make me more dependent, more vulnerable around him. Until I've mustered the courage to clarify our situation, I don't want to give in to the temptation of letting him pamper me. It'd be . . . wrong.

Except he's not the type to give up easily. All but ignoring my answer, he pulls out his phone and starts typing something on the screen, his fingers flying fast on the glass. "Don't worry about anything. Just give me a list of what you need: I'll have Phyllis arrange a delivery at the casino."

The *casino*? Is that where we're going? Also . . . "Who's Phyllis?"

His eyebrows jump before he composes himself, but in his eyes, the sadness returns, ever close to the surface. "She's my assistant. She was very happy to learn that we found you, and"—he inches closer, and there's a twitch in his shoulder, but the intent doesn't reach his hand; he doesn't touch me. He lowers his voice—"I'm happy too. I'm . . . so happy."

I look down and tuck a lock of hair behind my ear. "Even if . . . it's not . . . things are not like they used to be?"

If I only knew what "things" used to be between us. Was it casual? No, he wouldn't have done all that crazy stuff to save a friend with benefits, would he? *God*, I didn't want to have that conversation in the plane, not like this, with Dries and Isiporho watching, with nowhere to hide, no time to process any of this.

He does that thing again, where he looks at me in the eyes, and I can't think, drowning in all that blue. "Nothing has changed for me, Island. But I know . . . I understand it's too early for you." His features are taut with barely concealed pain as he adds, "For you, everything probably feels . . . complicated."

No. Complicated doesn't even begin to describe how I feel at the moment. There's someone else inside me, a girl listening to March, straining toward him, whose agony I feel yet can't connect to. There's someone else's pain tearing me up from the inside, and I want it to stop. My vision gets a little blurry; I sniff back, and I raise my palms in a feeble attempt to put some distance between us.

March tries to pull me back to him. His voice is so soft . . . and it hurts so bad. "Island, please—"

I shake my head. "Don't . . ."

When I try to back away, I end up bumping into Dries's chest. "Calm down, little Island."

I wiggle my way around him. I know he could catch me, but he doesn't; he watches me run to the one place I seem to always end up these days.

I need to go to the bathroom.

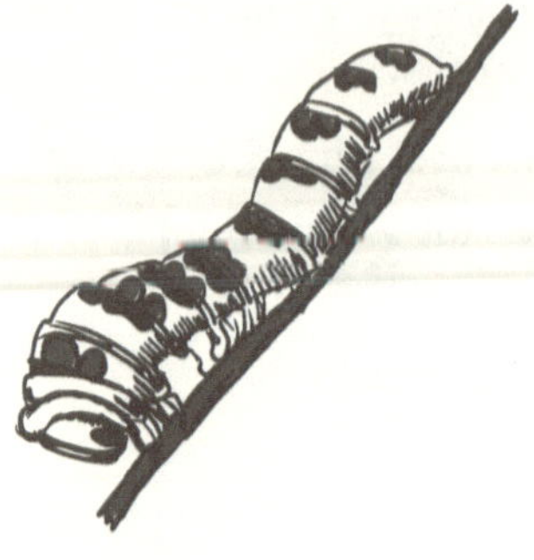

SIXTEEN
AEIOU

Dries came knocking at the door because he wanted me back in my seat for landing. So I exited the tiny lavatory and its stench of old urine with all the dignity of a girl who runs to the bathroom every time her boyfriend tries to talk to her.

March isn't the only man who wants something from me in this plane, by the way. For some unfathomable reason, Andrea has taken a keen interest in me. He waited in front of the door for me to come out, followed me on the way back to my seat, and sprawled himself in the aisle right next to me.

I grip the armrests, and my stomach heaves as we descend toward Constanta, aware of March's gaze on me like a continuous breeze tickling my nape. He never gave up on me—still won't—but does he realize he's trying to rekindle a flame I remember nothing of? Even those dreams I had . . . intense, vivid as they might have been, now they're just dry leaves on the ground. That doesn't make a tree and certainly not a relationship either. What if I never remember, or I do, but I've changed? Isn't love supposed to be something you can't forget? If I loved him, wouldn't I be sure instead of being terrified and feeling like he's invading a part of me I have no control over?

The wheels touch the ground at last, and the Beriev bounces down a runway in the dark. Bathed in the glow of a row of lampposts, a few planes await—Turkish Airlines and some Romanian company that doesn't ring any bells. Constanta—or rather MKA, as Jan calls it— seems like a small airport, with very little life on the tarmac save for a snowplow slowly clearing sludge from the apron under the eye of two employees leaning against the side of a luggage truck, cigarettes in hand.

After Jan is finished parking the plane in an isolated spot, we climb down that same rickety ladder and find ourselves on the frozen, silent tarmac, waiting while he goes to talk to the guys smoking near the luggage truck. I can't see very well what they're doing from where I stand, but I'm almost certain cash just changed hands. One of the men, wearing a bright-yellow vest, waves for the rest of us to follow.

Dries considers him with narrowed eyes, his hand inconspicuously reaching inside his coat . . . Next to me, March's hand rises to hover between my shoulder blades. I shiver at the brush of his gloved fingers against my parka but resist the urge to squirm away. "Island, please wait. They'll go first," he says quietly, tilting his head at Dries and Dominik, who are now treading toward Jan and his contact.

"Why? Is something wrong?" I whisper.

Isiporho looks around the tarmac, lifting his long coat's collar. "It's a little too quiet out here."

"It's 9:30," I counter. "Maybe there're no night flights."

"Maybe," March admits with a somber gaze. "But a little caution can't hurt, especially here . . ."

"Here? What's special about this place?"

Isiporho chuckles. "You're standing in the middle of a US air base."

"What?" I whirl around and scan the planes frantically, only to be stopped by March's arms around my shoulders.

"Don't worry . . . technically we're not inside the base. MKA houses a military base operated by the US and Romanian air forces. It's a logistics hub, a gate to the Middle East," he explains.

"The MiGs are over there," Isiporho adds, grinning at a cluster of barely discernible buildings toward the end of the runway.

Meanwhile, Jan, Dries, and the guy with the yellow vest are through with their palavers. Having ascertained that no tank awaits in the dark to run us over, Dries flicks his wrist in a discreet invitation.

Jan returns to the Beriev to guard it with Andrea while the rest of us follow our new guide inside an aged concrete building. In the deserted hall too, there's this strange silence, nothing but the clatter of our footsteps on the marble floor. Empty customs desks, only a few fluorescent lamps buzzing softly above our heads. March is tense. He might look his usual impassible self, but he hasn't said a word since we left the tarmac. I find I'm oddly attuned to him, to the slightest tic in his jaw, the way he moves. I can tell he doesn't like this bizarre atmosphere, and his unease gets to me too.

He stops, and I bump into his back, picking up the scent of mothballs. "Sorry," I say, rubbing my nose.

In front of me, March has pulled out his phone. He unlocks it with a quick iris scan, and I glimpse a bald, glaring ostrich in guise of a wallpaper. There's something familiar about it, but I can't place it—maybe something I saw on Animal Planet? Our little group watches him check data on the screen with raised eyebrows. When he's finished, he slips the phone back in his pocket and casually pulls out a silenced gun, aiming at the airport employee who led us here. Blood rushes to my temples, and my legs feel paralyzed as Dries, Dominik, and Isiporho react to the signal and draw out their own weapons like one man.

"That plane outside is a Dreamliner," March calls, his voice loud and clear in the silent lobby, as if he weren't talking to any of us but to some invisible assembly. "Turkish Airlines doesn't operate any of those, but I believe *you* own one. Please show yourself."

A trap? My gaze cuts to the Romanian airport employee who led us here. He's looking left and right, his cheeks deadly pale. He knows something . . . Dominik grabs the Romanian traitor by the collar, and at this point, he and I now have at least one thing in common: we're going to need new pants soon if the tension amps up any higher.

I wait, perfectly still, aware of my own breathing while bright-red dots appear on our chests, our heads, one after another, dancing like fireflies. Dries mutters a curse when a new set of footsteps echoes at the other end of the hall. A figure emerges from the shadows—an old man, wearing a black coat over a dark suit. He must be at least sixty, with gray hair and deep lines on his face. Not very tall or brawny, but he doesn't need that, right? I gulp softly when I see a red dot tremble in March's hair.

"It's all right," he murmurs without turning back.

"Is he one of your . . . friends?" I reply through gritted teeth.

March's arms move smoothly to set his aim on the newcomer. "No, but it's going to be all right. He won't hurt you."

Somehow I doubt that, especially since Dries looks pretty pissed to see this particular acquaintance walking toward us. The guy pulls something from his lips—a cigarillo, whose characteristic scent wafts our way.

"What a pleasure to see you back among the living, Mr. November. How have you been? Our Finnish colleagues insist you spend your next vacation elsewhere. They're still trying to explain to the Russians why a tank barreled through their border and destroyed a patrol vehicle."

Gravelly voice—no wonder, with the kind of stuff he smokes—and American. From the US base Isiporho mentioned then? March doesn't move a muscle, but I register Dries's soft, dangerous whisper to the treacherous airport employee still in Dominik's grasp. "Make no mistake, my little snake, you won't slither out of here."

The old guy smirks. "And isn't that Mr. Kovius? Risen from the waters of the Styx as well." He's now standing mere feet away from of us, and his dark, beady eyes are focused on March—no, on *me*? A smoke ring spins our way. "That's some very precious cargo you have there, Mr. November. You can trust us to treat it with the utmost care."

A muscle contracts in March's jaw, but his gun remains pointed toward the cigarillo man, his voice steady and almost cordial as he responds, "I'm afraid I'll have to decline."

That doesn't ruffle the asshole one bit. His forefinger taps the cigarillo, sending ash snowing to the ground. "Let's be reasonable. Mr. Kovius and Miss Chaptal are coming with us. And if they prove useful, you have a slim hope of seeing her again once I'm done with her."

A slim hope? I curl behind March, who seems oblivious to the red gem still gleaming on his temple. "You're acting far beyond your new mandate," he tells our host. "And you know I won't let you take her."

Take me where? And more importantly, what for? This whole ambush doesn't exactly scream official police business . . .

"Let's try this again, perhaps more serenely," Cigarillo-man replies before raising his hand and waving two fingers in the air. The red dots that had been marking us until now vanish instantly. He tilts his head to March expectantly, who lowers his gun in response. Dries and the others soon follow, but this collective gesture of goodwill does little to alleviate the tension in the lobby. It's in the air, in every shallow breath I take, dancing across my skin like static electricity.

Another cloud of smoke stretches our way while Cigarillo-man's gaze sets on Dries. "Miss Chaptal spent eight months with your brother. As you can imagine, I have many questions for her . . . and for you."

Dries glances my way; if he didn't look so arrogant all the time, I'd swear I just caught a flicker of worry in his eyes. How the hell does this guy know so much about us anyway?

Cigarillo-man's attention returns to March. "Once she's helped us, I'm certain we can come to a mutually beneficial arrangement, Mr.

November."

"How kind of you. However, I'm afraid Island needs urgent medical attention. No one questions her until she's seen Viktor and certainly not without me present," March retorts icily.

"Bugorski? Does Miss Chaptal know what kind of care he provides?" Cigarillo-man asks, cocking an eyebrow at me.

"What do you mean?" The question crosses my lips before I can stop myself. I'm getting a creepy vibe from this . . .

Dries steps in with what I gather he means to be a reassuring smile. "Don't worry about Viktor; he's a leading expert in his field."

Isiporho, who's been observing the exchange silently until now, points at the Beriev still parked on the tarmac. "He's the one who made Dikkenek's arm."

"Really?" I ask hesitantly—are neurosurgeons even supposed to deal with prosthetics?

"He's good," Isiporho confirms with a wink.

But that doesn't seem to satisfy Cigarillo-man. "In any case . . . I'd rather question Miss Chaptal before"—he makes a little show of searching his memory—"*Viktor der Butcher* gets hold of her."

Viktor . . . der *Butcher*?

March turns to check on me, reading the silent question in my eyes. "It's only a nickname they gave him in Germany; it really isn't as bad as it sounds."

SEVENTEEN
DOCTOR WHO?

"But *does* he have an *actual* license?"

It's the fourth time I ask, and the explanations I get are still as vague as they were ten minutes ago. So far, all I got is that Viktor Bugorski is supposedly a Russian "doctor" who ran into trouble with the East German state police when he worked for them in the eighties and subsequently fled to Thailand, then returned to Russia, then Ukraine, where he made a small fortune selling breast implants and borscht-flavored vitamins, but now he works here in Romania. What he did for those Stasi police guys remains wholly unclear though, just as much as what led them to want him dead at the time . . .

The cigarillo firmly stuck between his lips, our mysterious host watches the drama unfolding before him with an expression of boredom. Around us, a few soldiers wearing dark fatigues step out of the shadows, all carrying assault rifles and wearing weird goggles that make them look like giant insects. They too have taken an interest in the exchange, and from the corner of my eye, I see one of them scratch his head.

"Do you ever check whether your dentist has a license before sitting in the chair? I don't. What I check is whether I can trust the man," Dries insists while, next to him, Dominik and the Romanian traitor nod in agreement.

"What are you talking about? Is he a dentist or a neurosurgeon?"

March clears his throat. "He's a bit of a jack-of-all-trades like, say, Leonardo da Vinci."

Dries waves to his disciple. "Yes, exactly. Thank you!" He then towers over me with an accusing look. "Would you ask if da Vinci had a license?"

My eyes trained on the veins in the marble floor, I search my recent memory for passages I read in one of Anies's books, about the first guy who tested one of da Vinci's flying machines—and subsequently broke his leg. I come to a decision. "Bentsen was bad enough. I'm not getting near another mad scientist again."

"I can arrange for a reputed, licensed practitioner to see you immediately, Miss Chaptal," Cigarillo-man offers suavely.

"Out of the question," March snaps.

I gauge that old fart warily. "I'm good, thanks."

March moves to shield me. "I believe we're *done*. I'll make sure to contact you as soon as Island is well enough to be questioned, Mr. Erwin."

Erwin? I feel like I've heard that name before, but I'm not sure. I tilt my head at him. "Did we know each other before today?"

A thousand wrinkles appear on the guy's brow. March too sobers abruptly—well, if it's possible for someone like him to get any more sober, that is. I think he didn't want that guy to know about my amnesia.

"I like to think we know each other well enough, Miss Chaptal," Erwin says cuttingly.

Around my shoulder, March's fingers tighten, and Dries steps closer. "Who are you?" I ask.

This time Erwin tilts his head like a predator. He's figured it out. "A vast question. I work for the government of the United States. You could say I solve problems no one else will."

CIA. The moment the thought crosses my mind, it sounds so evident that I wonder what took me so long . . . In my brain, it's like the faces of a rusty Rubik's cube are slowly starting to rotate. "But you couldn't solve the plane bombing or what happened at the Poseidon, and you can't solve Anies."

Erwin's wry, scary smile returns. "Well, I can't without your help. But you seem quite . . . diminished."

"I remember nothing before April," I admit. "My long-term memory is pretty much shot."

He takes a deep, slow drag of his cigarillo, his eyes drilling holes through my skull, as if he could look in there and see the empty shelves for himself. "How unfortunate . . . and convenient. Nothing at all? I miss Agents Morgan and Stiles terribly—I'd been hoping you could reassure me they're—"

Agents? Like . . . CIA agents? The fear I can't control is rushing back in my veins. Pirate Morgan taping my mouth, Stiles's betrayal . . . "Y-you know them too? They worked for you?"

Through the curls of smoke, his voice becomes softer, almost enveloping. The gravel doesn't feel so rough as he says, "I'm not a monster, Island. My favorite weapon is compromise. I can tell there's a lot you need to know, and I believe we can help—"

March moves too fast for me to see, and on our bodies the shiny red dots reappear instantly. Dries steps in front of me, gun in hand, while the soldiers surrounding us have raised their weapons, ready to shoot. Around Erwin's nape, March's gloved fingers curl slowly. The old man remains perfectly calm as March pulls him close enough to whisper something in his ear. I can't hear anything, but I'm mesmerized by the slow movement of his lips, the faintest snarl as he finishes his sentence.

March lets go of his prey and raises his hands in a pacifying gesture. "Mr. Erwin and I understand each other."

Indeed. Again, Erwin gestures for his men to lower their weapons and tells March, "I give you twelve hours. Take her to Bugorski if you want, but know we'll be watching you. Once he's seen her, I *will* interrogate her." His gaze cuts to Dries, and I'm getting the feeling he's about to issue a challenge. "Mr. Kovius will remain our guest until then . . . as a guarantee."

My mouth falls open. Obviously he doesn't know Dries, as if a guy like him would ever . . .

"Acceptable. Dominik will send you a list of my demands. Don't expect me to sit down and chat if my comfort requirements aren't met." Dries adjusts his cuffs with an air of regal disdain, and I'm gonna need to pick up my jaw from the floor. "I hope for you that you know where to find French croissants and a decent bottle of cognac at this hour."

Dominik glares at the soldiers surrounding us, but Isiporho pulls him back with a shake of his head. March makes no attempt to step in either, and I search his eyes in dismay. This isn't right; I can feel it in the pit of my stomach, as if I'm getting seasick. How the hell can Dries surrender to that CIA douche without a fight, when he's basically been killing whoever dared stand in his way until now?

Dries walks away from our little group and allows the soldiers to circle him and take his gun, the haughty expression never leaving his face. When an overzealous goon attempts a body search though, he grabs his wrist lightning fast. "Let us all remain courteous to each other, and no one will get hurt," he warns with a carnivorous smile that bares his gap tooth.

"He's right, no need for that," Erwin confirms, prompting his men to take a step back. "Mr. Kovius will cooperate fully"—he marks a pause to look at me, his expression softening into something I could almost mistake for compassion—"for the well-being of his child."

The words fly in my face, prickling my skin like a slap. He knows. Dries's cold mask cracks, letting through a flicker of vulnerability that seems almost foreign on him. He doesn't say a word, but the wrinkles on his brow deepen, and whatever doubt I might still have entertained about him dissolves, washed away by a feeling I recognize. It's the same warmth, the same yearning as when I try to remember my mother.

"Don't go with them," I plead with him. "Don't . . ." *Don't leave me.*

"Island, it's going to be all right." March's arm snakes around my shoulder, warm and protective, but I don't want it. I stagger back.

Erwin's hands clasp together, the sound loud and sharp, rattling down my spine like a shock wave. "I understand there's a lot your little family needs to work through, Mr. Kovius, but I'm afraid it's time for us to leave, if you don't mind."

I look around in sudden panic, at March's sorrowful eyes, Dominik's hate-filled ones, and the men closing in on Dries to escort him away. They can't take him . . . not now, when I'm barely starting to understand how much I need him . . . "No! Please, I"—my mind races for a solution—"I'll go with you too. Let me go with him!"

My plea doesn't fall on deaf ears. A victorious sneer distorts Erwin's features through the smoke curtain. Of course, that's what he was trying to achieve.

"Miss Chaptal seems well enough to talk to us after all," Erwin notes sardonically.

I nod in agreement and elbow March when he tries to stop me, without much success—I'm not even sure he felt it. Erwin's men are taking Dries outside, toward a pair of black minivans that just parked on the tarmac. I free myself from March's grip for the second time and tell Erwin, "I'm going with you."

March is at my side again in a heartbeat, like a goddamn piece of gum. "Island, *no!* He's baiting you . . . Dries knows what he's doing."

Erwin doesn't move. He waits, his smile a terrifying invitation. I take another step forward when a powerful roar freezes me to the bone. "March, sorg vir jou damn vrou!" *March, take care of your damn woman!*

I stare at Dries through the windows, stunned. On the snowy tarmac, he's stopped and turned to face us, his gaze smoldering with rage. Yet he doesn't scare me. I instinctively know that his anger isn't directed at me or even at March. I leap forward; I want to go to him—

need to. It's my legs, my heart doing all the thinking now.

But I go nowhere, caught midair by March's arms. He hauls me back, and I shriek and kick in vain as Erwin's men usher Dries into one the vans and the door slides shut, leaving only black windows reflecting the snow and the lampposts' bleary light.

With the faintest shrug, Erwin turns his back on me and leaves, escorted by a few remaining men wearing ordinary suits rather than military gear. Like a vise slowly tightening around my torso, March's embrace crushes me, kills the fight in me. I pant, croak as the vans start driving away, but I'm too exhausted; I can't break free.

It's only after they're gone that March releases his hold. I scramble away and glare at him. "They'll never let him go, and you know it!"

A tired sigh deflates him. "Island, I think he made the right decision."

I stare down at the floor, at the tips of my boots, muddy. His, spit-shined. "Let me go," I grind out at last. "I don't want to see that Viktor guy, and I never asked for your help. I want to go to the US embassy, and I'll figure out my options there."

Isiporho runs a hand across his face while in front of me, March has turned to stone. His chest heaves, and his fingers curl, as if he is about to lose his temper, but they unfurl almost as soon. "I'm sorry . . . I can't do that."

"Then"—I swallow to steady my voice—"how are you any better than Anies?"

EIGHTEEN
BRACE YOURSELF

There was a car waiting for us on the airport's parking lot—a black Mercedes Dominik patted affectionately for a while, like he would have a horse. He eventually took the wheel while Isiporho climbed in the front. March sat with me in the back, and they head-butted the Romanian traitor and put him in the trunk, because March is after all a sensitive soul: he didn't want his brothers to shoot him in front of me—as if sparing me another bloodbath would somehow earn him back my trust.

My cheek pressed against the cool glass of the window, I watch headlights flash by in the fog, studying the continuous black ribbon imprinted in the snow by hundreds of tires. I've curled as far as humanly possible from March in the back seat and try to ignore his eyes, reflected in the window as he watches me with that beaten-dog look of his . . . The events of the night replay in my mind, over and over. I can still smell the cigarillo, as if the smell now clings to our clothes like an unspoken threat.

"What did you tell him?" I ask quietly.

In the reflection, March's eyebrows jerk, his expression one of incomprehension.

I turn to look at him. "That Erwin guy, he said you were trying to blackmail him. What did you say for him to let us go?"

In the mirror, I see Isiporho's mouth quirk in amusement. March appears to hesitate before he says, "I told him I was considering publishing my memoirs."

Dominik's eyes too dart to the mirror, full of curiosity. "For real?"

March gives a faint shrug. "I did start to write them. I had to find something to keep me busy in that hospital bed."

I meticulously file each word of his explanation. Erwin joked that March was back from the dead. Did he get badly wounded, at the Poseidon? I can tell I'm missing some essential piece of this new puzzle, hovering infuriatingly out of reach in the wasteland of my brain.

"You know, you should publish them anyway," Isiporho tells March with a chuckle. "I like your style. Easy to read, very direct . . . like a phone book."

"I'll consider your feedback," March replies tartly.

I have a zillion questions, but Dominik beats me to it. He gives Isiporho a befuddled side-eye. "You've seriously read it?"

The interested party nods. "A Million Little Bullets: Fifteen Years Spent Killing for Governments and Crime Lords Alike.*"

I stare at March in awe and horror. Governments—as in *US* government? You bet a guy like Erwin doesn't want to see that kind of best seller lining the aisles at Walmart . . . "You said you left the Lions," I recall. "What did you do . . . after?"

His jaw works silently at first, and I detect something that could be regret—or maybe guilt?—filtering through an otherwise masterful poker face. "I sold my services—as a private contractor of sorts."

Behind the wheel, Dominik snickers; I find nothing to laugh about. "You're a hit man."

"*Were.* I retired a little over a year ago."

It dawns on me that Isiporho and Dominik have stopped smiling and gone silent altogether when I ask, "Why?"

March's eyes fill with that tender sadness I've come to associate with him. I thought I could find it in myself to be stronger around him, to lock up that part of me that feels so raw, so powerless whenever he does that, but he wins again, and inside me, another wall collapses when he murmurs, "I wanted to be with you."

I take slow breaths to keep it together, stare down at my lap, the scar on my wrist. I don't think he understands what it does to me, how much it hurts every time he opens a tiny window to that life I've lost. It only serves to remind me that I'm standing in ashes, surrounded by strangers I have no idea how to connect to.

In part because I need a way out of that intimate trap, but also because I do worry about the immediate future of the poor dude we carry in the trunk, I change the subject abruptly. "The guy in the trunk . . . how are you going to kill him?"

March's eyebrows draw together. "Island, we're not going to—"

"Are you going to shoot him? Or is it Isiporho who's going to do it?"

The latter glances at me in the mirror. "We need to hear whatever he can tell us about Erwin's plans first."

A welcome rush of anger overpowers my fear as I remember March's words, back at the cabin. "You're going to question him? Like you *questioned* that man in Rio?" I snap.

He shakes his head. "It was a different situation."

"Is that what you tell yourself—"

"Dominik."

March's sudden bark startles me. I turn around at the same time that the Mercedes comes to a stop on the side of the road. I barely have time to see March's face before he steps out of the car, but I feel his anger, something in the air between us that doesn't need any words and bites into my skin.

Within seconds, the trunk snaps open. March pulls out our unfortunate traitor none too gently and rips off the tape from his mouth and around his wrists and ankles. My pulse picks up, and my hand hovers on the door handle, frozen. Deep down though, I already know where this is going.

The guy tumbles into the brownish sludge with a frightened groan, likely convinced he is living his last moments. My shoulders jerk when the trunk slams shut. Isiporho shakes his head with a sigh, and Dominik sends a pointed glare at March's silhouette in the mirror. Neither comments however when he climbs back in the car. Outside, the Romanian clambers away in a state of shock while the engine starts.

We resume driving in stifling silence, inches away from each other. In spite of myself, I'm focused on March's breathing. I listen, trying to gauge his mood. Maybe I should say something. He did let Brutus go, after all . . .

I risk a peek at his profile. He's staring straight ahead, like a wax statue. "Thank you," I mumble.

At first, I'm wondering whether he heard me, but after a couple of seconds, his posture relaxes, before he shifts to look at me. In his eyes, the ice has thawed, and that lingering sadness is back. I wonder if it ever leaves him. "Anything for you," he says softly.

And just like that, he rams through my defenses all over again. I have no snark left in me to fight him, so I nod and return to my contemplation of the window. Surely with enough self-conditioning I can convince myself that those butterflies in my stomach are because I'm hungry.

•••

All around us, the décor has changed. We were driving through deserted streets lined with decrepit concrete buildings, some of which looked ready to collapse, and then elegant stone mansions started popping up, one after another. Now there's a waterfront, a quiet road lined with wrought-iron lampposts, and a . . . castle?

I stare at the building's intricately sculpted façade through the window, my mouth open in a perplexed O. I gather that's the casino March was talking about—since that's clearly where we're headed— but it doesn't look like one. More like something out of a Disney movie, with all the columns and arches and that giant shell-shaped window overlooking the frozen promenade. On the walls though, the paint is chipping badly, and plastic sheeting hangs from one of the four turrets, dusted with pure white and billowing like a ghost in the wind. The whole thing feels like a twisted fairy tale setting, maybe in some long-forgotten kingdom awaiting to be freed from an evil spell . . .

"We've arrived," March says, when Dominik parks in front of the building.

I step out, dwarfed by the fifteen-foot arched window I gather is the main entrance. Lots of plastic sheeting here too, by the way—to conceal the inside from prying eyes?

"What is this place?" I ask. I'm probably getting a stiff neck later from all that staring, but it'll be worth it.

"It used to be a casino in the nineteenth century, but I think Viktor is turning it into a dental center," March explains.

"So he's restoring it?" Now that I'm getting a better look, I do see some scaffolding running along the casino's side, all the way to the seaside turrets.

Absorbed in my contemplation, I didn't notice that Isiporho is already walking away. He waves without turning back, and Dominik answers my question before I can even voice it. "You do your thing here. Porho and me, we're gonna see if we can find where they're keeping Dries."

March ducks his head in agreement. "Be careful; our little friends are remarkably obstinate."

I'm about to ask what he means by that when Dominik glances at the street running parallel to the promenade. His lips curl into a wry smile. Not all cars are covered by snow: one just parked right in front of the casino . . . Dominik responds with an equanimous shrug before he strides away to catch up with Isiporho.

"Wait," I call. "The car . . . won't you need it?"

He turns around one last time, a youthful, almost boyish grin on his face. He extends his arms in an all-encompassing gesture. "Cars, cars everywhere!" And off he goes, to steal some unsuspecting

Romanian citizen's car.

Meanwhile, I didn't notice that someone turned the lights on in the casino's hall. Through the transparent plastic, I glimpse a debauchery of chandeliers and mirrors, painted walls and so much stucco molding I'm expecting everyone inside this place to wear period costumes and frilly wigs.

They don't. Framed by a pair of burly bodyguards in blue uniforms, the guy who opens the door wears a red Adidas tracksuit and must be around the same age as Erwin. Interestingly, all of his hair migrated down from his skull to his chin to form a thick, curly white beard. I'm simultaneously reminded of Yul Brynner and Santa.

He whispers something to his goons, and they walk away with a wary glance in our direction. Once they're gone, Santa Brynner scans us with keen gray eyes. "Where is he?" I gather he means Dries . . .

"It's been a long night," March replies.

The answer seems to satisfy the guy, who opens the doors wide, not without a bit of a struggle and lots of creaking. "Welcome!" He puffs his chest. "To Viktor's Dental Palace."

He invites us in, one hand scratching a round and hairy belly under his sweater. A grin cracks through his beard, revealing yellowed teeth that could benefit from whatever it is that he does in here. He waves a dismissive hand at March. "I already know the favorite disciple. But you"—he tilts his head—"you're Island, right?"

I nod hesitantly.

"Good . . . very good. Do you want me to give you a little tour?"

No . . . Okay, maybe. I *am* kind of intrigued by that hall, the pink walls, and gilded moldings—like a little Versailles, but with fresh paint and plastic sheeting on the floor, and a half-finished white desk that looks like a space ship that warp sped its way into the middle of this rococo galaxy.

Behind me, March shakes his head. "Thank you, Viktor. Unfortunately, we don't have much time . . ."

The culprit gives a heavy sigh. "So, straight to my office?"

"Yes, please. By the way, did you receive—"

"That bag from your assistant? It's up there."

"Excellent." March's expression softens when he tilts his head at me. "We have some fresh clothes for you."

"Thanks . . ." But I wish he wouldn't have.

Santa Brynner cuts through our exchange with a pat on my back. "Come, come. I want to see that brain."

A lump builds in my throat, and I inch away from Viktor . . . *der Butcher.* "Wait . . . wait. What kind of doctor are you?"

"What kind of doctor did you expect?"

"Well . . . a neurosurgeon?"

He pumps his chest and attempts to tower over me, but it's not very effective because he's not that tall in the first place. "Petrozavodsk State University, neurosurgery, psychiatry, and a little microbiology too—I've always loved that."

I wince. "But your license has been revoked, and now you're a dentist?"

As soon as I've said this, Viktor's face falls, bushy eyebrows lowering into a conspiratorial expression. "Don't worry, *golubushka*; I'm not really a dentist."

"Actually . . . that's worse."

"No, no, you don't understand. I'm a businessman! I hire the dentists, and we make money. I'll show you on the way to my playroom."

I don't know if I should worry more about the fact that Viktor appears to cultivate loose medical ethics, at best, or him calling his office a "playroom." I feel March's hand on my back, both a reassurance and an encouragement to follow our host. He leads us up a monumental flight of stairs and to what looks like some kind of concert hall. Here, the paint is finished, and on bright-orange walls, delicate floral moldings have been painted in white and gold. It's a bizarre contrast to the two rows of perfectly identical dentist cubicles facing each other in the middle of the room. A medical scent floats in the air that overpowers that of old stones.

"We'll get rid of the stage," Viktor notes, gesturing to the tall arch showcasing an ancient wooden stage and worn red-velvet curtains. On the left, I recognize that incredible shell-shaped window taking up most of the wall, like a gate to another dimension. Time has made the glass foggy, and through it, Constanta looks like a cluster of blurry orbs glowing softly in the night.

Viktor grins at us, his arms akimbo. "So what do you think?"

"Very impressive," March concedes.

"The décor, the history: that's the kind of thing the international clientele want," Viktor explains. "With my palace, I put the *tourism* back in dental tourism."

I cringe. "Dental tourism?"

Undeterred by the hesitation in my voice, Viktor raises a victorious fist toward the monstrous chandelier glimmering above us. "It's booming right now! Too expensive to get your crowns done in America? Get them done in Romania for a third of the price, complete with a stay in a registered historical monument."

That raises March's eyebrows. "And you obtained the authorizations to turn it into a dental clinic?"

Viktor shrugs. "You ask me that? The killer who became an honest man, and the honest man who returned from the dead? *Net nichego nevozmozhnogo.*"

"I suppose, indeed, that nothing is impossible," March admits with a half-smile.

Viktor doesn't bother with a reply: he's already moving on, crossing the room toward a small door by the stage. We follow into a brand-new elevator—they haven't even removed the plastic film protecting the brushed-steel walls yet.

"We have fifteen rooms, and I set up my little den under the roof. Very nice."

"They're rooms for your patients, like a hotel?" I ask, trying to conceal the tinge of suspicion in my voice.

"Yes, they're for people who come here to get a lot of work done. Afterward, they just lie there, with their face swollen like a Botero." Viktor lets out a breathless laugh and mimics the effect with his hands as we step out.

Here too, the smell of fresh paint and detergent is overpowering. We're standing in a surprisingly modern hallway, almost like a regular hospital. The angled white walls are the only indication that we're indeed under the casino's roof. Hearing footsteps, I notice a couple of young women in turquoise scrubs strolling a perpendicular hallway. Viktor's employees work late . . .

"Come, come. It's this way." Viktor leads us toward a set of padded doors he shoves open to reveal a spacious office, complete with an examination table and what looks like a CAT scan room behind a window wall.

I send a worried look at March, who guides me toward the two transparent-plastic chairs facing Viktor's long desk. Before we sit down, he bends to whisper a soft reassurance in my ear. Maybe it's the effect of the stress, but when his lips brush my hair, the shivers dancing across my skin are . . . not all that unpleasant.

I nod and focus my attention to Viktor, who settles in an ample leather seat across from us, like a king in his throne. He smiles at me, but I get the feeling that it's no longer so warm—rather clinical, analytical. "What's the last event you remember before waking up after the dome's collapse, Island?"

NINETEEN
HARMLESS FUN

Somehow, I allowed myself to believe that Viktor was just this weird guy with a shady past and a tacky tracksuit who runs a bizarre dental center. Now that he's gazing at me patiently, his arms crossed on that mile-long glass desk, it's like I'm sitting in front of Bentsen again. I recognize the false kindness and genuine curiosity, the way he's trying to read my reactions while acting the part of the old friend I can trust . . .

March is watching me too but rather with a kind of contained febrility, something that flutters on his face but doesn't translate in his rigid posture.

I stare down at my hands on my lap. "Maybe . . . the water and Mozart . . . the Queen of the Night's aria. *Der Hölle Rache kocht in meinem Herzen*," I recite.

Viktor raises an eyebrow, and March leans a little closer. His fingers rap on his jeans nervously, but he curls them into fists.

"The first time I woke up at Ingolvinlinna, I thought I had been dreaming, and I couldn't remember the dream, but it was the only thing I remembered, and I thought it over and over. I couldn't remember the rest of the aria either, so I kept thinking about that line until it drove me mad."

"Do you know what that means?" Viktor asks.

"Yes. It means hell's vengeance seethes in my heart."

"Would you say it's an automatism, or would you understand something else in German if you heard it?"

"I still understand German, French, Afrikaans, or even Japanese, and my procedural and implicit memory is mostly intact, if that's what you're getting at. But my long-term memory is shot, and I can't remember how I acquired these skills or my personal history before I was brought to Finland. For example, I still know how to code, but I can't remember going to college or what I learned there. But the code makes sense when I see it. My automatisms are still here," I explain with a defiant frown.

A humorless grin cracks through his beard. "Well we have a smartass here." He nods to March. "She's a smartass."

Something that could be a smile tugs at the corners of March's lips but doesn't quite spread to the rest of his face. "She never ceases to amaze me."

I avert my eyes, a foreign pressure building in my chest at his compliment.

Unfazed, Viktor goes on. "Do you ever have . . . flashbacks, or dreams you believe might be memories?"

I gulp, and I can tell my ears are getting red. Hopefully my hair will conceal that. I make sure to avoid March's gaze as I say, "Maybe . . . I sort of guessed . . . that I knew March." Ignoring the jolt of his eyebrows, I soldier on. "I think I dreamed of him. When I saw him, I didn't know who he was, but at the same time, I recognized his eyes. They were giving me meds to make me slow, but after I started throwing them up behind Stiles's back, I was sharper and the dreams were . . . different."

The subject of my fantasies tilts his head in an effort to make eye contact. I stare at my lap harder.

Viktor raises a bushy eyebrow. "How so?"

I shrug, praying that my cheeks don't look as hot as they feel. "Just different."

A conniving grin cracks through his beard. "Well, you see, not everything is fried up there. Now strip, smart girl," he orders casually.

His words send a wave of goose bumps rising across my skin. "Wait, uh . . ."

Viktor tips his head to the scanner room. "We'll take a look at that fascinating device in your head." Without waiting for my answer, he presses a button on the phone sitting on his desk and mutters something in Romanian to a girl he calls Nadia.

Moments after, a blond woman in turquoise scrubs enters the office, whom I recognize as one of the two we passed earlier in the hallway. She's holding a folded exam gown, and she smiles at me. I bet she'd smile just the same if she'd shown up with a foot-long catheter . . . She gestures toward a white screen I didn't notice in a corner of the room.

I dart anxious eyes at March, finding in his gaze a hesitation that mirrors mine. Then again, if I don't take that scan, I'll never know for sure if there's really something in my head . . . With a final look his way, I go to change behind the screen. I pull up my sweater, grimacing when the tang of dried sweat hits my nostrils—nothing worse than smelling yourself. On my sternum, the butterfly still rests, warm and a little heavy. I tear it off and throw it on a chair along with the rest of my clothes. I know I should, but I can't bring myself to throw it away, maybe because I don't want to forget what Anies did to me, or maybe because it'd feel like killing the butterfly a second time . . . I'll decide what to do with it later.

I know they can't see me, but I'm wondering if they can make out some sort of shadow. I feel so naked, so aware of their presence. I rub my arms to fight the chills coursing through my body. When the camo pants and my jeans underneath hit the floor, I cringe at the sight of my legs; they're a little bony—nothing new here—but the day's adventures have left a trail of bruises all the way up to my hip.

The white gown fastens like a kimono; I tighten the string and smooth the front, like style still matters. I leave the relative intimacy of the screen to find that Viktor's colleague is already preparing a syringe for the IV contrast. I'm tempted to ask if she's a dentist, a nurse, or even a neurologist of the shadows like her boss, but I come to the conclusion that I prefer not to know.

"Normally, I'm supposed to ask you about allergies and medical history, but obviously . . ." Viktor trails off with a shake of his head. "No problem. Never seen anyone die from that anyway."

This . . . I'm pretty sure that's the kind of approach that cost him his license. March follows me into the scan room, looking equally circumspect. After Nadia has helped me lie on the table, I stare at the ceiling and clench my teeth. When I close my eyes, I see the dark room again, Pirate Morgan's sunken and scarred eyelid. It takes everything I have not to move, not to cry when she plunges that needle in my arm. I breathe fast as the heat of the dye spills in my veins, up to my neck and then my head. March's gaze trails on me one last time, lingering on the bead of blood where the needle pricked my skin, before he leaves the room with her.

And I'm alone, the table is moving, sliding into the scanner's mouth where bluish lights glint all around me. The suffocating fear is back. I feel the spider in my head, picture it crawling through my brain, frantically wondering if they can see it too. I hear Viktor tell me to calm down and lie still through a speaker. I will myself stiff and dead like a branch on the ground.

When it's over, I don't even wait for them to come for me; I jump down from the table, the tile floor icy under my soles, and hurry to the door. March opens it and tries to take me in his arms. There's a moment when my body wants this, seeks his warmth instinctively, but the fear is stronger, and I recoil. "I want to see the images," I say in a brittle voice.

Viktor points to the examination table standing in the middle of his office. "You go sit there, *golubushka,* and I'll show you everything."

Nadia goes to smooth a length of paper sheet over the table and crosses her arms, waiting for me. I walk to the table and sit under March's anxious gaze.

I see Viktor grab a sleek touch remote on his desk, and on the wall closest to the table, a panel slides up to reveal a large TV screen. After some amount of fumbling with the channels and a few seconds of Romanian pop, followed by soccer and a blue screen, the 3-D model of a human brain appears on-screen. My brain.

My chest constricts as the spider is now revealed in its terrifying details. The "body" is actually very flat, hardly bigger than an SD card, resting at the base of my skull, right above the first vertebra, like Isiporho predicted. The long wires reach deep, into the medial temporal lobe. Where my long-term memory should—used to?—reside.

Viktor's fingers glide on the remote to rotate the model. "Very nice, huh? Look at that level of detail. It's not even on the market yet, but Viktor has it!"

I can't find the strength to congratulate him for his state-of-the-art technology, but March's stony face does the job nicely. Viktor sobers and clears his throat. "So, what this is . . . well . . . I don't know."

My face bunches, but I bravely resist the urge to burst into tears.

He sees this and waves his hands at me. "No, no . . . what I mean is I've never seen anything like it. I didn't say I don't know what it does." His fingers tap on the remote repeatedly and a window pops up on-screen over the brain model, containing what looks like an EEG.

"Is that mine?" I ask.

"Yes and no. There's yours"—he taps once, and most of the chart flashes blue—"and there's a little extra." This time, another part of the chart flashes red, with perfectly regular spikes and waves, unlike the somewhat more random electrical activity of my own brain.

"These are very low-current electrical impulses. You don't even feel them," Viktor explains, "and they target centers in your brain that you need to access your long-term memory. The signal messes with your brain's activity and inhibits it." He nods to himself. "Your doctor did a wonderful job."

I go rigid on the examination table, sitting so straight my spine hurts. He probably doesn't even mean any wrong: I'm just another medical curiosity to him. He doesn't understand the magnitude of what I've lost.

March's voice is low, laced with warning as he reminds Viktor, "That woman erased her memories . . ."

The interested party seems unaware that he's seconds away from getting punched. "No, they're not really erased like data. Rather, if someone can light up the path neuroelectric impulses take in your brain to access your memories—which is fairly doable nowadays—they can block that path. She didn't completely empty the warehouse; she closed the roads."

A bubble of hope swells in me, soon overcome by fear. "Then how do you intend to fix this . . . reopen the roads?" I ask.

"We dig in." Viktor shrugs. "We open; we extract the device." Blood drains from my face, which Viktor seems to barely notice as he goes on. "Once it's done, we inject specific proteins into your brain to help neurons do the job, heal and restore connections between your cortex and hippocampus. But I'm not venturing any guess about what will be recovered. God only knows what else they pumped into your brain to screw your LTP."

I touch my nape reflexively, my stomach sinking at the very idea of anyone touching my brain again. "LTP?"

"Long-term potentiation. Synaptic activity in your hippocampus enables storage and access to memories. That's where the fun happens."

"But . . . the wires are inside my brain. Won't it be dangerous if you like . . . pull them out?" I'm picturing bits of gray matter being dragged along, and nausea rears its head, clutching at my stomach.

Viktor strokes his lips with his forefinger. "There's always a risk. In fact, there's a risk the moment we inject the anesthetic: that's how surgery works. But you're still young and healthy: you have no idea the things people can recover from. I could carve out half of your brain, and you'd walk out of here on your two—"

March's hand slams on a steel tray standing near the table, making me jump out of my skin, much like Nadia, who steps away with a yelp. His nostrils are flaring, and his features seem paralyzed by a mask of barely contained rage. "Please be mindful of what you're saying, Viktor."

I sit still, cold and terrified by that dark side of him as much as by Viktor's dubious treatment plan.

Viktor shakes his head, unruffled. "Interesting. Are you always this angry? Any palpitations, tremors? Got your serotonin level checked lately?"

March breathes out his temper. "Let's focus on helping Island instead . . . please."

"Yes, of course." He returns his attention to me. "So, if you don't want surgery yet, we could start by neutralizing the device's effects with something less invasive."

I bite one of my nails, considering him warily. "Like?"

"I'm thinking I could inject a modified podoplanin-based protein that will stimulate your hippocampus, after the ECT, of course."

I freeze. "*ECT?*"

"To fry the device and interrupt the signal."

March's eyes narrow. "Do you mean some form of electroshock?"

"We prefer to say Electroconvulsive Therapy these days. But don't worry; it'll only be a very brief, targeted discharge meant to deactivate the device, not even enough to induce a seizure. It's harmless fun, and she'll be anesthetized anyway." An ominous grin cracks through his beard. "We're not savages."

At last March appears to grasp the full implications of Viktor's offer: his expression turns guarded. So I'm not the only one who gets that a mad scientist who sells discount crowns with a revoked license wants to inject unknown substances into my brain and fry the spider with electroshocks. With no guaranteed results.

I'm waiting for March to voice an objection, for a sign that he's not actually considering going ahead with this madness. But they're both staring at me, Viktor like I'm a fascinating toy he's about to disassemble, March with a mixture of doubt and expectation. My stomach knots. He said it, back at the airport . . . that he wouldn't let me go. They're still looking at me. Fear creeps under my skin and becomes terror, fueled by the sick certainty that the choice won't be mine.

I can't focus on anything other than the blood drumming in my temples, harder and harder, until bright spots dance in my vision. A cold sweat makes the gown stick to my back. I can't see the door, but I know it's there, a few feet behind me. I want out. Away.

The moment I've made my decision, I feel the tension accumulated in my muscles explode in a burst of adrenaline. In a split second, I grab the instruments tray closest to me and hurl it toward March and Viktor with all my strength. March catches the tray midair—Sweet Jesus, that man is scary—just as I hop down from the table. My palms and knees meet the cool tile, and all I know is that I need to make it to that door. I scramble up and run, fueled by the panic swelling in my chest. From the corner of my eye, I see March leap to stop me, and Viktor shouts for him to get me.

He won't. The white padded doors are within reach, and when the doorknob turns, I feel wings sprouting in my back. They'll never catch me. No one is going to touch me anymore, play with my brain like Play-Doh, lie to me, or cage me like a fucking canary!

I crash through the door and barrel down the hallway. There I taste freedom for all of three seconds before I feel March's arms wrap around me from behind. Muscles clamp around me like a warm vise, pulling me backward and against his chest. I have nothing left to lose; I shriek at the top of my lungs. "Let me go! Let me gooo! Someone help me! Help!"

But in the doorway, Nadia averts her eyes and closes the doors, leaving me to fight alone. I sink my nails into his forearm and bite as hard as I can through the wool of his turtleneck. I roar so loud that my throat hurts, and my voice eventually breaks.

He only squeezes me harder and gets down to his knees, bringing us both to the floor. I feel his weight pinning me. Under him, I kick and convulse helplessly. "Let me—"

"Island, please . . ."

I feel him curl around me, his arms, his legs. He's caging me. "Island, listen to me."

I manage to elbow him, but he doesn't even flinch; he grabs my wrist and blocks my arm. The fight is over: my body sandwiched between his and the cold, hard floor, I can no longer move. I can't even find the strength to scream anymore; I just jerk in vain.

One of his hands is in my hair, stroking it over and over. "It's going to be all right. Please listen to me. If you don't want this, he won't do it."

"You're lying," I croak.

He combs away tear-soaked locks from my eyes. I didn't even realize I was crying. "I won't let anyone touch you."

"Except you. *You* do whatever you want. Touch me, lock me up." I sniff and hiccup, struggling to catch my breath. "I don't want you to touch me . . . Let me go!"

Around me, his hold loosens until he allows us both into a sitting position. I immediately crawl away from him, gathering the hospital gown around myself to preserve the remnants of my dignity. There're tears and snot smeared on the gray tile, glimmering under the harsh fluorescent light.

March's shoulders slump. He too seems suddenly old, exhausted . . . He runs a hand across his face. "What do I need to do for you to trust me? How can I prove to you—"

"Let me go," I repeat, this time more steadily, even as I struggle up on shaky legs. Perhaps to prove some sort of point I'm not certain I fully understand myself, I add, "Give me your car keys, and just let me go. I'll try my luck with Erwin if I have to."

I don't expect much from this desperate strategy—I don't even know if there *is*, in fact, a strategy. So when he pins me with that hypnotic blue gaze and hands me his keys, I'm kind of thrown off. I consider his upturned palm warily. It's an obvious trap. The moment I try to take them, he's going to ninja me, and I'll be back on Viktor's table of doom in a matter of seconds.

I take a step back. "Not like that. Throw them to me and, uh . . . drop your gun too. And kick it away."

With the faintest sigh, he gets down on one knee and reaches for the gun in his holster. My fingers curl into fists. My body is poised, ready to bolt. He places the black gun on the floor with slow, controlled movements and sends it spinning my way.

"Take it. If it makes you feel safer, you can have it."

My eyes never leave him as I bend to pick it up. The gun is heavy in my hand, still warm from the prolonged contact with his body. I'm surprised to realize that I know exactly what to do. Cold spills into my stomach. I've held a gun before . . . *Who the hell am I?* Like a robot, I thumb the side and find the safety lever. I flip it before cocking the hammer. I point the gun at his chest with what I hope is a menacing glare. He doesn't seem impressed, just fricking sad. Maybe it's because my mind is in shambles, but it gets to me, that despair in his eyes. I feel like crying again, standing in that hallway, aiming at this intimate stranger who wants me to trust him.

"The keys," I ask again, extending my left hand greedily. "I want the keys."

March tilts his head at me. "Island . . . are you sure you're capable of driving?"

"Watch me," I grind out, my features distorting into a snarl.

Behind him, I catch movement. *Shit.* Viktor decided March was taking too long to drag my ass back into the examination room. His brown eyes narrow as he takes in the scene before him. "Need any help with the patient?"

March replies without looking at him. "No. It's all right."

Under the silvery beard, the corners of Viktor's mouth tug down, yet he nods once and walks back into the room without so much as a second glance at us. He must know that my chances are almost as good as a chicken's in a nugget factory.

March returns his full attention to me; I feel his gaze searching me, probing, raising goose bumps all over my body. "No one will stop you, but I wish you'd put on a coat before you go outside."

I make a show of curling my finger around the trigger. "Very funny. Give me the keys, or I swear I'll"—I swallow, overwhelmed by the realization that I can never shoot. My stomach heaves at the mere idea—"I swear I'll do it!"

He gives no sign that my threat registered, his expression as soft and patient as ever. It reminds me of Stiles's good-guy act, and I'm about to say so when he tosses the car keys my way. I barely catch them and have to lower the gun, since motor coordination isn't exactly my strong suit these days. He had an opening, but he didn't move, didn't even blink . . .

When I feel the plastic fob and its heavy steel keychain in my hand, I clutch it to my chest. There *has* to be a catch. It's not possible otherwise. "I'm going now," I warn him.

He stands still, even as I take a series of slow steps away from him. I'm ready to spin on my heels and make a break to the stairs when his voice stops me. "Island."

I raise the gun and swallow hard.

"My coat is in the trunk. Please . . . put it on."

His quiet plea shakes my resolve. It makes no sense that something so simple could be so powerful, and for a second, I hesitate. I want to believe that this is real, that March is this knight in shining armor, the guy you only meet once in your life and who loves you so much he'll even open the door to the cage and watch the bird fly away. But Stiles and my—no, not my father, *Anies*—they too pretended to loosen the noose to better strangle me, and the more I trusted them, the easier it was.

I can't stand the way March is looking at me. I just want out. Now. I whirl around and run down the hallway and to the stairs. My heart threatens to burst out of my chest with every step, but my legs won't give up, carrying me with renewed strength. I stumble and nearly fall a couple of times, race past a few blurry shadows who make no attempt to stop me, until at last I'm on the first floor, scrambling down the line of cubicles in which Viktor's minions will start filling cavities at 8:00 a.m. sharp. I only run faster and crash through the entrance door.

Cold swallows me instantly, and it dawns on me that I'm now

standing almost naked on the promenade, barefoot on a blanket of fresh snow. Gusts of chilly wind bite at my skin through the gown's nonexistent protection, but I don't care: all I can see is the black Mercedes, still parked in front of the casino. Whatever game March is playing, I'll figure out later. I cover the final yards in a trance and raise the key fob with a shaking hand. The lights flash, the door unlocks, and none of it seems real. Even once I'm sitting behind the wheel, all doors safely locked, it takes me a couple of seconds to realize that he *really* let me go.

I told myself I wouldn't trust any of March's bullshit, and that I'd rather freeze to death than wear his coat, but I'm shaking badly, and I have to clench my jaw to stop the chattering of my teeth. All common sense and pride forgotten, I drop the gun in the passenger seat and get out to go grab the black coat that is, indeed, resting in the trunk. As I snuggle into the warm wool, enveloped by a comforting smell of mints and mothballs, my chest heaves with an emotion I can't understand. Something sweet and painful, overwhelming . . . that feels a lot like regret.

Even so, when I turn the key and the engine hums to life, I'm relieved to discover that I still know how to drive. Deep down, I know it can't be that simple, that March won't give up so easily, and he's probably watching me leave.

For now, however, I'm free.

TWENTY
THE BAPTISM

Okay, I did not entirely think this through. When I started driving, my plan was crystal clear: 1) Turn on the heat. 2) Adjust the goddamn seat. 3) Steady my grip on the wheel, because I nearly caused three accidents on my way out of Constanta, and I kind of scraped the side of March's car against a trash can—then again, there was snow everywhere; how was I supposed to know I was driving on the sidewalk? 4) Go straight to Bucharest without getting caught by Erwin, find the US embassy there and just get *home*, wherever that is.

Now that night has fallen and I'm driving through a seemingly endless plain on an almost-empty freeway, I'm starting to entertain doubts. For one, driving barefoot is hell. My feet are frozen, and the heat isn't helping much. I fear I'm gonna lose my toes at this rate.

Equally distressing is the prospect that knocking at the US embassy's door might prove to be a terrible idea after all.

Best-case scenario: I'm a US citizen *and* the real Island Chaptal—I've reached a point where not even that is certain—they take me in and, I guess, contact the FBI to let them know I'm no longer dead after all. Except Erwin implied that Stiles and Pirate Morgan are actually rogue CIA agents or something like that. What if they still have connections and find me? Do I want to take that risk?

Worst-case scenario: Nothing is real after all. I show up, and it turns out I hallucinated most of what happened so far. I'm not Island, the US embassy can't help me because I have no ID, I'm not a US citizen anyway, and when I look down at my arms, I see purple fur and realize I've been a Muppet all along. I can't help but check my hands on the wheel, just in case . . .

Also I'm hungry.

A bright-red sign that looks like a giant daisy flashes by, indicating a gas station a few miles away. Maybe I could stop and buy something to eat—I found a money clip with a couple hundred euros in March's inner pocket. I do feel some amount of misplaced guilt at the idea that I stole his car, his gun, and now I'm going to help myself to his cash too. I guess desperate times call for . . . well, larceny.

I pull right into the gas station and do a decent parking job, by my standards—I don't know if March would agree, but at least here on the median strip, I'm not blocking anyone. Stepping out barefoot on the wet, icy ground is the hardest part; the rest of me is kept fairly warm by the coat, although you could fit two of me in here. Once I'm steady on my legs, I trot toward the shop, drawn to the lights like a mosquito.

People stare at me when I enter, and some leering gazes make me all too aware of how vulnerable I am, almost naked under March's coat and alone in the middle of nowhere. I wonder if they'd look at my legs the same if they knew I'm hiding a gun in my pocket. I have no idea what a "tactical supergrade" is, but that's what's written on the barrel, and it makes me feel very powerful, even as I drop a pair of red Christmas-themed slipper boots, a soda can, and a chicken sandwich on the counter before a befuddled clerk.

I notice a row of flashy-orange Rompetrol sweatshirts lined near the register and grab one too before handing the young guy a hundred-euro bill with a regal gesture.

There's a beat of silence before he proceeds to scan my items and eventually gives me my change. I put on the slipper boots immediately in the middle of the shop. As I turn around to leave, I catch sight of my reflection in the window of a fridge. Staring back at me is a zombie whose face pops out of an oversize coat. The mess of tangled curls falling on her shoulders looks like she went through a wind tunnel, and that old guy with the grubby parka and the Heineken beanie keeps side-eyeing her insistently. I have a frightening epiphany: I'm 134 euros and one half-full tank away from becoming a crazy homeless lady who'll drag around a ton of plastic bags and talk to pigeons in the streets of Bucharest. I definitely should have thought this through.

When the Heineken guy attempts direct eye contact, I hurry out of the shop and run back to the Mercedes. Once inside, I feel safe, shielded from prying eyes by the tinted windows. I curl into the driver's seat and remove March's coat to shrug on my brand-new sweatshirt over the paper gown. Crazy homeless lady, indeed. Especially once I've snuggled back into the coat and I start an improvised picnic.

Soon the smooth black leather of March's seats is covered in bread crumbs. I shush my conscience, filing the pang in my chest as some twisted variant of Stockholm syndrome. I need something to silence the noise in my head, to numb my thoughts: I turn on the radio and browse through the stations until a familiar tune fills the car. Apparently, in Romania too, radio stations are legally obligated to air George Michael during the holidays. My throat feels tight, and the chicken doesn't taste so great as Michael croons that he'll give his heart to someone special for Christmas.

I drop the half-eaten sandwich back in the plastic box it came from. My eyes burn as if I'm about to cry, but the tears won't come. I hope this is it, that I've hit rock bottom, because I'm not sure I want to sink any lower. I'm about to drown my sorrows in a can of Fanta when I register footsteps and rustling outside the car. Someone is rapping on the rear window. Startled, I drop my soda on the floor mat. A sweet smell permeates the air as I watch the Heineken guy circle the Mercedes.

He slurs in a gravelly voice, "Esti înăuntru? Ieşi afară! Vreau doar să vorbim." *Are you inside? Come out! I just want to talk.*

Add Romanian to the growing list of languages my former self learned in another life. I don't understand everything, but my brain manages to piece together the general meaning of his—visibly drunken—exhortations. And no, I don't want to chat. I fumble for the keys in March's pocket with a shaky hand. If he keeps trying to look inside like that, I'm running him over!

Okay, maybe not. But if he had seen me drive, he'd move away. He doesn't; he keeps rapping, calls me *dragă*—whatever that means. I'm fastening my seat belt to get the hell away from here when the unthinkable happens. Heineken guy looks left and right and unzips his pants with a chuckle. From the corner of my eye, I see something dangle in his hands before a steady stream of liquid hits my window. I don't even want to know; I turn the key in the ignition.

Just as I'm about to hit the gas pedal, a shadow glides behind the Heineken Pis. I distinctly hear a deep voice say, "Good evening, sir," before the guy's face slams against the very window he just pissed on. My hands drop from the wheel, and I recoil with a yelp of panic at the sight of his bloody jowl grotesquely squished against the glass. It stays like that for half a second before sliding down, leaving a sickening red trail in its wake. A black-gloved hand hauls him away from the car, and he collapses a few feet away with a groan.

I don't need to look up to know who goes around beating up hobos at gas stations in the middle of the night. The doors are locked. I could wait. But he won't leave, right? I take a shivering breath, switch off the engine, and press the door's unlock button. The first thing I see when the door opens is a pair of spit-shined boots, as if I needed further confirmation that March never opened the cage. He merely toyed with me a little.

I step out, my eyes never meeting his.

"Island," he begins. "I meant to give you space . . . but Erwin's men followed you, and I was worried."

I look around instinctively, expecting some guy in a black trench coat hiding behind a gas pump, but all I see is a bald Santa in a red tracksuit waving at me. Viktor is leaning against a beige SUV I never realized had been tailing me. He shrugs. "I told him we should let them catch you when you leave the station, to teach you a lesson, but no one ever listens to me."

Meanwhile, the Heineken Pis is slowly sitting up, one hand clutching his bloody nose. The guy's noodle is still out of his pants, and for a second, I see pure hate in March's gaze. Fortunately for all parties involved, the offending appendage is soon tucked back where it belongs, and the guy staggers away until he disappears inside the cabin of a massive truck parked at the other end of the lot.

My attention returns to March.

"I'm not going back there," I say defiantly. "If you try to force me—"

"I won't. The choice is yours"—his voices catches—"if you don't want to try Viktor's treatment, I won't force you."

"But you can't give me my life back," I snap, more harshly than I intended.

His jaw tightens. "If you return to New York, you'll be at Erwin's mercy . . . provided Anies doesn't find you first. I need to keep you safe until I've solved this."

"Until Anies is dead or behind bars," I clarify. "But Erwin captured Dries, and he'll kill him if you don't take me back tomorrow."

"He'll never do that. Dries is far too valuable an asset, besides . . ."

"What?"

He shakes his head. "Never mind. No use in speculating at this point."

"March, if they manage to get rid of Anies? Will you let me go? For real?"

His voice sounds flat, remote, as he replies, "Once Anies is dead, if you want me gone, you will never hear about me again."

Isn't that what I wanted? Then why does my chest hurt so much I can barely breathe? Silence stretches between us until the revving of an engine alerts us to the fact that Viktor . . . just left.

I blink at the departing SUV. "He, um . . . he ditched you."

March seems equally dumbfounded. It's the first time I see him look like this, lips slightly parted in astonishment, like a little boy. I avert my eyes to conceal an involuntary smile.

"Indeed," he confirms before checking his watch. "All right. I've made good note that you don't want to return to the casino, but it's getting late. Let's find a place to spend the night, and I'll contact Erwin to sort out our options in the morning."

I shrug. "Okay, I guess . . ."

Honestly, I've stopped trying to think of the future, immediate or otherwise. At this point, I'm too tired and lost to do anything other than tag along. I walk to the passenger door like a robot, certain that March won't let me drive anyway.

He moves to climb in the driver's seat . . . and freezes.

My first impulse is panic. I'm thinking that he saw something; gunshots are about to erupt. In my legs, the muscles coil in anticipation, until I realize that what he saw are crumbs all over the front seats, and Fanta too.

I feel my ears grow hot. "I just . . . I used your money to buy dinner, but it's because of that guy, uh—"

"It's all right." The tremor in his voice tells me it's anything but. "Can I ask you to sit in the back for a few minutes? I'll turn on the seat heating; it won't be long."

"Sure." I settle in the back seat and watch him produce a mini wet wipe from his jacket's pocket. First, he wipes all crumbs from the driver's seat before he takes the wheel. We don't make it far: across the lot and straight to the car wash. What follows is a ten-minute ballet during which the front of the Mercedes is meticulously vacuumed, the dashboard wiped clean, the floor mat shampooed and thoroughly rinsed, then dried and put back in place. There's nothing to be done for the scratch on the side, but soap and water get rid of the last traces of the Heineken guy's bodily fluids, and at last I'm allowed back in the front seat. March returns behind the wheel and lets out a long sigh. "I'm sorry. I think it's . . . more comfortable this way."

Buried in his coat, I peer at him. I don't really mind that part of him, the cleaning. It's all so familiar . . . and yet I still can't summon any clear memories of this man before the ice-cream truck attack. Even in my dreams—my cheeks flush at the thought—he was only a shadow. Skin, kisses, whispers . . . pieces of a puzzle I couldn't solve.

"Do you have any mints left?" I ask.

"Yes." He searches his inner pockets for his precious tube.

"Take one," I say quietly. "You need it."

March's hand pauses before he can drop the candy in his palm. He tilts his head to study me, his eyes suddenly alight with curiosity. "You're right. I do."

TWENTY-ONE
STORY OF MY LIFE

He likes country. I was a little surprised when March synced his phone to the car radio, and Johnny Cash started crooning to a girl that he's been flushed from the bathroom of her heart. At first, I wondered if he had chosen that particular song on purpose, to convey some sort of . . . message. But the next track was some guy howling about his tractor being sexy, and I concluded that my shady ex is quite simply a country enthusiast.

So far he's kept his word: he didn't take me back to Constanta and Viktor's dreadful dental casino. There's a small town called Fetești-Gară not far from the gas station: that's where he takes me. We park in front of an austere concrete building that turns out to be a hotel, the aged sign proudly flaunting its only star. The inside could best be described as a sixties convent: clean and warm but sparsely furnished with the kind of stuff you'd expect to see in a flea market. March takes care of check-in while I tour the lobby and examine the lace doilies decorating threadbare velvet armchairs, the brown melamine sideboard above which a portrait of Jesus hangs on the wall.

"Island?"

I whirl around at the sound of my name. March is standing at the bottom of a staircase, waiting for me. The old lady sitting behind the reception desk is staring at me too. When her gaze slowly drags back and forth between the two of us, it hits me: we're going to spend the night together in this hotel, under the strict surveillance of our lord and savior. Which feels kind of weird. Shaking off my discomfort, I hurry past a dismal Christmas tree, whose branches seem to sag under the weight of a handful of golden balls, and follow March upstairs.

There're only a few rooms, and I have a feeling that we're the only guests tonight. When the door creaks open to reveal two beds, I address a silent prayer of thanks to a Virgin Mary icon hanging on the wall. March walks to the one closest to the window and lays a black suitcase and travel bag on the bed that he retrieved from the Mercedes's trunk.

He presses his thumb to a fingerprint lock on the suitcase, and I watch with no small amount of curiosity as a neat-freak-assassin's survival kit comes into view. There's a change of clean and perfectly ironed clothes on one side and a vast assortment of weapons on the other. Goose bumps bloom on my forearms when I'm reminded that this man has proven to be my most reliable ally so far, and he carries around hand grenades in his suitcase.

I don't know what to do with myself, so I pick the easiest way to avoid prolonged interaction. "I'm going to take a shower."

March gestures to the sports bag. "I retrieved it from the casino for you. It's fresh clothes and . . . other feminine products."

I secretly relish in his obvious embarrassment, like it's the thirties and tampons are still the harbinger of scandal and depravation. I take the bag with a small "Thanks."

"Will you need anything else?"

"No, I'm good."

The shower is too hot, but I don't try to adjust the temperature. I'm thinking that maybe my skin is going to peel off, and there'll be someone new underneath, someone whole. I step out eventually, and when the steam clears up, I'm dismayed to see that same girl in the mirror, only a little redder. She's not me. She wasn't Anies's daughter, might never be Dries's . . . she's not the girlfriend March lost. She's nothing but a stranger to the friends and family she once had. I massage my temples forcefully, fighting off the first signs of a migraine.

After a few minutes, I feel clear enough to wrap myself in a large towel and search the sports bag. It contains little more than the bare essentials, but clean underwear and deodorant have never felt so good. I slip on a pair of gray yoga pants and shrug on my Rompetrol sweatshirt. In the bedroom, March is checking something on his phone and types a quick message. He puts the device back in his pocket as soon as he sees me standing in the doorway. "How do you feel?"

"More or less okay." My gaze falls on his suitcase. "Hey, do you have maybe a pair of scissors in there?"

His brow twitches in suspicion. "Yes, why?"

I shrug. "Just . . . I need scissors."

He studies me, with those eyes that look like dark oceans.

"I won't do anything weird. I'm not gonna kill myself if that's what you're worried about."

His jaw tics. "The idea never crossed my mind."

I fidget in the bathroom's doorway while he retrieves a toiletry bag from his suitcase, from which he produces a tiny pair of scissors. "Will these do?"

With an eager nod, I walk to the bed to take them from him. As I'm about to close the bathroom door again, March's voice stops me. "Island?"

"What?"

"Can I ask you to leave the door unlocked?"

I'm not even going to dignify that with an answer. I glare at him and slam the door behind myself. Without locking it.

•••

"What do you think?"

March won't stop blinking, and he hasn't said anything since I came out of the bathroom. I fear my hair looks worse than I thought, probably like the result of a freak accident rather than a chin-length bob like the one I wore on EM Group's blog post.

"It's"—his mouth works in vain, until an unexpected smile lights up his entire face, creasing two dimples. It's the first time I see him smile like that, and he looks younger, just . . . *different*—"It's more like you. You look lovely."

I can't stop the blush that warms my cheeks at his compliment.

March gestures to the scissors in my hand. "I think one side is longer than the other. May I?"

"Yeah . . ."

He joins me in front of the bathroom's mirror. In the sink, eight months' worth of auburn tresses now rest in a damp heap. I feel better, lighter. I gaze at our reflection as March wets my hair and starts working on the right side of my bob with a frown of intense concentration. We stand in comfortable silence, the rhythmical snip of the scissors the only sound between us. Once he's put the final touch to his chef d'oeuvre, March straightens with an air of smug satisfaction.

I now sport an ear-length bob, and the sides are admittedly even, but on my forehead, the bangs are one-inch long, and I look . . . stupid. I think he was going for *Amélie*'s style, but the result is more reminiscent of Jim Carrey in *Dumb and Dumber*, and the orange sweatshirt doesn't help. My lips quiver, until I can't hold it anymore and let out a chortle. "Thank you. Please don't ever cut my hair again."

"You don't like it?"

I ruffle my hair with both hands. "It'll do, and hair grows back anyway."

"I'm terribly sorry . . ." He looks genuinely beaten, and I'm amazed that all it took was a bad haircut to bring down a man who

163

seems otherwise capable of enduring anything.

"Don't worry. Like I said, it's gonna grow back. Besides"—I crane my neck to better examine the sides—"I like it. It's almost a pixie cut. Do you think it'd look good if I dyed it blue?"

A self-explanatory grimace wrinkles his brow. "I prefer your natural color."

"Okay then."

Once we're finished cleaning the bathroom, and we're back in the bedroom, sitting on our respective beds, the silence returns. This time though, there's nothing comfortable about it. March won't stop looking at me, so I cross my legs and stare back to unsettle him. It's not fair that he looks so calm, and I'm jittering, my fingers drumming on the bed's scratchy brown covers. I almost wish he'd speak first, but he just sighs and looks down at his hands.

With a deep breath, I risk a toe out of my shell. "March."

"Yes?"

"What was I like?"

Confusion registers in his gaze, and when he doesn't answer immediately, I clarify. "I mean, before, when you knew me. Was I very different?"

My question seems to disturb him. When he moves to get up from his bed, I recoil instinctively. I'm not sure what I'm afraid of, but he takes the hint and sits back. "Island, you're not a different person, and I . . . I still know you."

"How can you be so sure of that?" I ask, my voice brittle. "I don't even remember where I first met you."

"In Tokyo. The day your mother died."

He might just as well have punched me. "You were *there*?"

"Dries wanted to capture her, to recover a diamond they'd stolen together."

I jump to my feet. "He *killed* her?"

"No. Anies had one of his men shoot your mother before Dries could capture her . . . I believe that's what started everything between the two of them."

Everything . . .

The throbbing pain I'm so used to is back, pulsing inside my skull. I cradle my head in my hands, and March is at my side in an instant.

"Let me give you—"

I push him away. "No! No meds . . . I don't want to take anything."

His chest heaves. "I understand."

"Just tell me about my mother, about Dries . . . Anies. Tell me what you know, please."

I return to my bed and curl under the covers. March sits back too, and I listen as he speaks. He's factual, concise; I like that. I have no idea how long we stay like this. I remember none of the things he tells me about—well, not consciously anyway—but some details make my chest tighten. He tells me about my childhood, the fifteen years I spent with my mother. He chooses his words carefully when describing her, but I read between the lines that she was part of the same world he and Dries are. A thief, a spy, traveling around the world wherever her next misdeed took her . . . with me in her suitcase.

Apparently I was homeschooled until the age of fifteen, probably because the longest we ever stayed in the same country was six months in Paris when I was eight. I'm surprised at how easily those new truths take root in my mind. Every word, every detail feels like evidence, and I come to realize that Anies skillfully blended real life and fiction to forge the lies he told me. I did spend my childhood globe-trotting, and I did learn several languages—including a bit of Romanian, obviously—just *not* with him. He was never part of the lives he stole. Already, his polished narrative about my perfect childhood with him seems to be fading away, like fog on a window . . .

March tells me about Simon, the man my mother chose to raise me, the other father who's waiting for me in New York. Simon works in investment banking, he's a curmudgeon, and he doesn't like tapioca because it constipates him. He's married to a woman named Janice, my stepmother, a retired economics teacher who's into yoga and veganism. Once again, it's a strange sensation to feel each new piece of information settle in my mind, click like a Lego brick, even when I can't picture any of these people, their faces, their voices . . .

"Do you have pictures?" I ask March when he marks a pause. "Of them, I mean."

"I can show you public ones; I don't possess any personal ones. I was never . . . formally introduced."

And I have a fine guess why . . . I give an awkward nod as he reaches for his phone in his jeans pocket.

When he hands me the phone, he's launched an image search that returned dozens of similar corporate pictures. Always wearing a suit, the man must be in his midsixties, with gray hair that's threatening to turn white and anxious, attentive blue eyes. There's this tension in the lines on his face, in every pic, even the ones where he shakes another businessman's hands or awards another some obscure M&A trophy. Simon worries too much, about everything, all the time. March didn't say anything about that: I just know it, or rather *feel* it. There's a stinging in my eyes: I wipe them with the back of my hand.

"He's kept all your things," March says softly. "He hasn't given up on you."

My things . . . Biting one of my nails, I let the full meaning of the words set in. My clothes, my books, my life. I focus again on Simon's stern face, transfixed. "In my place, in New York?"

"Yes," March confirms. "Joy's boyfriend moved in so she could keep the apartment on West 81*st* Street."

I almost let go of the phone. "She's . . . alive?" Surprise flashes in March's gaze, but I put the dots together before he can even confirm. "She wasn't at the Poseidon with us. She didn't die there!"

"No, Island." March places his hand on mine. The sudden heat of his palm feels a little strange, but I allow him nonetheless. "She didn't die. She's well . . . and she misses you."

I free my fingers to look her up in Google images, like I wanted but never could at Ingolvinlinna. The pics Anies showed me were real, and she does work in a law firm like he said. The simple ability to recognize her fills me with so much happiness, so much hope! She must have made me laugh all the time: her grin is infectious, and it's hard not to fall in love at first sight with her heap of blond curls and mischievous cornflower eyes.

Dammit, I'm gonna cry again. I fight it, blink back the first tears obstinately. Seeing this, March goes to the bathroom to pour me a glass of water. I sip it slowly while he sits back. "Do you want to stop here for tonight?" he asks.

"No, no . . . I want to know everything," I reply, gulping the last of my water. Mentally going through the list of my priorities, I remember our conversation with Erwin, back at the airport. "Erwin said Stiles and Pirate Morgan used to be CIA, and I"—a vision of a Roomba cat whirring around a nondescript living room flashes in my mind—"I think I knew Stiles . . . even before all this."

The blue in March's eyes darkens at the mention of his name. "You did. He used his position in Mr. Erwin's department to earn your trust."

He goes on to tell me about the way Erwin skillfully drew me into his net when he figured I was not only both March's and Dries's Achilles' heel but also potentially the warden of my mother's many secrets. According to March, Erwin didn't squeeze out much from me. Stiles, on the other hand, who diligently served Anies while pretending to defend the free world . . . that piece of shit became my Facebook friend and betrayed us all—I'm blocking and reporting him as soon as I can access my account.

My stomach lurches with a sense of impending doom as I ask the one question I can already feel I'm going to regret. "And . . . Morgan?"

March marks an unusually long pause: his lips pinch, and pinch, until I fear they're going to disappear entirely. "He used you to get closer to Dries. You were in a relationship with him," he says at last, his tone clinical.

My head spins, and nausea wells inside me. Did I call him Alexander? No, March says I called him Alex . . . back when I dated him, unaware that he was manipulating me to get revenge. Because Dries killed his entire family in a plane bombing. Morgan's father was a double agent who worked for both the CIA and the Lions, a frumentarius, March calls it. Dries hates those frumentarii guys since the man who shot my mother was one of them, and Morgan's family paid the price for Dries's grief, like countless others.

This time I just can't. Salty tears roll down my cheeks, and a violent bout of nausea has me running to the bathroom. I lock myself in, collapse in front of the toilet bowl, and the chicken sandwich I had earlier travels back up along with the Fanta in a revolting mess. March knocks to ask if I'm all right. I say yes because I don't want him to see me like that.

When I come out after having thoroughly rinsed my mouth, my legs are still shaking. "I can't believe"—I wrench my hands nervously—"I mean, he always creeped me out, but I never imagined . . ."

Maybe we can start over. It wasn't so bad, you and me, right?

Hearing his voice again, picturing the scarred flesh sealing an empty eye socket, I rub my forearms instinctively, overwhelmed by the urge to take a shower. "I feel . . . dirty. I can't believe I slept with that asshole!"

"You didn't."

"Oh? Okay . . ."

March's lips curve in a gentle, almost apologetic smile. I have a bad feeling about this.

"Are you sure? I mean, you can give it to me straight." I mentally brace myself. Please, *please* let it not be anything horrible like, "You didn't sleep with him; he raped you."

March clears his throat. "No, to the best of my knowledge, nothing happened when you two were together."

I give a trembling nod. "And he didn't touch me back at Ingolvinlinna . . ." I return to my bed and hug my pillow. Anies's innuendos about me building the future with that piece of shit Stiles ring back in my ears. "I don't think Anies would have allowed that."

Even so, March still looks uncomfortable, and that scares me.

"Is there something else?" I've been drugged for so long and my body was no longer mine. They could have done anything. I wish I could shrug out of my skin right now. "Was I"—my voice falters— "was I pregnant?"

March's eyes widen. "No, absolutely not."

"Then what's your fricking problem?" I mutter.

"You . . . well . . . unless someone—no, that's not what I meant . . . " He draws in sharp breath. "I believe you're still a virgin."

"I-I'm sorry, what?"

"You're a virgin," he repeats, his voice a little unsteady.

I sit up. Surely there's a misunderstanding. "But, um . . . you said you were my boyfriend."

"Hopefully I still am."

An excellent question, which I'd rather sort out later. No, what I need to hear is *how?* "Were we, like, really religious or something?" Even as I say this, I realize it makes no sense. March has killed at least ten people over the past forty-eight hours and admitted to having tortured a guy in Rio. Unless he pledged allegiance to ISIS, I'm pretty sure religion isn't his cup of tea.

His mouth purses. "How do I put this . . . our spirits were willing, but our flesh encountered . . . a number of obstacles."

"Like what?"

I listen, in a state of stupefaction as March goes over the many setbacks we've faced since the beginning of our journey. From that time he tried to kiss me in a car in Paris but a drunk bum threw himself onto our windshield—at least that one didn't pee on it—to a long series of ill-timed or otherwise interrupted attempts. People kept calling at the worst times, then he didn't have condoms, then his house exploded, then Dries barged into our room, then we were in an elevator and it wasn't the best time, especially since dolphins attacked us right afterward . . .

And I'm twenty-six. Still a virgin.

After I've processed this news, I blurt out the first thing that comes to mind. "So you've been trying to bang me for fourteen months?"

He strokes his chin pensively. "In a way, I suppose."

My jaw goes slack.

"I've been told I'm very persistent."

"That you are. But did you never want to just . . . give up and find someone else?"

All trace of humor vanishes from his eyes. "Never."

There's something hanging in the air between us after he's said this, and I don't know if I should ask, if I'm strong enough to hear his answer.

March tilts his head, his eyes searching mine. Yearning. "Island . . . can I see your left wrist?" he asks softly.

I chew on my lower lip and eventually murmur a hesitant, "Okay."

With slow, careful movements, he sits next to me on the bed. When the mattress sinks under his weight, I need to make a conscious effort to fight the instinct to curl, huddle, and keep my damn wrist to myself. I unfold my arm and extend it toward him, ready to snatch it back. His fingers wrap around my mine, warm and tentative. I'm starting to understand now where that deep-rooted fear comes from: I have no walls for this man. He knows my body, my mind. I can try to shut him out all I want: he's already in.

March remains silent for a while, staring down at our joined hands before his thumb moves to stroke the pale scar on the underside of my wrist.

"It was badly broken," I say, to break that unbearable silence. "They had to put in a plate."

He nods. "Do you remember what happened?"

"No . . . it was during the fall of the dome, right?"

"No. We went after the Crystal Whisperer in Croatia, but Anies sent Mr. Morgan to kidnap you."

I feel the blood drain from my face in a prickling sensation. *Him* . . . I think of the gianduiotti he offered me, and I'm going to be sick again. I actually *ate* them. "What happened?"

"You managed to escape him, but you broke your wrist when you ran away. You had a cast by the time we arrived at the dome, but"—he pauses and swallows hard—"your arm took several hits while we tried to escape the dome. I knew it was bad, but I didn't"—he draws a trembling breath, and when he looks at me, I see the way the blue in his irises shines. He's better than I am at holding back tears. His voice breaks though, and I can barely hear him as he says—"Island . . . I couldn't protect you and I'm . . . so sorry."

It's not fair. It's his eyes glistening; it shouldn't be me crying. The room and March's face turn to blurry sequins as hot tears rolls down my cheeks. I can't do this . . . I snatch my hand back and get up from the bed. "I'm sorry. I just . . . I need time to figure this out."

His voice is low, laced with tenderness and regret as he replies, "I know. Let's get some sleep. We both need it."

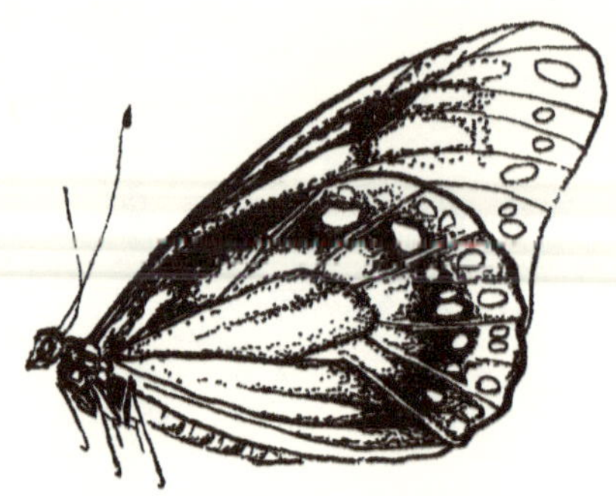

TWENTY-TWO
HOME

I can't sleep.

I kept the sweatshirt on, but the linen feels scratchy against my bare legs. I fidget and toss around in my bed, replaying the evening's events in my head. I suspect I've absorbed too much intel at once; my long-neglected neurons are working overtime . . . thinking of March sleeping in the bed next to mine. So close and so far.

It should make me happy. No, actually it should rock my world that I have this, someone who knows me intimately, who loves me enough to stick with me and persist against the odds of man and nature. Instead I feel lost, inadequate. I've forgotten almost everything about him. He's been looking for me for all this time, he fought off killer dolphins at the Poseidon Dome for me, and here I am before him, an empty shell with nothing to give back.

I'm not even sure how I feel about him; all I know is that pull when I'm around him, equal parts fear and need. It's like my heart is continuously breaking in slow motion, piece by piece. I fold and unfold my legs for the umpteenth time. How can he sleep so easily? I roll around and watch him in the dark. He sleeps on his side, bare chested, his back turned to me.

The street lamps outside cast a faint yellowish light that filters through worn net curtains. It caresses his skin, gilds an intriguing geography of muscles, veins . . . scars. Once my gaze settles on it, the disk of tortured flesh on his back is all I can see. It's about the size of a Frisbee, stretching from his left shoulder to the valley of his spine. I can't make out the details clearly from my vantage point. *But you've seen it. Touched it. You know* . . . The memory is at arm's reach, tantalizingly close to the surface. I need to get closer.

I slip out of the covers with excruciating care and venture a toe on the carpet. Then another. I hold my breath as I creep to his bed. I can't shake a sense of déjà vu about all this, me standing next to a bed he's sleeping in. After a moment of hesitation, I sit on the very edge of the mattress, like a sparrow ready to take off at the slightest threat. An odd combination of guilt and excitement sizzles through me as my fingertips graze the covers. He doesn't react. He should: any self-respecting killer would have been awake, gun in hand by now.

"Biscuit . . ."

The quiet echo of his voice makes me jump out of my skin. I nearly fly away to the other end of the room before I steel my resolve. I need to do this. I ball my fists and sit back. His leg touches mine through the covers, heat seeping between us.

"Do you want me to make some room for you?"

"I don't know," I whisper.

Even as I say so, my hand has moved of its own volition to touch him. The heat of his skin draws me. He lies perfectly still, allowing the journey of my palm up his arm, around his shoulder, until under my fingers, the flesh becomes a rough canvas of raised scars forming a lion head. My own skin prickles, aches for him as I explore the sadistically detailed pattern: triangular ridges for the fangs, a sinewy trail sliced through the skin that looks like a river, a multitude of symmetrical dents to represent a field, perhaps.

One word booms in my mind, taking a whole new meaning. *Broer.* I see Anies's hand on Stiles's shoulder, calling him his brother. At the time, I thought nothing of it. It was nothing but a way to reward a goon's loyalty, to tell him he was kind of part of the family too. But now that I see March's back, I think of the blood, of the hours spent in agony as someone carved that same loyalty into his flesh . . . I take the full measure of what it means to be one of Anies's "brothers."

"Why did you let them do that to you?"

March sits up, his arms reaching for me, and I'm on my feet and away from the bed just as fast. I hear the husky plea in his voice as his hand extends to beckon me back. "Island, please . . ."

I know that this whole situation is just as messed up for him as it is for me, but I can't help it: I'm still afraid . . . of him? I'm not even sure of that. My heart is beating fast, so maybe a little. I wish I were stronger, but my world had been so tiny, so slow, so foggy for all this time, and now the rush of the past few days terrifies me. It's a continuous free fall toward a glint of light down below, at the end of this rabbit hole. And yet, I need to overcome that fear and find my way back to him, because deep down, something tells me he's the safest rope to hold on to.

So, with cautious steps, I return to March's bed and sit by his side. I can feel his gaze on me, ever attentive, but I don't look at him yet. I need a little time to ease back into this strange intimacy. He makes no attempt to touch me, and I'm grateful for that.

Next to me, I feel him shift. "I didn't mean to scare you . . ."

"I know . . . I guess I'm a little on edge."

His reply comes with a sigh. "That makes two of us, I suppose."

In a way, I find it reassuring that we're on the same page. Are relationships like riding a bike, something you can't really forget, that comes back naturally if you give it a try? I scoot closer, until my shoulder is touching his arm. I reach for his hand, and his fingers close around mine, his thumb stroking my palm softly.

I peek up at the curve of his lips I can make out in the dark. What's the worst that could happen? Is my life going to get any weirder anyway? I free my hand to trace his jaw gingerly. I feel him startle and then relax as I trail down, drawing a path along his neck, his clavicles. His chest. My fingers splay across what can only be described as follicular nirvana. The hair is just like I dreamed it . . . soft, curly, fuzzy, dusting his pectorals and trailing all the way down a six-pack I want to believe can cure amnesia.

One of March's hands settles on the small of my back, and his breathing quickens as my palm glides down his stomach. His skin feels hot; it ripples under my fingertips when his muscles contract. I'm not naïve; I know what my touch is doing to him, but I'm not ready to venture that far down yet. I'm thinking that maybe I should stop when I feel a deep dent a few inches away from his navel. There, a patch of the divine fleece appears to be missing, and the skin feels a little different.

His head dips until his chin is brushing my cheek, the caress made rough by a little stubble. "I was very lucky. The second one did more damage."

The second one . . . My body tenses; a nameless fear spills in my stomach. "Where?"

March takes my hand and slowly guides it across his chest, right under his heart. The scar here feels shallower, but tracing it, I feel a jagged line running along his ribs.

He nuzzles my hair. "Dries dragged me out of the dome just in time, but he had been shot too, by Mr. Morgan. We were both in very bad shape when the Queen's men found us . . . On the bright side, I am now the proud owner of a 3-D-printed rib."

I wish I could smile, but around me the room is spinning. Mile-high glass walls are crackling, threatening to collapse on me. My dress is red, and March's blood is everywhere. A paralyzing terror freezes my limbs like ice. I can't move; I can't escape. We're being swallowed by water, and I hear Mozart again. I recognize the Queen of the Night's aria. Stiles. Stiles's suit. His sniper rifle. I try to hold on to March, terrified to lose him, but I can't save him and he's fading away in the darkness . . . Yet I feel his arms around me, strong, warm, alive, hauling me back to reality. In the safe cradle of his embrace, I break down and howl. "He shot you . . . He shot you!"

I barely register March's strangled gasp against my cheek. "You remember."

I'm swallowed by a tide of emotions I can't handle, and I let go. I taste salt at the corner of my mouth, and I have to squeeze my eyes shut because tears are blinding me. I bury my face in the crook of his neck, breathe a little soap and the deeper, unique musk of him. I know that scent. I love it. My fingertips claw at silky curls on his chest. I know this too, it's comforting and warm, and it's mine. March holds me tighter, rocking my tears away.

I think I've found my way home.

•••

It took me a little while to calm down. The room has become quiet again, our breathing the only ripples marring the silence. Under the covers, March and I made a little cocoon for ourselves, safe from the outside world, where we lie together. I'm safe, drained, and, after all that crying, strangely happy. His lips linger on my forehead, graze my temple. His hand rests on my hip; our legs are intertwined. He's all around me. I know it's corny, but the way our bodies are molded together, I'm thinking of the yin and yang symbol. A contented sigh fans against my cheek as he falls asleep.

He didn't ask whether I'm ready to return to Viktor's casino. We both know I am. I want my memories back. All of them.

TWENTY-THREE
ALESIA

Last night changed everything.

Here in this hotel room, huddled under the covers, listening to the water running in the bathroom . . . it's the safest I've felt in months. I peek out at the closed door. I'd be lying if I said I'm not thinking a little about what he looks like under that shower—not bad, if the muscles and magnificent rug of chest hair I caressed can be filed as topographical evidence. If we've never been all the way, have I ever seen him entirely naked? I did get a good look at his upper half last night, but we were in the dark, and, well, it was a different kind of intimacy, an aftermath. We were both exhausted, and neither of us were truly in the mood to explore beyond the comfortable boundaries of this newly reawakened tenderness between us.

I bite my lower lip, fighting a secret grin against my pillow. I have a boyfriend, and this morning, in the bleak light of dawn, my world feels different. Broader, brighter. There's an *us*; it's no longer just me groping my way in the dark. March walks at my side, carries my memories, a part of me. A treasure box he kept for me until I returned. I want to make the most of the life he promised to give back to me. I want to tell my father and Joy I'm alive; I want to see my old apartment, walk in New York streets, and rediscover all the people, the places I've forgotten.

But that can't happen yet. Now that I'm fully awake, the weight of reality slowly settles on my shoulders again. March was right: if I go home now, all I'll accomplish will be leading either the Lions or Erwin right to my family's doorstep. Like a seed taking root in my heart, I feel the need to protect them grow stronger. I can't go to them yet, but I'll find my way back to them.

For now . . . my stomach is growling. There's a bottle of water and a bowl of complimentary vanilla wafers sitting on a small wooden desk by the window. Still floating in my now thoroughly wrinkled Rompetrol sweatshirt, I sit up in bed and rub my hands. Breakfast is served.

I turn the TV on and plop myself back on the bed. Careful to eat above the bowl because I know March is going to freak out if he sees crumbs in his sheets, I flip through the channels, looking for any kind of English-speaking news. I've been deprived of actual reliable information for far too long to settle for teleshopping . . . I grunt in appreciation when I stumble on CNN between a soap opera and an ad for pizza-flavored chips.

I munch on my wafers and watch with interest as the anchors discuss President Steed's recent decision to appoint Steed International Broadcasting's CFO as Secretary of Commerce—it doesn't help that the guy is Steed's cousin . . .

Meanwhile, March seems to be done with his shower. The door opens to reveal a freshly shaven Prince Charming. I swear this man was born with a no-wrinkles setting. He dusts something on his sleeve—I don't even know what; there's *nothing* there. His gaze immediately sets on the bowl in my hands, like a laser pointer. I hastily place it on the nightstand, flushing with irrational guilt. "I don't think there're any crumbs . . ."

He clears his throat. "I didn't see any."

So he *was* checking . . . March walks to the bed and sits by my side while, in the background, the anchors keep droning about unemployment rates for December. I'm no longer really paying attention because March's knuckles are slowly trailing down my cheek.

"How do you feel today?"

I lean into his touch. "Okay . . . No, pretty good actually."

His hand skims up and down my arm. His lips graze my hair, my ear shell, trace my jaw, silently asking for permission. I inhale his scent, his aftershave, and something citrusy, soap maybe. His hesitation, mine . . . it's so much like a first kiss. Feeling bold, I rest a hand on his shoulder and seek his mouth. I feel his smile when my lips brush his. I cup his cheeks in my palms, the skin there almost smooth from a close shave. With a trembling intake of air, I take the lead, capturing his lower lip and tasting the sweet, minty flavor of toothpaste.

It's easier than I imagined it'd be—instinctual, really. I'm not even scared when he kisses me back in earnest, and the kiss gets a little wet, a little desperate. In fact, I never want to stop. March is slowly bringing us down into the pillows. I touch the tip of my tongue to his, and make a silent prayer that this moment will last.

He's eventually the one who pulls away to stroke my cheeks with his thumbs. "I missed this so much . . ."

"Me too," I whimper, and it's true. I just didn't consciously know it.

His mouth finds a wonderful spot on my neck, right under my ear, one that's apparently deserving of a thorough hickey. His voice is deep and breathless against my skin. "I missed you so much . . . every day . . ."

I'm not entirely sure where this is going, and I vaguely remember I was supposed to get ready, but one of his palms is reaching up my thigh, working its way to my hip. I'm in for the ride. I wrap my legs around him, and my eyes roll back in delight.

Odysseus.

The word registers in my brain like a blade slicing through our little bubble of lust. I jerk against March and scramble to a sitting position on the bed.

For him too, the bubble has burst, and the usual lines of worry have reappeared, weighing on his features. "What's going on?"

"I-I need to listen to this," I stammer, grabbing the remote to raise the TV's volume.

...A difficult hearing tomorrow for newly appointed NASA Administrator James Zwicky. All eyes will be turned to the House of Representatives as the committee on Science, Space and Astrology asks: Where is *Odysseus?*

It's been 197 days since *Odysseus*'s disastrous launch attempt that claimed the lives of nine American astronauts. "The costliest calculation error of aeronautics history," to quote Vice President McLean, is still purported to rest some 18,000 feet underwater at the bottom of the Litke Deep, an oceanic trench located to the northeast of Greenland.

The red planet was at hand's reach, but *Odysseus*, a pharaonic seventeen-year-long project reported to have cost nearly a trillion dollars to the United States, will not be. The first of its kind, the spaceship was designed to dock a 130-feet-wide habitable artificial-gravity ring currently orbiting Earth and carry it all the way to Mars in four months to establish the first permanent settlement on the red planet.

But the dream has turned into a nightmare, as experts have been working nonstop over the past six months to recover the ship and its third-generation nuclear ion reactor. Today, after Greenpeace announced a plan to deploy two small submarines to look for signs of potential radioactive contamination in the area, NASA issued a statement to reaffirm that the main reactor was never started, as the ship crashed before reaching orbit, during the disassembly of its Falcon 13 rockets.

I stare blankly at the TV, as the off-screen voice comments on images of the wheel-shaped living quarters that awaited *Odysseus*'s crew in stationary orbit. Portraits flash one after another, listing the lives lost during the failed launch. Hillstone, Chopra, Beauchamp, Jamal . . .

I rub the heel of my palm against my forehead, trying to remember what's so important about this. "Anies . . . he mentioned something about *Odysseus*." I search my memory and see Stiles again, giving him the absinthe. "He toasted us. He raised his glass to *Odysseus*'s journey!"

March's brow creases in doubt. "He could have been referring to something else. Are you certain he meant that ship?"

"I don't know . . . Maybe Erwin would. Do you think we could try to sort of . . . trade intel with him? Or just drop the hint and see if he reacts?"

"Island, I'd rather work on severing all ties with him at the moment." He gets up from the bed and walks to the window. "Starting with the two agents who spent the night outside."

I watch in curiosity as he parts the threadbare beige curtains just an inch, enough to glance down the street. He doesn't close them though. He scans the place, his eyes progressively narrowing.

"What is it? Is there something wrong?"

"I'm not certain, but we need to leave."

I jump from the bed and slip on my yoga pants, an unpleasant prickling rushing down my spine. "Right now?"

He doesn't answer. Instead, I see the magic suitcase in his hands. One, two silenced guns get secured in a double holster around his torso while I put on my boots. He grabs a couple of magazines that go into an extra pouch on the side. A handful of mints from the precious tube that never leaves him before he takes his dark-plaid blazer . . . and throws it at me. "Wear it."

"Why?"

"Island, we don't have time."

I'm about to demand an explanation when the bedroom's phone rings, a shrill, old-fashioned metallic sound. March shakes his head silently, but the phone won't stop ringing, each attempt whipping my heart rate up a little faster. I shrug on the blazer, registering its unusual weight on my shoulders and the stiff material underneath the lining—bulletproof?

March slams his magic suitcase shut and presses his thumb to a tiny fingerprint scan on the side. A small digital screen lights up, glowing blue against the case's sleek black material. He types in some sort of code and holds out his hand for me. "Bathroom window," he hisses.

He can't be serious. "We're on the second floor!" I protest, a rush of cold air hitting my face as he opens the window.

"There's a garage below."

It's the only explanation I get before he grabs me by the waist and hauls me up onto the toilet lid and then through the window. Oh God . . . there *is* a row of snowy tin roofs right under the window, but they look so far, miles below . . . I scan the cracked concrete buildings surrounding us and grip the wooden frame, willing myself to take the leap. In the bedroom, the ringing has stopped.

"Island, jump!"

Does it count as domestic abuse if your boyfriend pushes you through a window? I'm not given any time to ponder this as March shoves me, and I land ass-first on the roof. The powdery snow cushions my fall somewhat, but a crack of pain announces a bruise. March follows right afterward, his weight making the structure shake dangerously.

I'm a heartbeat away from cardiac arrest, and I still have no idea what's going on, or who we're fleeing from, until I see a black Hummer parked down the street that looks nothing like the tired Dacias scattered on the nearby parking lot. Definitely not from the neighborhood. Like the four men who just jumped out and are now running toward us. They're wearing ordinary civilian clothes, but the guns in their hands tell another story . . .

"You said Erwin's men were watching us—" I yelp as March helps me roll down the roof and onto the ground. Barely protected by the yoga pants, my knees protest at all that scraping and bumping in icy weather.

"They're dead."

Cold fear prickles down my spine. That can mean only one thing: Anies's "brothers" have found us.

We take cover between two garages when the first shots tear through the air, some slamming into the sturdy brick walls shielding us. Reddish brick chips explode mere feet above my head, and I shield it reflexively, huddled against March. He takes my hand and pulls me, forcing my legs into action. Gunshots crack above us, coming from the bathroom's window, as we race along the line of brick and concrete sheds toward the safe haven of a garage that seems to be missing one of its doors.

We're almost there when I register that above us, the shooting has stopped. There's a beat of unnerving silence before a deafening boom rips through me, shattering glass and stone. I turn my head to see the gaping hole that was once our bathroom window vomiting clouds of black smoke. The magic suitcase—it was still on the bed—I'm figuring whoever touched it shouldn't have . . .

While, behind us, the Lions are probably looking for their bearings after the explosion, we tumble inside the open garage. There, a dismembered car and rusty tools are slowly fading under layers of grime and dust. March drags me toward a corner and drops me unceremoniously behind a stack of old tires. "Stay here."

I wish I were strong enough to hold him back, but I can barely control my own fear as he moves a few feet away to take cover behind the car's brownish carcass, with a perfect vantage point to the street outside. Several rounds of shots clank into the garage's remaining wooden door, and I press my hands over my ears to block the painful buzzing in my eardrums. I can hear footsteps crushing gravel outside, distant screams—panicked neighbors, no doubt. Near the doorway, a shadow briefly grazes the ground before vanishing just as fast. They're circling the garage.

Guided by faint scraping sounds coming from the other side, March aims one of his guns at the worm-eaten door. Slowly. Calmly. I watch in morbid fascination as his arm follows the imperceptible movements of an invisible target outside the shed. His face is perfectly blank; there's no life in the blue eyes I know, only cold calculation. A little chunk of me shatters at the thought that maybe the man I spent the night with isn't here anymore . . . I clench my fists to stop the tremors shaking my body.

Under the black wool of his turtleneck, the muscles in his arm bunch, ready to absorb the recoil. He's perfectly still as he presses the trigger, and on the other side of the door, a man collapses with a groan of surprise. The second after, March has rolled away from his hiding spot and the barrage of bullets that shreds the door. Curled behind the tires, I clasp my hands over my mouth in a desperate effort not to scream.

March retreats into a darkened corner of the garage. With the door now destroyed, he takes another shot, and I glimpse a blond guy falling to the ground in the street. *Stiles?* No . . . it's not him. The remaining men momentarily retreat, right before one of them throws something our way that clanks onto the concrete floor and rolls under the car. I immediately picture a grenade, and panic explodes in my chest. But instead I register a low hissing sound, and a thick, acrid smoke starts filling the shed.

March roars, "Island, cover your face!"

I lift my sweatshirt's neck to protect my nose and mouth . . . a second too late. The first inhalation makes me choke and cough through the fabric. My eyes are stinging so badly tears blur my vision; the men storming the garage are little more than terrifying shadows. Over the blood pounding in my ears, the hoarse shouts, and the gunshots, I manage to focus on a single goal: hinder their progression. One after another, I kick at the tires stacked in front of me and send them rolling toward the blurry shapes barreling inside the shed. A few feet away from me, a chilling scream echoes through the smoke, and a splash of blood arcs into the air, landing with a splatter on the car's rust-covered side. I grit my teeth, panting fast. *Please . . . not March. Please!*

I crawl toward a pearly gray smudge that could be the sky outside, the heavy bulletproof blazer hindering my progress. In the midst of the confusion, I recognize the sound of March's suppressed gun right before a body crashes to the ground inches from my right hand. Lifeless eyes see past me, and the blood runs and runs, dark, from a wound on the man's forehead. I look away and drag myself toward the light, hoping I'll be able to breathe, see something at last, and maybe March already got out, and we can escape . . .

I hold on to that tiny sliver of hope, and when gravel scrapes my palms, I barely feel it. All I know is I made it out. I try to scramble up and find my bearings, but the moment I start to rise on shaky legs, pain explodes in my ribs. I roll onto my back, blinking up at the ghost who kicked me back to the ground. It's when he bends down to grab my hair that I see the eye patch, and an inhuman scream rips through my throat. Pirate Morgan hauls me to my knees while I desperately claw at his gloved hand to ease the agony blazing across my scalp. I struggle for oxygen, certain that he's going to tear my hair off if he tugs any harder. Around us, more men have gathered. There's no escape.

"Party's over, Mr. November!" Morgan yells cheerfully. I see a blade snap open in his left hand; I go perfectly still, frozen at his feet. "Please get the fuck out, or I'll be delivering daddy a one-eyed bitch."

Seconds tick, one after another. In the garage, the chaos turns into quiet rustling. March tears through the smoke and walks toward us, unarmed and flanked by two men. He's a mess, covered in dust and blood that I'm not sure is his—but he looks okay, and it's all I care about.

"On your knees," Morgan orders.

March's eyes are set on him. He still wears that odd, impassible mask, like his features are paralyzed, but his gaze . . . it's deadly, focused. If they give him the slightest opening, I know those rings of dark blue ice are the last thing Pirate Morgan will ever see. Yet he obeys. He looks at me and drops one knee to the ground. My heart breaks into a thousand razor-sharp shards.

"He wants you both . . . unharmed," Morgan admits with a huff of disappointment.

"Then you might want to let go of her," March warns, hate

cracking through the thin veneer of civility in his voice.

A snarl bares Morgan's teeth. "Believe me . . . the only thing keeping me from gutting you both right now is that I know he'll hurt you more than I can."

In his hand, the incurved knife remains, but his grasp on my hair eases a little. I let out a trembling exhale and I block everyone else to focus on March. I feel our bond, beating inside me like a second heart. I hold on to it. We're alive; nothing else matters right now.

The sound of an engine snaps me out of the moment. Behind us, a long black Citroën sedan has stopped. The rear door opens, and the first thing I see is a gray suit. My stomach knots as I recognize Stiles's eternal black tie before he's even stepped out. Butterfly stitches cover the wound March inflicted to his forehead yesterday, yet his gaze is as compassionate as ever as he walks to us. Maybe there really is no anger in him after all, nor any kind of moral compass . . .

Morgan acknowledges his presence with a disdainful glance. "I told you it wouldn't be hard. Honestly, I have no idea how you managed to fuck up twice in a row."

Stiles all but ignores the jab and flashes March a cordial smile. "I'm glad to see you again, Mr. November, but you never do anything quietly, do you?"

Indeed. Glancing up, I notice terrified faces observing us through the surrounding buildings' windows, most half-hidden behind their curtains. And that concert of howls growing louder in the distance: someone called the cops, and probably the fire station too . . .

March's eyes narrow as he replies in an emotionless voice, "Dries was very surprised to see you alive at the Poseidon. He almost didn't recognize you, in fact."

With a chuckle, Stiles bends to free me from Morgan's grasp, who lets go with a hateful glare—one that's child's play compared to the expression on March's face when Stiles's gloved hands touch me. The muscles in his neck and jaw bulge, as if he is ready to pounce.

Stiles strokes his chin. "It's been over fifteen years, and some days even I still don't recognize myself," he muses, his tone deceptively soft, even as he adds, "but I've gotten used to my new face. It ain't so bad, considering I didn't even expect to survive after he was done with me."

As he says this, I stare at him, trying to find evidence of some sort of surgery in his drab, regular features. He could be anyone; I can't find the other man underneath, the one Dries left for dead . . . I avert my eyes as he helps me up. It's already taking all I have to stand straight and not tremble. He tips his head to the sedan. "We're gonna have to leave. Island will be riding with me."

With this final push, March detonates. His elbow flies into the face of the man standing to his right with a nauseating crack. The man's body is taken by spasms, and he collapses, his nose cleanly shoved all the way up into his brain. Past the millisecond of shock, a second goon pulls out his gun, but with a swift movement March breaks his arm and takes the weapon while the guy staggers back with a groan of pain. March leaps forward, almost fast enough to reach me. But not fast enough to dodge Morgan, who jumps in the way and . . . aims his gun at me.

March freezes, his finger on the trigger.

Stiles makes no attempt to help me this time, watching coolly as Morgan presses the barrel against my temple. "I've been told I got some serious anger-management issues," he hisses. "And you're wasting my fucking time."

March's hand is shaking as he lowers the gun. He's fighting himself. I wish I could tell him he didn't fail me, that it's going to be okay, but Stiles steps in at last. He places his hand on Morgan's gun, casually pushing it away. "Enough . . . Mr. November knows we can trust each other."

With this, his arm wraps around my shoulders, and I register a flash of despair in March's eyes when Stiles opens the door for me to climb into the sedan. I look at March; I try to keep our bond alive as long as possible, even after the door slams shut and I'm alone with Stiles in the back seat. The engine starts, and I still look, until Morgan kicks him hard, over and over, and they drag him away to the Hummer. I feel hot tears rolling down my cheeks, and my mouth falls open, but no sound comes out, only air whizzing from my throat in a silent sob.

There's no sign on Stiles's features that he understands the depth of my distress, but the compassionate smile never wavers as he hands me a tissue. "There, don't cry. You're gonna be fine."

TWENTY-FOUR
THE BLUE DANUBE

My tears have dried, and I've retreated as far as possible from Stiles in the back seat, but there's nowhere to escape. With a sigh, he presses a button in the arm of his door, and a tinted privacy screen slides up. Now it's just the two us. I shudder.

His tongue clicks, the sound unnervingly loud in the silence. "Island, when did you stop taking your treatment?"

I press my forehead against the window. We're driving away from Feteşti-Gară and toward the Danube, across a white countryside that blends with the ashen sky like watercolor. I wrench my hands on my lap. "What are you going to do to March?"

"Me? Nothing. But I'm afraid Anies is going to make an example of Mr. November."

My gaze settles on the mirror outside, where I can see the Hummer following us. My stomach heaves at the idea that March is in there with that sick piece of shit Morgan . . . "Why do you keep calling him that? Is that his real name?"

"No. Just a nickname." He leans back in the seat, crossing his arms. "Island, you didn't answer me. When did you stop taking your meds?"

"About a week ago," I admit.

"Thought so. Why? What happened that made you decide that?"

My head snaps up, sudden anger flaring in my veins, as if he'd branded me. "Do you even need to ask? I *trusted* you, and you drugged me . . . *Every. Fucking. Day!* You stole my life. You took *everything!*"

"I obeyed Anies's orders."

I ball my fists, trembling with a mixture of pain and rage. "So you and I could build the future together?"

He tilts his head, studying me with curiosity. "Do you want to? I thought you'd chosen Mr. November for that . . ."

"You people are all insane . . . How could you ever think—"

"Spare me that." His lips curl up, and the mask falls—gone is the sympathetic smile, replaced by a smirk that suits him much better. "We both know you'd have given in eventually if Dries and Mr. November hadn't come back from the dead." His expression softens again as he summons the old Stiles back. "I was growing on you, wasn't I?"

"No! I never thought of you like that, and when Anies started hinting that's what he expected . . . all I wanted was to get away from you."

"You're breaking my heart." He chuckles. "But do you understand what Anies really needs? He wasn't playing matchmaker for fun, you know."

"I started thinking about it after I learned Dries was my father. Anies . . . he's old and ill, and he doesn't have children, but he wants to leave some sort of . . . dynasty. And Dries's genes were good enough for that, right?"

Stiles ducks his head in confirmation. "Correct. He's hoping to start a hereditary tradition."

"A bloodline," I murmur.

"He thinks it's the only way to avoid another succession war."

I'm mentally picturing the greenish, milky absinthe sloshing in a heavy crystal glass. The peace on Anies's features every time it took over his mind and body. My eyes widen in realization. "He's dying."

Stiles shrugs. "Aren't we all? But yes, he's running out of time, and there are things he wants to achieve before he's gone."

"*Odysseus?*"

One of his eyebrows cocks in surprise. "There's that. And there's you. Believe it or not, I think you actually matter more than *Odysseus* to him."

I gave you everything I couldn't give your mother, Island . . .

Anies's words take their full meaning as they ring again in my ears. I am my mother's ghost, and she's alive in my heart, my blood, even though I've lost my memories of her. I wonder if he ever saw me at all, or if it's been her all along in his sick mind. "Was it what he wanted to do with my mother? Did he want to cage her like that? Is that why"—my voice falters and I have to force the words out—"is that why he killed her?"

Stiles gazes through the window at the faint outline of a truss bridge over the Danube, emerging from the mist ahead of us. "I've been at his side for a long time, but there are things even I don't know. I think he never got over your mother's rejection though."

"She rejected him . . . and he murdered her," I manage through gritted teeth, feeling a surge of hate electrify my body.

Stiles shakes his head with a sigh. "These things are always complicated . . . Here, I brought something for you." He produces a small plastic bag from his pocket, which he hands me. "You forgot it in Constanta. I thought you might want it back."

My heart skips a beat. Covered in dried blood is the butterfly in amber Anies gave me. I left it in Viktor's office, when I changed for the scan . . . I breathe fast through my nose, clutching the red-stained plastic. "W-what happened to Viktor?"

He winces. "Let's just say he won't be able to operate on you. I'm really sorry about that, Island."

I slip the packet into the breast pocket of March's blazer with a trembling hand and sit still, straight. Viktor, who tried to help us, is dead.

Next to me, Stiles checks his watch, his gaze still locked on the steel beams supporting the bridge we're now crossing. "Island, fasten your seat belt."

I look at him in confusion. He's stopped smiling, his eyes focused and unblinking.

The muscles tighten in his jaw, rippling under his skin. "It's an order."

There's a coldness and an authority in his voice I don't think I've heard before. My hands jerk and automatically reach for my seat belt. I manage to secure it in spite of a case of terminal jitters. I see Stiles reach inside his coat—for a gun?—and it takes me another whole second to notice the shadow growing in the distance, speeding on the Danube and tearing through the layers of viscous fog.

Under the sedan's wheels, a low rumble shakes the bridge. All I can do is watch, petrified, as a dark shape storms toward us in a massive cloud of water. Less than a hundred yards from the bridge is something I can neither clearly see nor identify. That long, aerodynamic body could be a jumbo jet, except I don't think I've ever seen six . . . no . . . *eight* engines sitting atop the head of any aircraft. The wings are way too short for that thing to possibly take off, like they got chopped in half . . . and the dual tail? It must be, what . . . a hundred feet wide? What the ever-loving deuce?

Unfazed, Stiles is removing his coat. He shakes his head. "Your father was never subtle."

Dries? But . . . how? All I can process at the moment is that this giant jet-like thing that doesn't fly isn't going to stop, and it's headed straight for us: now would be a good time to start panicking. Panting erratically, I grip my seat belt and the door handle as the sedan takes a powerful acceleration, likely to avoid impact. But the unidentified gliding object doesn't hit the bridge; rather, it barrels underneath in a deafening roar. For a moment, the car is shaking so badly I'm sure the entire structure must be collapsing. Yet the road is still here, and we drift through a titanic downpour, like a giant, surreal car wash. Waves crash against the car's windows, engulfing the road, as the monster slows down under the bridge. I can practically feel my skull buzzing from the continuous roar of its engines.

When the sedan spins to a stop, Stiles grips my shoulder, steadying me before I smash my head against the window. He too has fastened his seat belt. A dry laugh shakes his shoulders. "Hold on. I'm afraid we're only getting started."

Which is exactly why I'm craning my neck and straining desperately against my seat belt to see the Hummer that took March. A black blur drifts past us, hits the railing and topples dangerously before coming to a stop. "March! He's in there, I have to—"

Stiles flattens his hand over my chest roughly, blocking my movements. "Don't worry about Mr. November . . . his fairy godmother watches over him."

What the hell does he mean by that? Before I can ask, I register two loud shots, like a cannon just got fired. Through Stiles's window, I see several projectiles rise in the air with a hissing sound, connected to some sort of metal rope. They bite into the side of our car and the stranded Hummer's with a clanking sound. Grappling hooks? *Oh shit* . . . Around us, the bridge's massive steel beams rattle as the mystery machine's engines pick up, soon enveloping us again in a storm of vaporized water. I pick up the ominous moan of metal straining under pressure, and that's when I feel like we're . . . moving. Slowly, inexorably, we're getting dragged toward the railing by a powerful pull.

This isn't really happening.

Against my better judgment, I grip Stiles's forearm, clutch it until my nails dig into his skin through his jacket. "Oh my God, oh my God, oh my God! What are they doing?"

Already resting precariously against the rusty and damaged railing, the Hummer topples first: I scream March's name, witnessing, powerless as the vehicle takes a fifty-foot plunge into the icy waters of the Danube.

"Calm down!" Stiles shouts—the last thing I hear before the sedan hits the railing hard. There are a couple of excruciating seconds during which the car teeters and tilts, tilts, until I see the steel beams above us, then the clouds, and with a rush of horror, I know it's over; I feel the railing give way with an earsplitting creak, and we go down. I'm weightless, conscious of the fall until we hit the water, and it's like my body shatters, pain erupting from all sides. My shoulder and knee hit the door hard while my head slams against the headrest.

Through my daze, I see greenish water splash on the windows while the car rocks and tilts downward, sinking in the river, it seems. Through my panicked daze, I'm vaguely conscious of Stiles undoing my seat belt, of his voice. "You're gonna be fine . . ."

No I'm not! He's a shadow at the edge of my vision, and I reach for him as he seems to drift away . . . before I become aware of water rushing in. Nothing could have prepared me for the shock of being immersed in this icy tomb. Air whizzes out of my lungs, I gasp for oxygen, and by the time the ring of ice clamps down around my neck, I'm disconnected from my body, disoriented. My legs jerk uselessly, perhaps in an attempt to swim, but I can't.

With a final desperate gulp of air, I go under. In the murky water, I glimpse shadows undulating away from the car—swimming. My brain wants to, urges me to paddle, move, do anything, but I'm struggling in icy treacle, my muscles petrified by the cold. Even reaching the door handle seems impossible. I strive toward it uselessly, but I'm not the one to open it. Hands clasp around my shoulders, someone snakes an arm around my torso, and I'm being hauled out of the car.

I recognize March's black turtleneck right before asphyxia kicks in. I hold on to him and fight the urge to breathe, as hard as I can, until my lungs betray me, and I inhale pure ice. Spasms shake my body as I start drowning, but all of a sudden, the cold becomes a prickle on my face, an icy wind biting my skin. My head is out of the water, and I cough until I'm on the verge of throwing up. March is little more than a shivering blur, but I feel his chin against my cheek, and I can't believe I'm still alive.

Splashing sounds alert me to the presence of several men around us. Most are swimming away, crawling toward the shore. Amid the chaos, I glimpse an eye patch, and Morgan's face, distorted with rage. Renewed chills threaten to make me suffocate when I hear March's pant in my ear. "Hold on tight."

Am I not? I'm not sure; my arms are so numb. I'm trying to squeeze him, but maybe I'm slipping away. I don't get what's happening until I see his fist, closed around a grappling hook similar to the ones that dragged us into the river in the first place. Suddenly, we're gliding so fast I'm sure it's not March swimming like that. I mean, he's amazing, but he's not a dolphin. Or a speedboat. My eyes flutter shut, choosing to close the curtain on reality and replace it with bright, colorful spots and dolphins, dolphins everywhere.

I think I've passed out.

•••

"For God's sake, does he need to be under the blanket too? He looked fine! A little swim never killed anyone." That hushed growl . . . it's Dries, bitching to someone from behind a door.

I'm warm. Almost too much, in fact: there's a burning ache in my extremities. My head hurts too; a lingering headache throbs under my temples. As I come to my senses, a single thought boomerangs in my skull. *March* . . . is he okay? My rising pulse eases at the feeling of hot skin against mine and the best chest hair in the entire universe tickling my shoulder blades. His breath fans over my cheek; we're spooning on a narrow mattress under something weightless and shiny that hurts my eyeballs and my brain when I crack an eye open. I immediately screw it shut. No light for now. I stir painfully while March nuzzles my hair and readjusts the thermal blanket over us. "Take it slow, biscuit . . . You're safe."

I roll to face him with a wince. Braving the wretched glare, I make another attempt at opening my eyes to examine his face. I stroke his cheeks, the soft bristles on his temples. There're bruises on his forehead, at the corner of his mouth, a shiner under his left eye . . . all eclipsed by that warm, boyish smile I realize I've come to need like oxygen. I feel his dimples crease under my fingertips, and I can't help but grin too. "Let's agree to bring floaties next time," I rasp.

His smile falters. "Island, I'm sorry I—"

I know what's coming next; I press my lips to his to silence his apology, tasting him. If I never learn anything else in my life, at least I can say I understand the meaning of *carpe diem* better than most people ever will. And true to that motto, I intend to make the most of each passing second, savor them while I can . . .

I let March pull me closer, noticing for the first time that we're almost naked, our underwear the last shred of propriety standing between us. I do experience a fleeting moment of embarrassment, but it's little more than an ingrained reflex. In truth, nothing has ever felt so good, so right as his body stretching atop mine. The kiss grows feverish, exploratory, and I don't miss the way his hands stroke my sides, massage me, eager for more . . . but ultimately shy. He gives one last tug to my lower lip. "Biscuit, I really wish we could keep going but—"

"We're not alone," I complete with a sigh, taking in my surroundings for the first time. The continuous hum in the background suggests a plane, and indeed, we're in a small cabin, entirely lined with a dull combo of gray plastic and carpet. *Hold on* . . . Through a pair of round windows on the wall, I glimpse stormy weather muddying the sea horizon. So that thing I saw on the river *was* a boat after all? I sit up, fighting the shivers coursing across my skin when cool air insinuates itself under the thermal blanket. "Dries . . . I heard his voice. He's here? What happened?"

March presses a kiss to my shoulder. "A lot. First let's find you something to wear and a hot drink."

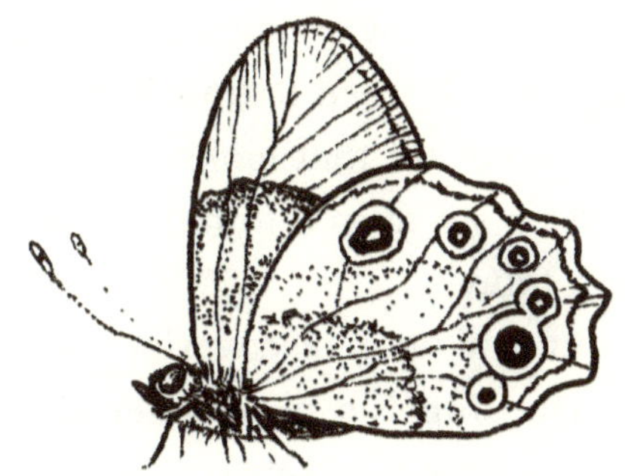

THE SEA MONSTER

I'm getting used to wearing whatever I can scrape together to cover my temptress body. Like those black mechanic pants I found in our cabin's closet—I actually think they're cool—and a green Springboks sweatshirt, courtesy of Dominik. The only other clean T-shirt in his bag read "It won't suck itself" on the front; we both averted our eyes and tried to pretend I hadn't noticed.

Isiporho lent March some clothes, since they're about the same size, so he at least gets to look normal, in dark wool pants, a gray sweater, and a clean white shirt underneath. As soon as he's put on the sweater, he sets to rolling the sleeves up with meticulous gestures. Two perfectly equal folds, measured using the cuff, and thoroughly flattened. Once he's through, he inspects the result with a satisfied huff.

"Feeling better?" I ask.

He nods, but his eyebrows pinch in concern. "I know this isn't ideal . . . I contacted Phyllis; she'll have a suitcase ready for you in Istanbul."

"So that's where we're going?"

"Yes—"

The cabin's door slams open before March has the time to finish his answer. Yup, Dries somehow escaped Erwin's claws, and it seems my biological father never learned to knock. He gauges me, regal in a navy striped three-piece suit that looks like it came straight from dry cleaning. He takes a sip from a fuming coffee mug in his hand. "Come, I'll give you a tour."

We follow him out, and upon discovering the rest of the ship, my confusion deepens. The ship *is* a plane after all. I gather the small bedroom March and I warmed ourselves in is located at the tail, and the long, cathedral-like cabin we just entered looks every bit like the inside of a military plane: no windows in sight, and rather than the smooth plastic covering the walls of commercial aircraft, it's steel, levers, and buttons everywhere, completed by large nets meant to secure cargo. Two rows of seats face each other on the sides, all empty—save for two.

The usual carefree grin lights up Isiporho's face when he sees us, and he rises from his seat. Dominik's hand jerks in the semblance of a greeting, but he doesn't look up from his laptop, his fingers rapping feverishly on the keyboard. I don't think he's that busy: more likely he doesn't want to make eye contact with me after the T-shirt incident.

Isiporho looks up to the plane's ceiling and gestures to the imposing structure with a swipe of his arm. "Not bad, huh?"

"It's amazing," I concede. "But . . . what is this thing?"

Dries's chest swells with pride. "Let me show you."

We follow him to the other end of the cabin, up narrow stairs, and to the cockpit door. On the other side, Jan and Andrea sit respectively in the pilot and copilot seats, cocooned in a jungle of wires, switches, buttons, and dials. It's the stormy sea stretching as far as the eye can see that steals my breath though. I instinctively squeeze March's hand, an astonished grin taking over my face. We're not in the sky. We're racing, gliding above the Black Sea at dizzying speed. Yet, inside the cockpit, there's only this continuous hum, like we're in a quiet bubble, sheltered from the tons of water we lift in our wake.

I know this. I can't remember where I learned it, but the physics principle behind the magic is still here, engraved in my mind. Short wingspan combined with low-altitude flight, close to the ground: reduces drag, increases lift, allowing it to hover over any surface at incredible speed. "It's a ground-effect craft!" I squeak.

"Meet the Caspian Sea Monster!" Dikkenek confirms with a cheerful bellow, echoed by Andrea's excited bark.

Dries seems in an equally good mood. "It's a Soviet ekranoplan prototype they built in the seventies, a Lun class. Those poor idiots dropped the program and let that beauty rot on dry land. I bought it from the Russians in the nineties, but Anies never really saw the point. We renovated it, but we didn't do much with it either."

"She's been waiting for years in a hangar in Odessa, and all she wanted was to fly!" Dikkenek laughs.

Dries toasts him with his coffee mug. "Twenty to forty feet above the water." He points to one of the innumerable dials on the dashboard. "Four hundred miles per hour under radar-detection level." He shakes his head. "Anies never saw the point, but believe me, I do . . ."

At the evocation of Anies's name, the past few hours rush back to me, and chills run down my spine. *Stiles.* He knew it was Dries as soon as he saw the ekranoplan, but I'm getting the feeling that there's more to this. His southern drawl echoes in my head again. *Don't worry about Mr. November . . . His fairy godmother watches over him.*

"What happened?" I ask Dries. "How did you escape Erwin? How did you know where to intercept us?"

He takes a long sip, his golden gaze darkening, almost amber in the dim cockpit light. "One thing at a time. Let's sit down and have a little chat."

•••

There's some uncertainty regarding when exactly the cocoa powder that went in my mug was produced, but Dries said it's fine, that these things never go bad and that Soviet-era cocoa was mostly beet sugar and color additives anyway. That's precisely what I feared, but I'm starving, so I'm dipping my third Soldier Fuel peanut butter bar in the brownish water in my mug while March watches me with no small amount of concern over his coffee cup. Isiporho joined us, but he noted that the only thing he trusted in the ekranoplan's galley was the tea—March hasn't touched his coffee since.

After I've gulped down the last bite of my energy bar, I take a circular look at the three men gathered with me around a table in the aircraft's briefing room. A continuous drizzle hits the windows, coming from the massive trail of surf we leave in our wake. I rest my elbows on the melamine and lace my fingers. "So, how did you find us?" I ask. "Was it because of Erwin's men? They were following us before the Lions killed them."

Dries chuckles. "At least they were useful once in their life."

"But how did you escape?" I probe.

He waves his hand dismissively. "There was no need to escape . . . What did you think? That I couldn't deal with that deplorable clown? He *needs* me. Right now I'm his only hope to ever crawl out from the archives."

I frown. "The archives?"

March chimes in. "Well, much like the rest of us, Mr. Erwin has been going through a bit of a rough patch since the Poseidon incident."

"They flushed that malodorous turd . . . Good riddance." Dries snorts.

Okay, I'm increasingly lost . . . "*They?*"

"Mr. Erwin used to be the unofficial head of the Directorate of Foreign Operations," March explains. "But with two rogue agents joining a criminal organization, six hundred victims in the plane bombing, and an entire vacation resort sunk in the Pacific . . . the agency decided it was time for new leadership."

I nod. "So he got fired? Or is he in charge of the archives now? But he had all those soldiers with him . . ."

"To the best of my knowledge, he's been offered a position within the declassified archives department, to oversee the sorting of all cafeteria-related complaints from 1947 to 1990," March says.

I wince. "I . . . I don't think that's what he's doing right now."

"Neither do I. He may not have the ear of the new administration, but he siphoned considerable sums from his budget over the years, and he's well connected. I'm assuming he's using those resources to go after Anies."

"On his own?"

Isiporho shrugs. "Possibly, but you never know with men like him . . ."

"No." Dries considers his empty cup with a smirk. "He's hunting alone, probably hiring ex–black ops. Steed and his team don't trust the agency. They purged the old dogs and replaced them with a bunch of brain-addled brown-nosers. Good for our business. Bad for Erwin's . . ."

I listen, trying to put the pieces of the puzzle together. "So you made a deal with him?" I ask Dries.

"Not quite, but he understands I'm after Anies too, and his best hope to take him down is to let me lure him out."

"Unless it's the other way other around," Isiporho notes dryly.

I stiffen. "What do you mean?"

Dries fishes something from his inner pocket that he tosses onto the table. Casting a faint golden hue on the melamine is my pendant. Or rather two halves of it. The amber has been shattered, and with it, the frail wings of the butterfly. I touch it tentatively, both relieved and ashamed. It might have been Anies's gift, but it was also a precious archeological piece, and now it's been destroyed. "Did it break in the river? It was in my pocket . . . but it was intact when Stiles gave it back to me."

March reaches to take my hand in his as Dries growls, "He's playing with us. I should have dumped that little cunt in a meat grinder when I had the chance . . ."

Around me, I feel the walls tilt, and I'm getting seasick. I squeeze March's fingers to anchor myself. "*You* broke it." And I think I know why.

Isiporho shakes his head with a bitter smile. "We were so focused on that thing in your head and the plate in your wrist that we never thought to search for a bug anywhere else."

March points to the golden metal loop and the larger piece of metal that used to secure the disc of amber. "It's high-end technology, undetectable when it's not actively transmitting. The signal itself was short range, but we believe the tracker was capable of hooking on to unsecured wireless networks as well. I believe that's why it took them so long to locate us in Finland. They didn't have precise coordinates."

"And when we landed in Romania, the pendant found a network to connect and signal our position," I complete, my voice tight.

Dries takes one of the pendant's broken pieces and studies it with piercing eyes. "At least now we're free to move."

I fight the laces tightening around my throat. "But Viktor is dead."

Isiporho nods, an unexpected sadness shadowing his eyes. "We found him at the casino."

Killed by Stiles, or one of his men . . . I look down at March's and my joined hands. A lone spark lights up in my long-abused neurons. "*Odysseus* . . . did Erwin say anything about it?"

That sends Dries's brow shooting upward in an expression of genuine surprise that looks almost foreign on his features. "Is anyone not looking for that wreck these days?"

Excellent question . . . "So he mentioned it too?" I say, springing back to life. "Stiles told me he thought I was even more precious to Anies than *Odysseus*. I *knew* there was something!"

March strokes my wrist pensively, searching Dries's now-shuttered expression. "There's a nuclear reactor inside the ship . . . do you think the Lions could have stolen it? To bargain with the US government?"

Isiporho leans back in his chair and runs a hand across his chin. "*Eish* . . ."

Dries gazes past us, through the window, as if lost in a world of his own. It seems the energy that continuously drives him past all obstacles has deserted him. "'All men dream,'" he says slowly, "'but not equally. Those who dream by night in the dusty recesses of their minds wake in the day to find that it was vanity: but the dreamers of the day are dangerous men, for they may act on their dreams with open eyes, to make them possible.'"

I get the feeling he's quoting someone, but there's nothing to retrieve from the empty shelves of my brain. "Is that from somewhere?"

He remains silent. I don't like that he shut down on us—or maybe what upsets me is the realization that even he can be rattled.

March eventually answers for him. "Lawrence of Arabia wrote that, in the *Seven Pillars of Wisdom*."

"Okay, so . . ."

"We're going to need your boy," Dries tells March, his knuckles rapping on the table—a sure sign that his personal brand of unflappable determination is back. "That little *poes* who hacked Auben's phone in Rio. What was his name?"

"Colin," March replies. "Colin Jeon."

"Who's that?" I ask.

He winks at me. "Someone who'll be happy to see you."

Isiporho leaves the table to retrieve a small laptop from a metal case, which he hands to March. "I installed your game. Is that really how you contact him?"

March nods, his fingers flying fast on the keyboard to launch a colorful window. I watch in perplexity as he logs on to . . . *Kawaii Farm*. He selects his character, a little ostrich with huge eyes wearing jeans overalls and a straw hat. God, it even has a little rake: this is so cute! The map loads, and March's ostrich runs across flower fields and orchards, guided by the direction keys.

I go through the stats panel at the bottom of the screen. Whoever this Colin person is, March didn't play Kawaii Farm just to contact him . . . 67 orchards, 223 crop fields, over 400 hamsters working the fields full time for minimum wage, a staggering ten million "coinz" stashed at the Kawaii Bank of Investment, gold-shovel medal, platinum-wheelbarrow trophy . . . March's ostrich has built an empire.

Meanwhile, the bird leaps among coconut trees and tropical pink flowers, all the way to another farm. He knocks at the door of a turtle-shaped house, prompting the launch of a chat window.

He starts typing. "Would you be interested in purchasing a mithril rake?"

Dries, Isiporho, and I wait with bated breath as the door creaks open, and a little turtle with equally large and shiny eyes appears—a ninja turtle, judging by the shuriken secured to its shell by a yellow belt.

"Anyone else bidding on it?" the turtle asks.

March's lips stretch into a rare grin. "No, only me and my girlfriend."

Barely a second after he's pressed the enter key, the 3-D scenery dissolves into a shimmering dust of pixels until the screen turns black and a video conference window pops up. A young Asian guy sits in a big blue gaming chair behind a cluttered desk. Jet chin-length hair curtains his glasses, and I make a mental note of his green Teenage Mutant Ninja Turtles T-shirt: someone's a fan . . . He combs his bangs back with his fingers, and an ecstatic grin lights up his face. "Oh my God, you're seriously back!"

I smile in return, because the joy bubbling inside me instinctively tells me he's a friend. "Yeah . . . I guess I'm back."

Behind the glasses, his eyes train on March, and his mouth purses in solemn admiration. "You're hardcore . . . If you print Struthio T-shirts, I'll buy one."

"Struthio?" I ask March, searching my memory for everything he told me last night. "It's that private security business you founded after you stopped . . . um . . . killing people?" I realize as I say this that he hasn't really stopped, but at least he tried, so I guess it's a good start.

Colin's eyebrows pinch at my comment about Struthio. I offer him an apologetic wince. "Sorry . . . I don't remember everything. I'm still catching up."

Shock registers on his face and, right afterward, sadness. "But . . . you remember me, right?"

On the table, March's hand squeezes mine as I answer, "No . . . I'm sorry. No."

Colin slumps in his chair, looking even younger as he clasps a hand over his mouth, looking devastated. Somehow I feel like I've failed this guy I don't even remember, and that's only the tip of the iceberg: there's an entire life to learn all over again, and so many people who'll feel like Colin . . . like March felt when I wouldn't let him in.

"It's gonna be okay," I say softly. "We can get to know each other again, and maybe someday I'll remember."

Colin gives an uncertain nod and seems to relax until Dries pops up behind me. The moment he sees him, his face scrunches up in visible dismay.

Dries greets him with a carnivorous smile. "Yes, it's me again. And you're going to sing for me, or I'll find you, and I'll plastinate your—"

"That's unnecessary," March cuts him off dryly. "I already explained to you that our relations with Mr. Jeon are nothing but cordial."

"That little snitch works for the NSA," Dries snaps. "He might as well report to Erwin directly . . ."

"But I don't!" Colin counters in outrage. "And he already told you not to threaten me like that."

"All right, all right." Dries waves off Colin's complaint. "*Odysseus*—what do you know about it?"

Colin sobers and leans on his desk. "That it was awesome, but NASA lost it at the bottom of Litke Deep, and their congressional hearing won't go well?"

"And what can you tell us that we won't hear on television?" March probes.

He cringes. "One day they're gonna find my body, and it'll be all your fault. You know that, right?"

Dries glares at Colin. "And they'll find it much sooner than you expect if you don't start talking."

I elbow him discreetly with a disapproving look while, behind me, Isiporho stifles a laugh at their antics. Colin shakes his head and starts typing on his keyboard. On-screen, a map of the Arctic Ocean pops up in a new window. A cursor appears over a dark blue spot, not far from a cluster of frozen islands. "That's Litke Deep, about a hundred miles north of the archipelago of Svalbard." The cursor glides half an inch down. "And that point here, that's where they think *Odysseus* crashed."

"That's not in Litke Deep," I say. "Was it carried north by sea currents? I mean, it weighs two thousand tons . . ."

Colin sighs. "Probably not." Another window flashes on-screen, containing what I recognize as a spectrogram. Represented with a pattern of bright colors forming columns is a series of powerful, low-frequency sounds. There's a date in the bottom right corner: October 17—recorded two months ago. "What did they record?" I ask.

"A whale, of course." When he sees my mouth twist in doubt, Colin laughs. "That's what Zwicky is gonna tell Congress tomorrow anyway."

"That a giant whale sank their trillion-dollar spaceship?"

"That should go over well . . ." March comments with a sigh.

Colin shrugs. "Better than telling them we suspect it's a nuclear submarine signature."

My jaw goes slack, and I hear March's eyebrows shoot up.

"Unconfirmed?" Dries asks, his fingers rapping on the table.

"Kinda not entirely confirmed," Colin replies. "Let's put it like this: you'd need something pretty powerful to tow a hundred-foot ship, and the docking would be noisy . . ."

"And?" Dries insists, his nostrils flaring.

Colin squirms in his chair. "Something like the brand-new type 099 the Chinese lost a year ago, along with a dozen nuclear warheads. Which is totally a rumor, and maybe it's still being tested in a secret location like their official news agency is telling everyone . . ."

There's a beat of silence in the briefing room as the enormity of the news sets in. It's Isiporho, having been listening quietly until now, who first manages to speak. "The brothers . . . stole a nuclear submarine to tow *Odysseus*?"

Colin's eyes widen until I fear they're going to roll out. "Oh, my fucking God! The Lions did it?"

Dries sends him a murderous glare. "They didn't," he hisses. "And the quieter you are, the longer you'll live."

In my ears, their voices are muted, a distant din when my thoughts have concentrated, narrowed down to a single point. The butterfly. Anies brought it back from his trip to the factory . . . "It's in Ecuador," I say out loud.

March's fingers lace with mine, his features taut with worry as he listens to me.

"Anies said he'd take me to Ecuador with him when his project was complete. He's been shipping things there for months; it was his obsession. He said"—my voice falters—"that it'd be a surprise."

And what a surprise. If he really crossed that line . . . I can't imagine what he's cooking there, but none of the scenarios my brain slaps together are any less than disastrous. With the combined power of *Odysseus*'s reactor and the warheads that were in that Chinese submarine . . . he could wipe a small country from the map.

I'll give you even more. An entire new world . . .

I'm still breathing, but my throat is so tight I'm not sure the oxygen is reaching my lungs. "We need to find that ship . . . I think he's gonna make a huge mistake."

A strong, warm hand squeezes my shoulder. I look up to find Dries gazing at me. In his eyes, the gold darkens as he tells March, "I'll go make a call of my own."

TWENTY-SIX
THE MERMAID

After Dries locked himself in the cabin to make a call that seems to have added ten years to the lines on his face, March confirmed that our next stop would be Istanbul. He remained evasive as to what we'll do once we're there. He keeps saying he'll keep me safe, but we both know that's not what I'm asking. Anyway, that would be my second most immediate concern. The primary one being whether I'll live long enough to see the Blue Mosque at all . . .

Dries said the whole thing is perfectly safe, but like with most of his plans, I have doubts. It's too late to chicken out though: I'm sitting between March's legs in the long and narrow speedboat, my life jacket is secured, and in front of us, the ekranoplan's massive rear-loading ramp is opening as the aircraft slows down, revealing a trail of crashing waves and whirlpools of foam. Cold air rushes in, along with the engines' deafening noise. Around my waist, March's arms tighten their hold. "It's going to be all right."

I grip his hands, my breath coming in short pants. I'm starting to identify a pattern: he always says that sort of thing before shit hits the fan . . . I get that Jan has to hide the ekranoplan, that it'd be a bad idea to cross the Bosphorus Strait in plain sight, with its populated shores, constant patrolling, and in a country that's barreling fast toward dictatorship on top of that. So yeah, it's a great idea to drop us twenty miles away from the strait so he can turn back and seek refuge for Dries's "baby" on the safest shores of Bulgaria. But I didn't sign up to be tossed into a washing machine, and since we all had to put on waterproof coveralls and goggles, I'm getting the feeling that it's exactly what's about to happen.

At the front of the boat, Dominik checks the Kevlar line connecting us to a winch while, in the back, Isiporho gets in position by the outboard engine, ready to lower it as soon as we hit the water. Sitting next to me, Dries grins at the whirling, roaring hell under us. "Best time of the year for a cruise!" he yells.

It's the only warning I get before a whirring sound announces that the winch is spinning fast, and we're being dropped. I grit my teeth, and screw my eyes shut as we accelerate down the ramp and toward the sea. We're weightless for a split second before the boat hits the water and bounces on the turbulent rolls, shaking us like lotto balls. The next few minutes feel like a race in rapids as the ekranoplan's trail drenches us in cold, salty water. My nails dig into March's hands when a powerful wave threatens to make the speedboat capsize. It gets better though. Around us, the sea goes quiet, and we're now rocked by a lazy swell as the aircraft becomes a blurry dot in the horizon.

"Woohoo!"

We all turn to Dominik, who just confirmed my suspicions that he's a complete adrenaline junkie . . . He shakes his head to partially dry the water dripping from his skull and face. "Let's do that again."

"Perhaps some other day," March offers before removing his goggles and running a hand through his own water-soaked hair, much in the same fashion Dries is.

Isiporho lowers the engine into the water. It gives a low gurgle and hums to life, and soon we're gaining speed on the tranquil surface. When he notices that I'm still sitting frozen against him and give no sign of uncurling, March combs my hair back, squeezing a little water from the damp waves. "Biscuit, are you all right?"

I glower at Dries's smug expression. "Let's *never* do that again."

"See?" he tells March. "She's fine."

The weather is kind enough that we're eventually able to shrug out of our coveralls, and it doesn't take us long to reach the Bosphorus. Hills rise and fall past us on each side, peppered with tile roofs and shrouded in afternoon mist. As we progress toward Istanbul, the number of seagulls circling over our heads increases exponentially. Villages become towns and harbors until modern buildings and beautiful white villas crowd the shores. I start to worry about the patrol boats cruising the straits, but Dries shrugs it off with a comment that Turkish coast guards have enough on their plates with the rubber dinghies on which thousands of refugees risk their lives every day to reach Greece: with only five passengers and a razor-sharp silvery hull that screams "rich tourist toy," they couldn't care less about us.

Against all odds, I lived to see the Blue Mosque. I shift on March's lap to get a better look when we reach the southern mouth of the Bosphorus. There it is, overlooking the bay and competing with the equally majestic Hagia Sophia basilica. I squint at the complex stack of richly adorned domes guarded by six minarets, like arrows reaching for the sky.

March rests his chin on my shoulder, following the direction of my gaze. "When they built it, the Mecca mosque was the only one in the world to have six minarets. They had to build a seventh one there to keep up."

"Gotta have standards," I say in a laugh.

"Exactly . . ."

We sail west, around the old district of Fatih, the jewel that travelers once called Constantinople. Concrete progressively replaces old stones as we reach Bakirköy, a commercial district on the European side of the city, where Atatürk Airport lies, surrounded by shops and hotels. Our destination is a tiny marina south of the airport, right in front of a park. You'd think the winter weather would deter the locals, but there're quite a few people sitting on benches or enjoying a drink in nearby cafés. The place must be a little summer paradise, if the number of yachts lined along the pier is any indication. We moor between *Simarik* and *Latin Lover* in the general indifference of the Istanbulites strolling by with their kids.

Once we've left the speedboat behind us, Dominik's eyes scan the area until a predatory grin curls his lips. My money is on that blue Land Rover . . . and yep. With a casual stride, he crosses a patch of lawn to reach the coveted vehicle. He's so quick, so sure-handed that to the external observer this must look like nothing more than a man briefly fumbling with his car's key lock.

We follow in his footsteps, and I shush my guilt when climbing into the back seat between March and Dries while Isiporho sits in the front with Dominik. Dries pats my shoulder, watching his disciple switch the engine with smug satisfaction. "He's almost as good as your mother. She had gifted hands . . . and expensive tastes," he adds with a wink.

I stare at him in amazement. This isn't much—almost nothing, really—but he's never talked about her until now except that one time back at the cabin, and all I had to jog the ruins of my memory were Anies's lies and March's faithful but limited account.

"How did you meet her?" I ask eagerly while we drive past shops and palm trees toward Atatürk Airport.

A wistful smile softens his features. "In a circus."

"*What* were you doing in a circus?"

"Nothing. It was in '87; we'd just finished a job in Rome, and with nothing to do for the next twenty-four hours, I went for a walk around the city."

"And you ended up in a circus?"

He rolls his eyes. "The great Federicci circus . . . They'd set up their tent in the northeast, and it was . . . pathetic. The crowds were scarce, and they were barely making ends meet. Have you seen *Down and Dirty*, by Ettore Scola?"

I shake my head, unsure whether to answer "no" or "I don't remember."

"It was something just like that. Filthy trailers, haggard clowns . . . and the ringmaster's wife—what was her name?— Mandorla . . . No, *Mandorlina* . . . 'Little almond.' Who must have weighed a quarter ton and dyed her hair blue, because she had this act . . . as a mermaid in a water tank."

Behind the wheel, Dominik snickers, and March and Isiporho too can't contain a smile.

"And my mom worked there?"

"Oh, yes, she did . . . It was in August, and the heat was crushing. I walked around that dump, bored and curious, I suppose. And I saw a sign on a trailer that said they had lions, so I looked for the cages, and I then saw *her*." He pauses, visibly pleased by his little effect on an audience that's now captivated by his story. "She was standing there in a bikini, hosing two mangy lions." He shakes his head. "They were poor beasts, declawed, with their fangs filed down. But her . . . she was barely twenty, and you should have seen her . . ." He clasps his hands in a silent prayer to the goddess who lives in his memory, the young woman with long red hair and mysterious green eyes I saw in the sparse pictures Anies showed me. "It took me all of five seconds to make a move."

Something is happening in that stolen car: for a moment, Anies and his terrifying plans have been forgotten, and a concert of laughs rises: deep chuckles—Isiporho's and March's—echoed by Dominik's breathless chortles and my giggles.

"What did you tell her?" I ask. On my left, I glimpse planes waiting on the tarmac, and I want to hear more, to make this moment last before reality catches up with us.

Dries crosses his arms with a grin. "It's like for women with children: you always pet the baby first to break the ice. So I went for the lions. I played with them, showed a bit of dominance to impress her."

I clasp a hand over my mouth, my shoulders shaking in hilarity.

"And it worked," he goes on, nodding to himself. "We chatted a bit. She had this magic act back then: pulling rabbits from her hat, card tricks . . . She'd tell everyone she was a Romanian orphan who had fled Ceauşescu's dictature." He wiggles his eyebrows. "Sandra the Romanian wonder."

My brow flies up. "You can't be serious."

"Dead serious. She had a little side act lifting the parents' wallets while the kids petted the rabbit. We got to know each other better, and I discovered she knew her way around safes too . . . I did a little digging up on her, and it turned out that trouble seemed to follow the Federicci circus wherever it went."

"She was a thief . . ." I complete, my joy turning bittersweet.

"*Artist* would be more appropriate in her case. It's not every day that you meet a twenty-year-old who does jewelry stores without getting caught."

"How long did you stay together?" I probe.

Dries draws a sigh and goes quiet. I gather he doesn't want to get that personal with his disciples listening. "It never really ended," is all he says before Dominik parks the SUV a hundred yards away from a low building on which a sign reads General Aviation Terminal.

Dries clasps his hands, his confident façade falling back in place. "At least we'll be flying into the storm first-class."

Next to me, I feel March stiffen, but he doesn't comment and instead opens the door for me. I look up at the cloudy sky from which a light drizzle has started to fall. With a sigh that's part exhaustion, part delight, I inhale the damp air, heavy with the scent of gasoline and wet grass.

Once we're inside the terminal, a nice ground attendant leads us to a bright, spacious lounge. I sink into a blue-suede-upholstered couch while Dries locks himself with Isiporho in the business-meeting room to have what appears to be a private conversation. From the corner of my eye, I watch them nod to each other through the tinted glass isolating the room. Possibly to divert my attention from their plotting, March brings me apple tea in a plastic cup before he goes to retrieve two suitcases he had his assistant deliver at the desk. One is a sleek black little thing that I'm afraid looks every bit like his previous magic suitcase—I hope they're not too fussy about scanning hand luggage at Atatürk. The other is a regular rolling suitcase I'm guessing is for me.

He returns to the lounge at the same time that Dries and Isiporho exit the meeting room. Dries plops himself onto the couch next to me and casually wraps an arm around my shoulder. I tense involuntarily—it's the first time he's touched me like that since our reunion. It's not uncomfortable, just a little foreign, the smell of his spicy cologne, that warm weight. There's something intimate about it that I never realized existed between us until now. We're family after all.

His gaze seeps over me, an odd tenderness laced with his usual smugness. "Our roads part here, little Island."

I freeze.

"Isiporho and Dominik are going to check something for me at the Paris temple. You'll go with them." He sends a pointed look at March. "And I trust Mr. Menahem to keep you safe while we solve our differences with the brothers."

I have no idea who Mr. Menahem is—another Lion?—and I also make a mental note that March mentioned those "temples" back in Finland. There's apparently something going on with them that matters a great deal to the brotherhood. But it's not what makes the blood rush to my head and my mouth quiver with sudden anger. I glare at Dries. "You're not getting rid of me."

He welcomes the statement with a chuckle. "Yes, I am, but I recognize your—"

"Shut up," I snap, before turning to March. "I want to discuss this with you."

Without waiting for his answer, I get up and walk to the business-meeting room. A couple of guys in suits are already in there, but I barge in, fuming. "Sorry, gentlemen, we're going to need the room."

The oldest one, a paunchy Arab guy pushing sixty, turns to me and looks me up and down with obvious disdain. "Not free. You go away."

He shouldn't have. I've taken enough shit in a short two days. I take a deep breath, puffing my chest, and without warning, swipe his papers from the table angrily. The guy steps back, his nostrils flaring in outrage, and I'm about to unleash my fury on his tacky gold MacBook, but March stops me just in time, catching the laptop before I send it crashing to the floor.

The second occupant, a young guy with a pink tie and a gelled mohawk, gets to his knees to pick up the papers with trembling hands and grabs the precious laptop. He squeaks something that sounds like Arabic, seemingly urging his colleague to get the hell out of here.

With cautious steps, they draw a wide berth around me to reach the door. *Yeah, that's right; look down: I am the law!* The second they're gone, the door closes behind us. March crosses his arms and gauges me with hard blue eyes. He's been nothing but kind to me since he rescued me from Ingolvinlinna, but this time, in his irises the waters are dark and dangerous. I sustain his icy gaze bravely as he says, "Are you done? This is hardly like you."

"How would I know that?" I shoot back.

"Island, I won't be dealing with a tantrum—"

My palm slams painfully hard onto the meeting table. "I'm sorry, a *tantrum*? Anies killed my mother, he locked me up, he wiped my brain clean . . . he *erased* my entire life! And now that stuff with *Odysseus*, and you're telling me to wait in Paris with Menahem-whatever-no-one-cares?" I yell, my breath short.

He takes a step forward, his expression completely blank save for a twitch in his jaw. And his eyes . . . they pin me in place, compel me. I swallow and try to control my breathing when I realize he's got me trapped against the table. "My mother died when I was thirteen," he says in a flat voice, like he'd comment on the weather. "She overdosed in our bathroom, on speedballs that my father gave her. I found her body." His Adam's apple rolls in his throat as he continues. "After the ambulance took her, I cleaned the floor. She had bled from her nose and . . . emptied her bladder."

I grit my teeth, shivers coursing through my body as his pain flows to me, like poison I'm absorbing. He's not finished, and I wish I could look away, but he's taking me with him kicking and screaming somewhere I'm not sure I'm strong enough to go.

"You're not the first woman I've loved," he continues, the same cold anger enveloping each word.

This time I flinch and avert my eyes. I'm still standing, but it's like I'm losing my footing. "Who was she?"

"One of Erwin's agents. Her name was Charlotte and I was"—his brow quivers, and he shakes his head, as if rejecting that particular memory—"I would have done anything for her, but she didn't love me. She left me because she didn't want . . . that level of complication. I scared her, and she was probably right to go."

One of my hands lets go of the table edge to rest flat on his chest. His skin burns under Isiporho's wool sweater, like he has a fever. "March . . . what are you trying to tell me?"

He wrestles his features back into an emotionless mask. "She died too. She was killed during a mission in Ivory Coast. I struck a deal with Erwin to go rescue her, but I made it too late. The soldiers necklaced her."

Each beat of my heart echoes painfully all the way up to the back of my throat and I think a deeply buried part of me already knows, fears what's coming next. "Necklaced?"

March takes a sharp breath. "They trap the victim's body in tires, douse them with gas, and set them on fire. She was barely alive when I found her, and all I could do was end it . . . I shot her. I killed her myself."

My eyes squeeze shut, and I clutch his sweater. A vision of a charred body flashes behind my eyelids. I picture March's finger, pressing the trigger. I steel myself. He weathered my pain and my anger; I'll shoulder his. I stroke his chest soothingly. "March, I am . . . so, so sorry."

One of his arms snakes around my waist while his free hand cups my cheek. "Island, I lost them both because I couldn't protect them.

Like I lost you once already. You can't"—his voice catches as he holds me tight—"you can't ask me to bring you back to him."

It dawns on me that because March bared himself to me like that, I'm now carrying a little part of his memories, as he carries mine. I understand how he feels, and I measure the magnitude of the gesture, from this man who shields himself so much. I only wish I could let him protect me the way he wants to. Life is a bit more complicated than that though . . . I relax in his embrace and return his hug. "Was I like that before?"

"What do you mean?"

"When you told me to do something, when you wanted me out of the way, did I obey?"

A pained chuckle rumbles through his chest between us. "Yes. You were . . . very reasonable. And you always let me keep you safe."

"Nice try. I must have been a dream girlfriend then."

His lips press in my hair, the words muffled against my temple. "You were bliss and chaos . . . still are."

"I need to do this," I say quietly. "I need answers; I don't want to spend the rest of my life looking over my shoulder, hiding and being afraid. I want a life with you, but for that, we need to end this first. And you'll need me; if Stiles was right, I'm Anies's weakness as much as I'm yours."

"Island, I'm not certain that's what I want to hear . . ."

He's right. No amount of rational arguments will change the fact that he wants to protect me and I want to fight this battle. I know what he needs to hear, words I'd have never imagined saying two days ago, and which now seem so evident. They tumble from my lips, hushed yet confident. "Je t'aime." *I love you.*

Against me, I can feel his posture relax. "You're not playing fair," he murmurs. "But I love you more than anything."

"Then keep me with you." I smile, nuzzling his chest.

"What do you make of Dries's opinion?"

"I think he'd want his child to show some balls."

March's chest shakes with suppressed laughter. "That sounds wrong on so many levels."

We were wrong. Dries wanted his *disciple* to have balls. His anger has been slowly simmering under a stone-cold mask since March and I came out from the meeting room and announced a minor change of plan. He led us in dignified silence to a damp tarmac glistening from the afternoon drizzle, and waited, as Isiporho and Dominik said their good-byes and wished us good luck with a respectively heartfelt and reluctant bro hug.

As soon as they're out of sight, the pressure cooker of Dries's fatherly resentment explodes. "Is that how you thank me?" he hisses at March as we make our way toward a long navy-blue jet next to which a ground attendant awaits us. "My leg hurts every day, you know."

My gaze drops to said right leg, the one I noticed was sometimes a bit stiff back in Finland. Did he wound it when dragging March out of the Poseidon?

"It hurts," Dries goes on while March follows him in cautious silence. "And the pain gets even worse when an ungrateful little maggot who owes me *everything*, including his life, stabs me in the back."

"Look," I begin. "It was my decision and—"

"Silence, young lady!" He flashes me a withering glare. "You shouldn't even be here." He points to a distant point at the other end of the tarmac. "You should be on that plane, bound for Paris!"

My neck shrinks into my shoulders, and March shakes his head in silent encouragement not to egg the beast on.

As he's about to climb onto the airstair, Dries freezes and spins on his heels with surprising ease for a fifty-three-year-old guy whose leg is supposedly causing him constant agony. His eyes turn to hateful slits as he tells March, "I'm rescinding the authorization I gave you to touch my daughter." He pauses for dramatic effect and adjusts his jacket. "Permanently."

It could be a trick of the dying daylight, but I think I just saw despair flash across March's face.

TWENTY-SEVEN
THE MARK

Gender stereotypes be damned, this jet is the work of a woman.

Sitting next to March in a ridiculously soft leather seat, I grip my armrest as the jet gains speed on the runway. Low vibrations travel through my body as we take off in the closest thing to heaven I've experienced since leaving the poisonous cocoon of Ingolvinlinna. It's obvious that extreme care went into every detail of the plane's interior, from the soft white and beige palette of the furniture, to the vibrant gold of embroidered silk cushions strategically flung on a long couch—all matching the bed's linen in the small bedroom I noticed at the back of the plane. Black peonies rest in a Ming vase on a lacquered cupboard right next to a wall-mounted screen, and of course, there's a ceiling shower in the bathroom.

So yeah, a woman was here, and I don't mean the flight attendant Dries is wooing behind us. I know I shouldn't, but I listen, because this is basically a master class in seduction. A suave compliment about the beauty of her ebony skin got her to admit her mother was South African. What a coincidence—so is he! And which town does the *hartjie* come from? The darling—whose name is actually Isabelle—is from Johannesburg. Another coincidence! Why doesn't she sit down for a moment and share a flute of champagne with a fellow *Joburger*?

Perhaps sensing a trap, Isabelle declines with a gentle but stern reminder that she can't drink on the job, and much less with passengers. Damn, foiled!

Next to me, March dozes, his eyes half-closed. His gaze follows Isabelle when she retreats into the galley, probably out of a deeply ingrained habit to scan any potential threats. She's pouring a flute of rosé champagne for Dries. Threat level: low.

I pat his thigh. "I'll go take a shower and change."

He nods with a tired smile. "Take your time. You need to relax."

What a gentlemanly way to say that he's the one who needs to relax and that he'll fall asleep as soon as I'm gone . . . Dries pays little attention to me as I pick up my suitcase and head to the bathroom. His lips resting against the rim of his glass, I can tell he's mentally undressing Isabelle. She tucks a stray curl back into her tightly braided bun with a gracious hand and smooths imaginary wrinkles from her navy blue dress. For all her professionalism, I'm not entirely certain she minds his attention . . .

Once I'm alone in the bathroom, I immediately proceed to strip from Dominik's Springboks T-shirt and the black mechanic pants I'm floating in. I tumble into the futuristic oval shower stall with a sigh and rest my forehead against the glass panel as warm water pours over my head like a summer rain. I let myself slide down until I'm sitting in the tray and gather my knees against my body. I think of Anies, who promised we'd go to Ecuador together. The prospect of facing him again has been kind of abstract in my mind until now, but now I'm on this plane, and it's becoming real. Strangely, I'm not scared as the droplets hit my back, drip down my chin. I'm well aware that there are still a number of ways he could hurt me if he wins this round, but the whirlwind of these past few days has made my skin a little thicker. I've tasted despair and, with it, found a renewed hunger for life. I scramble up and grab a bottle of shower gel with a determined huff. We're going to get the world rid of at least one sketchy uncle.

I don't remember Phyllis, March's assistant, but *she* remembers me: every single clothing item neatly folded in the suitcase she had delivered at the airport for me is a perfect fit—including the underwear, I realize with a blush. Also those trashed jeans and the gray T-shirt featuring a cartoon cat double-flipping its audience off is likely what I would have gone for if left unattended in a shop. I fumble in the little bag with a smile. It's a bit silly, a drop of water in the grand scheme of things, but having forgotten my entire life, I'm inordinately happy to discover the bottle of perfume. I spray some on my wrist and inhale the clean, flowery scent. I decide that my former self made sound decisions: I indeed love White Musk.

I come out of the bathroom to find Dries sitting on the couch with Isabelle—looks like she finally agreed to share the champagne with him. I register the hushed notes of a guitar playing in the background while he tells her about the beauty of Oman, especially at night. Has she ever been there? No? Maybe he should take her then. I purse my lips to contain a sigh—as long as they don't start making out right in front of me . . .

Still in his seat, March is hunched over a tablet, seemingly—or willingly—unaware of the fact that he's been made an extra in an Enrique Iglesias video. I shake my head and return to my seat. He didn't seem the type, but March is deeply engrossed in crosswords. I watch him beat a particularly tough definition before victoriously typing *prurient* in the remaining empty squares. I offer a round of applause while he sets the tablet on the mahogany table facing our seats.

He studies my new appearance with a tender smile. "Much better . . ." His head dips to my neck, to inhale the fragrance clinging there.

"How do you like the Queen's Gulfstream, Island?"

I jump at the sound of Dries's voice, and March's head snaps up. I'm reminded of March's tale about Dries barging into our room on his yacht when we were about to . . . Then there was Dries's claim that March is no longer allowed to touch me, as per some unwritten rule he made up and intends to enforce. An imperceptible sigh deflates March; his mentor isn't done with him yet.

I wrestle my wince into a smile. "It's a beautiful jet . . . But what kind of queen are we talking about? A *real* one?" I've come to understand that Dries remains a powerful man even after his downfall, but somehow I didn't picture his connections including royalty.

Suddenly a notch cooler, he glances at the puzzled Isabelle, who's still curled on the couch with her half-empty flute of champagne. "Why don't you go take care of dinner, *hartjie*? I'm starving."

Ouch . . . *rough* douche move. Thirty seconds ago, she was a goddess he planned on taking all over the world with him, and now she just got relegated back to the kitchen. What a complete dick he can be. Regardless, once she's disappeared into the galley, Dries sits across from us and crosses his arms. "It's a pity you forgot about her, because Guita hasn't forgotten about you."

"Guita?"

"The Queen."

"Of what?" I insist.

"Of the Board," March clarifies. "It's a large criminal organization. Many, if not most criminal networks answer to the Board one way or another."

"Or rather used to," Dries corrects.

My gaze travels between the two of them. "And is there a king?"

Dries chuckles. "No. He'd be long dead. Guita doesn't like to share."

"But she lent you the jet," I counter.

He clasps his hands. "Let me put this in a way I'm certain you'll understand: the Board used to be instrumental in bringing balance to the force." My ears perk up as he goes on. "The Poseidon, which Anies destroyed, belonged to the Board. It was both a tactical and symbolic asset. The Board's most influential members used to meet there, and it was also a considerable source of revenue."

My head bobs up and down as I process all this. "And destroying the Poseidon rattled the whole organization?"

"Precisely," March confirms. "The Queen's leadership was brought into question, and with Erwin losing control over the Directorate of Foreign Operations around the same time, the Board's cordial ties with the CIA have been all but severed. This means no more cooperation or mutual protection for the players on either side."

"What kind of cooperation?"

Dries shrugs. "The usual . . . Act like you didn't notice me buying opium from some despotic fruitcake ruling over a hellhole in central Asia, and I'll pretend I don't know your agents are actively funding the next revolution there."

I wince. "So the Queen is basically after Anies because he ruined her business?"

"In short, yes." Dries nods. "But it goes deeper than that. He destroyed a very delicate balance, which we, the Lions, were part of. Our role was to fight the Board's battles and eat the carcasses."

I smile bitterly. "But that was no longer enough for Anies . . . He wanted more than just leftovers."

"I'm guilty of sharing that dream," Dries admits with a shrug. "But the difference is that I woke up." His eyes set on March, an unexpected spark of affection in their depths. "I thought a lot about what you told me back in Tokyo . . . You were right. The Lions were never meant to rule over anything."

March shakes his head. "But Anies thinks otherwise, and now that both Erwin and the Queen are out, the brotherhood has been busy." He goes on, for my benefit, this time. "As Dries told you, Guita was forced to step down from the Board following the destruction of the Poseidon. There's a succession war going on between the supervisors of the Hong Kong and Moscow subdivisions. The Lions have taken advantage of it and have been plundering the Board since, killing its members, taking over their operations."

"They've been on a rampage," Dries notes, a twinge of admiration in his voice.

"But Erwin knows about all this, right? Can't he . . . do something?"

A husky laugh bursts from Dries. "Have you forgotten he's under new management?"

"President Steed? Yeah, you said he doesn't trust the CIA, and he replaced old farts like Erwin."

"The agency tried to prevent his election with all sorts of quite hilarious leaks. That wound hasn't closed yet," Dries confirms. "And he's been busy with internal politics since his election. He's trying to ignore that he'll need them sooner or later."

"Speaking of which," March interrupts. "Perhaps it's time we show Island what's bringing us to Ecuador."

He takes his tablet from the table and connects it to the wall-mounted screen in front of us.

"Erwin had the right intuition," Dries begins, as March opens various scans of bank documents and waybills on-screen. "He was trying to prove that Aidan Keasler and Anies are, in fact, the same man. He knew about Keasler Industries, and he could tell that the amounts of cash flowing through KI were not only massive but highly suspicious. He simply didn't know where to start." A smirk cracks through his silvery beard. "But then you came back to us, with fascinating tales about a factory in Ecuador . . ."

I fidget in my seat as he zooms in on the logo on one of the invoices. "Saraya Mediasat? It is one of Anies's businesses?"

"Yes," March confirms. "He bought it through a shell company based in the Caymans three years ago."

Dries shakes his head, his mouth quivering into a snarl. "And here I was with my biltong factories."

"Saraya . . . launches satellites," March states, eyeing the data in the screen with the closest thing I've seen to fear in his eyes so far. "They operate a space center fifty miles south of the Colombian border."

"In the middle of the jungle . . ." I note, when his fingers swipe on the tablet's screen to open a satellite map. "Maybe they'd have the technology for a launch . . . but if *Odysseus* was there, wouldn't it show up on satellite surveillance?"

"There's nothing," Dries admits. "But what you see are the past twenty-four hours."

I nod. "Supposing that's where he took the ship, he's had months to hide it."

"You mentioned shipments," March adds. "Perhaps you won't be surprised to learn that KI's activities have been primarily geared toward Saraya over the past two years. The rest of the group is little more than a cash machine financing Saraya."

Frowning at the screen, I tap the tip of my nose—there's something familiar about the gesture, but I can't remember where it comes from. "That's what Erwin wanted from us. He wanted to understand what's the deal with Saraya. But now we have enough evidence for the US government to look into it, right? They could, I don't know, send a bunch of agents there . . ."

Dries snorts. "They won't." He takes the tablet from March to open a series of grainy pictures. "Here comes my favorite part."

I fight a shudder when I recognize Anies's black mandarin suit. As for the other guy . . . his face is a little too blurry, but the fiery-yellow comb-over billowing in the wind looks familiar. "Hold on. Is that Steed?"

"Oh, yes, it is," Dries replies in a smooth, dangerous voice. "Saraya launches Steed Media Global's satellites for a very competitive price."

March shakes his head. "The US's diplomatic relations with Ecuador have been strained over the past decade, mostly over intelligence issues . . . Steed won't trust Erwin's word unless he can prove with absolute certainty that Saraya is behind the theft of *Odysseus*. Until then, I doubt that Steed will ever green-light an operation on Ecuadorian soil, and targeting one of his most strategic business partners no less."

"So we need to find that ship," I conclude, pointing at the map. "If we can prove it's there, or even just parts, Anies is going down."

Dries looks at me then and smiles. Not a douchey smile or even a smug one. A genuine dad smile, if my instinct is correct about it. One that makes me feel strong, pumped. He tips his head to the galley door, through which a rich scent I identify as truffle wafts to us. "Now, is anyone hungry?"

•••

As I suspected, the Queen knows how to live. I wolfed down that plate of prosciutto and truffle pasta and even ate the edible flowers decorating my strawberry-and-pistachio cake. Next to me, March remained quiet and dignified as he ate his portion of pasta. Then a second one, before the rest of his tray was meticulously cleared, down to the slightest bread crumb. Dries, for his part, hit the champagne harder than the food but requested a second slice of cake from Isabelle—I suspect that we share a sweet tooth on top of a gap tooth.

After Isabelle has picked up our trays, I fall back in my seat with a moan of delight. "I'm in heaven!"

"Would you like to rest?" March asks. "Isabelle prepared the bed."

Dries's head snaps up from his cake. His eyes turn to slits.

"It's okay. I'm not really tired yet. Plus, when we land it should be around 5:00 p.m. in Ecuador, right? So I'd better not sleep too much during the flight," I muse out loud.

March doesn't seem fully satisfied with this answer, but Dries is. He rises from his seat, towering over his disciple, all disdain and warning. "Ek hou jou dop." *I'm watching you.*

He's not, actually. He disappears into the bathroom, and a minute later, I hear the shower running. Because I have no respect for authority, I immediately shift in my seat to press a kiss to March's lips, tasting of sugar and strawberries. It's over too soon when his eyes dart over to the galley to which Isabelle retreated again. "Perhaps at another time," he whispers.

I give a reluctant nod. He's right: I don't really want to be caught in the middle of a savage making-out session, either by her or Dries. Besides, there's something else I need to discuss with him. Ever since we parted ways at Atatürk airport, Isiporho and Dominik's strange mission has been at the back of my mind.

I place my palm against my window, watching the sun set and burn the sea of clouds beneath us. "March . . . the temples, what are they?"

There's a pause before he replies, "Landmarks for the brotherhood. Over the centuries, the Lions have often been scattered by wars or political shifts. They'd disappear and relocate. The temples are safe places they built over time, places where they could hide valuable documents and artifacts . . . The Lions would tell you they're where their heritage is kept alive."

I turn to look at him. "And what's so special about the Paris temple?"

"It's where they keep records of the mark each brother carries."

"You mean like that scarification on your back?"

"Yes. It's all a bit arcane, but there's a meaning behind each mark. There's a unique code number but also symbols that represent who you serve, your abilities, and what position your master intends for you to fulfill in the brotherhood."

"So Dries wants information on someone's mark . . ." The missing piece falls in place in my mind. "Stiles?"

"Yes. I think Dries wants to know if Mr. Stiles was ever carved in the first place, and if so, who did it, and what's in the mark."

"Anies kind of hinted he had big plans for Stiles."

"But that could only be true if Mr. Stiles was a Lion," March completes.

So Dries too suspects Anies wants to make Stiles his successor . . . "Back when I was at Ingolvinlinna, I noticed Anies looked ill," I recall. "He'd cough all the time, and he drank absinthe to numb himself." March's eyes narrow in curiosity, but he remains silent, allowing me to go on. "And in the car, Stiles said that it was true, that he was dying."

He nods slowly. "Dries didn't realize Anies was getting out of control, and it was perhaps too early for him to detect external signs of illness."

"But he'd have found out eventually, and he was the vice commander: he'd have been next in line. Anies got rid of him eight months ago, probably before Dries could take over and ruin his plans."

"Possible," March agrees, his gaze somber. He takes my hand and squeezes it, his thumb stroking my palm tenderly. "Island . . . there's something I've been meaning to ask you . . . but I don't know if I should."

I shrug. "Dries kept an amputated hand under his seat. He passed it to Dominik, and then Dominik returned it, and he put it back under the seat. So ask. Nothing you can say can beat that."

March's eyebrows draw together in contrition. "Island, I'm profoundly sorry—"

"Ask."

He does, in that quiet, straightforward manner he does everything else. "When I saw you in Hamina, you were with Mr. Stiles."

I feel suddenly a little cold at his evocation of the Christmas market. I knew nothing at the time; I was putty in Stiles's and Anies's hands. "Yes," I confirm.

March takes a deep breath that makes his nostrils flare, like he's trying to contain something that might otherwise explode inside him. "Did he touch you?"

There's so much loaded in those four words. I see myself again, laughing while Stiles picked a reindeer costume for his cats, his hand on my shoulder. Then I saved his life back in the woods. Begged for it, really. And he spared us in Romania, whatever his motives were. I wrench my hands nervously. I can imagine how things look from March's perspective.

I shake my head. "No. It was never like that. He"—funny how I was about to say *he took care of me*. I can't though; the very notion twists my stomach—"I trusted him," I finally say. "I thought he was taking care of me, and obviously I had that wrong. Anies wanted"—*he wanted to breed me*. I look down at my lap, shame burning my cheeks at the idea of wording Anies's intent out loud—"I think Anies would have wanted me to get closer to Stiles, so there could be . . . more potential successors. But Stiles never did anything. He never took advantage of me."

The half lie makes me cringe internally. Stiles never crossed that line, but he was getting ready to. He and Anies thought I was ripe for the taking, and I don't want to imagine what would have happened if Dries and March hadn't rescued me. Would I have eventually capitulated like Stiles said? So that Anies could play Sims with me and his favorite goon? An involuntary grimace twists my mouth. I hate that feeling that my body was no longer mine, that it was just a thing to drug, to modify . . . to use.

March brings me against him; his lips brush my ear. "Island. If I see him again . . . " he murmurs, the words soft but laced with razor-sharp warning.

I bury my face in the cotton of his shirt. "I know. You'll kill him."

"Yes."

TWENTY-EIGHT
THE T-REX

I tried to stay awake as long as possible. Since there was no other outlet to our sexual frustration, March and I did some level-six crosswords together under Dries's disapproving gaze—*buccinator* is one of the most ridiculous words in the English language, by the way, and "solicited by the neonate" isn't a definition, it's an intellectual scam. I eventually got *vanquished* by *dormancy* and 10 hours breezed by at 650 miles per hour.

Still curled against March's shoulder in my seat, I stir and take a bleary look at my surroundings. Someone—probably him—covered me with a purple fleece blanket. It's the click of a lock that fully rouses me. Isabelle exits the bedroom, looking a little . . . flustered. She secures a black hair tie around her messy bun and readjusts her navy blue dress. She greets me with a nervous smile that I return drowsily before settling back against March. His shirt smells of fresh laundry, and he wasn't wearing those jeans last night; he must have changed at some point. He presses a gentle kiss to my forehead. "Good morning, biscuit. Did you sleep well?"

"Yeah, those seats are incredible." I grin, patting the cushy white leather. "What time is it?"

He checks his watch. "Four thirty p.m."

I rub my eyes. "Okay . . . not gonna sleep much tonight—"

"There she is, fresh as morning dew!"

I look up to see Dries toasting me with a cup of fuming coffee whose pleasant aroma soon fills the cabin. He's standing in the bedroom's doorway, looking pleased with himself, as usual. Uncharacteristically, he's not yet wearing his full three-piece suit, only beige linen pants and a clean shirt whose opened top buttons reveal a patch of gray hair.

Hold on. Bedroom. Isabelle. Dries . . .

Rusty gears rotate with slow, painful jolts as my sleepy neurons do the math. My nose bunches. Dries's gap-toothed grin stretches a little wider, a little smugger, if that's even possible. In the galley, Isabelle is zealously fixing meal trays. A rebellious curl springs free from the bun she hastily fixed, and she won't look at me. So I turn to March instead, hammering a silent question. He averts his eyes and clears his throat.

Sweet Jesus, Dries banged the flight attendant while I was sleeping. Less than twenty feet from us, he committed the unthinkable, and now she's going to serve us a meal, and I already know that my omelet is going to taste awkward.

I straighten in my seat and shake my head at Dries, who winks at me in return. I can't believe he pulled that kind of shit when he kept playing outraged nineteenth-century dad with March—God forbid we so much as kissed . . . while he was busy nailing Isabelle!

The dreaded omelet is eaten in silent outrage—mine anyway, because Dries looks peachy, and I figure that after years of celibacy, March has developed the indestructible mental armor of a yogi. I'm sure that whatever he thinks of Dries's stunt, he won't comment. But his plate speaks for him. I take an anxious peek at the artful tableau he's created in the white porcelain. Grapes, watermelon cubes, and blueberries, all sorted apart in perfectly parallel lines. One single blueberry rolls out of line and threatens to touch the omelet: he tucks it back in place. The faint creak of his fork against the plate is nerve-racking. This is a man who's been tested beyond endurance, and all that sorting is the only way he knows how to deal with it.

After we're finished, I give March a hug—one he's earned, regardless of Dries's snort—and go to the bathroom to brush my teeth and freshen up. I'm not touching that shower stall with a ten-foot pole; God knows what happened in there too. I slip on the canvas sneakers Phyllis found for me and strike a ninja pose in front the mirror. Lecherous dads, supervillain uncles: I can handle it all.

In the cabin, March is adjusting the cuffs of a navy blue jacket over his white shirt. I freeze in the doorway as I take in the broad-shouldered silhouette whose back was turned to me in my dreams. Always wearing a navy jacket and dark jeans. Spit-shined shoes. Black leather gloves. I manage a trembling smile. "You were in my living room . . . and there was a pink knife."

A crease forms between March's eyebrows, but the curve of his lips tells me he's happy. "You and I had a bit of a rough start . . ."

"How rough?"

Guilt flashes in his eyes. "I roped you on your bed with your own tights."

My mouth falls open at the same time as Dries's, but while he looks ready to strangle March, it's a giggle that bursts out of me. "What? Seriously?"

"Yes." He nods with a chuckle. "But I had to let you go when you threatened to throw up all over the bed."

I peer up at him from beneath my lashes. "Is that how you seduced me?"

"No, I took you out to eat fried pork and squid-ink ice cream for that. And I showed you my—"

"Enough!" Dries's neck has turned a nice shade of burgundy under his shirt, and his features are taut with meteoric rage.

March turns to him, his expression perfectly blank save for a twitch of his mouth, which etches a dimple in his cheek. "Website."

I grin excitedly, ignoring Dries's menacing glare. "You have a website?"

"We had to close it down," March admits.

"Because you had to disappear and Struthio Security along with you?"

"Yes. It's a pity; we had a lovely brochure—I didn't even really mind that it was an emu instead of an ostrich on the cover. I kept some, as a souvenir."

I take his hand, lacing my fingers with his. "Maybe once this is all over, you can reopen Struthio."

He squeezes my hand back. "Who knows?"

"March?"

"Yes?"

"What's with the ostriches? Is it, like, a fetish?"

●●●

Actually, it's not sexual. They're just March's favorite animal because he likes their soft, thoughtful gaze, and he's convinced that they're smarter than they let on—star-nosed moles only come second, although he admitted to finding them fascinating as well.

I first imagined we'd land in Quito, but we've started our descent toward an airstrip that's been hacked into the jungle, south of a winding brownish river. Dries has cooled down a little, since March is no longer talking about tying me up—I need to ask for details about that, because while he doesn't strike me as a wannabe Christian Grey, I'd rather have some forewarning if I'm dating a potential ropist.

I hold my breath as the jet's deceleration buzzes in my ears. The Gulfstream's wheels caress the runway in one of the smoothest landings I can remember—which is technically not that many. After Isabelle has opened the door and the airstair is in place outside the jet, March and I get up from our seats first and take our respective suitcases, but Dries has a little something to settle first. I feel a pang of sympathy for the young woman as her fingertips trail shyly down the front of his vest. She whispers something in his ear; he smiles, but his eyes remain distant. I don't think he's going to call her.

It will be at least another hour until the sun sets, and on the sunny tarmac, a group of men awaits in front of several Jeeps and pickup trucks. Shirts, jeans, ordinary civilian clothes . . . but those who don't openly carry a gun barely hidden under half-open jackets—

Sadly, I'm getting used to this sort of welcome committee.

"Do they work for the Queen?"

"No," March says. "For one of the Board's members. He lives and operates primarily in South America."

What kind of business our host *operates* remains to be seen . . . I scan the testosterone-fueled crowd on the tarmac. Amid the dark clothes, rugged beards, and leather jackets, a patch of color billows softly in the late-afternoon breeze. A young woman stands, wearing a long white blouse embroidered with multicolored flowers over tiny shorts. My gaze trails down, from the black braid flung over her shoulder to the stripe of bronze skin I glimpse underneath her blouse. Unless it's a trick of the light, she's heavily pregnant under the garment.

The teen—because upon further examination I conclude she can't be over twenty—waves at us excitedly and runs toward the airstair. March responds with a gentle smile; is she someone he knows?

Dries goes first, but she barely acknowledges him. Her almond-shaped eyes are set on me—or is it March?—and she's quivering with excitement, her full lips pressed into an impatient pout. Because I can't just stay stranded up there, I trot down the airstair nervously. The second my feet touch the solid ground, she pounces, pulling me into an excited hug. I blink and breathe a flowery perfume as she squeaks, "Oh my God, you're Island! I wanted to meet you so much!"

I send a questioning look at March, whose mouth opens to offer an explanation, I presume. Before he can do so, however, our hyperactive host drags me away and pulls out a golden smartphone from the back pocket of her shorts. "Selfie!"

She pulls me against her and wraps her arm around my neck, bringing our cheeks together. Once she's adjusted the phone in front of us though, the corners of her mouth fall. She lets go of me and whirls around to glare at March. "*You* don't get to be in the selfie."

March takes a step back and raises his palms in surrender. One, two, three pictures get taken, which she promises she'll send me, and we're led to the car. When he attempts to climb in the same Jeep as me and the girl, March receives another glare—he doesn't get to ride with us either and is relegated to another vehicle with Dries. At this point, I expect someone to show up any moment with a can of spray paint and write "box of shame" on the hood.

Once I'm sitting in the back seat with her and the doors have slammed closed, I overcome my stupor to ask the obvious. "Thank you for welcoming us. But . . . do we know each other?"

She rolls amused eyes at me. "I'm Beatriz!"

As we drive away from the aerodrome on a road crossing that lush valley we saw from the tarmac, I glance at our driver's sunglasses in the mirror, searching his shuttered expression for answers. There are none to be found.

"I'm Antonio's wife!" Beatriz insists.

Here we go again . . . Maybe I should print out warning cards that I'll give to people every time they expect me to recognize them, like deaf people and Jehovah's Witnesses. "I'm sorry," I say with a sad smile. "I've got amnesia. I don't remember you, or Antonio."

Her eyelids flutter in a series of rapid blinks as she digests the news. "It's okay. Maybe they never told you about me anyway, but Antonio . . . he's going to be so sad." She pouts. "Maybe you could pretend you remember him?"

That sounds like the premise of a bad Adam Sandler movie . . . So no. "Beatriz, I'm not sure it'd be right to lie . . . but maybe you can help me and tell me a little more about him?"

Beatriz clasps her hands and nods eagerly—I'm diagnosing either hyperactivity or joie de vivre in this girl, probably both, but I decide I like that. As it turns out, March rides in the Jeep of shame because he tried to kill Antonio a year and half ago . . . and failed to do so when I bravely stepped between Beatriz's love and March's gun. She explains to me that it all started when her big brother, a certain Angel

Somoza, lost his temper upon learning that then-eighteen-year-old Beatriz had been seeing a handsome and tenebrous Mexican hero almost twice her age—Antonio Romos. So Angel hired March to kill Antonio, because that's apparently how he deals with family issues. I'm obviously not going to cast the first stone here.

Anyway, March let Antonio go, who subsequently vanished back in the shadows . . . for about three weeks before resuming his torrid affair with Beatriz, this time with a luxury of precautions—none of which included condoms. Angel's legendary short fuse blew up again when he discovered his sister was pregnant, but this time March was unavailable to shoot Antonio—being presumably dead. Beatriz used her secret weapon—the waterworks—and her brother begrudgingly agreed to let Antonio live if he made his sister an honest woman.

And so, in a couple of weeks, Beatriz Romos will give birth to a little girl whose future uncle, the temperamental Angel, may or may not be an international arms dealer.

"You know we're going to call her Isla," she says, her tone now more subdued. "Because she wouldn't be here if it wasn't for you."

I feel my ears grow a little hot at the compliment. I'm not sure I'm deserving of such honor, especially since I can't even remember the circumstances in which I allegedly saved her husband's life in a heroic display—I'll have to ask for March's version of the events. I stare down at my lap to conceal my embarrassment. "Thank you . . . I'm very honored."

"You deserve it!" she replies, the electric joy that seems to power her returning fast. "I'll show you my ultrasounds. She looks so beautiful. Like a lump, but a beautiful lump, you know?"

I can only nod: I'm pretty sure I'll unleash hell if I dare to question whether a parasitic lump growing inside you like an alien can truly be beautiful. In spite of my lack of enthusiasm, one of my hands moves to rest on my stomach almost instinctively. That's what Anies wanted from me . . . and the idea filled me with horror. But I guess it's different when it's a lump you really want to have, with someone you love. To the best of my knowledge, I never gave the idea any consideration until I saw Beatriz's proud baby bump. I gulp, mentally praying that my biological clock isn't catching up with me at the worst possible time. I frown down at my belly. No, I don't want a lump. Not in the immediate future anyway . . .

"Do you want one too?"

I snap back to reality. Beatriz is watching me, her large brown eyes full of curiosity.

"Um, no. Maybe in a few years." If I can project myself that far in the future, that is.

She draws a compassionate sigh. "I know; you need to find someone first."

I'm about to remark that I *do* have someone—even if she doesn't like him—but for the time I notice that it's gotten a little darker in the car. We passed a few clusters of small houses with tin roofs, but now we've left the road crossing the valley for a narrow trail, and around us, the dying sunlight is now filtering through dense tropical vegetation. "Are we going into the jungle?" I ask.

Beatriz nods. "We're almost there; the Refugio is on the other side of the Rio San Miguel."

As she says this, the Jeep tears through the emerald lace we'd been enveloped in until now. Sure enough, there's a recently built steel bridge crossing over a river reflecting a fiery-pink sunset. Somehow, I doubt that those heavy-duty steel cables and surveillance cameras are the work of the Ecuadorian government . . . The Jeep's wheels clank on metal boards as we drive across until we're back on the rough terrain of the trail. I notice a grayish smudge in the trees, and crane my neck to catch a glimpse of the furry creature hanging upside down from a high branch. "Oh my God, was that a sloth?"

Beatriz grins proudly. "Yes, it's very quiet around here, so they like it. Sometimes they even enter the garden, but I have no idea how they do that. Angel keeps asking Ernesto to check the surveillance tapes because he doesn't like that. He thinks it's personal, that they're trying to defy him."

I plaster a smile on my face to conceal what would otherwise be a wince. The more I hear about Beatriz's volatile brother, the more I worry . . . like when the wall comes in sight. I stare through my window at the tall concrete fortification that just burst into view, slicing neatly through the sea of trees. It must be at least fifteen feet high, topped with barbed wire and, again, cameras—Jurassic Park comes to mind. Are they keeping a T-Rex in there or what?

The Jeep jolts to a stop. Beatriz's hands fidget on her huge belly, and her feet tap the floor mat impatiently as huge steel gates whir open to let us in. When she notices the hesitation on my face, her smile turns a little apologetic. "Angel likes his privacy."

Makes sense. If he's really that bad and he hangs around with that Queen person, the man had better make sure security is tight in his crib. And what a crib it is . . . My nose flattened to the tinted glass, I take in the madness that is Angel Somoza's "Refugio": a Rubik's cube of glass, steel, and concrete in the middle of the jungle. On three floors, long rectangular units pile up, overlap, some connecting to others like bridges. At least one of them contains a fricking pool, which glows a peaceful turquoise through the windows encasing it. All around this marvel of modern architecture, a garden stretches, delimited by a tangle of trees: the little chunk of jungle that's trapped inside the compound behind the walls we passed.

Maybe I should try selling Kalashnikovs to despotic fruitcakes, like Dries said.

The cars stop in front of the villa's entrance, where more goons await. That's when I notice that there's a clear dichotomy going on here: half of the guys follow the same dress code as our driver and his colleagues—jeans or cargo pants, dark shirts—some revealing abundant rugs of chest hair, but none that would ever stand comparison with March's, by the way. There's the occasional gold chain or leather jacket but mostly unostentatious, practical stuff. And then there's the other half . . . A bunch of guys that look like Matrix agents, in identical, perfectly fitting black suits. A couple of rebels do wear their hair in carefully slicked back ponytails, but the rest of them boast short, well-kept haircuts, a far cry from the messy beards and wild locks of many of Somoza's men.

Either Angel couldn't decide over a dress code, or these are someone else's watchdogs . . .

"Antonio!"

Beatriz's loud squeal draws my attention to a man in his midthirties walking toward our car with his arms wide open. Pretty handsome, with short black hair and a little mustache, wearing a burgundy shirt over dark slacks. His most striking feature though is the tattoos covering his face. Various numbers on his forehead and his neck, delicate tears running down his cheeks, and a crown on his chin—that I first mistook for a goatee. Beatriz opens her door to jump out of the car and directly into his arms. On his hands, I notice more numbers, bullets, and a heart transpierced by three swords. She didn't specify what Antonio did for a living: I'm starting to suspect he's in the same business March used to be in . . .

Beatriz pulls her husband close for a deep kiss while I step out of the Jeep. When they break their lip-lock and he sees me, Antonio's smile becomes a full grin. He extends one arm to invite me into a group hug. From the corner of my eye, I notice that March and Dries exited the Jeep of shame. I briefly hesitate before trusting my instincts and allowing Antonio to wrap his arm around my shoulders. The greeting that rolls off of his tongue is enveloped in the same warm Latin accent as Beatriz's. "Let me see you, *querida*. So tough even the Lions couldn't eat you."

"I've heard you're pretty tough yourself," I say, raising an eyebrow in amusement.

He shrugs, his expression turning mysterious. "*Antonio* is immortal."

Against his chest, Beatriz giggles in response. I love the way he puts emphasis on his own name like a brand. This guy sounds like a lot of fun. March walks to us, but Dries keeps a safe distance, eyeing Antonio with a sort of watchful contempt. The culprit lets got of Beatriz and me to shake hands with March, who takes on the offer with a good-natured smile.

"And it looks like death spat you out too, *Surafricano.*" A hard glint flashes in Antonio's gaze as he adds, "Good thing you're not here for me. There can only be one immortal . . ."

March chuckles. "I'll remember to bring my sword next time."

That's when Antonio seems to take notice of Dries standing behind March. His expression sobers, and he strides to him, a challenge gleaming in his eyes as he extends his hand.

Dries stiffens and adjusts his linen jacket with a sharp tug. "You can't be serious. That clown cunt fired a rocket in my dining room; I don't even know why I'm letting him live," he informs no one in particular, before spinning on his heels and marching into the villa, right past a guy who was apparently coming to welcome us and stands there dumbfounded.

I blink at March and Antonio alternately. "What is he talking about?"

That's when the shift occurs on Antonio's features that tells me he's figured something is wrong.

March relieves me of the burden of having to inform Antonio that I remember nothing of his glorious deeds. "Island suffered memory loss. She might sometimes need a little context on past events."

Antonio's expression softens. I read pity in his gaze, and I hate that . . .

"I hope you at least haven't forgotten me," a soft female voice remarks with a touch of amusement.

All eyes set on the pair of newcomers standing in the villa's doorway. The man with the indigo shirt, there's nothing familiar about him. He must be in his thirties, and at first he reminds me of Pirate Morgan because of his wavy black hair and the thick stubble covering his jaw. The woman though . . . her presence makes me shudder with a sense of déjà vu. Faint lines around her mouth suggest she must be in her late forties, but her honey skin is otherwise flawless, and her white tapered dress hugs lean curves. Black tresses fall onto her shoulders, framing a single pearl around her neck. It's like a photograph, something once printed in my brain and long forgotten. I know, without a doubt, that I've seen that pearl before.

Her gaze sets on Dries, balls-shriveling cold. "I believe we need to talk."

There it is, the T-Rex they're guarding in these walls.

TWENTY-NINE
ANGEL EYES

This has yet to be stated explicitly, but I have little doubt the woman we're following inside the villa's lobby is the Queen. Which would make the man with the scary face . . .

"Angel, you have to tell me who decorated this place," the T-Rex says in her silky voice as our little group makes its way across the heart of the Refugio, a hall whose glass walls showcase the illuminated garden outside. A complex chandelier made of hundreds of white origamis hangs above our heads, dominating the room. She's right, by the way: Angel's furniture is an interesting blend of modern and retro with very little color, mostly a camaïeu of grays with touches of black lacquer and reddish wood. Nice stuff.

Angel—because yes, that guy in the indigo shirt is apparently

Beatriz's fearsome brother—flicks his wrist in the direction of one of the henchmen sandwiching our procession. "Ernesto . . . you find the name of the architect."

Ernesto, a fiftysomething guy with a loose linen suit and an elaborate gray mustache, takes note on his phone with a nod.

We're led down a hallway sloping to a set of tall black doors. The walls around us look like a thick concrete tomb—I'm guessing this is some sort of bunker under the villa. When one of his goons opens the doors to reveal a large meeting room, Angel freezes and, for the first time, turns around.

I gulp.

A little shorter than March, all lean muscles and hawkish angles, Angel Somoza isn't good-looking in the conventional sense of the term. His high cheekbones are a rough terrain, plowed by old acne scars. A deep track runs from his Cupid's bow to his ear, clearly the result of some grisly punishment—the cut looks too deep and too straight to be the product of a mere accident. And his eyes . . . let's just say I'm glad it's Beatriz he's burning holes into with that dark, intense gaze. She doesn't flinch though; huddled against Antonio, she sustains her brother's cold glare bravely.

His scarred mouth twitches in apparent irritation. A deep, husky voice echoes around the concrete walls, unnervingly loud in the silence. "Beatriz. Ve a tu cuarto." *Beatriz. Go to your room.*

Her nose bunches, and her hand squeezes Antonio's, but she eventually looks away, defeated by the command without a fight.

Aw, *come on*, what is this, the eighteenth century? I'm keenly aware that it's a disastrous idea to step in, but my mouth starts working before I can stop myself. "Should the two of us go too?" I ask tartly, pointing to the T-Rex.

Angel's eyes widen briefly, as do his guest's, but she looks mostly amused while cold furor flares in his black irises. I ball my fists and inch closer to March, just in case.

"Your woman can go too," he growls in March's direction, ignoring me completely.

Around us, Beatriz and Angel's goons await the next move with bated breath while Dries runs a hand across his face, perhaps to conceal some amusement of his own. March's shoulders lift in the slightest shrug. "I'm sorry. I'm afraid I have no control over this untamed Amazon."

I press my lips together in a desperate effort not to smile. At last, Angel deigns to look at me, gauge me. And I wilt. I can't deny he oozes charisma, in the same frightening way Dries does, but when he locks that stygian gaze on me, I feel my spine turn to a popsicle. I grit my teeth and force myself to stare back. This is the hill I've chosen to die on, for feminism! "I'm staying," I snap. "And Beatriz is an adult; she's past the age to get sent to her room."

Angel takes a shuddering breath that makes his nostrils flare, and next to me, March tenses. Okay, this *is* the hill I'll die on. If Angel looks at girls like that, they probably end up chained in his basement. And if that's the look reserved for his enemies . . . I doubt he has that many left. A soft giggle dispels the electricity in the air like a breeze. Angel's eyebrows pinch in confusion at Beatriz, who's smiling shyly while Antonio whispers something suave in her ear. She nods and allows him to turn her around, toward the lobby. As they walk away together, he looks back one last time, a challenging glint in his eyes. I'm guessing the message here is basically, *I know how to handle your sister, and you owe me one.*

Angel flashes me a contemptuous look. "Are we done?"

Look at that . . . Stellar macho douche Angel Somoza now addresses me directly. Like a real person. I stand a little straighter. "I guess so."

Inside the meeting room, Ernesto fumbles with the remote to a fat multiscreen display covering one of the walls. I swallow not to drool. I want that; I want it so bad . . . We all sit around a mile-long glass table, at the end of which the T-Rex is given a place of honor, in an oversize black leather chair. She crosses her arms, waiting for the screens to light up. The aerial picture of a vast industrial complex appears. I recognize the octagonal shape of Saraya's facility. The launching ramp is clearly visible at the center of a wide concrete plate, along with a cluster of buildings.

Angel points to the picture. "*This* is my problem. And I understand it is yours too, my Queen."

I glance at March, who gives a little nod of confirmation. It *is* her. I watch her with renewed fascination, wondering what it took to get where she did, how many sacrifices . . . Even now, I have the intuition that this woman holds more power than many heads of state ever will. A deceptively gentle smile curves her red lips. "I'm sorry to hear that, Angel. What did Mr. Keasler ever do to upset you so?"

Next to him, that Ernesto guy presses a button on the remote, and the aerial picture turns into a 3-D model, which he rotates to focus on a river bending around the facility—possibly the one we crossed coming here.

"He needs the water," Angel begins. "Their pumps are here, and here." As he says this, red crosshairs flash in two different points, where concrete structures can be seen rising from the brownish water. "He doesn't want anyone snooping around Saraya, and he's trying to lock up a twenty-mile perimeter." This time a red line snakes through the jungle, encasing the facility. "He blew up my airstrips and killed my men. I lose time and money reorganizing my shipments to Colombia, and I see *his* men, patrolling *my* land, threatening *my* people"—a snarl distorts his scar—"all the way to Palma Roja."

The rumble of a low chuckle rises from Dries's chest. He tilts his head and gives Angel a look that's part amusement, part paternal scorn. "So he steps on your feet, and he gets in the way of the gifts you send to your little narco friends. That's terrible, Angel . . . terrible. Well, hear this: if our hunch about what he's cooking up in that space center of his proves correct, all your troubles will be gone. Along with you and everything that stands between here and Quito."

"We think he stole a ship," I say quickly when the rage in Angel's eyes threatens to reach all the way down to his clenched fists. "With a very powerful nuclear reactor. And he probably has warheads too, at least twelve intercontinental JL-3s."

March chimes in as well. "The JL-3s contain both multiple warheads and decoys. Think about it: even if he used a single one . . ."

Angel's fingers uncurl, and for a second, I get the impression that he's getting pale.

The Queen offers him a compassionate smile. "We need your help, my dearest friend, and this time, the stakes are bigger than any of us."

He sits down and leans back in his chair, eyeing Dries and March warily. "I have men; I have toys; you already know that. What else do you want?"

"Well," the Queen begins, "Mr. Erwin landed in Quito this morning with a little escort of his own, but he certainly has no sanction to raid Saraya with mercenaries . . . unless we give him reason to."

"You want us to break in and search for that ship?" Angel asks. "It's risky, but maybe through the water system. The pipes are large enough, if we blow up the pumps . . ."

"No," the Queen replies, her voice pure silk. "In truth, what I want is to pull out every single inch of Mr. Keasler's intestines and keep him alive to watch." Her impeccably manicured nails rap on the glass slowly. "But before I get to enjoy this spectacle, we will indeed need to find *Odysseus.* Once we have hard evidence, leave the rest to the Americans. All I want is Keasler alive."

I avert my eyes with a soft gulp. I could almost feel for Anies . . .

An oddly tender smile softens Dries's features. "I told you you'd be glad to see me again," he tells the Queen.

The corners of her mouth tug down in response. "Bring me your brother, and when that is done, if you're still alive, I may consider forgiving you. That being said, it would be more elegant for you to die there."

I look back and forth between the two of them. *Did he . . . ?* "What did he do to you?" I ask her.

As soon as my question echoes in the room, March clears his throat, and pretty much everyone around the table blanches.

I blink. "What? I actually want to know."

Next to me, Dries is evidently stifling a laugh while March's mouth purses tightly. "I'm terribly sorry for this," he tells the Queen.

Whatever I said, she considers with benevolence though—real or fake, that's anyone's guess.

Angel squints his pitch-black eyes at me in an evident attempt to induce self-combustion. My skin prickles, and I actually wonder if it's working, if that terrifying gaze has that power. "You don't address the Queen unless she asks you a question."

I frown. "But you and Dries—"

"I have killed enough men for her to earn that right," he hisses.

That still doesn't tell me what Dries did, but March looks genuinely embarrassed. I decide to drop the issue for his sake. I lower my eyes. "I'm sorry I asked, ma'am."

"Your father betrayed me," she says quietly. "He and your mother stole something from me."

My head snaps up. I hear March again, recounting the life I don't remember. *Dries wanted to capture her, to recover a diamond they'd stolen together.* The Queen was the one who missioned my mother to steal it. It all . . . "It all started with you," I say, my voice brittle.

She nods. "And it ends with me, it would seem."

I wonder if that sudden vision of my mother smiling in a car is real or if my brain reconstructed it based on March's account. My mother lets go of the wheel. Her head lolls softly; she slumps in her seat. She's asleep, and blood runs slowly, like a dark river, from the wound on her temple. Drop after drop, *drip, drip* . . . The hood is blue, and flames are rising because we hit another car that was parked at a gas station. I see myself die . . . until March's arms are around me, the smell of mint as he pulls me out of the car. And it all started for the Queen's diamond, because of Anies's anger, Dries's weakness.

I'm shaking, and the dripping won't stop, rolling down my cheeks, hitting the glass table silently. And March's arms are around me again, anchoring me, like that very first time in Tokyo. "It's all right . . ."

No. It's not. They're all silent, staring at me. I feel their disdain, their pity, and I'm suddenly angry at them. At Dries, the Queen . . . I wipe my eyes with the back of my hand and set my sights on Angel, the arms dealer who's going to save the world. "You've been fighting

Anies for months, just for your little chunk of territory; how do you think you'll manage to break into Saraya?"

He glares daggers at me. I don't feel them. "Who do you think you are—"

"It is, in fact, an excellent question," the Queen interrupts. "And the answer is very simple: we will need a solid diversion, something that would require his men's full attention." Next to me, March raises a suspicious eyebrow as she goes on. "I'm going to deliver the three of you to Mr. Keasler."

Dries's eyes close briefly, like he's trying to contain a fury that might otherwise surge and overflow.

March's fist clenches on the table, and he breaks the rule. "Dries and I will go, but Island must stay here."

I place my hand on his, squeezing it with all the strength he gave me. "No . . . she's right. Anies wants me back. If I return, he gets what he wants, and he's going to be focused on me, at least for a little while. It could be the opening we need."

March shakes his head; he's breathing fast. "No, that's . . . I won't—"

"I'll be surrounded by the best," I say with a quivering smile. "What could go wrong?"

Angel shrugs. "Nothing ever goes wrong with me." I'm certain that no bigger lie has ever been told . . .

To everyone's surprise, the Queen gets up from her chair and walks around the table to March. She places a hand on his shoulder. There's something tender about the way she touches him, and he looks up at her in that way I know will make her feel like they're alone in the room. I fight a pang of jealousy.

"You served me well all those years," she purrs. "To the best of your abilities, I believe." Her thumb strokes his deltoid back and forth. He's not moving, and I'm boiling. "I ask for one final sacrifice."

He sustains her gaze, his expression open and guileless, as he answers, "No."

One of her eyebrows arches and quivers. Her nails dig into his shirt, and I just can't. I grab her hand. Angel explodes from his chair, and half of the goons around us reach either to their back or under their jacket. I don't let go. "I'll go," I say, steadying my voice and locking eyes with her. "Not for you. Because *I* need closure. And March doesn't owe you any more sacrifices. You should be thanking him for remaining faithful to you through good and bad."

Under my fingers, I feel her grip on March's shoulder lessen. "It's always the women," she says softly. "Men are never that strong."

With those final words, she lets go of him and leaves the meeting room silently, without looking back.

After the doors have closed behind her, everyone in the room stares at me, speechless, some wide-eyed, some with their faces scrunched up in mild confusion. March too seems in shock; he looks at me like he's seeing me for the first time.

I comb back a strand of hair behind my ear with nervous fingers. "What?"

Dries's baffled expression morphs into a grin. He shakes his head as if he'd just downed something incredibly strong. "Nothing . . . I believe there's one last point we didn't discuss."

Angel settles back in his seat and reverts to his default "cold angry mask #1". "Speak."

Dries raises his palms questioningly. "In what plane of reality does Anies accept a gift from Guita without suspecting a trap?"

Angel's lips curl into a terrifying parody of a smile. "It won't be a gift, and it won't come from her."

THIRTY
ICARUS

If this was a movie, we'd be at the scene where the frame freezes with a record-scratch sound effect before my off-screen voice asks, "How did it come to this?" and then answers my own question with some snarky comment about terrible life choices and too much jungle juice.

So yeah, how did I end up in Angel Somoza's dreaded basement—dirty, sweaty, bloody, stripped down to my underwear, and handcuffed to a steel chair? My bare toes curling on the dusty floor, I whimper through the rag gagging me as the razor blade caresses me, trailing across my chest, up my neck and then my jaw, slowly, leisurely. His fingers wrap around my throat and direct my face to the camera lens gleaming in the darkness.

Against mine, his cheek feels hot and rough, the bristles abrasive. I inhale his scent, something aggressive, made of spice and sweat. The blade threatens to bite into my skin as he speaks to the camera. His voice rumbles through me, raising goose bumps all over my body. " . . . So now, my friend, we negotiate."

I grit my teeth when chains rattle in a corner of the room, followed by the dull thud of a powerful punch. A coughing groan echoes in the concrete tomb as Antonio and another guy I recognize as Beatriz's driver drag March and Dries in front of the camera, their clothes blood-soaked rags clinging to their flesh. Angel moves away from me, but my relief is short-lived: he delivers a few vicious kicks to March's and Dries's stomachs and sides while his goons film every growl, every gasp of agony.

After he's wrapped his little home movie, Angel makes a note that it would have been more realistic if he'd castrated either of them. On my skin, the sweat now feels icy.

Antonio holds out his hand to Dries, who mumbles he'd sooner die. March gets to his feet and is at my side in an instant, unfastening the handcuffs locking my wrists to the chair's bars. I spring up and wrap my arms around his chest. Behind me, I feel Dries pat my head briefly with a gruff reassurance that we're done.

I squeeze March harder and feel his tension thrumming through me: it might all be a little act meant to convince the Lions that Angel caught their most wanted and wants to bargain for control over his territory, but the dirt covering our bodies is real, and I know this basement and the filthy clothes March is wearing are probably the closest thing to hell for him.

He locks eyes with Angel. "I appreciate your . . . dedication. However"—his hand wraps around my waist possessively—"that was perhaps a little more *realistic* than I expected."

Antonio nods in agreement, and Angel ducks his chin, a smirk curling his lips through the dark stubble on his jaw. "The devil in love . . ." he drawls before his head snaps up. "You get one. Because if another man touched my woman like that, I would cut him up . . . slowly."

Before I can ask what March is supposedly getting, he lets go of me, and the punch flies, lightning fast and powerful enough to send

Angel crashing onto the chair I was strapped to less than a minute ago. A satisfied grin stretches the tattoos on Antonio's cheeks, but none of Angel's men otherwise lift a finger to help him up. I think they know better. Sprawled on the chair, Angel massages his jaw with a low, threatening chuckle. "Now all of you get out of here before I change my mind and kill you."

•••

"You don't worry about anything!"

Even if I wanted to worry, it'd be difficult to resist the hurricane that is an angry Beatriz. She ran to us when we reappeared in the villa's lobby following our trip to the basement. Behind her, a young woman in a frilly red apron came to the rescue with three towels for us and is now rolling frightened eyes as she takes in our state of disarray.

"I-it's okay, Beatriz," I stammer, taking my towel. "Please don't be upset . . . Stress isn't good for your baby."

"I'm not upset. I'm pissed!" she squeaks, glowering at Antonio, who stands behind us with an air of genuine contrition—behold, the power of an irate wife. "¡Vete y golpea a Angel por mí!" she orders. *Go and punch Angel for me!*

He cringes and raises his hands in a pacifying gesture. "Quizás no esta noche, mi vida . . . " *Maybe not tonight, love of my life . . .*

Meanwhile, Dries has taken his towel and, in perfect Spanish, asks the young maid if she can lead him to his room. She nods eagerly, and I refrain from a face-palm when I overhear him compliment her hair as they walk away . . .

Beatriz eventually drags me to my bedroom while Antonio guides March down a hallway toward a secondary bathroom. I actually wanted to go with him and make sure he was okay, but I'm starting to realize Beatriz exerts the same kind of power as her brother, only through soft bullying rather than senseless violence. Less than a minute after my abduction, I'm standing in one of the cubes I saw from outside, a spacious bedroom whose glass windows open to the garden. Veil curtains protect our privacy, billowing softly in an

251

evening breeze that carries the heady scent of grass and flowers into the room.

I look around at the king-sized bed and the minimalistic fifties furniture. I wonder how many guns Angel had to sell to purchase a Le Corbusier chaise longue . . .

Beatriz switches on a mile-wide flat-screen and selects a track on YouTube. "You like Delfin Quishpe?" she asks with a cute smile that would almost make me forget her previous outburst.

I have no idea who that is. Apparently that guy wearing a fringe leather jacket, a cowboy hat, and hopping around to the sound of what can best be described as . . . Andean techno. He's not even really singing at first; he just yells stuff. Kitschy doesn't even begin to describe it.

Beatriz gazes at the screen, her hands joined on her belly while her hips jerk instinctively to the rhythm. "I love him . . ."

"Me too," I admit. It's true. The guy's bizarre dance moves and off-tune singing have . . . enraptured me. I watch him, slack-jawed, vaguely aware of Beatriz going to the bathroom to turn on the taps of a long stone bathtub. Jesus, his name is written in huge capital letters on his pant legs. This Ecuadorian hero is fearless.

"Your suitcase is in the closet," she says, "and there's a surprise for you in the bathroom."

"Thank you . . . You really shouldn't have."

She comes closer and pulls me into a loose hug. "Antonio says I have to go. He'll take me to the airport tonight. We're going to his place in San Pancho."

I pat her baby bump awkwardly. "Maybe it's safer for your little lump. The man we're looking for, he's . . ."

"I know. Angel says Keasler is crazy. I think he's actually afraid." She giggles, but this time the joy doesn't quite reach her eyes. "I mean, Angel of all people . . ."

I understand then that it's not just about telling me good-bye. She's scared of losing that strange brother of hers, who sells antitank ammo but thinks the sloths breaking into his garden are after him, who gives and takes with equal ferocity. I return her hug in earnest.

"It's gonna be okay. If anyone can pull this off, it's March and Dries. Plus Angel is gonna help us."

"I know." She sighs. "You're still kids, all of you."

I look at her curiously; it would have never crossed my mind to call someone like March a kid, much less Dries.

"Antonio, he understands," she goes on, her gaze falling to the ample bump under her blouse, "that he can't be a kid anymore."

I'm tempted to contradict her, but maybe she's not entirely wrong. Would I make the same choices if a little lump freeloaded on me? I think of my mother . . . who tried to flee with me to Tokyo, to escape Dries, to protect me. Did she decide to grow up too late?

"You should tell Angel that," I eventually say. "Before you go, you should tell him you want him to leave the playground."

Beatriz doesn't answer. This time her nose bunches, and tears roll down her cheeks.

•••

She's gone. Antonio dried Beatriz's tears and took her to the car. Dries said he was a clown who once blew up his dining room with a bazooka, but the man who told me good-bye tonight was more than that. There was certainly a bit of playfulness in his brown eyes as he called me *querida* and made me promise to come to him if I ever got tired of March—thank God Beatriz took that joke well . . . But there was also gravity, when he asked me one last time if I wanted to change my mind.

I didn't. I'll stay a kid a little longer, but Antonio has officially become a dad.

After they were gone, I went to the bathroom at last. The tub was full and Beatriz's surprise sat on a wicker armchair, wrapped in a red satin ribbon: an elegant black leather toiletry bag . . . filled to the brim with strange and wonderful things. I tossed a handful of bath bombs in the tub and dove in—or so to speak, because if you dive face-first into a stone tub, you die.

Soaking chin deep, lulled by the birdcalls echoing in the jungle, I relax completely. My body gives up, dissolves in the fragrant water.

Through the sheer muslin curtains, I gaze at the darkened garden sculpted by the light of the torches, bloodred hibiscus flowers and leaves shivering in a soft breeze. It's only been four days since my last bath, but those ninety-six hours have felt like an eternity. I died, and I was reborn since, so I indulge to celebrate this new start in life. I test every single product Beatriz gave me. Exfoliating gel, face cream, hand cream, foot cream: I spend at least an hour scrubbing and slathering every inch of my body with mysterious substances.

After I'm finished, I contemplate myself in the mirror with a sense of deep satisfaction, feeling clean, new. I wrap a fluffy white towel around my body and smile to myself when it brushes my now-baby-smooth legs. A blush creeps to my cheeks; I've shaved places I know I'll sorely regret to have subjected to such treatment in a couple of days, but for now . . . the flat-chested, bruise-covered war prisoner looking back at me in the mirror is the epitome of sexy.

Prepare your old ass, Anies, for I wear pineapple lip balm and used a questionable Brazilian cream that claims it'll make my nipples pinker: Island Chaptal is back!

When I step out of the bathroom, the first thing I notice is March's navy jacket, neatly laid on the chaise longue. The window is still open, and through the milky veil of the curtains, I see him, standing on the terrace with his arms crossed, enjoying the garden's quietude. He's changed back into a perfectly pressed white shirt and dark jeans whose creases appear to have been ironed extensively—maybe to make up for the twenty minutes of hygienic hell Angel put him through. I tiptoe to him, but his sixth sense kicks in, and he turns around before I've even reached the window. Dammit.

A tender smile pinches his dimples when he sees me, and I feel myself melt a little. It's the calm before the storm: by dawn, the Lions will receive the product of Angel's directing efforts, and all the players will gather for a poker game where the loser gets nuked. Until then, I wish time could slow down. I want to be alone with him in that room forever, warm, safe. He walks to me and trails the back of his knuckles down my arm. Delicious shivers dance across my skin in the wake of his touch.

"Do you have everything you need?" he asks.

"Yeah, Beatriz spoiled me."

"Excellent." He's still smiling, but there's sadness lingering in his eyes, creasing lines on his brow. He knows it too, that we can't stop time . . .

It could be the effect of the mysterious nipple cream, but gazing into in all that blue, I feel strong, happy, and I want the same for him. I want to share this feeling with him, reassure him that I love him, and that we're gonna be okay, somehow.

I want us closer . . . connected.

I'm barely conscious of the movement of my hands undoing the towel. It slips from my body, falls to the floor with a whisper. The second after, the breeze raises goose bumps on my chest, and my shoulders jerk with the instinctive need to cover myself, but I don't, because March is looking at my naked body, silent, his features frozen in an unreadable mask.

When he ducks his head and moves away, I think that maybe I was too bold and made a terrible mistake. He walks to the dimmer switch and grazes it. The light bathing me becomes comfortable darkness, dim rays streaking the room, licking my skin. Then he takes his phone from his jeans pocket and taps the screen twice before setting it on the desk. A faint buzz signals that the volume has been turned off. I swallow softly.

He returns to me, and this time I'm no longer afraid. His hands glide around my waist, down to the back of my legs, to pick me up. I look up at his jaw, outlined by a ray of light, as he carries me to the bed and lays me down on the mattress carefully. My pulse is thrumming fast under my temples in breathless anticipation.

March sits by my side and bends to brush his lips to my forehead, trailing down my nose, my lips. He pauses to kiss me deeply before his mouth resumes its journey. I arch against him when he reaches my neck. My hands fumble blindly for the buttons of his shirt; he helps me, and soon it slides down his shoulders. I smell soap and warm skin, something that's just him. The moment my palms splay on the warm rug on his chest, an ecstatic grin tugs at my cheeks. I stroke those silky, springy curls over and over while, in a moment of pure transgression, March tosses his shirt on a nearby armchair. It lies in a heap, wrinkled. I register the rustle of his belt sliding out of the loops of his jeans before it joins the shirt, similarly discarded.

When his mouth finds mine again, there's no longer any doubt that we're past folding things. Past self-control. I wrap my arms around his neck as his lips seek mine, tugging and nibbling. I taste the mint on his tongue, and I want more. Slowly, he lifts me up until I'm straddling his lap. I caress his hair and let my fingertips trail down to the lion on his shoulder while we break the kiss to catch our breaths.

I smile against the corner of his mouth. "I love you, Mr. November . . . and I really want you naked."

March buries his face in my neck, his voice down to a husky sigh as he replies, "I love you too . . . I love you . . . so much."

Those precious words wash over me like a warm wave, seep under my skin, and I hold on to him as he moves atop me. His lips barely leave mine as the rest of his clothes hit the floor. It's official: I've introduced a little spark of chaos into the perfect order of his life, and I have no regrets.

It's exactly the way I dreamed it, his skin merging with mine, heated kisses and soft bites as he works his way down, exploring sensitive territory that's entirely his. I throw my head back, and my fingers dig into his scalp when his head disappears under the covers. His hands linger on my breasts, unwilling to let go of the prize, but his mouth . . . *Oh my God* . . . Yes, it's definitely going down. A trembling exhale makes my stomach dip when his lips graze my inner thigh. My hands reach for his, gripping them tight.

An appreciative growl rises from under the comforter, before I see stars and fuzzy unicorns. Disjointed thoughts collide in my mind like a chime; I wonder if he knows exactly where and how to touch me because we've done this before. Then I can't think anymore. There's pure sunshine between my legs, pulsing through my veins. Bright spots dance under my eyelids, and inside me, something coils and coils . . . My mouth parts in a silent scream until sounds overflow and spill from my lips, culminating in a high-pitched moan. It's over too soon, and I crash back to Earth, in the bed, still holding March's hands with a trembling grip.

As he emerges from under the covers, a knowing smile on his lips, I take several gulps of air. My body goes limp, spent from the high—except for my legs; they're still shaking a little. March molds his body to mine, nuzzling my neck and stroking my thigh while I recover.

"How do you feel?" he asks, his voice laced with a suave undercurrent that tells me he already knows the answer to that question.

"Eeek!"

A thick silence falls in the bedroom. We look at each other.

"Th-that wasn't me," I stammer. The endorphins clouding my brain are now dissipating, quickly replaced by confusion.

March blinks. "I know, biscuit . . ."

"Eeeek!"

This time the plaintive squeak whips us both to a sitting position. We look around the room for the source of the noise.

I roll to the edge of the mattress. "I think it's coming from under the bed."

March gets up to check, and I indulge in some shameless ogling in spite of the gravity of the situation. That's a damn fine butt . . . on a body that a Greek sculptor would have carved in marble for posterity. He kneels by the bed with a frown, his eyes scanning the shadows, until his eyebrows jump. I peer anxiously as he reaches under the bed and the squeaking intensifies. *What the hell?*

When March rises to his feet, my mouth falls open in silent shock, and two thoughts flash through my mind. The first one is that we are indeed cursed: dark forces work against us to ensure that I'll never lose my virginity, and March will forever tread a path of thorns and utter frustration. The second one . . . is that someone needs to come up with a calendar of hot, naked men holding sloths. That stuff would sell like fake piercings at Hot Topic.

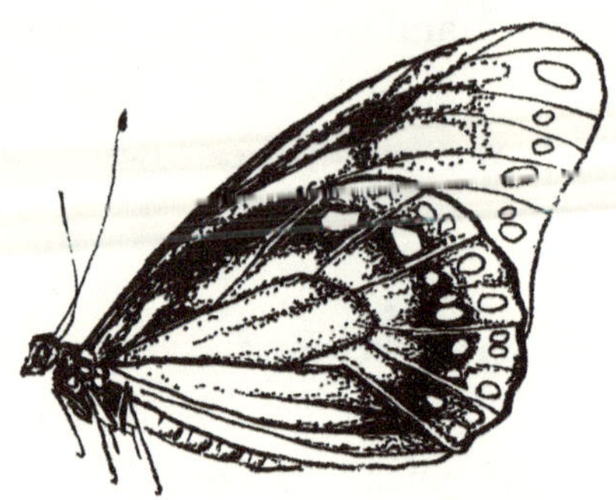

THIRTY-ONE
THE CROSS

Yep. A goddamn sloth.

In March's arms, the furry little guy—I'm not entirely sure if it's a he or a she, by the way: there's nothing sticking out—has stopped squeaking and is now thrashing . . . very slowly. Its short legs pedal uselessly against March's stomach while its lanky arms curl around his shoulders.

"Um . . . it must have sneaked in when I was in the bath. Beatriz told me they sometimes manage to enter the garden," I venture. No wonder Angel hates them, if they hide under his bed too while he does . . . whatever it is that he does to women with those terrifying eyes of his.

March doesn't reply. He stares down at the beatific smile

permanently etched on the creature's lips, his expression something halfway between befuddlement and dejection. The face of a modern Icarus who was about to touch the stars when a squeaking sloth burned his wings and sent him plummeting to the ground. My gaze trails to his lower body, and I bite my lower lip in disappointment. Yeah . . . everything is going down.

I leave the bed, pick up my towel from the floor, and cover myself. "I'll dress and take him back to the trees. I'm sure he can find his way out."

"I'm certain he will," March concurs, in a flat, remote voice.

With a compassionate wince, I extend my arms and allow our unexpected voyeur to latch onto my body. "I'm really sorry about that . . . but I won't be long," I say, stroking the strangely rough fur covering the small body—maybe it's a baby? The sloth is lighter than I expected and sort of . . . limp, like it's barely holding on to me in spite of its long claws. I suppose it's—understandably—freaked out.

A muscle tics in March's jaw. "It's . . . all right, biscuit. I suppose these things happen."

I'm afraid the curse is actually ours alone, but I'm not going to tell him that because he looks crestfallen enough as it is. Better get the sloth to safety before it gets shot.

•••

I slipped on a pair of panties, a light cotton dress, and my sneakers to go free Hadrian—I decided that would be its name. I'm not sure why, but I think it sounds cute. Ignoring the strange or otherwise amused looks a few of Angel's guards send my way, I hurry across the garden to the nearest tree. I don't care what they think—or rather I prefer not to imagine—I have a sloth to save, and then I'm gonna run back to that bedroom, tear my clothes off, and jump on March! I'll let him take the lead right afterward though, because obviously, he's the most qualified of the two of us.

Dammit. The guards won't stop staring at me . . . I hope no one actually ever mentions the incident in public. I'll probably have to change my name and go prowl the badlands, alone on my Harley. Like a renegade.

Hadrian alerts me that we've found the perfect tree with a faint squeak. He's right: a ground light gilds the rough bark, lighting up a path back into the safety of thick foliage. Just what we need. I help him latch to the trunk and watch him slowly climb up. I wiggle my forefinger at his departing butt and hiss, "Yeah, that's right, back to the jungle, mister. And you'd better pray I don't find you under my bed again!"

"What in the world are you doing, little Island?"

I whirl around in mild panic. Sweet Jesus, there's a witness to eliminate! Dries is standing on the lawn a few feet away, shadowed by a pair of palm trees. When he moves into the light, I notice that he too must have been chilling a bit. His white shirt hangs lose over a pair of linen slacks.

"Um, I was just . . ." I shake my head to collect myself. "We found a sloth in our room, and I went to help him back into the trees."

His eyes turn to slits. "*We?*"

"March and I," I clarify.

Under his silvery beard, his lips go thin. "I see . . ."

I give a tentative smile. "You don't need to be like that, you know."

"You mean a responsible, concerned parent?"

Uncontrollable laughter shakes my frame in response, and it takes me a good thirty seconds to recover under Dries's irritated stare. "Sorry . . . sorry about that. But yeah, what I'm trying to say is that you don't need to play dad. I'm old enough to—"

"You're vulnerable."

I blink in surprise. There's no contempt to be found in his admission, only raw anguish. Deep lines of worry wrinkle his brow, crease his eyelids, and I recall with a shiver the way he exploded back in Finland, when he realized what Anies had done to me. It's easy to forget that Dries is a human being because he hides it so well most of the time; everything seems to glide over him like on the scales of a fish. But it doesn't. The pain, the blood, it ravages him from the inside, and I see that devastation now, carving its way out.

I glance back at the darkened window and the room in which March still awaits. Such is our curse . . . I sigh and take a step toward Dries. "Do you want to walk?"

He gives me his arm like an old-fashioned gentleman, and we tread in silence across Angel's lawn, away from the ground lights and the guard, in the comfort of obscurity. We eventually sit together under a tree, near a patch of fragrant orchids.

"Think of it this way," I say as Dries settles against the trunk, stretching his legs in the grass. "I could have fallen madly in love with Angel. Wouldn't that be marginally worse?"

"I should have strangled him with his own cross back there." He grunts.

"His cross?"

"He hides it under his shirt. He's a *Catholic*." He spits that last word like it's actually worse than being an arms dealer.

I shrug. "Okay . . . whatever floats his boat. What I mean is that I'm an adult, I make choices, for better or worse, and you can't protect me from everything and everyone. Also you don't get to criticize March when you *banged* the flight attendant practically *right* under our noses. I can't believe you did that . . . Seriously!"

His lips curl in the dark. "She was a fine little thing."

I let myself fall on the lawn. "Can you at least feign contrition?"

"I never apologize." He chuckles. "That's my religion."

I let his words sink in, gazing at the star-studded night sky, the crushing beauty of space one can only witness in the absence of any light pollution. "Dries."

"Little Island."

"What happened with Alexander Morgan? With his family?"

He doesn't say anything at first. I register some rustling, and he moves to lie by my side. "I was under the impression that you already knew . . ."

A wave of sadness washes over me, that numbs me, engulfs me whole. "March said you had Morgan's family killed when he was twenty-two. His parents and his little sister. He said that Morgan tried to use me to take revenge on you, and you shot him, and you . . . you took his eye out to punish him." My eyelids briefly flutter shut as I remember those minutes of overpowering fear I spent alone with Morgan and his demons, back in the dark room. "I think that's why he went crazy."

"Are you making excuses for him?"

"No. I'm just trying to understand."

Because if my father truly killed a sixteen-year-old girl and her mother in cold blood . . . I don't know how I can deal with that. It hits a raw nerve, makes me think of my mother.

His chest heaves, and the deep exhale that follows smells faintly of the cigar he must have smoked before he joined me. "He's probably not the only monster I created. There're two things you can never fully control in our business: side casualties, and . . . what you might call the ripples. Everything that will unfold once the job is done."

I shift to look at his profile, barely outlined by the distant glow of the Refugio's lights. "So that's what they were, Morgan's mother and his sister, side casualties?"

"They weren't supposed to be in the plane." In the dark, his hand moves to take mine, like a big, warm paw squeezing my fingers a little too tight. I startle before gripping it in return. "But it's no use living in the past; I'm not asking for anyone's forgiveness," he adds gruffly. "Morgan should have never touched you. He should have come to *me* and faced me like a man. I would have given him a fair fight."

"You would have killed him," I correct him.

Dries's thumb strokes my palm. "Of course."

"So he went to Anies instead . . . like Stiles did."

He jackknifes up with a look of outrage. "Please don't tell me you feel sorry for that clown too!"

"Not really . . . more like this impression that . . . it never ends. They take revenge, you take revenge, and it goes on and on."

Dries's lips curl in disdain. "He was a low-grade frumentarius who traded intel behind my back—"

"I honestly don't care what he did fifteen years ago," I say wearily. "Don't you ever have regrets? You never wish you'd have worked nine-to-five in your biltong factory?"

"And missed out on all this?" He chuckles, waving at the Refugio and the jungle around us. "No. But when Léa left . . ." His voice softens, hesitates before he goes on. "I found out she was pregnant a few months later, and I was too proud to beg. I told myself that if she wanted out, she could go to hell for all I cared."

I reach for his hand again, gripping it under the stars while my heart breaks silently.

"I should have gone after her, kept you both."

I sit up in my turn and huddle against him. I smell the sandalwood and the cigar. My father's scent. "You would have made a terrible dad," I say, wrestling the word past the lump in my throat.

"I know."

•••

When I return from the garden, I find March lying on the bed with his eyes closed, his breathing soft and even. He almost fools me into thinking he's fallen asleep, but he never lets his guard down: he stirs the moment I make it past the muslin curtains, as if that mere whisper was enough to alert him to my presence. I strip down to my underwear to join him back in bed and curl against him. The room goes silent, save for the occasional birdcall past the walls of the Refugio.

He gathers me close and presses a kiss to my forehead. "I saw you chat with Dries; I didn't want to interrupt."

"Don't worry; we're safe. He doesn't know what happened with the sloth."

"I get to live to see another day," March notes, a smile playing on his lips.

"Is it true that Angel is super Catholic, by the way? It sounds—"

"Strange?"

"Kind of."

"It's true. He thinks God needs monsters like him too. I'm still not entirely certain how he reconciles the path he chose and the demands of the Lord—he tried to explain it to me once, but I thought it was very convoluted, and we were watching his men bury half a dozen bodies in the jungle at the time." He sighs. "But he thinks God is sending him signs once in a while. He accepted Beatriz's wedding because Jesus came to him in a dream and told him Antonio was his cross to bear."

I caress his chest, threading my fingers in the silky curls there. "Do you think God sends you signs too?"

"I don't know. Religion never made much sense for me. But I'm starting to think he's looking down, and he doesn't want someone like me to defile you."

This time I snort in laughter. "March, I honestly think the sloth was an accident."

But March doesn't laugh; he looks at me, his irises shining with an emotion I'm not sure I can read in the dark. "Maybe he believes you deserve better—"

"You're all I need."

He goes silent, his hand rising to caress my cheek. I lean into his touch as he smiles, and he replies, "Then I suppose I'm Dries's cross to bear."

THIRTY-TWO
THE RABBIT HOLE

Time slipped away too fast. The sun hasn't risen yet, and I recognize Dries's deep voice and March's smoother intonations. I push back the comforter and peek in the direction of their hushed voices. March is standing in the bedroom's doorway and is listening, shirtless, as Dries delivers the news. ". . . Retreating north . . . accepted the deal."

Anies took the bait. He's easing up his iron grasp of Angel's territory in exchange for us. After they're done, March returns to the bed and sits on the edge. I don't know what to say that could possibly reassure him, so I just crawl out of the comforter and kiss his cheek. A low purr rises from him in response. "It's time, biscuit."

"I know."

We don't shower. No need to when we're supposed to have spent the night in Angel's basement, and we're going to wear filthy cargo pants and shirts anyway. I get a tank top too—one that must have been white decades ago. The three of us meet with Angel's men in the lobby. I can see the muscles work in March's jaw as he tries to adjust to the grimy clothes they made him wear. We get a little dirt smeared on our faces for good measure; I lace my fingers with March's when I see his throat constrict while Ernesto's fingers swipe at his cheeks. I remind myself, with a shudder, that it's probably nothing compared to the rest of the day awaiting us.

We're led outside, where three armored station wagons await, their black paint gleaming in the golden light of dawn. It rained a little, and the temperature dropped during the night. Fresh air engulfs us, heavy with the scent of earth and damp leaves. Angel walks to us, carrying hinged handcuffs. Before he can lock mine in place, Dries pulls me to him. The pink sky and glistening vegetation spin around me, their colors blend. I close my eyes and block it all out while my father hugs me tight. His voice is a low rasp meant just for me as he says. "Now you have my blessing, little Island."

I bury my face in his chest, dirt be damned, and I squeeze him. I eventually let go with a sigh and step back to slap his arm. "Now man up, *poes.*"

A deep laugh shakes his shoulders as he allows Angel to handcuff him. March's turn comes. "You know what to do," Angel tells him once he's finished. I examine the handcuffs now securing his wrists. Rigged? When it's my turn, Angel's touch is unexpectedly gentle, guiding my hands into the thick steel trap. I feel March's eyes on us, a flicker of jealousy hovering close to the surface of those blue pools. Angel ignores him though, and his fingers wrap around my arms, rotating them carefully in opposite directions. "You need the right angle," he explains. "Then you apply a little pressure. You don't need to push hard, but do it fast, like you want to snap them off."

I flick my wrists the way he showed me, and to my amazement, the handcuffs give way with a sharp click. Satisfied, Angel closes them again, and they snap back in place. One of his men opens the door to one of the station wagons for me. I'm about to climb inside when I notice a flash of white at the edge of my vision. A ghost has been watching us. Standing atop the stairs in front of the villa's entrance, the Queen is here. The pristine silk of her jumpsuit billows around her body as she walks down, flanked by her bodyguards.

She plants herself in front of March. "Never show yourself before me again."

The words are harsh, but the rueful curve of her lips tells another story. After twelve years, she's setting him free, for good.

I offer her a tentative smile. "Thank you."

She shrugs it off. "There's little guarantee either of you will live anyway." She then walks to Dries, and jaws collectively drop when she places a hand on his chest. Her smile turns coy as she leans closer to whisper in his ear, "You are forgiven after all."

I stare at the two of them in complete disbelief, at the boyish glee in his eyes, the sway of her hips as she walks away, regal, indeed. *Oh God* . . . I send a distressed look to Dries, who cocks a suggestive eyebrow in return. For the first time, I notice the thin gold chain under Angel's shirt when he clutches the tiny cross nested between his collarbones and utters a low expletive in Spanish. March was right: Angel has Jesus on speed dial.

And by the way, the true Lion king struck again.

•••

The station wagon jostles through the jungle along the Rio San Miguel, shrouded in the morning fog. Sitting by March's side, facing Dries and Angel in the opposite seats, I watch palm trees flash by, lining the muddy banks. We pass wood-and-tin shacks overlooking the murky waters in which the occasional canoe glides by. I can feel my pulse slowly rise as we approach a rickety bridge marking the limits of Angel's territory. I wish I could take March's hand, but feeling him next to me will have to be enough.

I take deep, slow breaths.

"I'm with you," he murmurs.

I startle and look up at him. His face is a perfectly blank mask, but I know better. We share the same fear, and it's oddly comforting to think that we're so attuned to each other. It's been a while since we saw any house, and through the foliage, the bridge comes in sight.

Dries's eyes narrow when we get close enough to discern a procession of black SUVs waiting on the other side. "Here we go . . ."

In spite of our audience, March bends toward me on an impulse, to kiss me. A brief swipe of his tongue against mine earns us a low hiss from Dries—"Fokenwil . . ." *For fuck's sake . . .*—before the doors open, and Angel gets all business. He shoves us out with controlled strength, and his men drag us toward the bridge, in the middle of which a group of men now awaits. I recognize the black uniforms I had gotten used to seeing everywhere at Ingolvinlinna.

My sneakers skid in the fresh mud, each step harder than the previous one. In my legs, the muscles tense and protest, my self-preservation instinct kicking in to stall my body, warring with my will to keep walking. I can do this. I'll return where it all started, in the cradle of Anies's palm.

March darts anxious eyes at me, but we keep going, stumbling under an occasional vicious shove—Angel's men take their job very seriously. Under our feet, the squishy ground becomes solid wood that creaks ominously with each step. We're on the bridge. Our improvised captors stop and aim their guns at us. We cross without looking back, toward the mist from which shiny black hoods emerge.

When we reach the middle, Anies's Lions encircle us, their guns drawn much in the same way Angel's men have done. As they escort us silently to the other side, I glimpse the rear window of Angel's car rising. He's watching us go. Our fate now depends entirely on whether he and the Queen can successfully storm Saraya while we entertain Anies with our much-desired presence . . .

We've crossed the bridge. The trail on which the SUVs parked appears to zigzag back into the jungle. Into the depths of Anies's small kingdom. The door to one of the cars snaps open and a lean figure steps out. I shiver, but it's almost a reflex. Seeing Morgan's eye patch and his leather jacket tear through the fog, I'm overwhelmed by anger, and sadness most of all. That's it; he has what he wants, and the grin cracking through his stubble says so. Like me, he's reached the end of the rabbit hole, and his reward awaits him. Dries is at his mercy.

He walks to us and holds his fist in front of his mouth, like this is all too much joy. He looks like a little boy opening his Christmas presents. He sizes Dries up and down, his gaze burning with the madness that consumes him. He laughs and shakes his head. "Whew. I kind of worried Somoza would kill you. But you're here." He shivers in apparent delight. "And you're all mine."

Dries returns his smile. "Am I? Or did Anies order you to bring me to him?"

Morgan's joyful mask wavers. "Don't get your hopes up. I have his word. Once he's done with you, you and I are gonna spend some quality time together."

Dries shrugs off the threat. "What are we waiting for then?"

With a jerk of his head, Morgan signals for his men to take us to the cars. "They ride with me," he says, looking at Dries and me. "And do something about Mr. November. I didn't like what happened in Romania," he adds, sending a hateful glare March's way.

As soon as he's said this, one of the men produces a syringe from a pouch on his jacket. He tears the plastic wrapping with his teeth while two men take hold of March, who strains against them before submitting with gritted teeth. Dries tenses—he probably didn't expect that. I leap toward March when they stab his neck. "No!"

Morgan pulls me back roughly and fists my hair. I shriek in pain as, before me, March sways and falls to his knees, his breathing increasingly labored.

"Island, calm down!" Dries shouts.

I draw a shuddering exhale and relax in Morgan's grip. He's right. There's nothing we can do for now. We need to bend, because that's how we'll resist. I let Morgan drag me toward one of the SUVs while his men haul March's prone body into another vehicle.

Once the doors have slammed, I find myself sitting regrettably close to Morgan while Dries is sandwiched between two Lions in the opposite seat. Morgan tilts his head at Dries as the car starts driving, racing so fast down the trail that outside, the dense vegetation is little more than a greenish blur flashing past us. "What were you seriously going to do?" he asks with a chuckle. "Raid Saraya with the last retard who still follows you? All of that . . . for the three of you to get caught by Somoza like rookies . . ." His gaze hardens. "You're fucking pathetic."

Dries shrugs. "What can I say. I'm a dreamer. Always have been."

Morgan stares at him and clasps his hand around my thigh, massaging roughly. I freeze in pain. Dries's jaw tightens; his mouth becomes a pencil-thin line.

"You should have seen her back at Ingolvinlinna . . ." He spins his finger against his temple. "Completely fried. She'd do everything we asked like a good girl." His smirk turns feral. "I wondered who she was gonna suck first, me or Stiles."

Dries's eyes screw shut, and in that moment, we're connected. I feel as sick as he looks.

"He's bullshitting you," I tell him, forcing a smile to my lips. "Anies would have never let him touch me. He's just a goon."

Morgan's fingers dig into my flesh hard enough that I know they'll leave a bruise. I hiss in pain, and that same agony registers on Dries's face. "Don't worry, little Island," he says through gritted teeth. "Mr. Morgan won't see the sun set."

That psychotic asshole lets go of my leg with a snort. "You're so full of shit . . . By the way"—he points to the windows with his thumb—"take a long, good look at that."

I glance sideways, and my eyes go wide, as do Dries's. Angel's wall was a joke compared to the sight that greets us when the vegetation disappears. All around Saraya, the jungle has been razed to establish a security perimeter, and we're driving in the shadow of a ten-story ribbon of concrete. We pass a first checkpoint, a simple barbed wire fence delimiting a zone inside which I'm pretty certain anyone who gets caught gets shot, human or animal. Ahead of us, gates open in the wall, guarded by more armed men. Even if they manage to sneak inside Saraya's water-drainage pipes, how the hell will Angel's and the Queen's men take over this fortress?

The gates clank shut behind us, and we're now . . . in a mostly empty industrial complex. The launching ramp I saw on the satellite map is here, but there's no one around it, and I'm starting to realize that with its few buildings and hangars, the actual space center is fairly small compared to the size of the octagonal area enclosed in those massive walls.

Dries and I look at each other in doubt while the procession of cars drives toward one of the hangars.

An adolescent grin quivers on Morgan's lips. "You're gonna love this shit."

Somehow I doubt that either Dries or myself will enjoy anything that goes on in these walls. The hangar's doors slide open. Here too, I'm getting the impression that we're not getting the entire story: the place is empty and almost entirely dark, save for fluorescent light illuminating a spot at the center of the building. We drive to that improvised stage, and I notice yellow paint stripes on the floor, marking off a circular area, a dark line that looks like a continuous cut in the asphalt. Muted whirring sounds rise from beneath the car, and a low vibration comes from the floor that reverberates in my chest. The yellow disc we parked in is rotating slowly . . . and we're going down.

I watch, wide-eyed, as we're engulfed into an underground elevator. I try to evaluate how far down we're being taken, but I lose track of the steel platforms we glide by after having counted at least five. At last, the elevator stops with a jolt, and there's a well-lit tunnel ahead of us, entirely lined with white panels. I'm getting the feeling that this tunnel too is circular. Numbered gates flash by—1, 2, 3, 4 . . . each number on the wall glows red from a dotting of LEDs. I register movement at the edge of my vision, and for the first time, I see humans in this facility. A little group of technicians in gray coveralls and wearing bright-orange safety helmets strolls past us in the tunnel, without so much as a glance for the procession of SUVs.

As if they're used to it.

The car slows down in front of gate number 8, and Morgan flashes us a smug look, visibly pleased by our aghast silence so far. Gate number 8 blinks green, and its steel doors slide open with a whoosh. I distinctly hear my jaw unhook itself and hit the floor mat at my feet.

To quote the dramatic statement of that CNN anchor, where *is* Odysseus? Here. Sitting in the middle of a concrete dome so high I can't even get a feel for its size, surrounded by scaffolding in which a flurry of orange helmets and black fatigues hustle and bustle in deafening noise . . . there it is

THE LAST SUPPER

We're driving through the dome, but I barely pay attention to the hubbub around us, the mini trucks driving by, loaded with spaceship components. My eyes are glued to the bullet-shaped stack of three modules apparently still undergoing some touch up. The lowest one, that's the nuclear ion thruster, a mad engine capable of propelling more than a ton per kilowatt. All around the ship, large dents in the hull will allow *Odysseus* to dock to its gravitational ring . . . once it leaves the atmosphere.

I squint at the ship, trying to identify the various sections. The longest one must be the habitable quarters, then the control, both pressurized. A huge electronic arm is working on a third unit, some sort of long tube secured to the underside of the ship. I hope—pray, really—that it's not what I think it is . . .

I still can't fully process the fact that Anies seriously did it. In the opposite seat, Dries too seems to have momentarily forgotten Morgan's presence. His gaze is riveted to the spaceship, his face completely blank. His hands though, they're shaking a little, and knots form in my stomach when I notice it. The car stops in front of a large glass tube—another elevator. Morgan rubs his hands in anticipation when the doors click open. A group of Lions surrounds the car, all carrying visible guns at their belts. Two men detach themselves from the group to open the rear doors. Anies definitely isn't taking any risks this time.

Morgan pulls me out of the car none too gently while his men do the same for Dries, immediately encircling him afterward. I turn around to check on March and see men drag him out of the second SUV. I clench my teeth, the urge to run to him boiling in my veins, hammering in my chest. He no longer seems fully asleep, but rather in a daze. They haul him to his feet and support him because the effects of the drug they injected him with make him virtually unable to walk. I can't stand seeing him like this, his head lolling on his chest. I take a step toward him, but Morgan's hand immediately clasps around my arm. "It's this way," he chides.

We're escorted to the glass elevator in religious silence while, around us, workers and Lions alike go about their business and appear to blatantly ignore the fact that Anies just kidnapped people who look in poor shape. The words *collective moral failure* come to mind.

At least in this confined space, I'm closer to Dries and March. His head rises weakly, and he sees me. His eyes are half-closed, and he blinks repeatedly, as if struggling to keep them open.

"It's gonna be okay," I whisper to him.

"It's not," Morgan shoots back without looking at me, adjusting his black leather gloves. "Not for him anyway."

I barely resist the temptation of ramming into that asswipe and biting anything my teeth can reach. The elevator is taking us to the top of the dome, and *Odysseus* now rests below us, majestic, its white hull even brighter under the artificial light. In the scaffolding, one of the orange helmets is busy erasing the US flag painted on the side of the main unit with a laser. For all the Lions have accomplished, I find there's something pathetic in that single move. Like a reminder that this is nothing more than grand theft after all.

When the concrete ceiling looms dangerously close and we must be 150 feet above the orange ants hurrying at our feet, the car slows down to a stop. The elevator's glass wall slides open with a hydraulic sigh. I turn around and freeze at the sight awaiting us, but Morgan grips my arm tighter and drags me forward. The salon's stone walls are the same, an exact replica, down to the faint musty smell, and each painting hangs exactly where it should. The couches and the brocade armchairs are in the same place, facing each other. In the fireplace, logs crack and pop softly as flames consume them. The bar is here too, and the absinthe fountain stands on its mahogany countertop, the glass vessel gleaming gold from the fire reflected in it.

I'm back at Ingolvinlinna.

It takes me ages, or maybe just seconds, to realize that someone is sitting in one of the armchairs, facing away from us and toward the fireplace. On the burgundy armrest, a hand moves. I already know the black suit, the mesmerizing green glow of the absinthe swirling slowly in the crystal glass. He extends his arm to place the glass on an antique table and gets up from the armchair.

Anies turns around to acknowledge us. At my side, Dries stares at his brother, his gaze devoid of anger, only an unfathomable sadness. When one of the guards shoves March and he collapses at my feet, I shrug off Morgan's hand and get to my knees, trying to balance myself with the handcuffs. I can't touch him, but I feel the heat of his body against mine, and I find the strength I was lacking. He may not be at his best, but I read determination in his irises. He can still fight this, and we can be okay.

"Come closer; let me see you both," Anies says, his voice hoarse from what I suspect was a recent fit of coughing.

With one last look at March, I allow Morgan to help me to my feet, and I follow Dries as he walks toward the fireplace. In a corner of the room, a heavy oak door opens, its hinges protesting with a creak. Anies's lips curl into a wry smile. "It isn't like you to be late, *broer*."

A shudder dances down my spine when Stiles appears in his eternal gray suit and black tie. There's nothing but tenderness and compassion to be found in his pale-blue eyes as he takes in my state of disarray. Too bad none of it is real.

"Bring us the bottle," Anies says.

With a nod, Stiles walks to the bar and retrieves a red wine bottle from a finely sculpted cupboard. He pours a glass with careful, practiced gestures and brings it to Dries.

"Romanée-Conti," Anies comments. "Still your favorite?" Without waiting for an answer, he flicks his wrist to Morgan, who seems to hesitate before resolving himself to obey his boss's command. His mouth is a tight line as he produces a universal key from his inner pocket and proceeds to unlock Dries's handcuffs. I watch the key turn in the lock with gritted teeth, silently praying he won't notice the way Angel rigged them.

Dries accepts the glass without a word or even a glance for Stiles. He takes a slow sip, his eyes closing in delight. "Enlighten me, *broer*," he says. "What is going on in here, exactly?"

Anies waves the question off. "Nothing you need to concern yourself over. Enjoy your wine, sit down, and relax. You've earned it."

Dries chuckles. "No, thank you, I'd rather die standing."

"As you wish," Anies replies, his voice a notch colder.

Dries takes another long sip and considers his brother over the rim of the delicate crystal glass. "Nuking the world, huh? *Ma sou skaam wees...*"

Anies coughs a laugh. "I'm afraid Ma would be ashamed of every single thing you and I have done since we left home. But let me ease your mind. I don't want to destroy the world—I have enough on my plate as it is. Let us say I'm trying to rescue my kind."

Hot anger flares in my veins at his words. "*Rescue*...You're bringing terror!" I shout.

His golden gaze sets on me. The same as Dries, as mine, suddenly softer. "I'm happy to see you, Island. I knew you would come back to me."

I step back instinctively.

"Oh, yes, that's something else I wanted to discuss with you . . . I believe you stole my child, and took her mother from me," Dries notes, in a chilling conversational tone.

"Jy weet ek het die regte besluite te neem." *You know I made the right decisions.* I seldom, if ever, heard Anies speak Afrikaans, save for the occasional endearment to his brothers . . .

"Vir wie?" *For whom?* Dries's congenial mask falls as he spits the words. He throws the glass to the ground. It crashes on the aged wooden floorboards. Wine spills like blood, and each crystal shard is set ablaze by the flames reflecting on its edges.

But it's not to him that Anies answers. His eyes are set on me as he says, "I was very happy when your mother obtained the Cullinan for us. I trusted her, shared my vision with her, and I offered her a place at my side . . . I would have given her everything."

"But she refused," I say, shaking from all the pain, the rage.

He looks sideways at Dries. "What a misfortune . . . that she was the one thing we both loved the most."

Dries stares at him, like the words didn't fully register. So I say it, and I can feel my voice breaking with each syllable. "You killed her."

"She would have become a problem. I made a rational decision at the time."

I think I see Dries's fingers quiver, the only warning before he sends the table on which the absinthe glass rested flying into the fireplace, and he lunges at his brother. He grabs Anies's throat with both his hands and squeezes, and I feel it in my neck, in my bones too. Anies barely resists, but Morgan and his men instantly leap to protect their dear leader. I scream when I see them gang up on Dries like beasts, grabbing his arms, his neck. March tries to get to his feet. I realize that his gaze holds renewed sharpness—his body isn't quite willing yet, but his mind is clear. His shoulders flex. He's summoning the strength to snap out of Angel's handcuffs.

"No!"

Dries's roar booms over the grunts of the men trying to restrain him. He's seen March, who freezes in a kneeling position.

"No . . ." Dries repeats, this time in a breath of exhaustion as he gives up the fight and allows Morgan to bring him down to his knees with a powerful kick to his weakened right leg. The very one that got shot and shattered when Anies destroyed the Poseidon.

Tears are building in my eyes, and each breath I take burns my lungs. I understand, and yet I don't. If March frees himself now, when he can barely stand up, it's over. We don't stand a chance. But I can't accept this, seeing Dries like this, defeated. Two guards close in on me as well, clasping their hands around my shoulders in silent warning. In my legs, the muscles coil with the need to cross the distance in the room to him, but I can't; I stay petrified as Morgan pulls out a long combat knife from a sheath in his boot.

Through it all, Stiles has remained perfectly still. He made no attempt to stop Dries. He watches, like a sphynx in the middle of a sandstorm.

Morgan presses the blade to Dries's cheek while his men hold him still. "I want to start with his eyes," he rasps.

Anies sighs and walks to his protégé. He places a hand on his shoulder, in a paternal, almost tender gesture. "We are just," he says softly. "And we abhor unnecessary cruelty."

Morgan's features distort with equal hate and frustration, but he mumbles a barely audible, "I know."

I draw a breath of relief.

A derisive smile cracks through Dries's beard. The gold is fading; he looks exhausted. He looks up at his brother. "You'll fix my daughter. No matter what it takes, you'll fix your mess."

Anies nods, but it dawns on me that Dries is looking past him. At Stiles. I don't think Anies noticed it though. Icy fear creeps up my spine when I hear him tell Morgan, "You deserve justice more than anyone else in this room, Alexander."

Blood freezes solid in my veins. March too seems to pick up the renewed threat in Anies's voice; he straightens, the muscles in his forearms rippling, ready to fight back. But again Dries shakes his head imperceptibly. He's looking at March and me, an odd peace relaxing his features, something foreign . . . that could be love.

Anies's voice sounds distant, unreal as he says, "Clean and quick, please."

The blade moves so fast I don't have time to scream. Pain explodes in my chest as it plunges effortlessly through the skin, slicing neatly through Dries's carotid. The blood flows, dark and fluid, on his neck, his chest. It drips onto the floor, and a howl builds from deep inside me, that won't come out, that just can't. I watch him tremble and go lax in Morgan's grip. His body jerks one last time and hits the floor with a soft thud, his eyes still open but unseeing. A whimper escapes me. I need to see him more, just a little longer, but my vision is getting blurry. I feel salt pooling at the corners of my mouth, and March . . . he's gone quiet in the arms of the men holding him. He's gazing at Dries in stupefaction, his Adam's apple rolling painfully as he swallows several times.

A sob bursts from me. "Oh no . . . No, no, no, *no!*"

But Dries can't hear, and no one else in this hellish den will. I lost him before I could even remember him. I lost my father. Through my tears, I see that Morgan's only remaining eye is glistening too. He's looking down at Dries's prone body, at the warm blood that splashed on his hands and boots. The blade still rests in his hand. His tongue darts to swipe at his lips as if they were dry, and he smiles, the guileless smile of a child who got his Christmas present at last.

Anies's gaze softens, filling with the false kindness he used to bathe me with. He pulls Morgan into his arms. "You did well, Alexander. You've served your purpose."

Morgan rests his sweat-soaked brow on Anies's shoulder. Around the knife's grip, his fingers shake a little. He exhales with difficulty. With infinite care, Anies takes the knife from his hands as a happy sob rakes through Morgan's body.

"You did well . . . " Anies repeats, his voice coarse silk.

The knife flips in his hand and sinks into Morgan's side with ease, tearing through his ribs and left lung. In Anies's arms, he stiffens and takes a gasping breath, his eye wide with incomprehension. With a flick of his wrist, Anies turns the blade in his chest. Morgan's ribs snap with a sickening crack, and the blade reaches deeper, probably to his still beating heart.

Each thump of my own heart feels like an earthquake reverberating through my entire body as I try to process what just happened. Blood gurgles from Morgan's throat, streaking down his jaw. His knees shake, and he too collapses, mere feet away from Dries's body.

In Anies's eyes, the fatherly kindness dissipates like fog on a window. He extends a hand wordlessly, waiting for one of his men to go fetch a hot towel from under the bar. He wipes his hands meticulously, including under his nails, until Dries's and Morgan's blood has entirely transferred to the white terry, mingled. He gives the stained towel back to his henchman without a glance for him or the bodies lying at his feet.

"Mr. Stiles."

"Yes, sir?"

"Please take care of the rest," he orders. "I'll go introduce Island to Claire."

It's the mention of my name that snaps March out of his own stupor, and this time the volcano I know to rest dormant inside him, ever close to the surface, erupts. Risk or not, Angel's magic handcuffs snap open, right before the forearm of the man holding him back snaps in its turn. Nausea pushes at the back of my throat when I glimpse the dangling limb's unnatural angle. The guard closest aims his gun at him and four consecutive shots shred the brocade of an armchair, sending delicate feathers flying in the air. Half a second too late: feathers snow around March as he leaps at the guy's throat. One heartbeat later, there's an ugly bruise where March's fist shattered his windpipe and the gun now rests in March's hand while his victim slowly suffocates, wide-eyed.

When new gunshots crack in the air, I strain against my own cuffs in panic, trying to reproduce the trick Angel taught me. I give several desperate tugs that nick my skin while blood and brain matter splatter onto the elevator's incurved glass wall—an imprudent Lion got shot directly in the face. The salon descends into chaos, and bodies hit the floor as Anies's men try to stop a now-armed March—or maybe just survive. The moment I finally manage to free my hands, I register a flash of black at the edge of my vision. Anies hauls me to my feet and tries to drag me with him toward the oak door Stiles disappeared behind seconds ago. My feet skate in blood as I claw at his hands, fight him with all I have.

At first, I mistake the booming sound and the shock wave that rip through the room for a grenade, but through the windows overlooking the launching area, I see flames and coal black smoke rise from a gaping hole at the base of the dome.

Distant gunshots crack in the facility, followed by screams, and soldiers pour from the newly formed wound in the wall, clearly wearing various types of gear, some light, some black. Time stops, and I forget how to breathe. The Queen really did it. To go after Anies, to get her revenge, she raised an army of fortune, an improbable alliance of mercenaries, Ecuadorian gangsters, and black ops who trusted Erwin's instincts and remained faithful to him, against all logic.

A rough hand grabbing my chin brings me back to the pandemonium roaring around me. Anies's fingers dig into my cheeks, his gray eyebrows quivering over wild eyes. "Island . . . Did you play me?"

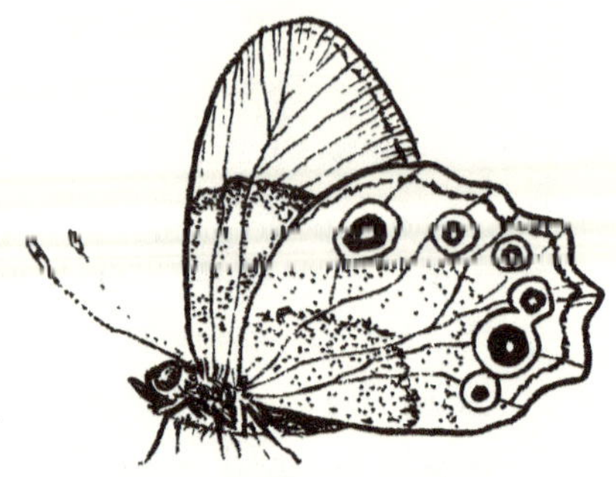

THIRTY-FOUR
THE RING

Shielded behind the bar, March has seen Anies trying to take me away. Several rows of bullets blast into the sculpted mahogany in an explosion of wood shards. Not good . . . He can't cross the room until he's gotten rid of the three remaining men, and that's without taking into account the elevator. It went down a few seconds ago, and whether it's coming back up full of Lions or the Queen's men will determine whether we live or die.

I kick and jerk in vain in Anies's grip as the door gets ominously closer, and his men slowly back up in a cluster to protect our escape, guns and rifles in hand. There's no time left. When I hear renewed gunshots coming from behind the bar, I expect to see March jump out in the open, but that's not it. Above our heads, the crystal chandelier illuminating the room tinkles and creaks dangerously . . . before crashing to the ground, taking out one of the Lions in the process. My eyes briefly screw shut at the sight of the sea of blood-covered crystals now covering a copy of Anies's favorite Persian rug.

One of the two remaining men, the one with the rifle, switches to automatic, and proceeds to literally shower the bar with bullets while Anies forces me to cover the remaining feet toward the door, kicking and screaming. I know for sure that March fires back, and there's only one guy who makes it out of the room before the oak door slams closed and the digital lock on the wall blinks red. I look around frantically; we've jumped back to the future and into a sterile circular hallway. Here too, large numbers on the walls indicate various gates leading back inside the dome. Their LEDs have all turned red. They've locked up the place, no doubt to stop the progression of the Queen's and Erwin's men.

Behind us, a loud bang shakes the oak door. I scream, "March!"

The Lion escorting us darts cold, gray eyes at the door. "Commander, ons moet nou gaan." *Commander, we have to go now.*

Anies lets go of my arm to fist my hair brutally and gives a tug that threatens to snap my neck like a twig. His voice is a low growl that raises goose bumps on my skin. "One thing I've learned in my old age is to forgive, Island. You've tested my patience, but I will forgive you once more, because the future matters more than the past." He tugs harder, and I cry out in pain. "Any more missteps would have grave consequences."

That man made me an orphan: no need to elaborate on what consequences. I find no snark left in me to respond to his threats as he drags me along the hallway to the only gate flashing green. Number 1.

On the other side, in a long white room about the same size as the salon we just escaped, crates of equipment await next to a row of black pressure suits. At the other end of the room, near a wide circular air lock marked with yellow safety stripes, a group of men and a woman are ready. Their suits are on, and they carry round helmets whose visors reflect the bright fluorescent lights above our heads. Legit astronauts wouldn't have holsters strapped to their thighs and torsos though . . .

They're looking at me, and suddenly I see two ghosts. *Hillstone, Chopra* . . . The names and faces I saw on television flash in my mind, and I recognize that tall black woman with the short caramel brown hair, and the young Indian guy with a fierce mohawk, who gives the impression that he's hiding behind her. Commander Claire Hillstone, Flight Engineer Bahjin Chopra. Both supposedly dead along with their seven unfortunate crewmates.

"Claire, help her," Anies orders.

He can't be serious . . . He just can't. But she's walking toward me, her dark eyes full of determination, and the Lion who escorted us to this room gives me a little shove. Anies gauges me coldly. "You have ninety seconds."

With this, he grabs one of the pressure suits and disappears with one of the evil astronauts behind a set of sliding doors that engulfs them with a low hiss.

As soon as he's gone, she grabs my arm roughly and pulls me toward a similar door, with Anies's personal watchdog following us. When I resist, she slaps me hard, the impact made even worse by the thick gloves she wears. "Millions of people out there would sacrifice everything to be in your place."

I'm sorely tempted to snap back *they can take it,* when the doors slide closed and she throws a stretchy gray leotard at me. Primed by fear and some amount of unbidden humiliation, I strip hastily in front of them and slip on the jumpsuit. The material is strange; the moment it clings to my skin, I feel a little cooler—something meant to regulate my body temperature inside the pressure suit?

She's approaching with it, by the way. God, whatever March and Angel are doing out there—whoever they're killing—I hope they hurry the hell up, because that bunch of illuminati is seriously considering literally putting me in orbit. Once I've slipped my legs in the lower half of the suit, Claire and the guard help me shrug on the top, made heavy by a small and flat backpack—compressed air supply, likely. She seals the two halves of the suit's steel belt together and screws the helmet on my head. Once it's safely in place, she fiddles with a digital screen integrated in the suit's arm. Air is expelled with a soft hiss, and I feel the pressure suit tighten around my body until I can move my arms and legs more or less freely. I look down at the data glowing green on the screen; I'm breathing 78.09% nitrogen, 20.92% oxygen, 0.93% argon, and 0.06% carbon dioxide.

Okay. One minute from now, someone is going to pop from behind a door and say they filmed everything, and I've been punk'd. This is the only rational outcome I can envision. But there's no camera, and Claire seals her own helmet while the guard invites me to come out first with a flick of his gun. In the white room, everyone else has their helmets in place and their suits tightened around their bodies like mine, including Anies. I swallow hard. This man isn't just evil, or even a complete psychopath. He's lost his shit, and his followers are too blind to see it.

Praying he can hear me through the helmet, I blurt out the first rational argument that comes to my mind. "We . . . we're gonna eat up to 4 g during takeoff. I'm not trained for this, and your lungs . . . Even if this thing doesn't fail and kill us all, I'm not even sure you can *survive* that kind of acceleration!"

A faint smile stretches his lips as his voice filters inside my helmet, relayed by a speaker. "I don't intend to die until I've reached for the stars, and you won't either."

I wish I could be as confident—or as dangerously deluded— because ahead of us, the air lock is opening slowly, and I'm not ready. I'm panting hard, and the glass of my helmet starts to fog as Anies and Claire each place a hand on my shoulder and push me forward into a tunnel leading to a second air lock—*Odysseus*'s.

Cut from the outside world inside my suit, I have no idea what's going on out there, but I pray with every fiber of my being that someone damaged that ship, and it can no longer take off or something. No . . . wait, *wait*. If it's damaged . . . it could blow up, with us inside. *Oh God*, I regret ever dreaming of going to space.

The second air lock rotates and, tormenting inch after tormenting inch, opens. I glimpse dark walls covered with glowing screens, buttons, wires everywhere. Windows. Anies's men help me fold into one of the nine horizontally placed seats and secure my seat belt straps, pulling them tight—intentionally, I suspect. At last, I can see what's happening in the dome. Chaos unfolds all around us, with some of the scaffolding around *Odysseus* destroyed, orange helmets and soldiers running in all directions, smoke everywhere . . . rising to the cloudy sky. I look up and see the concrete roof of the dome slowly parting, the two halves retracting inside the walls.

"You can't launch in these conditions . . . The whole place is coming apart!" I yell while his men strap Anies in the seat next to mine.

In the pilot's seat, Claire starts flipping switches as a monotonous male voice crackles through the ship's speaker, informing her that it's T minus ninety seconds before launch. "Your friends had better get the hell out of here if they know what's good for them," she shoots back. "The boosters are going to clean up the place."

When the full implications of her words register, I go rigid. She's right. If they can actually start the rocket boosters, the entire dome will turn into a blazing inferno while *Odysseus* ascends. I strain against my seat belt. March! He's down there somewhere. I roll panicked eyes at the window, hoping not to see him anywhere near the ship.

On the dashboard, a light starts to blink red.

"It's the payload unit," that Bahjin guy says, his fingers flying fast on a keyboard to track the origin of the alert. "Hull integrity is okay, but maybe they didn't seal it properly . . ."

Before he's done going through the ship's data feed, the button stops blinking and turns back to a reassuring green.

Claire turns to him. "False alarm?"

"Do we have time to postpone launch and check?" Bahjin asks tartly.

Anies's bark cuts through their exchange, "False alarm, we're launching."

In my helmet, the voice keeps on talking, devoid of emotion.

Odysseus is now running off its nine onboard electrical cells . . . We have a go for auto-sequence start . . . *Odysseus*'s onboard computers now have primary control of all the ship's critical functions . . . T minus fifteen seconds and counting . . .

The cabin starts vibrating much worse than any plane takeoff, a rumble that twists my stomach, tears through my eardrums. I grip the armrests. This isn't real, and if it is, I just want March to be safe, away from this hell.

Five . . . four . . . three . . . two . . . one . . .

Lose the ignition . . . lift off.

White smoke engulfs the ship, and I stare at the patch of sky barreling toward us. We're moving too fast, and I try to breathe, but the Gs pile up, crushing my throat, my lungs. It seems barely a few seconds flash by, before the voice says we're three miles in altitude, and we broke the goddamn sound barrier . . . Next to me, Anies seems lifeless, his arms folded on his chest. The engine revs up. My eyeballs are drilling inside my skull; blood hammers in my temples and, with it, agonizing pain. Through it all, I hope that rotten piece of shit actually died in his own ship.

I blink, and for a moment, everything goes dark. The next thing I register is Claire's voice, announcing that we've reached sixty-three miles in altitude, and we're traveling at five thousand miles an hour. Around the ship, the sky has become an indigo blanket as she drones into the speaker that we're more than halfway to orbit and a little over a hundred miles away from *Odysseus*'s gravitational ring.

This is a nightmare, and I'm gonna wake up. If not, at least I made it through the acceleration . . .

Anies's voice rasps in my helmet. "See? We're both alive."

"You're completely crazy . . . What are you gonna do now? Take us all to Mars along with your missiles?"

Bahjin's laugh bursts through the speaker. "We're not going to Mars. Actually we're gonna stay real close to Earth. Like, uncomfortably close!"

I squirm in my seat to stare at Anies's profile. "What does he mean?"

"Island," he asks, "do you know the speed of the fastest ballistic missile currently deployed on Earth?"

"Mach 22," Bahjin quips from the front seat.

Anies gives a nod inside his helmet. "And can you imagine how fast a projectile would hit the target if fired from outside the atmosphere?"

I look around the ship, at the eight sickos riding with me. I think of the long tube I thought was part of the payload—a launching ramp. My supercooling suit does little to stop the sweat from beading on my forehead as the truth dawns on me fully. "You modified it so it can fire missiles." I take a shuddering gulp of air. "You're gonna use reentry speed to fire missiles so fast the interception systems won't able to keep up."

"Mach 26," Claire confirms in a cold voice. "Once we've docked to the ring, it will absorb the recoil, and we've reprogrammed the command center to control the launch. Depending on the orbit, a missile shot from *Odysseus* will take less than thirty seconds to hit the target. It's the ultimate nuclear dissuasion."

Bahjin removes his helmet, grabs a candy bar from a pouch in his pressure suit and starts munching on it, speaking between mouthfuls. "It's completely awesome. Take your average ICBM, Topol-M, Dongfeng, whatever . . . you fire it, and then sure, it's flying fast, but you gotta cover thousands of miles to hit your target. Those guys, on the receiving end, they literally have ages to detect and intercept you.

"Now, take *Odysseus*: you just use your boosters to get in position above your target. You dash at seventeen thousand miles per hour outside the atmosphere: they can't do anything about that. Then you've got, what, two hundred miles tops to cover, with a missile that can hit twenty thousand miles per hour at cruise speed." He shakes his head and waves his half-eaten chocolate bar at me. "You know that Exoatmospheric Kill Vehicle the air force has been testing?"

I shake my head slowly. I have no idea what he's talking about, but I figure it's going to come in handy if Anies actually goes through with this madness and fires a missile to Earth.

"Well," Bahjin replies, "even if it could actually intercept something—and right now it's intercepting shit—it wouldn't be enough to stop us. We're at the top of the food chain, like, really at the top."

"But the Chinese missiles," I say. "They're not designed for atmospheric reentry . . . aren't they going to blow up?"

"We were primarily interested in the warheads they contained," Anies replies.

Bahjin's voice echoes his. "They were crap . . . We had to redesign them almost completely, but at least we had the warheads," he concludes with a snort, right before a series of LEDs start blinking red on the dashboard. "They've spotted us," he snaps, his tone suddenly cool and focused. "They're trying to access our systems."

"As expected," Anies says. "But they're too late."

I gulp. "The US government wants its ship back?"

Bahjin chuckles. "You bet they do. But they don't know who they're dealing with. I reprogrammed everything in there. Bahjin Chopra, PhD is awesome!"

That's when I feel the change in my body, and I notice the sky all around us, or lack thereof. The thruster has stopped, and we're gliding in the immensity, weightless. Beneath us, Earth's atmosphere is a graceful blue arc blending with the dark horizon. We're in space.

I stare through the window for several endless seconds, having forgotten how to blink, how to breathe. I'm brought back to reality by the clatter of Bahjin typing furiously on his laptop. "They managed to connect to the ring's system; they're trying to lock it up to stop us from docking."

Anies leans back in his seat. "I trust you," he simply says.

"Strength and honor, sir," Bahjin grunts as he battles NASA's attempts to shut him out of *Odysseus*'s orbital ring.

Strength and honor . . . I've heard this before, but I can't remember where. I gather though, that like Morgan, Claire and Bahjin basked in Anies's light and let that sun blind them. *Frumentarii.* That's what March called those who sell their souls to the Lions, like Morgan. Do they know Anies killed him? Or maybe they just don't care . . .

In the front, Bahjin raises a victorious fist in the air. "I killed the last connection to their satellites; we're in command."

Anies's lips twitch. "By the time they manage to launch an emergency mission, we will be long done."

In that moment, I don't know whether to be horrified or admire his uncanny ability to always plan ahead of his adversaries. We continue to drift until a white shape comes into view. My jaw goes slack, and air whizzes in my throat as I gaze at the terrifying beauty of *Odysseus*'s ring.

THIRTY-FIVE
XX121

Seen from afar, *Odysseus*'s orbital ring looks almost smooth, the complexity of its weaving of ceramic panels and air locks invisible from a distance. It's a giant wheel in space, and dire as my circumstances might be, I can't help staring in silent awe. When we get close enough, I can make out the arms connecting the ring to a long docking platform in its center, bigger than the ship.

"Starting automated docking sequence," Claire announces.

I know what relative speed means, but I never imagined that I'd ever experience it in space: the entire docking feels like a slow dance between the ship and its cradle. We're cruising at seventeen thousand miles an hour over the Pacific, and I just don't feel any of it: I'm free from gravity, a little dizzy, held secure by my seat belt as we turn around to align with the docking platform. My head is upside down, but I have no physical sensation of it.

The cockpit shakes as the ship imbricates itself in the center of the orbital ring with a muted clank that echoes in my helmet. Earth is far and close, incredibly blue and peppered with clouds that stretch for miles and look like little more than cotton candy from here.

Hunched on his laptop, Bahjin hammers at the keyboard with a satisfied huff. "I got this; the ring is connected to our reactor."

Holy fricking Raptor Jesus and all his saints . . . I still can't fully process the magnitude of what I'm experiencing, but they did it: they actually stole that ship and completed its assembly. I tremble in my seat when more clanking ricochets around the cockpit, coming from the ship's underside, where the launching ramp is now imbedded into *Odysseus*'s central docking platform.

"The payload is secure," Claire announces, as electronic arms work on transferring the ship's deadly cargo. The missiles. They're being stowed in that platform, ready to be fired.

Anies's hands move to undo his seat belt. "Excellent, let's board."

He and Claire go first. They unbuckle, and my jaw goes slack as I watch them float away from their seats. This is real. Once they undo my seat belt, the same thing will happen to me. Oh my fricking God, this is *real* . . .

My eyes screw shut in anticipation while Anies's goons free me from my seat. I float up and their arms immediately clasp around mine to guide me toward the now-open air lock. We float down a narrow arm lined with thermal foil that connects the ship to the ring's command center.

"Once artificial gravity kicks in, it will take you a while to get used to it," Claire warns us. "You're going to feel seasick."

I brace myself when I see her flip a series of switches next to the final air lock. Bahjin's excited whistle rips through my eardrums as the orbital ring starts spinning slowly around *Odysseus* and the connecting arm along with it. Once again, I'm disoriented; my brain struggles to reconcile the factual knowledge that we're spinning with the lack of actual sensation. As gravity sets in and pulls me down toward the air lock, I do feel queasy but also anchored. At least now I can find my bearings.

The final air lock whirs open, and they push me through. Or rather I tumble into the ring, betrayed by the very gravity I wished for. For a second, I see myself smashing into the wall ahead of me and destroying equipment that's worth more than my life, but arms catch me just in time. I register the door hissing shut behind me and look up. The dark-skinned guy gripping my arms . . . he's wearing a white space suit with a US flag, and he wasn't in the ship with us. There's a second guy, with graying hair and angry blue eyes.

The rotation team. It took NASA fifteen years, mission after mission, to assemble the ring and there're always at least a few astronauts watching over the US government's baby. Did Anies corrupt them too? *All of them?* There must be what, at least five or six people up here and—

"We're ready, sir," the blue-eyed astronaut barks while, around me, everyone starts to remove their helmets. I fumble with mine, and it's Anies who unclasps it, with a benevolent smile that makes my skin crawl. I hate having to, but I accept the arm he holds out to me because that spinning ring messes up my senses. My internal ear and I try to come to terms with the fact that we're standing . . . horizontally, in a wheel that completes roughly 5.5 rotations per minute.

Claire leads us down a white hallway lined with pipes, valves, and electronic equipment. Through rectangular windows, I see the darkness of space, studded with stars, unreal. We pass two air locks whose iris-scan systems get defeated by Bahjin's laptop. As Bahjin is getting ready to open the massive security door barring the way to the command center, I notice a reddish smear on a series of switches on the wall to my right. Blood.

I glance at the two men who awaited us inside the station. There's another stain on the sleeve of the black guy's space suit. *We're ready, sir* . . . I inhale slowly to keep my fear under control. I don't think Anies managed to convince the rest of the rotation crew to destroy the world for him . . . and that's why they're nowhere in sight.

When the final air lock slides open, Bahjin raps on the scan lens with his forefinger and says in an exaggeratedly deep voice, "Nothing can catch up with a Steed!"

I wince and glance at Anies's impassible features. Shortsighted tycoon Reginald Steed probably never expected that his regular meetings with "Aidan Keasler" would result in his space program being used against him—and with his favorite slogan, no less.

Oh my God, this is like *Star Trek*. We're standing in *Odysseus*'s vast command center, facing a giant screen on which Earth can be seen rotating peacefully, unaware that a bunch of dangerous douchebags threaten it. More screens line the brand-new helm and launch consoles behind which the captain's seat stands empty on a central platform, like a white throne in the middle of this orgy of cutting-edge technology.

Claire walks to the helm console and trails a reverent hand over the black glass top and its integrated tactile dashboard whose keys glow a soft, snowy white. She presses her palm to a fingerprint lock on the glass, and the dashboard flashes green before a multitude of keys and buttons starts lighting up. She turns to look at Anies as he settles in the captain's seat, flanked by his faithful Lions. For the first time, a radiant, poignant smile illuminates her face. His lips curve in response, and she's staring directly into the sun, burning before my eyes. What did he tell her? What did he promise that makes her beam with pride and gratitude like that? It must have been exactly what she wanted to hear, what she needed. Because that's what he does, how he controls people . . .

Next to her, Bahjin sits behind the launch console and is now busy removing the plastic film from his new screens with a delighted sigh.

"Come here, Island," Anies orders.

My eyes dart to the brawny guy standing at my side and the ones guarding Anies. A third one guards the air lock, but the rest of them left the command center along with the two traitors from the rotation team to go check the first missile, which now awaits inside the launching ramp. I decide to play along until I can come up with a plan that would allow me to defeat nine overtrained killing machines, one Indian nerd, and one dying supervillain who could still force-choke me in his sleep.

Anies's goon hovers behind me as I cover the distance to the captain's seat and climb onto the platform to stand at his side. I don't look at him; I stare straight ahead at the control screen, on which data is now flashing. They're targeting something in Alaska . . .

"What do you think will happen once you strike?" I ask, reining in the tremors in my voice.

His gloved fingers rap on the armrest slowly. "For the rest of mankind? Nothing they'll notice."

I spin on my heels, anger burning in my cheeks. "Are you fucking serious? You really think you can murder millions of people—"

"Seven hundred at most," he corrects.

"What's there?"

"Only Fort Greely," Bahjin answers with a sigh of annoyance, like he's watching a kid relentlessly try to shove the cube in the circle hole. "It's the US's main interception base. That's where they test their antiballistic missiles. They have like thirty interceptors ready for launch, crazy stuff . . ."

"Soon they'll have none," Claire says quietly.

Anies's gaze sets on the red dot blinking in the middle of Alaska. "We're not declaring war, Island, and there will be no unnecessary violence. All we're doing here is establishing a new balance in the equation of nuclear dissuasion, one that will ensure our voice is heard and our word followed."

I shake my head, a fear I can't contain washing over me and paralyzing my body. "Please stop . . . You're never going to rule the world."

A laugh rises from his throat, which he coughs out, along with blood that stains his lips. "Is that what you imagined? That I'm here to proclaim some sort of global takeover?" I stay silent and let him continue, because, well . . . yeah. "I don't care what kind of idiot or dictator holds the leash, as long as he makes the right choices. Choices that drive mankind forward and preserve our resources and civilizations. Choices that *aren't* being made as we speak." His jaw sets in determination. "Someone needs to tip the balance of the world in the right direction or else we might not even survive as a species."

"Blackmail," I grind out. "You're hanging a sword of Damocles over their heads to get them to do whatever you want."

His lips quirk. "I do intend to provide some amount of counseling . . ."

On the screen, the single red dot still blinks steadily at the center of a series of orange circles, delimiting the potential impact radius. Thirty-five miles. A blast that will not only obliterate the base but the nearest town as well. Outside, *Odysseus* is locking down on its target. Estimated time to cover the 218 miles of space and atmosphere separating us from Fort Greely: 43.9 seconds. Not even long enough for them to detect the missile and launch one of their interceptors.

"Fort Greely will be a simple warning," Anies says, ice enveloping each word. "An invitation to discuss our options."

Blood roars in my ears, and I consider begging, screaming, but I'm petrified as outside, the end of the launching ramp slides open. With small, controlled releases, *Odysseus*'s lateral boosters rotate us into position to face the target, like the eye of a Cyclops staring down at Earth.

Quivering with excitement, Bahjin announces that all systems are clear to launch. Claire's fingers tremble over the keyboard. She turns to look at Anies, her gaze seeking not just his authorization, but more: reassurance . . . love, maybe. "We're ready, sir," she says, steadying her voice.

I'm looking at her, unaware that it's Anies I should be looking at: when I turn around, I see his hand hovering above a touch screen integrated into the captain's seat's armrest. A red circle pulses steadily on the dark glass. My heart hammers against my rib cage in tune with it, each beat a deafening bang in my ears. I need to do something. I need . . . Like *Odysseus*'s formidable thruster, adrenaline explodes in my veins and propels my legs. It's like the whole ship is shaking around me as I leap, so fast, so high I never thought it possible.

No, wait . . . Oh God . . . Oh shit!

I take off and fly right above Anies as the ring stalls and stops spinning, sending us all floating around like goldfish in a zero-gravity bowl. All lights go out in the command center, and the red glow of the emergency lighting bathes our weightless bodies. Anies secures his seat belt just in time, even as his legs lift effortlessly. Taken by surprise, his men float away but manage to latch onto the handles running along the walls. The Lion closest to me grabs my leg when I fly past him, his fingers crushing my ankle. I gasp in pain while, under me, Bahjin and Claire struggle to buckle up too. I vaguely register Bahjin's voice, yelling that something went wrong with the power cells in section five of the ring and that we're switching to auxiliary.

Within seconds, an electric hum revs up, and the lights come back. The ring resumes spinning with a low, lazy moan, and my heart plops straight into my stomach when gravity claims me again. I fall on top of one of Anies's Lions and immediately roll away from him when the guy groans under me. He doesn't look okay. He's pale, and his eyebrows pinch and quiver as he struggles up. I blink at the spectacle of his agony and realize with a dash of hope that I literally busted his balls. One down, ten more to go!

"What happened? Can you fire?" Anies asks Bahjin when everyone is more or less back in place.

He doesn't answer immediately, his fingers flying fast on his tactile keyboard as he tries to evaluate the situation. "I don't know. It looks like a power failure in section five. Power has been restored in sections one to four and seven to twelve, but we're disconnected from sections five to six . . . No, seven . . . seven is out too!"

"Can we fire?"

"We . . . Not yet, sir!"

Next to him, Claire orders Anies's men to head to the damaged sections. A snarl twists her lips, and the warm brown of her skin seems to be turning gray under the artificial lights.

"What's going on?" Anies barks. "Give me a visual."

On the main screen, several windows pop up. External cameras: something happened to the ring in the three sections connecting to the launching ramp. The lights are out in there, and there's a little smoke escaping section five. Holy shit, the hull is compromised!

It takes Bahjin a little while to reconnect some of the cameras. He can't access any of those in sections five and six, but after some effort, we get a live feed from the cargo units in section seven.

Bahjin goes silent, his mouth working in vain as he takes in the scene filmed by the cameras. Anies's fingers curl around his armrests until they turn white, and I'm thinking his bones might snap. Hope and terror lace in my chest and constrict my lungs. Three of the Lions who had been overseeing the launch in section five lie on the ground and blood is everywhere, pooling on the floor, splattered on the missile containers, staining the walls in long carmine trails.

"W-what the fuck?" Bahjin asks, typing—punching, really— on the keyboard to collect data. That's when section eight goes dark.

Claire yells in her headset, "Omega Six, Omega Nine? Answer me!"

But those men aren't answering either, and whoever—or *whatever*—killed them and just took another section of the ring offline is now progressing toward us. The command center is section twelve; we don't have much time left.

Sweat runs in cool beads down my nape. None of this makes sense, but honestly, considering the day I've been having so far, I half expect to see the glistening black exoskeleton of a Xenomorph dash across section nine. But it goes dark, and I see nothing. Outside, the windows turn pitch black, as does our camera feed. I swallow hard. Maybe one of Anies's men turned on him. Maybe he realized decent people don't start nuclear wars with the first world power, and he said, "That ain't right. I'm gonna eat everyone in here to stop this." Oh God, I'm making no sense, and I don't want to die up here, in the dark, without March.

When section ten goes dark, and Bahjin has nothing to offer but furious typing and a sweaty brow, Claire undoes her seat belt and pulls out a black gun from the holster around her thigh that looks like some prop straight from *Blade Runner*, with a strangely bulky barrel. "We need power in section five to fire. I'm going there," she says, her delicate features set in a grim mask.

Anies nods for her to go, and she's halfway to the door when the lights go out. In front of his screens, Bahjin switches from one camera to another feverishly. Section nine, section ten, nothing, *nothing*. Section eleven . . . on the other side of the air lock isolating the command center. His hands freeze over the keyboard as the main screen displays the silhouette of a ghost in the darkened hallway, ten feet away from the door. A shadow among shadows, revealed more clearly only when he switches to night mode. Blurred lines become a man in a pressure suit, holding two guns and standing perfectly still.

Anies's men and Claire get in position on each side of the door while Bahjin intensifies the image to identify the newcomer. It's weird because my heart is still thumping so hard I can hear it in my ears, but I'm no longer scared. I know before the computer is even done filtering the camera's feed. No one else could be obstinate enough to destroy a fricking spaceship. There's another beast onboard *Odysseus*, one much more dangerous than any Lion, and Anies, who gazes at the screen in fascination, a muscle twitching at the corner of his mouth, knows it.

"Who's that?" Bahjin gasps, when the camera reveals a square, blood-soaked jaw and icy eyes staring at us.

"March," I tell him.

THIRTY-SIX
BLACK PEARLS

I have no rational explanation. He wasn't with us inside the cockpit; I'm sure of that. The cargo unit wasn't pressurized, but he's wearing a suit too, so . . . *maybe?* Hope rushes through me and, with it, renewed energy. We can find a way out of this.

For now, we're in a pinch though: Anies isn't stupid; he's probably calculating that if he opens the air lock, he gets a chance to get rid of March, but mostly he'll trigger a massacre. I wait, every single muscle in my body tensing the longer he stares at that screen.

"Bahjin," he says. "Can you stop the ring?"

A slight wince flashes across Bahjin's face. "Are you sure . . . sir?"

"Yes. On my command, stop the ring, and depressurize section eleven."

I check the screen. March isn't wearing a helmet, and I see none around. Oh no, *no* . . . anything but that. Anies's gaze meets mine; he reads my distress, plain as day. There's not a single trace of regret to be found in his eyes as he says, "I'm sorry, Island."

I have no time left to think and certainly none to cry. Loud cracking outside the room makes me whirl around with a start. March is trying to shoot the lock.

Bahjin shakes his head. "All beef . . . no brain. Everyone buckle up; stopping ring auxiliary engine in twenty seconds."

I'm out of time; I act on instinct. The Lion whose balls I inadvertently crushed is still standing close behind me, ready to block any escape. I fall to my knees and grip his leg desperately. "Oh God, no! No, please, don't let them do this!" I scrunch up my face, summoning some waterworks—something regrettably easy to accomplish given the level of stress I've been under these past few hours. I sense him startle. I bawl harder. "We love each other! Don't depressurize my boyfriend, please!"

"Island!"

Anies's angry shout is the final distraction I need. I grit my teeth and punch the guy with all my strength. My fist hits something soft and a little squishy under his suit. Air instantly escapes his lungs in a loud huff, and he folds inward with a muffled groan. The other Lions lunge at me but not before I manage to elbow my victim in the side of the knee. There're kneepads integrated in our suits though, and for that reason there's a distinct possibility that the move hurts me more than it does him. Agony pulses in my arm, but he drops to his knees in surprise at this exotic self-defense combo.

I have half a second to either flee or fight back before two six-foot Lions pounce on me. It could be the adrenaline blazing through my system, but I think I'm starting to understand how March does it. The trick is to trade self-preservation for efficiency. I roll over and grab the Blade Runner gun strapped to Busted-nuts's thigh. Self-preservation: aim and hope to hold them with the threat alone. Efficiency . . . my thumb finds the safety, and my eyes screw shut as I press the trigger blindly over and over.

I register a grunt. Did I hit one of them? I need to hold them back. I need more time for March, just a little more . . .

My vision blurs and goes black when the man closest to me knees me hard in the stomach and rips the gun from my hands in one quick move. Stars dance under my eyelids, and I gasp for oxygen in vain when his free hand grips my throat to immobilize me fully. I see the sweat on his brow, his dark eyes narrowing at me, daring me to move.

Steps echo somewhere behind him. Black boots appear, integrated to a suit. Anies looms above me. The Lion lets go, and I feel Anies's hand glide in my hair before he pulls hard. Pain lashes at my scalp and I let out a broken howl.

"I don't have time for this, Island. And I warned you there would be consequences." His sighs fan over my face, carrying the mephitic breath of a dying man. "Her hand," he tells his goon.

I jerk in panic when the guard grabs my right wrist and forces it still, crushing it to the floor. Someone separates my suit's glove and pulls it off, and I see the black blade in Anies's hand that the third Lion just handed him. I scream and thrash in vain. Claire and Bahjin watch, their gazes blank, unfeeling. Anies trails the blade across my palm and nicks the skin, drawing a drop of blood. "You're going to tell me which finger," he asks, his tone eerily calm, almost tender.

I writhe, arch until I'm sure my spine is going to snap from the effort to free myself. "Uh . . . no . . . no! Let me go!"

"Which. Finger. Island."

When the blade presses against my pinkie, I know he's chosen for me. I shake and cry hysterically, willing myself out of this reality as the pain increases.

"Oh fuck, he's found the auxiliary cable!"

Bahjin's scream is the only warning we get before the lights go out, and I am effectively lifted from this reality. The Lion's hold on my wrist loosens as he floats toward the ceiling, like the rest of us. I find myself looking upside down at the screen, on which March is as powerless against zero gravity as we are. Around him, the remnants of the electric cable powering the ring's rotation engine dances gently, like seaweed in a quiet ocean. He won't give up. A light kick against the wall propels him to the door, and he tries the manual-opening lever over and over, his features twisting in rage and exertion.

I blink in realization. I get it! He cut the power because he thought it'd allow him to go manual. But we're in the command center, and one of the cells still powers our computers to protect the launch system so, logically, in the event of an electrical failure, you can only go manual . . . from this side of the door.

I spin around and scan the air lock at the other end of the room. I see the lever, outlined by the red glow of a series of switches. I try to find a way to float toward it, but arms wrap around my waist like a vise. I look up to see Anies's face in the dark, a terrifying war mask sculpted by the red light bathing us. In that single second, I know this face will haunt my nightmares for the rest of my life if I survive this.

The blade he holds glints crimson in the darkness as his fingers wrap around my throat, exposing it. Panic floods my system, and a vision of Dries's blood flowing from the wound in his neck flashes before my eyes. I know I have to fight this, that this time it's not about cutting off my pinkie. I try to elbow him and arch away from the blade in his hand. My feet hit something—the captain's seat. *Drop self-preservation; be efficient,* I remind myself. I stop struggling and feel his hold tighten around me. The blade closes in on my carotid, grazes it in a chilling caress. I breathe out my fear as my feet find leverage against the back of the seat. I push hard to propel myself. Zero gravity does the rest; we both barrel toward the air lock.

I spot shadows in my peripheral vision: Anies's men are coming to help him. Time is running out, but I'm so close . . . *so close.* I strain with a howl of rage, of despair. My fingers reach, claw at the air, even as the blade starts biting into my skin. I need more leverage, I just need . . . One of the Lions floats close, to block my legs. *Just a little more leverage.* I kick back as hard as I can, using him to propel myself one last time, away from Anies and toward the manual-opening lever. A moan of agony buzzes in my ears. Forgive me, Nut Jesus, I think I kicked that poor guy in the balls for the third time. But I feel the lever's cool steel in my hand; my fingers curl around it! Almost instantly, Anies's hand clasps around mine to stop me.

He tugs hard to tear my hand away from the lever. I let him.

Relief washes through me and makes me go lax in his grip for a heartbeat. The air lock slides open with a satisfying hydraulic hiss, and in the dark, in the chaos, I see March's face, his hand reaching for mine.

Anies hauls me back, and I register suppressed gunshots cracking through the room. Fear explodes in my chest; here, in zero gravity, there's no way to easily dodge. I see March wrestling one of the Lions in a corner of the room while another one floats past us, blood bubbling out slowly from a wound between his eyes. I struggle against Anies's grip, spurred by his labored breathing in my ear. A fit of coughing rattles through him, my cue to push him hard and break free. Air and blood gurgle together from his throat, and his shaking hand lets go of the blade. I catch it when it flies past me and grip it, terror and rage surging in my veins.

"Island," he rasps. "I never . . . wanted anything else than to give you all of this."

A wave of nausea wells in my stomach. All of *this*? My parents' blood? The life of a doll? Or maybe all the lives lost, threatened? There's so much I want to say, to shout, but seeing him like this, defeated, while March is butchering what's left of his men, I know there's only one thing that could hurt him more.

I hold out the blade defiantly, to keep him at a safe distance. "I tread on your dream. I fucking *trample* it."

In the darkness, bathed in the red of the lights and the delicate blood bubbles floating around us like rubies, shock registers on his face, like he only just realized it's over. The orbital ring won't start again, and the power in section five probably can't be restored to complete the launch.

Yes, now he understands and . . . I pedal in vain as he lunges at me, too fast, his face ravaged by unfathomable hate. His hands are on me, around me, and I thrash in panic. I don't feel the blade tear past his suit and go in; it's already in his side when I see black pearls float between us, pouring from the wound. I go still, petrified. My hands shake around the blade, and I let go. His eyes are wide, his features paralyzed. He's trying to breathe, but he can't anymore. I remember Morgan's face when Dries's body hit the floor, his tears. I don't know if mine are the same. They blind me and I can find no joy, no relief, only horror.

Behind him, a ghost floats toward me. Claire's features emerge from the darkness, painted by the red light, and the sound . . . the broken howl erupting from her lips crawls under my skin, twists my insides. She welcomes his lifeless body in her arms and screams, screams, and that's when I fully process that Anies is no more. *He's dead. I killed him,* I repeat to myself, the words impossibly loud in my mind.

I just float, drained, broken. I watch her kiss his forehead, and I see the shift on her face, the tipping point between pain and hate. She draws her gun so fast I don't understand. I stare at the barrel inches from my face, numb and confused.

Her finger tightens on the trigger but never presses. A single black dot bursts between her eyes, and she too falls asleep amid the black pearls flowing from her wound.

This time, when unseen arms envelop my body, I'm not afraid.

"It's all right, biscuit . . . It's over."

Part of me wants to shout that it's not, that we're floating in a sea of blood. and we broke a spaceship we'll never be able to pay for. I also want to ask what happened to that guy drifting past us, because his neck doesn't look quite straight. But I'm so tired. I spin around, throw myself into his welcoming arms, and I cry, sob the stress, the pain out. March squeezes me tight, rocks me against him, and we stay like this, weightless, truly suspended in time and space. I kiss his jaw blindly, breathe him. I don't care that he smells of sweat and blood; the animal in me knows only his body against mine.

I never want to let go, but at some point, March stiffens and maneuvers us apart gently. "I'm sorry, biscuit. Give me a second."

I watch in confusion as he uses the handles running along the walls to propel himself across the command center . . . in pursuit of the shadow that just slipped through the air lock. I hesitate before grabbing the handle closest to me and following him. I find him floating in section eleven's hallway, shoving a dark silhouette to the wall. A flash of red from the emergency lights above their heads reveals Bahjin's wide-eyed face squished against a window.

March presses his gun to Bahjin's nape. "Please. Land. This. Thing."

He whines. "I can't; you ruined the auxiliary cable!"

The hair on my nape stand on end in a prickling sensation. "You mean you can't fix it?"

"I don't know, he damaged stuff in section five too."

Oh my God . . . We're potentially stranded in space. With a complete douchebag. March and I exchange a look. I read my fear in his eyes. Will we have to eat Bahjin to survive until a rescue mission comes? Will they even send one?

A soft sniffing sound rises from Bahjin. "This time they'll never renew my H-1B." He offers me a trembling smile. "Do you think you could testify I treated you well, so they don't put me in jail?"

March lowers his gun and releases his grip, allowing Bahjin to float a few feet away. He runs his hand across his face with a tired sigh. "I doubt you'll ever go to jail if we spend the rest of our lives in space."

Bahjin blinks at him. "I meant when we get back, with the reentry pod."

THIRTY-SEVEN
STARS AND SATELLITES

March keeps a wary eye on Bahjin as the latter hurries around a massive spherical white pod in section three of *Odysseus*. He drifts from one dashboard to another along walls lined with storage compartments and wires, flipping switches, entering parameters into a long, tactile screen. A final pull on a big lever causes a low hum to rise from the reentry pod.

"Okay, now we suit up," he announces.

March and I help each other seal our respective helmets. Once it's done, I look into his eyes, the lines of worry and exhaustion around them. Mr. November really doesn't like space, this beautiful immensity he has zero control over . . . I take his hand and pull him with me toward the pod. Somehow, each in our little bubble, with about a million layers of various insulation systems between our skins, we've never been closer.

Once the three of us are strapped in our seats, the pod's air lock closes slowly and hisses shut. I look around at the two rows of three seats and the big, round window while Bahjin programs the pod's boosters to propel us back into the atmosphere. I crane my neck to check the back of the pod. There're two crates of dry food and drinking water encased in the walls, along with medical equipment. Most of the space is occupied by some sort of long and large back seat. The whole thing was probably designed to be minimally habitable in case the astronauts land in the middle of the Arctic Ocean, and it takes days to rescue them—and they have to eat the weakest one in the end . . . Jesus, I should have never read that book about the Franklin expedition. It messed me up.

Next to me, March is silent in his seat, his nostrils flaring slightly with each breath.

"Are you okay?" I ask, taking his hand.

His voice echoes inside my helmet, sounding frayed. "Yes . . . but let's agree to never go to space again."

"What happened? How did you get into the ship?"

He squeezes my hand. "Let's say I'm not entirely certain Mr. Stiles was ever loyal to Anies."

"He helped you?"

"Threw the suit at me and shoved me into the cargo unit, really. But yes, he went to great lengths to ensure *Odysseus*'s mission failed."

I try to compute the news. Has he been some sort of triple agent all along? For who then?

"You fucked us up, dude . . ." Bahjin mumbles to March through the radio while the pod starts to move, carried by an electronic arm toward a large air lock.

"So you traveled in there," I muse, ignoring the input from the sociopathic douchesac—who's admittedly saving our lives—in the front seat.

"Those missiles were a little too close for comfort," March admits.

I wince.

"We're going out," Bahjin announces, as a series of soft clanks outside indicates that the metal arms are releasing us. I watch them through the window as we float away into the star-studded void. They look like they're waving good-bye. I remember that this place is a tomb and avert my eyes.

With the help of the boosters, *Odysseus* shrinks away until all I can make out is a white spot in the dark blanket enveloping us. My head lolls, and I think I close my eyes a few times, holding on to March's hand as we drift, drift . . .

"We're seventy-five miles downrange; it's gonna get a little shaky," Bahjin warns us.

A bold understatement. I grip March's hand as the pod starts to tremble and, indeed, shake badly. Fiery arcs of light flash through the window, yellow, orange, and then a bright, beautiful pink. "It's the plasma trail," I yell excitedly in my helmet while my body is otherwise threatening to come apart as we barrel into Earth's atmosphere at four thousand miles per hour. March turns his head to look and consents to a stiff smile while, around the pod, compressed air ignites and engulfs us in fireworks so vibrant, so beautiful that maybe it was all worth it, just for that moment. March still doesn't like space though.

The pod's trail blaze eventually dies, replaced by an endless blue sky. We tear through a gradient of indigo, cobalt, azure until Bahjin's voice yells in our helmets, "Hold on tight; the chute's getting released!"

I brace myself, expecting to feel the same kind of jerk I experienced when March and I jumped from the helicopter back in Finland, something that will make my stomach heave all the way up to the back of my throat. But we didn't fall at the speed of sound in a two-ton capsule at the time . . . and it's *bad.* Shaking-and-mixing-your-internal-organs bad, three-thousand-mile-high-roller-coaster bad. We spend several seconds dangling at the end of a giant yo-yo, and I fear brain commotion is on the menu, when at last, the ride comes to an end.

The parachute is rocking us gently as we descend toward turquoise waters and pale sand. I let out a deep breath as the pod plops into shallow waters, swaying a few yards away from a beach.

March removes his helmet with a deep sigh. "Nie meer ruimte reis." *No more space travel.*

"Where are we?" I ask Bahjin as we both remove our helmets.

He checks the screen in front of him. "About six miles northeast of Nassau. Rose Island. Just so you know, the pod is emitting a signal, so the men in black are probably gonna show up in a few hours to get it back." He unclasps his seat belt and seems to be searching for something under his seat. March tenses, and his hand reaches for the gun in its holster.

But all Bahjin pulls out is a big orange bag. He flips a couple of switches, and the pod's door unlocks before whirring open. He gives a sharp tug at a string hanging from the bag before tossing it into the water. March and I watch in mild confusion as a self-inflating raft unfolds and swells into shape.

He turns to look at us. "Is it okay if I go?"

March's jaw tics.

"I mean, you're good now. And they have condoms in the med kit if you want. They added them after they figured some engineers had been testing the pod after hours—totally gross." When he sees that the two of us are staring at him blankly, he swallows. "I'm making things awkward . . . No, no, I get it. That was . . . awkward."

Bahjin and I see March reaching for his gun at the same time, and our savior's wince mirrors mine. "I thought we were good? Come on, man . . . Is it because I'm Indian? Blame the immigrant for everything, is that what this is about?"

March's chest heaves, his lips set in a thin line, and I'm sure I know what's coming, but Bahjin doesn't. He gives us this candid and expectant look that turns into panic when March lunges at him. There's little suspense as to the issue of the fight as March efficiently locks Bahjin's arms behind his back—a shiver of sympathy makes its way down my spine. The way his elbows are bent looks painful. Bahjin squeals in vain as March drags him out of the pod, and they plop together in the raft.

Water sloshes, laps at the orange plastic, and there's a lot of scuffling and protesting as March straddles Bahjin before he grabs a handful of the parachute's lines floating all around the pod . . . Oh my God, I knew it: he's secretly into bondage. My eyebrows rise higher and higher as I witness his expert trussing of a squirming Bahjin. The guy's wrists, legs, and ankles get secured with tight knots before March performs his finishing move, using a loose nylon strap to gag his victim. After that, Bahjin's screams dial down to muffled, exhausted grunts.

"Are you gonna leave him in the raft like that?" I ask, unfolding from my seat to better examine March's handiwork. "What if seagulls try to eat him?"

The interested party writhes in terror as March casually answers, "They'd need to tear through his suit first, but they're very smart creatures. They'll start with his face."

I study our prisoner with a sorrowful sigh. "Maybe we could cover him with something, just in case?"

•••

March agreed to cover Bahjin with the parachute so seagulls won't gouge out his eyeballs, and after he secured the raft to the pod, we closed the door to get some much-needed privacy. He'll be fine . . . I guess.

It's not that bad in here, and it helps that we're in the Bahamas and it's 80.6 degrees. I'm starting to get why the engineers liked the pod so much. We got rid of our space suits and made ourselves comfortable in that giant back seat. I rifled through the various storage compartments in search of things to steal. You wouldn't believe the things NASA slaps its logo on . . . I found wet wipes to freshen up, a clean white tank top and a matching T-shirt for March— so keeping those—but also NASA toothpaste, blue NASA blankets, and even a few Milky Ways. These guys thought of everything.

Once March is done with his second candy bar, he proceeds to fold the wrappers repeatedly, until all that's left is a compact square that he puts in the pod's tiny trash compartment. He did the same with his wet wipes, and I'm almost scared at the idea of how clean his place must be.

When he returns to the back seat with me, I curl against his shoulder while his lips linger on my forehead.

"March, there's something I need to ask you, and I'm so sorry if it sounds . . . awkward."

Around my shoulder, his hand pulls me a little closer, as if he's afraid I'll drift away. "I have no secrets from you."

"I forgot your name," I admit bluntly. "I know you have this nickname, Mr. November, but *March*, I have no idea if it's your first name, your last, or even some sort of . . . codename. I'm sorry, I don't remember." God, that sounded almost as bad as "Who are you and what are you doing in that pod with me?"

"March is the name my mother gave me, and I never told you my family name," he admits quietly. "I wanted to be Mr. November for you, someone . . . right. So I never told you. I gave up my name when joining the Lions . . . and I thought you wouldn't have liked the boy I used to be much, anyway."

"It was you, even then, and I think"—a sob builds in my throat that I can't contain—"I think Dries liked the boy you used to be too."

He draws a tired sigh. "I never imagined I would say this one day, but I'm going to miss him."

"He was a flamboyant asshole," I concur. March chuckles in response. "But I feel like I lost such an important part of me." My vision blurs again as I say this, and he pulls me into a tight hug that eventually results in our spooning in the back seat.

"We'll find a doctor to remove that thing," he murmurs in my ear. "And there's a big part of yourself awaiting you in New York. It's been a very difficult eight months for your father and Joy too..."

March is right: the warmth in my chest as he mentions them reminds me that I miss them, need them. Their memory has been wiped, yet my love for them remains, like a glimmering outline in my mind. I roll around to face him, caress his cheeks, his jaw, made rough by a little stubble. "You're a very important part too." *Perhaps the most . . .* "But you still haven't told me. Who's my boyfriend?"

He whispers it against my lips, like a secret just for the two of us, and I smile. It's a good name. I can get used to that. I close my eyes when his lips roam away from my mouth, tasting my neck, my clavicles. His hands sneak under my tank top—I think he's trying to say it's in the way: I pull it over my head and drop it in the crate closest to me. March's T-shirt joins it right afterward.

I indulge in some chest-hair therapy, caressing it over and over while his fingertips skitter across the territory they already know, making me squirm. "You're tickling me!"

"My apologies, I would never . . ." is what he says before launching a vicious attack on my sides.

"A penny for your thoughts." I gasp after he decides I've suffered enough.

His eyebrows rise comically. "Are you certain?"

"I can handle the truth," I proclaim with a firm nod.

He brings me close to his body, so I can feel exactly just how much all that tickling affected him. My hands roam on his shoulders, linger on the rough canvas of the lion that was once carved into his skin. He welcomes the attention with a purr, and I feel the mood shift. "I'm thinking," March begins, "that this is perhaps the only place in the world where no one will call or barge in." His body moves atop mine as he goes on. "Additionally, I checked under the bed and determined we are sloth free."

I press a trembling kiss to his chin and tug at his underwear. "What about the men in black? What if they knock to get their capsule back?"

He stifles a strained laugh in the crook of my neck. "I've reached a point where I'm shooting whoever interrupts us. Human or animal. No exceptions."

"You're a menace to society."

I think he says, "Indeed," but the word gets lost in a deep, meticulous kiss that leaves no part of my mouth uncharted. I feel my panties slipping down my legs, the caress of his hands as he helps them past my ankles. I hold on to him and lose track of time, forget everything but our skins gliding, our hands and lips exploring urgently.

I'll be eternally grateful to the lewd engineers who first explored the pod's potential, because we quickly reach a point where each touch is simultaneously too much and not enough. March's breaths become husky sighs. He says we really need a condom, but his hands won't listen, caressing my thighs and bringing my hips ever closer to his. How we manage to stop kissing long enough to disentangle ourselves, I have no idea.

It's a strange pause, a few seconds of shivering anticipation, when he moves away to take a little blue foil packet from the pod's medical kit. I'm not really scared, but I become aware of my inexperience; everything feels new, the smell of the condom, the way March's body molds to mine with intent. I look into his eyes, finding tenderness and hesitation that mirror mine, and I know that bond is all I'll ever need.

My heart beats fast, elated, and when the pain comes, I embrace it. I bury my head in the crook of March's shoulder, breathing a little sweat and tasting salt. It's done, and that single precious moment belongs to us both.

Above me, March isn't moving yet. I feel the tension coiling the muscles in his shoulders; they strain under my palms with the effort to support himself and keep still. "Biscuit, I'm so sorry . . . are you all right?"

I look up at him and nod, too overwhelmed to form words at the moment. It hurts more than I expected—enough to for me to briefly consider that penetrative intercourse is to foreplay what the Gremlins are to Gizmo, really—but I need him to know that it's okay, that there's nothing to apologize for. Because we're making love.

I cradle his jaw in my palm and feel it quiver under my fingertips. His features are taut like he's in pain too . . . but a wonderful kind of pain. Our hands join on the fleece blanket, his lips find mine, and little by little, we learn each other, find our rhythm.

I let that gentle swell rock me and lose myself in March's eyes, blue galaxies where his emotions lie bare: the need, the joy. The pleasure. All too soon, he strains against me, draws in a hissing breath, and I know it's over. He's falling from the stars, and I hold him all the way down, until his body grows heavy atop mine, exhausted. He rolls over, his hand never letting go of mine, even in that sweet aftermath.

Curling against him, I listen to my own breathing and feel my heart rate slowing down with a sense of wonderment. From a purely physical point of view, it wasn't exactly stars and satellites, but nonetheless, a giant step for all twenty-six-year-old girls named Island who love their hit man boyfriend . . . Also, to be honest, my lower regions *are* tingling quite a bit, and not just from the lingering ache. That whole Lego business does sound very promising.

After he's recovered from the high, March draws the blanket over us, and his thumb swipes at my cheeks. "I'm sorry . . . I hurt you."

I lick a salty drop from my upper lip. I didn't realize I've been crying. I shake my head. "Not that much."—I swallow back more stupid tears—"I think it was awesome."

He draws me close, wrapping his arms around me like a safe cocoon. "You're too generous with me. I'm sorry that you didn't . . . that it wasn't quite—"

"It was the best sex I ever had," I say to rescue him, burying a smile in the holy rug covering his pectorals.

I feel his laughter rumble through his chest. "The things you do to my ego, Miss Chaptal . . ."

We stay like this for a while, sated, sleepy, cuddling and whispering to each other the silly things you can say to someone who officially knows every square inch of your body. I can't say we're really concerned about who will come to recover the pod or when— the later the better.

That is, until a distant droning reaches us through the thick titanium walls. I prop myself on my elbows to glance through the window . . . and fall back with a groan.

"Helicopter?" March asks, rather rhetorically.

"Yeah."

"Biscuit, I'm afraid we have to give the pod back."

I stifle a hiss of pain as I get up—I didn't realize I was that sore . . . "I'm keeping the toothpaste and the underwear."

"I'm certain they won't mind," March concedes with a wink before reluctantly slipping back into the pressure suit. Because it's those or greeting the men in black in our birthday suits instead.

As the droning grows in intensity, we open the pod's air lock. March jumps onto the inflatable raft to check on Bahjin, who remained safely roped and gagged. He looks fine, but I still feel a little guilty that we left him outside like that while we . . . Well, he was going to nuke a US airbase after all.

As expected, a navy blue helicopter is hovering above our heads, the wind of its rotor raising a crystalline mist around us and swaying the raft gently. When the ladder drops down, my knees quiver, and I hesitate. For all I know, that's another first for me, and I thought the US government had secure procedures for this kind of stuff rather than G.I. Joe–style stunts. But I remind myself that I broke the sound barrier *twice* today. I flex the couple of muscles in my arms. I can do this.

March helps me latch on to the ladder, and I try my best to ignore the way it swings back and forth as I climb, one torturous rung after another, with the wind lashing at my face. *And, for the love of Raptor Jesus,* I repeat to myself, *don't look down. Don't!*

I inwardly squeal in relief when I feel strong hands taking mine and helping me inside the chopper. It takes me less than a second to figure what's wrong though. It's the black fatigues every man is wearing that tip me off. Or maybe the fact that behind their sunglasses, none of these guys seem genuinely pleased to see me. March's expression too darkens when he reaches the top of the ladder and discovers the rescue team.

I'm not entirely certain that those Lions flew all the way to Nassau to congratulate me on successfully murdering their commander.

THIRTY-EIGHT
THE TEMPLE

Okay, let's not panic. I count six men—two in the front and four in the back, all armed with worryingly elaborate assault rifles. A couple of them sandwiched us after strapping us tightly to our seats. One of them took March's gun and scanned us quickly with some kind of flashlight—a handheld metal detector, I suspect. Another went down the ladder to go get Bahjin, whose smiling face appears in the doorway. After the Lion is done helping him into the back seat opposite to ours, Bahjin winks at us with a shrug. I grit my teeth and glare at him in return. We should have let that asswipe get eaten by seagulls . . .

Goose bumps prickle all over my body as the rest of the men stare at us through their sunglasses. Black-gloved fingers await on the triggers of their weapons, and you could cut the tension in the cabin with a knife—which of course they brought, I note with a wince, spotting the incurved hilt of a karambit tucked into one of the men's tactical vest. March places a hand on my shoulder and sits still. I think he knows better than to try something for now . . .

Bahjin turns to the Lion sitting next to him, a guy with a short blond beard—their leader, maybe? It's subtle, but there's something in that guy's features that suggests he's more relaxed than the rest of his little gang. Yep, that one's in charge.

"Strength and honor!" Bahjin barks happily over the roar of the rotor as the chopper flies away from our little pod.

Blond-beard remains silent. He searches the pockets of his tactical vest for something. I barely have the time to identify a syringe before he casually stabs Bahjin's neck. Bahjin's eyes go wide, and his mouth works in vain for a couple of seconds before he passes out.

"Could never stand that kid," Blond-beard shouts to our attention.

Obviously. I gulp, wondering whether we're next. Rather than playing doctor though, the Lion sitting to my left lowers his rifle and opens a compartment between our seats to retrieve two headsets. He hands me one while his colleagues ostensibly aim at March when he reaches to take his—at least they're learning from their brothers' mistakes. I adjust my headset hesitantly. In the opposite seat, Bahjin has been reduced to a ragdoll held together by his seatbelt's strap, his head lolling gently against the headrest. I don't know what to make of all this. I thought they were basically here to rescue Bahjin and take us prisoner, but I pick up . . . mixed signals.

"Better?" Blond-beard asks with the hint of a smile once the headset is secured on my head.

"Is this an invitation we are free to refuse?" March asks coldly.

Blond-beard's lips quirk through the golden bristles, and he replies, "I was told the lady would be well rewarded for her attendance."

I try to read his eyes through the sunglasses, to no avail. Are we talking rewarded as in *free T-shirt* or rewarded as in *Ha-ha-ha, a slow death shall be your reward, traitor?*

In a moment of rare self-awareness and honesty, March stares into the guy's sunglasses and replies, "If you hurt her, I will kill you all. I will carve up every single one of you until there's only meat left."

I freeze in my seat when two barrels rise to point at his head in response.

"So I've heard," Blond-beard says, the *r* rolling softly off his tongue. "But there'll be none of that. We're here to deliver a peace offer."

"From who?" I probe cautiously.

He shrugs one big shoulder. "You're gonna have to follow us to find out."

"What guarantee do I have that Island will be safe?" March retorts.

"You have the word of a Lion, *broer*. Isn't that enough?"

Now that's a good question, and one that does *not* call for an honest answer, for the stark truth might vex our new friends. So, I pinch my lips, and really, March's disdainful glare speaks for itself. The rest of the flight is spent in religious silence, under the calm scrutiny of Blond-beard and his bros. Holding March's hand, I watch through the helicopter's windows as the sun sets over Nassau, painting pristine beaches and luxurious resorts with shimmering gold and coral pinks.

Beneath us, the airport comes into view, and soon enough, we land at the end of a runway where a lonely black jet awaits us. I have this incongruous thought that if this was a romance book, a muscled billionaire would be awaiting us in the jet to fly us to the other end of the world and do filthy things to us in the privacy of some well-guarded mansion. But the only muscles are those of our deadpan escorts, and I don't think March would want to surrender to a billionaire anyway.

"You'll have breakfast in Paris," Blond-beard announces before one of the men takes our headsets, and the helicopter's door opens.

March and I exchange a look. Paris. Where Dries sent Isiporho and Dominik . . . Where the answers await?

"Let's see this through," March says softly. "I'm with you. Whatever happens . . . I'll be with you."

I give his hand a squeeze as Blond-beard and his men escort us toward the jet. "I know," I murmur. "I'm not scared."

It's when I reach the airstair that I notice they're not taking Bahjin with us. His prone body just got loaded into the back of a white van that stopped a few yards away from the helicopter.

"What are they going to do with him?" I ask Blond-beard.

He shrugs one big shoulder. "He has a date of his own."

I wouldn't exactly call it an answer . . . March's hand rests on my back, a silent encouragement to leave Bahjin to face his own judgment. But that little speck of guilt at the back of my mind simply won't be ignored. "Are they going to kill him?" I insist.

"No," Blond-beard replies with a finality that suggests I'm gonna have to take a Lion's word for it.

At last, March and I follow him up the airstair and inside the jet. Unlike the Queen's little flying palace, this plane, while comfortable in its own right, speaks of sobriety. Beige factory furniture, simple plastic closets, and a tiny lavatory that will at least allow for a little cleaning up if no one pulls out a gun and says, "No water for you." But I don't think they're going to do that. We're guests after all, formally invited and stuff, and this is no kidnapping, since everyone here boarded of their own free will. Perhaps to better live that lie, a younger Lion goes to retrieve clothes wrapped in plastic from a closet after takeoff. He hands them to us and flicks his head to the lavatory.

See? Five-star service, not a kidnapping at all.

Half an hour later, I've freshened up, and I'm wearing a knee-length blue cashmere dress and elegant high-heeled pumps that look like a wardrobe malfunction on me. I come out of the lavatory to find March similarly disguised, in a dark suit that's really not him at all. But the dimples creasing his cheeks when he sees me, they're his, and it's all I need.

When it becomes clear that our hosts still won't talk to us, I curl up in my seat and fall asleep, safe at March's side.

•••

I'm floating in the dark with Anies, each crease and angle of his face sculpted by the red light. He's looking down at me, and his hands are around my neck, squeezing. I gasp for air in the void of space. I'm cold, and there's no way out, no knife, no one to save me . . . *March!*

I jerk upright in my seat and directly into March's welcoming arms.

His palm rubs my back in soothing circles. "It's all right, biscuit; we're landing."

As my heart slows down, I massage my eyes with the heels of my palms, fighting a slight headache. Through the window, I see a gray tarmac glistening with rain. That's Paris all right, where all colors fade between November and April, and the asphalt is the same color as the sky—which also happens to perfectly match the buildings and the ashen faces of the Parisians.

I realize with a derisive smile that this is, yet again, one of the things I can't remember ever learning. But I've been here before; I can tell. The strange concrete curves of Roissy Airport's massive dome are familiar, as is the heavy French accent of the ground attendant who welcomes us. She seems perfectly unfazed at the sight of a bunch of paramilitary creeps pouring from the jet—she must be used to seeing much worse. Prince of Thailand worse.

I hesitate to ask whether we should be showing passports somewhere, but Blond-beard and his bros behave like they own the place, and that pair of French cops actually opens the gates to the parking area for us—the things you can accomplish in this world with a dash of glamour and corruption . . . We're led to a pair of dark Mercedes SUVs. Blond-beard sits across from us in the back, along with the young goon who gave us the clothes. It's hard to tell because of the glasses, but I pick up a sense of self-satisfaction in the air. We glide away from the tarmac in solemn silence, until all of a sudden, in the speakers, Selena Gomez's voice starts cooing sensual encouragements to kill us with kindness.

Blond-beard jerks in his seat. March's and my brows rise in sync when the smoked-glass partition separating us from the driver slides down, and he barks, "Louis, we're working here."

Louis glances at us in the mirror. He must be forty; the temples of his black crew cut are graying. His mouth curves down in something I suspect to be half-contrition, half-protestation. "He said it was allowed because he likes that one!"

The mention of the mysterious "he" appears to settle the conflict: Selena keeps singing as we enter the freeway and race toward Paris. Her voice urges us to remember that no war was ever won in anger, and by then, I'm pretty sure I know who summoned us, who finds his solace in pop when he rides . . .

Soon we're driving along, Haussmannian stone buildings, cafés, and naked trees lining the street—on the Seine's right bank, if I'm correct. We take a few turns left onto small streets, reaching Paris's historical center, where the oldest mansions still stand. The SUVs park in front of an ancient stone wall in which a set of wrought-iron gates bars access to a private French garden.

"We're at the Paris temple," March says.

I suspected so. I think of Isiporho and Dominik: Did they make it here? And more important, if so, did they make it *out*? Alive? My fingers briefly lace with March's before we climb out of the car, seeking reassurance. As the gate creaks open, his palm lingers on the small of my back, a warm reminder that whatever happens, he's at my side.

We follow our sort-of-but-not-quite captors into the garden. Our feet crush gravel as we make our way toward a neoclassical *hôtel particulier*, whose heavy wooden doors are guarded by two fierce lions roaring for eternity in the sculpted stone. The doors open and warmth engulfs us. It's now a soft Persian rug under out feet, over a parqueted floor whose heavenly beeswax scent tickles my nostrils. An ample flight of stairs leads to a series of salons on the second floor. Crystal chandeliers gleam softly above our heads, the floorboards sigh under our steps, and Roman warriors watch us with eyes of marble. This atmosphere could only get any Frenchier if someone pulls out a beret.

After we enter a salon whose walls are lined with cream brocade,

Blond-beard invites us to sit on a baroque sofa lined with burgundy velvet. I gaze at the dead trees in the garden, past windows that reach all the way up to a fifteen-foot ceiling where angels frolic among gilded moldings. I remember March saying that the temples are museums of a sort: I concur.

Blond-beard goes to knock at a set of doors at the other end of the room. They come ajar, and a few words are exchanged in hushed tones. March watches the exchange with narrowed eyes, and I peer in anxiously, hoping to get a glimpse of our host. The door opens at last, and the first thing that comes out, well . . . suffice to say that my jaw goes slack.

Blond-beard and his colleague stand in quiet dignity as the orange tabby rides past them, enigmatic and regal on its black Roomba. The noble steed whirs around the room, vacuuming the Ghum silk carpet's intricate pattern with steady alacrity.

"The commander will see you now," Blond-beard announces, his gaze straight, as if he didn't notice the Roomba now bumping against his boots repeatedly while the cat stares up at him with guileless turquoise eyes.

March and I get up and enter the room in a state of mild stupefaction. A war has been won without being fought, and indeed without anger. Stiles stands before us, wearing his eternal gray suit and soft, bulletproof smile.

He walks up to us and holds out his hand to shake with March, who stands still—some wounds won't close anytime soon.

I manage to find my voice, not without some effort. "You . . . took his place."

"It was time for some change, and I can't thank you enough for your help." He's talking to me, but his eyes are set on March as he adds, "My friend."

March gauges him, dark ice crackling in his irises. "Never."

Stiles gives a good-natured shrug. "The offer remains on the table."

Meanwhile, I've managed to swallow my shock. "You used us

against him . . . from the start."

He walks to a finely adorned liquor cabinet standing behind a long Napoleon desk covered with papers. "I'm a romantic at heart," he says. "When we found Auben and his fingers in Rio and it became clear that Mr. November was still in the picture, I had an inkling that love could move mountains, with a little help, of course."

March's lips set in a hard line. "You would have never gotten your way through rebellion, not in Anies's dictatorial system. So you undermined him and chose Dries and me to strike the finishing blow. It couldn't be you killing him, nor one of your men."

Stiles gestures to the row of rare spirits sitting inside the cabinet. "A drink?"

March remains silent, but my eyes widen when I recognize the green hue of the absinthe bottle. Stiles notices the direction of my gaze. Pure kindness shines in his baby blue irises as he says, "Oh don't worry; I wouldn't give you that. Never to a friend."

My throat constricts. "You were poisoning him; that's why he was sick."

His mouth purses comically, like a little boy caught stealing from the cookie jar. "He did have terminal pancreatic cancer, but you know how it is . . . Sometimes the schedule needs a little adjustment."

And Stiles adjusted Anies's schedule . . . weakened him so he'd die faster. I'm starting to think he could almost scare me more than Anies, this kind killer. Because in the last moments, I saw Anies for who he was—I saw a man and his madness. I can't find that in Stiles. I stare at him, scan every line on his face, the pleasant and banal features forged by surgery fifteen years ago, and I can't find the man underneath. I sense no anger, no weakness. Sweet Jesus, that new boss is gonna be much worse than the previous one . . .

He closes the liquor cabinet with a sigh. "I know you're angry, and I'm sorry I had to play you both a little. It was for the best. No more nuclear warheads," he announces, his voice suddenly a notch sterner. "We're going back to our roots. There's a lot of work that needs to be done to preserve the temples and a lot of people who need a little shove to the other side. That's what we do best; we're not cut for the light."

That's true, but listening to him casually mention the people he's going to kill, I see no major improvement in the Lions' line of business.

"And I'm working on smoothing things with the Board and the agency," he adds. "Mr. Erwin was very happy to collect our friend Bahjin in Nassau. And the Queen . . . well she wasn't exactly pleased that Anies died before she could get a hold of him, but I think she likes this new direction we're taking, and of course, we'll help her regain her position. We need that balance between all the players; your father was right about that."

My heart tightens unbearably when he mentions Dries. "You watched him die," I rasp. "You didn't lift a finger."

He shakes his head sadly. "We'd have ended up with another succession war on our hands. There was no other solution, and your father knew it. Both he and Anies had to go. We needed a clean slate."

"Or rather you didn't want to risk competition after Anies's death," March grinds out, his chest heaving with the same pain and anger I feel crushing mine.

Stiles winces. "You really won't give me any credit, will you? Well, let me tell you this: Dries and I had our differences in the past, but it's all water under the bridge. I forgave him a long time ago." He tilts his head at us, in that attentive, predatory way I'm pretty sure he inherited from Anies. "I could have executed his men when they came here to search the archives."

March's jaw works silently while I try to remain indifferent, my spine rigid. He knows about Isiporho and Dominik's mission.

"But I let them take what they wanted because I didn't mind. We need to stop killing our own brothers like that all the time or else we're gonna have to lower our recruitment standards," he muses, sending a pointed look at March before opening his arms wide. "I want reconciliation. If they ever want to recover their place among us, tell them they're welcome."

I listen to Stiles's little tirade warily, wondering if he let Isiporho and Dominik live out of the goodness of his Southern heart or rather because he wanted them to succeed and let Dries know that Anies's reign was coming to an end one way or another . . . "So you really won't go after them?"

He shrugs. "Not unless they give me a good reason to. By the way, Island, in the same spirit, I want you to know there'll be no retribution for your heinous crime under my watch."

The floor seems to collapse under my feet, like I'm free falling again in the reentry pod. "I'm sorry, my heinous—*what?*"

Stiles tuts me. "Island, you murdered the Lions' commander. Anyone else would face dire penalties for that."

"Don't even try to go there," March warns him, his fists clenching.

"Calm down, Mr. November," Stiles chides. "You're always so testy . . . I didn't bring her here to point fingers." His eyes cut to me. "I brought you here because your father asked something from me, and I intend to deliver."

My vision blurs a little as I picture Dries's peaceful golden gaze again, the last seconds . . . *You'll fix my daughter. No matter what it takes, you'll fix your mess.*

"Follow me," Stiles requests.

He leaves the office and returns to the salon where his tabby is still ambling around Blond-beard and his pals. Stiles kneels, and the cat immediately leaves its Roomba to trot to him. He pets it amorously and picks it up. "Bring her in," he orders his goons.

The salon's doors open, revealing a lean and elegant gray-haired woman clad in a pink turtleneck and beige pants. I instinctively take a step back, my stomach heaving. He didn't kill Bentsen. The faded gray-blue eyes that used to pick me apart during our sessions gaze at me, quiet fear now simmering in their depths. She doesn't want to be here any more than I do.

Next to me, March has gone still. His nostrils flare. I wrap my hand around his clenched fist in an attempt to placate the storm I can feel roaring inside him.

"You will take this thing out," March orders, his usual politeness frightening in its absence.

She crosses her arms and stares through the window at the bare trees outside, unable to sustain his gaze. "The procedure is invasive. Island should recover well, but there might be some marginal loss."

March inhales sharply, but I take the hit without flinching. Without really knowing it for sure, I've come to terms with that possibility. I was ready to live again even if I didn't recover any of my memories: the sacrifice of some of them suddenly feels trivial in light of everything that happened to us.

I nod slowly. "When do we start?"

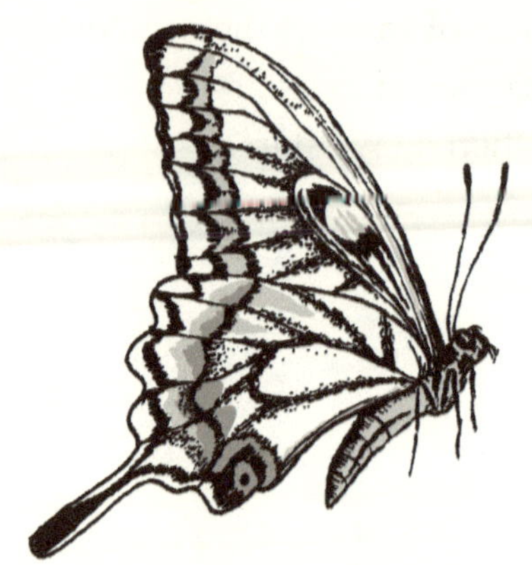

THIRTY-NINE
THE PHONE CALL

> "Ramirez lay in a pool of his own corrupted blood, his thick mustache forever still. Rica gazed down at his mutilated groin. 'You and your evil shaft can sell cocaine in hell! I defeated you, Ramirez!' Rica screamed, shimmering tears streaming down her beautiful eyes and soaking the perfect globes of her breasts."
>
> —Kerry-Lee Storm, *The Cost of Rica #4: Vengeful Passion*

I remember that the hallway was very white, that March held my hand all along, until I closed my eyes and dreamed. I came out of the operating room with a bald spot and twenty-nine grams lighter.

The dream lasted another five days, my mind wandering in a place that wasn't death but wasn't yet life. March watched me dream and waited for me to find my way back to him, surviving on hospital meals and crosswords. I was reportedly carted out of my room at the clinic on the sixth day. I remember nothing of that, but that's okay. Eight months of retrograde amnesia has the merit of putting that kind of minor disagreement in perspective. I'm a survivor: now all three parts of *The Hangover* sound like a joyride to me.

I have vague memories of March making a phone call after the ambulance ride, of his voice speaking over the phone in French to someone and telling them that I was getting dehydrated, and I wasn't fully comatose because my eyes would occasionally flutter open, but I still wouldn't move or speak, and he was worried.

What I do know for sure is that on the dawn of the seventh day, I blinked awake, for good this time. The first thing I saw was March's back, clad in his usual white shirt—wrinkles in the cotton suggested an end-of-the world situation, but the room was actually quiet. I lay on my side, in a large bed, buried under a gray comforter. The whole thing felt as fluffy as my brain as I blearily took in my surroundings. I stared up at the intricate floral moldings decorating the ceiling, then down at the chevron parquet and marble fireplace at the other end of what looked like a nearly empty bedroom. I wanted to scratch my skull under the gauze taped to my nape, but I feared that my brain might leak out in some horrific and never-before-recorded medical accident. I decided against it.

I touched his back tentatively, and he jerked awake, rolling to his side in a heartbeat to check on me. Sweet Jesus, end of the world indeed: I took in the circles of exhaustion under his eyes, and not one, not two, but probably *three* days' worth of whiskers. He was looking at me, haggard; I brought my fingers to his jaw, feeling the rough bristles there. I smiled. Dimples pocked his cheeks in return, and he shifted closer to kiss my forehead. "Welcome back on Earth, astronaut."

"Island has landed," I confirmed with a croaky chuckle.

"Are you thirsty, biscuit?"

I ran my tongue over my dry lips. "Yeah, parched, actually."

"Wait for me here," he commanded before getting up from the bed.

Not that I was going anywhere. Not without a beanie, obviously. He brought back a glass and a bottle of water; I sipped some with cautious gulps, dehydration and hunger making my stomach knot in protest. After I was done, I handed him the glass back and glanced through the window. "We're still in Paris, right?"

"Yes, Ilan found the apartment for me."

Ilan . . . It was like my neurons had just gotten whipped—hard— but they too were still waking up. They stalled, and I felt March's anxious gaze on me, until a face flashed in my mind, a black-haired man in his late forties with piercing green eyes, a graying beard, and leathery olive skin. With him came another memory: that of a beautiful black woman, her long hair, her warm smile. I was in their apartment; we talked together about March. *Kalahari.* March's nice ex, Ilan's wife, and the one who had first told me about . . . Charlotte. New emotions welled in my chest; joy and pain laced together as the memories surfaced, one after another, like bubbles in a mile-deep pool.

"Ilan . . . he worked for the French secret service, but now he kind of . . . freelances, and he has a weird friend who sells burgers and depleted uranium rockets," I droned, in a mild daze.

Relief lifted ten years off March's features. He nodded. "Yes . . . exactly. We can see him later if you'd like. I thought it might jog your memory to convalesce in Paris."

Convalesce . . . My face bunched. "No convalescing. It's all I've been doing for the past eight months," I mumbled, pushing the covers aside to get out of bed.

His arms automatically snaked around my waist as I sat up. "Island, you need to take it slow."

"But I don't want *slow*," I whined. "I need to move, to do stuff . . ."

What kind of stuff remained to be determined, but already I could feel the cogs spinning in my brain, names, faces, ideas hovering close to the surface. For the first time in almost a year, I felt like my old life was at hand's reach.

"Wait here a second," March said, letting go of me. "I have something for you. I thought it might cheer you when you woke up."

I watched him get up and leave the bedroom through a set of French doors opening to a long hallway—typical of a Haussmannian apartment. Through the window, I noticed the spire of Notre-Dame, turned grayish by a bleak morning light. Since I had a direct view on the east end of the transept, I gathered the narrow bridge crossing the Seine had to be Pont Saint-Louis—which would place us somewhere on the west side of the eponymous Île Saint-Louis.

March returned with a bag he placed on my lap, a lovely pink thing tied with a white satin ribbon. He sat back on the bed while I inspected its contents. Upon discovering the book inside, I was reminded of Bentsen's warning that removing the implant wouldn't restore my memory exactly like it was before but rather allow me, with some effort, to access data that had been sealed away until now. I studied the cover silently. The muscular chest and ornate red font were familiar, and I could tell I was happy, that my heart was fluttering with excitement in fact, but the reason why hovered frustratingly out of reach.

My lips pursed as I flipped the book to examine the back cover. I grinned. Yes, this was . . . "Oh my God. *Cost of Rica* four came out?"

Relief lit up March's face. "Yes, a few months ago."

"Oh, thank you. Thank you, thank you, *thank you!*"

I leafed through the brand-new pages in utter delight. "Have you read it?"

"I might have skimmed through it while you were asleep," he admitted, ducking his chin to conceal a guilty smile.

"Is it good? Does it end well this time?"

"I don't want to spoil it for you. I'm fairly certain you'll enjoy it though."

"I'd better . . . I mean, Rica's been fighting Ramirez for ages, and I don't think I've ever seen anyone get kidnapped and raped so many times. This guy seriously needs to die. Also that cliffhanger in the previous book? Give me a break. I hate authors who do that! What was the point? We all know she's going to end up with Ricardo anyway. Seriously—"

My rant was silenced by March's arms flying around me, squeezing me tight. Against me, he was shaking. I returned his embrace and tucked my head under his chin while he let out all the stress, the fear, and the pain in a long, hoarse chuckle. And he laughed and laughed, and at some point, I started laughing too, because Rica would probably end up chained in Ramirez's basement again, and I loved March so much my heart might burst.

After we'd both calmed down, I looked up at his face and traced the dark circles under his eyes with my thumbs. "When was the last time you slept, Mr. November?"

His tired sigh breezed against my forehead. "Two days ago."

I placed the book on the nightstand and nuzzled his neck, all the while pulling him toward the inviting heap of pillows. "Come here; you're the one who needs to convalesce."

•••

March slept at my side, a gun under his pillow, and his arm flung across my belly as if to make sure I wouldn't vanish again. Once in a while, he'd shift or make a little snoring sound from the back of his throat, perhaps riding his ostrich through the wild immensity of Kawaii Farm's plains . . . Propped against my pillows, I couldn't stop thinking, tugging at strings everywhere in my brain, unraveling them one after another. My mother's smile, Dries sharing ice cream with me in Tokyo after he'd tried to kill March, because that's what supervillain dads do. And normal dads too.

It was 7:00 a.m. in New York, and Simon Halder was probably putting on his tie and watching CNN in the mirror. Then he'd have a cup of black and a bagel with organic soy spread instead of cream cheese and chive like he wanted, because Janice, his wife, was trying to turn him vegan. I crept out of bed carefully and padded down the hallway.

I found a phone in the living room, sitting on the birch sideboard by the window, bathed in the gray light of winter noon. I didn't remember the number; when I tried to visualize it in my mind, I couldn't. But my fingers still knew it; they hadn't forgotten.

It rang. Once, twice, over and over.

Until a grunt at the other end of the line answered me. "Simon Halder speaking, and it'd better be important, because you're calling from a goddamn hidden number before I've had my coffee."

The tears started rolling before he was even done ranting, and my throat was too tight for any words to come out.

"*Who* is this?"

I got scared he would hang up before I could produce any sound. I sniffed hard and tried again. "Dad . . ."

The silence that followed shattered me a thousand times. I tried to breathe through the sobs shaking my frame.

But then . . . he spoke. "Island?"

I didn't think I'd manage, but at last, the words I needed so desperately erupted. "Dad, I want to come home for Christmas!"

Other books in the Spotless Series:

SPOTLESS

(Book #1)

BEATING RUBY

(Book #2)

CRYSTAL WHISPERER

(Book #3)

APACHE STRIKE FORCE

(Novella #4.5)

(Book #5)

Acknowledgements

A billion thanks to Tiffany Yates Martin, Lindsey Nelson and Regina Dowling, who work on the Spotless series a lot more than I do, to Jovon Sotak, without whom this adventure would have never happened, to Benoît, for putting up with me, and to every single one of my readers. You guys are the reason I write those books, and going through your desperate messages on Facebook fills me with malevolent glee. Maybe for my next series, it'll take even longer for the characters to sleep together . . . Who knows? Have you read *The Emperor's Edge* series, by Lindsay Buroker? Muahahaha!

About the Author

Camilla Monk is a French native who grew up in a Franco-American family. After studying business in Paris, she taught English and French in Tokyo before returning to France to work in digital advertising. A self-taught programmer, she spent ten years building rickety websites for financial companies, before publishing Spotless, her debut novel. 

Camilla is now a full-time writer and lives in Montreal, where she keeps a close watch on the squirrels and complains on a daily basis about the egregious number of Tim Hortons.

For more (questionably useful) information, visit: